COLOR BLIND

ALSO BY JONATHAN SANTLOFER

The Death Artist

JONATHAN SANTLOFER

wm WILLIAM MORROW *An Imprint of* HarperCollins*Publishers*

This book is a work of fiction. The characters, incidents, and dialogue are drawn from the author's imagination and are not to be construed as real. Any resemblance to actual events or persons, living or dead, is entirely coincidental.

HarperCollins books may be purchased for educational, business, or sales promotional use. For information please write: Special Markets Department, HarperCollins Publishers Inc., 10 East 53rd Street, New York, NY 10022.

FIRST EDITION

Designed by Jessica Shatan Heslin

Printed on acid-free paper

Library of Congress Cataloging-in-Publication Data

Santlofer, Jonathan, 1946–
    Color blind / Jonathan Santlofer.—1st ed.
       p.   cm.
    ISBN 0-06-054104-0
    1. Women art historians—Fiction.   2. Ex-police officers—Fiction.   3. New York (N.Y.)—Fiction.   I. Title.

PS3619.A58C65   2004   2003067666

---

04 05 06 07 08 JTC / RRD 10 9 8 7 6 5 4 3 2 1

To my daughter, Doria,
the best kid a dad could ever hope for

In order to use color effectively it is necessary to recognize
that color deceives continually.
—JOSEF ALBERS

There is nothing there. What you see is not what you see. What
you see is nothing. . . . What you see is what's in your mind.
—AD REINHARDT

COLOR BLIND

PROLOGUE

His hands sweat inside thin, white cotton art handler's gloves. His underarms are damp and itchy, legs achy, feet falling asleep. In the deep pockets of his disposable jumpsuit is a brand-new handkerchief, wide silver duct tape, a white bristle paintbrush, a small bottle of chloral hydrate, three knives, and two pieces of primed artist's canvas, rolled up.

He peels down the edge of his glove and squints at the cool green numbers on the illuminated, paint-splattered Timex: 4:38. *Where is she?*

He thought he had her routine down pat. He's been watching her for a week. The last three nights she'd stopped turning tricks by 3 A.M., met her pimp—tall, rail-thin with waist-long dreadlocks—on the far west corner of Zerega and 147th Street, a neighborhood he'd like to forget, but can't.

He closes his eyes, hums along with the tune that has just clicked on in his jukebox brain: "Like a Virgin." A song she liked to play over and over. He can even remember the picture on the cassette, the "material girl" done up like some whore bride.

He shakes his head against the music, not with it, trying to dislodge the tune along with the pictures that are now playing, bouncing along to the simple four-four beat, and all those sounds: cot squeaking, moans coupled with faux endearments—*Yeah. That's it. Give it to me. Baby, you're the greatest. So big. So strong.* And the smell of sweat and beer and sex and sadness.

The click of a key in the lock.

The pictures fade; music shuts off; adrenaline kicks in.

He can barely stand still.

Just a minute. Hang on, sloopy—

The darkness in the closet has added to his affliction. Nothing. Total blackout. No color at all.

But he can wait. Soon there will be more than enough color.

Footsteps. Heels click-clacking against hard wooden floors.

He shifts his weight, and a dress or blouse slides across his face, thin fabric teasing his cheek, perfume, something flowery, cheap, in his nostrils, a bit like *hers*.

The edge of the hanger grazes another, the slightest ping.

The footsteps stop.

Has she heard?

His gloved hand grabs hold of the offending hanger, the rest of his body gone rigid.

No, there they are again, the heels against floorboards. She must think she imagined it, or she's too tired to care—one too many blow jobs to care about anything.

He pictures her counting out bills, figuring her take after the skinny pimp has gotten his cut, losing count because she is so stupid.

That's it. He's had it with her.

Closet door thrown open, and he sees her, but only for an instant. Her features blur, morph into that more familiar face as he charges toward her.

He doesn't hear her scream, but knows enough to clamp his gloved hand over her mouth as he wrestles her to the floor, throws himself on top of her, knocks the breath out of her. Just enough time to retrieve the roll of silver tape, tear off enough to seal her mouth shut.

A flash in the back of his mind: mouth taped, hardly able to breathe.

Her struggling brings him back to the moment and he gets a grip on her arms, twists them behind her back, unrolls more tape, wraps it around her wrists, again and again until all that are left free are her legs, kicking, aimless, like she's doing some futile aerobic exercise.

It doesn't take much for him to get hold of them too, tape her ankles together.

She continues to struggle, her bound form on the floor doing a pathetic bump and grind. It's hopeless. Even she knows it. He can see it in her eyes, which stare up at him, beseeching. What color? Blue? Green? Something light.

He glances around the room at the cheap furniture, fake leather couch. Brown? Gray? He squints, blinks, reaches out for the table lamp beside her bed and clicks it off.

Ah, much better.

A comforting dimness in which to work.

He empties his pockets. First, the pieces of canvas, which he carefully unrolls, one a painted street scene, the other blank.

Next, his knives, which he arranges in a row, like a surgeon. One long and thin. Another with a heavily serrated edge. The third small, delicate, and pointy.

When she sees the knives she starts squirming all over again, and beneath the tape she is making low, guttural noises from deep in her throat.

"Shhh . . ." He strokes her forehead, has a flash of that other face, so clear, and of himself, as a young boy, crying. No. Not what he wants to see.

A tune: *Do you really want to hurt me?*

He shakes his head, focuses on the woman's nipples, visible beneath the thin cotton of her tank top, inserts his knife at the bottom edge of the fabric—just above her exposed belly button, which is pierced with a gold hoop—and with one quick move the material falls away and her chest is completely exposed, naked.

He arranges himself on her pelvis, his weight holding her in place, knees beside her head.

For a moment he is gone, does not, cannot see or hear her, his brain a jumble of noise: *Thomas's promises—Billie Jean is at my—Four out of five dentists—*

Then she squirms, and he's jolted back, her face coming into focus, a gray monochrome.

He touches her hair, wonders about the color.

He has to know.

He raises the long, thin knife, then brings it down. Fast. It pierces her chest easily.

Her eyes widen. She gasps behind the tape.

He douses the handkerchief with chloral hydrate, holds it over her mouth and nose, watches as her lids grow heavy, hiding those blue? green? gray? eyes. No need for her to suffer unnecessarily.

He closes his eyes too, pushes the knife in deeper and knows it's over for her.

When he opens them, there is blood everywhere, dark, deep cranberry—no, mulberry—spreading over stark paper-white skin, and her hair—so blond, so yellow, no, more dandelion or goldenrod or sunglow! Yes, that's it: Sunglow!

His head is swimming; he's practically swooning.

The walls are green. No, electric lime, or jungle green, or mint? Yes, mint. He imagines himself inside a bucolic landscape—periwinkle sky, pine green grass, shocking-pink flowers.

He studies her flesh. Is the pale peachy tone beneath her brassy make-up draining? Are her freckles losing their apricot hue?

No. It's too soon. It can't be.

He grabs hold of the paintbrush, dips it into the blood pooled in the girl's navel, the gold hoop sticking out, a half-moon, a relic. The blood maroon, or is it strawberry? *Who cares? It's gorgeous.*

His paintbrush comes away crimson, dripping liquid roses.

He expels a breath, mouth open, ecstatic, touches himself. He's hard. Close.

Oh. Oh. Oh.

It's almost too much.

His hand is shaking as he draws a thick scarlet stroke onto the blank canvas. Then another, and another. *Beautiful. Beautiful.*

Now with the short knife he shears off a lock of that sunglow hair, and presses it into the blood strokes on the canvas.

He switches to the serrated knife, digs deeper, uses it to saw through ribs. Then, with gloved hands, he pushes away flesh and bone to get to those deep-purple organs. That's what he wants to see. There they are in full chromatic splendor: Orchid! Eggplant! Cerise! Magenta! Purple Mountain's Majesty!

Oh, God!

His eyelids flicker; his body shudders.

A tune is playing, far away—in his mind, or in reality? He has n[...] A man and woman singing a banal duet: "Deep Purple." Iro[...] dreamy number from a cassette she picked up in some discount st[...] compilation of oldies.

And then the pictures begin again.

No. He doesn't want to see them, doesn't want anything to inter[...] with this precious moment. All this color.

But there they are, on a bed, oblivious to the song or the room or [...] young boy watching.

No, no. Not now! They are ruining it, wasting it.

Too late.

When the images finally fade and the room and the girl come back into focus, that gorgeous purple is already turning pale lavender. Within seconds, pewter.

No!

He touches her hair—the dazzling sunglow yellow has gone ash. And the room is going gray. And all that ripe-tomato blood is fading to black.

He shuts his eyes.

When he opens them, everything is dull gray, and beneath the coverall his shorts are wet, and he feels deep, soulful shame.

He closes his eyes again. He might as well. There's so little purpose now, everything colorless.

Squalid memories crowd his mind like ants on sticky candy—grim corridors, dull furniture, dead air. One colorless indistinguishable tenement after another.

He stands, resigned. Starts to pack up, though it's not so easy—his gloves are soaking. Gingerly, he lifts each of the items—the knives, brushes, tape, knockout drops—and places them back into his pockets.

Then, very carefully, he props the painting he's brought with him— the street scene—against the toaster on the kitchen counter, tears off a paper towel and cleans a smudge of the girl's blood from the canvas's edge, steps back to admire his work.

Fuck. He forgot to look at it, to see how he'd done, how close he'd come to getting things right.

Damn. What's Donna going to say?

the same, him getting lost in the moment. Donna will a good friend.

one time he remembered, just for a second, before it

t particularly liked what he'd seen.

hy he keeps forgetting to look. If he had a therapist, it.

discussing this—*this*—with one of *them,* makes him

rough a kitchen drawer, finds a roll of Saran Wrap, peels h, and carefully wraps it over the canvas painted with rned with a lock of hair. He can't help feeling disappoint- es it now, the blood strokes gray-black, the hair so colorless. h the effort. Though the moment, that was something.

of vermilion—or was it purple?—flashes in his mind's eye. n't hold on to it.

ghs, enervated from all the work and the inevitable letdown. akes in the drab room—dark curtains, pale walls—and the life- dy on the floor. He leans over, lifts open one of her lids and stares e dull gray iris.

ay too late.

Another thing he forgot.

Damn. Jessica never forgets anything. He should be more like her.

He spies the woman's handbag beside him on the floor, opens it and removes a stack of bills, mostly tens and twenties, and stashes them in his pocket.

He pulls himself up, shoes slogging through blackish blood as he heads toward the door, his body gone heavy with frustration and regret.

He even has to remind himself to remove the bloody gloves, peel the plastic Baggies off his shoes, and not be depressed that he never got to see the color of her eyes.

After all, there's always the next time.

ONE

H old on a sec." Kate unhooked her black lace bra, lay back onto the all-white bed, pillows, silk spread pushed aside.

"I was just getting to that."

"The bedspread or my bra?"

"Who cares about the spread?" Richard smiled, crow's-feet deepening at the corners of his dark blue eyes.

"I do. And I'd think you would know that after almost ten years of marriage."

"Is this going to be a discussion?" Richard's lips grazed one of Kate's breasts.

Kate shivered, then sighed. "No discussion." She slid her arms over his neck, thinking how much she loved him, perhaps even more so now than she did when they had first met and he'd courted her—Richard Rothstein the dashing bachelor lawyer, Kate McKinnon the Astoria cop. Talk about an odd couple. At least on the surface. Not so different once you stripped away Richard's glossy facade to find the boy from Brooklyn; or added the polished veneer that Kate had worked so hard to acquire after she'd left the force, returned to her first love, art history, earned the Ph.D. that became the art book that became her very own PBS series, *Artists' Lives*. All of it a surprise to her still.

If anyone had bothered to ask the young girl from Astoria where she'd be at forty she would never have predicted any kind of fame, certainly not riches. Exchange a row house for a penthouse? Sometimes even Kate had trouble believing it. She was lucky and she knew it. Perhaps that was why she devoted half her time to the educational foundation Let There Be a Future—the one that funded inner-city kids from grade school through college.

Saving kids. Hell, she didn't need a psychiatrist to explain that one to her—the motherless girl from Queens. Though when she could finally afford to she'd spent some time on the couch trying to get past it, or at least understand it: her mother's early death—a suicide—and all the guilt she'd felt, as if somehow she'd been the cause.

It was the shrink who got Kate to see that following in her father's footsteps—becoming a cop—had more than a little to do with trying to please him and make up for his losing his wife, who, by the way, if anyone cared, happened to be *her* mother.

Just about every other man in her family—uncles, cousins—had been a cop. Kate was the first woman. And even with her making detective in two short years, getting her father's attention and approval had proved elusive. But when they assigned her to runaways and she'd gotten the chance to save kids, it all became worth it. Back then, Detective McKinnon thought she could save everyone—but those missing teens had taken a toll.

How many times can I have my heart broken?

A question she'd put to herself, her shrink, her chief in Astoria, and later to Richard, who had promised to try and mend the many fissures and cracks when he proposed marriage and offered her a way out. And so far he'd done a pretty good job.

"Love you," she whispered.

Richard smiled at his wife, took in her unconventional beauty—the long straight nose, expressive brows over piercing green eyes. He ran his hand through her thick dark hair that Kate had only recently begun to spend way too much money on—having the few gray strands spun into gold. A gift to herself for her forty-second birthday.

"Anyone ever tell you you're gorgeous?"

"No. Not recently." Kate leveled a stare at Richard. *"Get it?"*

Richard painted a sheepish grin across his features. "Sorry."

"Forgiven," said Kate, moving her hand down Richard's back and under the waistband of his pajamas—ones she'd bought in Florence when she was there to deliver a lecture on up-and-coming American artists at the Accademia only last month.

Richard rolled off her, pushed his pajamas down, kicked until they fell off.

Sometimes, thought Kate, observing her tall, athletic husband kicking away, he seemed like a little boy, even with his forty-fifth birthday only a week away. Maybe, she mused, as he maneuvered himself back on top of her, all men are boys, which, at the moment, was just fine with her. Kate kissed his mouth, then ran her lips lightly over his ear.

Richard moved to Kate's neck, tongue skiing along her collarbone until reaching her breast.

Through half-closed eyes Kate took in Richard's brown-gray curls, freckles on the tops of his shoulders. Was it only a year ago she'd come so close to losing him; to believing he had betrayed her?

The Death Artist.

An image flashed behind Kate's eyes: Richard's onyx-and-gold cuff link half-hidden under the edge of a Persian rug, catching a hint of light, but enough to be noticed—at the scene of a murder.

"Richard, you won't ever lie to me again, will you?"

Richard's shoulders sagged. "What? No. Why . . . now?"

"Nothing. Sorry. Never mind."

Richard expelled a loud breath, sat up. "What's the matter?"

"Nothing. I—I was just . . . remembering,"

"We've been through it, haven't we, Kate? A dozen times. I thought it was ancient history."

"It is. Forgive me." Kate was sorry she'd spoken, wanted to take it all back, have Richard's hand on her thigh, tongue on her breast. "Tell you what," she said, laying her hand on his cheek, "I promise to shut up completely if you just go back to where you left off, okay?" Her fingers flitted over the hair on his chest, then down, lightly skimming his half-erect cock, back and forth, feeling it get hard again.

"Deal," said Richard, burying his head in her neck, adding a playful bite.

"Ow!"

"You're not allowed to say anything, remember?"

Kate lay back, closed her eyes. But a second later another image flashed: a body on a kitchen floor—and blood everywhere. *Shit.* No way she wanted to see that. Certainly not now. She'd worked so hard to forget. But how could she? The death of a young woman who had been as close to her as any daughter she was ever going to have.

She opened her eyes, stared at the architectural detail in the ceiling, anything to banish that horrendous image. She would not see it. It was over. Finished. The Death Artist was history. She and Richard were fine. No, they were great. She clasped Richard to her.

"Honey, you're strangling me."

"Oh." Kate loosened her grip. "Sorry."

"You sure it wasn't intentional?"

Kate laughed, lightly slapped Richard's back. She was okay. She would not think about any of it—Richard lying to her, Elena dying—it *was* ancient history.

She let out a long breath.

"Hey, you sure you're with me?"

"Absolutely." Kate slipped her hand between Richard's legs.

"Ummm . . . Very nice." Richard reciprocated, one hand between Kate's legs, the other under her ass, fingers teasing.

Kate's turn to moan. Richard still had the touch. How could she ever have suspected him of anything?

Richard skimmed his lips across Kate's belly, head coming to rest between her thighs, tongue beginning a slow dance.

Kate took a deep breath, all those bad images totally erased from her mind.

The feel of her skin, the scent, the taste of salt and oysters on his tongue, Kate's slowly writhing body—all of it was working its voodoo on Richard.

More than a decade and there was still no woman he'd rather make love to than his wife; no fantasy needed to stay interested either. Kate was more than enough for him. His lover. His partner. His friend. Kate, the one who had helped him become not only one of the best criminal lawyers in New York, but one of the most respected.

Nowadays, Richard Rothstein had more money than he knew what to do with. So why'd he still want more? Was he making up for those humble Brooklyn origins, the feeling that no matter how well he did or how much he acquired, it could all disappear? No way he was going to let that happen. He'd do almost anything to protect his Central Park penthouse, his home in the Hamptons, his silver Mercedes coupe, his enviable collection of modern and contemporary art. Just thinking about them made him hotter, his tongue move faster.

"You'd better stop doing that," Kate whispered. "Or it will all be over before we begin."

Richard drew his body up along Kate's, kissed her mouth.

Kate could taste herself in his kiss. She gasped ever so slightly as Richard slid inside her.

Kate's breathing was deep, regular. Richard could see she was asleep. So why wasn't he? After sex he usually fell into a coma. He stared at slivers of moonlight winking in between the heavy bedroom curtains.

He should have had it out with Andy this afternoon. At least have discussed it, figured out what was to be done. Now it was going to keep him awake, play over and over like a song stuck on repeat. *Damn.*

He glanced over at Kate, a thick lock of wavy hair falling across her cheek. He lifted it off her face with his fingertips, gently let it drop back into place.

Should he have told her? But what, exactly? No, no point in that. And really, why worry her? It wasn't Richard's way of doing things. Dissect the problem. Come up with a solution. Right.

A siren was wailing in the distance.

Richard pushed the blanket aside, quietly got out of bed.

In the bathroom medicine cabinet he found the vial he was looking for, shook an Ambien into his palm, broke the sleeping pill in half. Enough to give him a few hours of sleep and still make it into the office

in the morning without feeling drowsy. He washed down the tiny nugget
of promised dreams with a handful of water.

His reflection in the mirror looked old. Circles under his blue eyes.
Lines around his mouth deeper than usual. Worry, that's what caused it.
Richard frowned, looked away.

By the time he slid his legs back under the comforter, he thought he
could feel the pill taking effect. He'd talk to Andy before he took off for
the Boston depositions. Everything was solvable, always had been. In
Richard's world everything would always be fine.

Kate stretched, opened her eyes, the all-white bedroom coming into
focus—paintings on the walls, pottery on handcrafted shelves, the
glowing incandescent numbers on her alarm clock: 8:22.

She blinked. Could it be? She almost never slept past seven. She
hadn't even heard Richard leave.

She glanced over at his side of the bed—rumpled pillows, pajama bottoms in a heap on the floor. She plucked the pajamas up as she headed
toward the bathroom. Clearly there was no way she was ever going to
domesticate that man.

The aroma of Kiehl's tea tree oil filled the shower. Kate took her time,
a quiet day ahead of her: lunch with her women friends, a manicure, a
quick stop at Let There Be a Future, after that, dinner with Nola, since
Richard would be away.

Nola Davis.

Kate's second chance at a surrogate daughter.

Kate had been mentoring Nola since the ninth grade, when the girl
from East New York first entered Let There Be a Future. Not always a
smooth road. The sleepless nights that girl had put her through! And
now, with only a year to go at Barnard to finish up her B.A. in art history,
Nola had gone and gotten herself pregnant. Kate had just about wanted
to kill her—at first. Of course once she'd gotten over the shock she'd
started interviewing baby nurses and trying to convince Nola to move
into the Rothsteins' twelve-room apartment for a few months after the
baby was born. She'd been fantasizing about the room she and Richard
had originally planned as a nursery finally being occupied—hanging new

wallpaper, maybe painting clouds on the ceiling. But Nola wasn't sure. She was considering a temporary move to Mount Vernon to live with her Aunt Gennine, the one who had taken care of her after her mother's death, which was okay with Kate, she would not push—though she had to admit that the thought of a baby here, in her apartment, was thrilling.

In the bathroom, she used a couple of tortoiseshell combs to hold her hair in place, brushed mascara onto her lashes, ran gloss over her lips. She put on a simple gray cashmere sweater, charcoal slacks, and stepped into flats. She was tall enough. Almost six feet. Why add the extra inches? There was no one she needed to intimidate these days—and that was the way she liked it.

Richard's suit jacket was slumped over the back of a bedroom chair like a bad mood.

Kate hooked her thumb under the collar. She didn't want to leave it for Lucille. Bad enough there was a stack of dirty dishes in the sink. Lucille was their housekeeper, not their slave. Kate still had trouble letting someone take care of her, let alone wait on her.

The dark stain on Richard's jacket lapel made it clear why he hadn't worn it. Red wine, Kate guessed. Something for the dry cleaner's, or the Goodwill. She'd add it to the pile of cleaning. She made a quick check of the pockets. Richard was forever leaving things in them, then complaining when an important legal document was washed, dried, and pressed beyond recognition. A few coins in a front pocket, a folded bank statement jammed into the breast.

Kate dropped the change onto Richard's night table along with the bank statement, which had a yellow Post-it on top with the word *Andy* scribbled in red ink in Richard's unmistakable scrawl.

Kate took it in quickly—a list of deposits, withdrawals, check numbers, dates—and was about to turn away when she noticed the two entries circled with Richard's red ink. One for $650,000. Another for almost a million.

Numbers like that still impressed her. Always would. More than a bit of the Astoria girl who wore her cousin's hand-me-downs still lived inside the grown-up woman, no matter how chic or secure Kate might appear.

She studied the numbers again, but they didn't mean much to her—a bank statement, that's all.

Kate dabbed her throat and wrists with Bal à Versailles, her mother's scent, now hers, though it had taken her years to be able to wear it.

A quick look in the full-length mirror confirmed to her that she looked okay.

The truth—if you asked even the most casual observer—Kate was a knockout. She smoothed her hair, then headed down the hall past framed Mapplethorpe photos of sumptuous, erotic-looking flowers, past the eclectically decorated living room, where designer furniture and flea-market bric-a-brac coexisted perfectly. The walls were a mix of modern and contemporary paintings, with a couple of medieval artifacts that Richard was particularly proud to own displayed with a kind of studied nonchalance: one leaning on the mantel, the other on a side table beside a dozen art books, the cover of the top one sporting a Picasso self-portrait which happened to be hanging on the wall just above it.

For a split second it made Kate sad. Paintings instead of family snapshots, artifacts rather than the baby pictures or formal shots of kids in caps and gowns she'd always imagined.

Yes, they had tried. Over and over. Even going for in vitro fertilization. Nothing had worked. Of course they'd considered adopting, and probably would have if Kate hadn't become so involved in Let There Be a Future, and all of those kids who needed her that came along with it. A blessing. Kate glanced at the wall of living room windows that displayed the park below better than any painting, her vision blurred. Tears? Kate swiped at them with the back of her hand. No way she would allow herself any self-pity. Not with her life, her luck. Ridiculous. Anyway, she'd gotten over the idea of having children of her own years ago. The fact was Let There Be a Future had supplied her with plenty of kids. So what if they weren't her biological kids. They were all terrific, and they all needed her help.

Kate turned away from the paintings and the spectacular view.

At the front hall closet she reached for her jacket and stopped. For a moment she had the feeling that something terrible was about to happen—or already had and she just didn't know it.

She tried to shrug it off, thinking she was not so different from the mother she'd lost way too young—or every one of her Irish aunts who were forever crossing themselves and looking heavenward and saying Hail Marys, who were tied to every damn superstition known to mankind, and loving every one of them. Man, the fears those women had.

No, Kate was not like them.

She slid her arms into the sleeves of her jacket, pulled the collar to her neck.

There it was again—not so much a chill as a sense of foreboding, nothing specific, but the kind of feeling she used to get all the time when she was a cop and things had gone really wrong.

But she wasn't a cop and nothing *had* gone wrong.

Kate shook her head against the dread. She was late. That was all. She'd go to her luncheon, have her manicure, meet Nola for dinner, and everything would be fine. Just fine.

TWO

Floyd Brown brought his unmarked NYPD Chevy Impala to an abrupt stop beside the three battered trash cans that no one seemed to use—the street, curb, everywhere was littered with garbage. It was one thing to have shit piling up in front of the run-down tenements that lined most of these streets, but in front of the police station? Brown made a feeble attempt to shove some of the debris closer to the bins with the side of his foot. *Damn.* Didn't these cops have enough respect for the job to take a minute out of their precious day to clean up this mess?

Nothing changes, thought Brown, as he mounted the pitted stone stairs of the Bronx precinct, his old station. Eight lonely years walking a beat. Until the year when he'd finally made detective. That's what got him over to "the city," to Manhattan.

Of course being the detective who broke down the Gutter—the name given to the serial killer who literally scooped out his victim's insides and took them as souvenirs—didn't hurt. Floyd could actually smell the guilt on that guy. Nerdy, Buddy Holly–type glasses, wispy goatee, a real librarian type. No one, not the other cops, not the FBI robots, thought this was their guy. They'd brought him in because he lived next door to one of the victims. That was all.

But when Elliot Marshall Rinkie walked into the interrogation room, took off his polyester jacket, Floyd smelled it: a mixture of sweat and something . . . feral.

He'd broken the guy down in less than three hours, had him crying, snot dripping out of the little creep's nose right into his stupid little goatee.

After that Floyd not only got respect, but a nickname—the Nose—which, thank God, the guys tired of pretty quickly. But the other thing he got was a promotion and a chance to join an elite homicide squad in Manhattan. And that stuck.

Floyd liked it, was good at it too—going on the hunt, sniffing the psychos out, bringing them in, getting them into stiff-backed chairs in airless little rooms where he could go at them. Unfortunately, the cooler ones did not give off any tattletale aroma, no eau de killer. But there were other ways of getting to them. Floyd had learned a lot in his fifteen years as a homicide detective in New York City, had seen things that most people couldn't even imagine.

He pushed through the heavy wooden precinct doors, memories coming at him faster than scenes in a Jackie Chan movie—dark street corners, lukewarm coffee in Styrofoam cups, hookers, pimps, con men, junkies.

Floyd had been on the brink of retirement a year ago, would have done it too, if it hadn't been for the case that was supposed to be his last big one and an ex-cop named Kate McKinnon, who became his de facto partner. Man, that first day he'd despised her—the way she had strutted into the police conference room looking like Park Avenue, having all the answers.

But he'd been wrong.

McKinnon was good police. Despite the fact that she'd been out of the scene for years, her instincts were intact and she never pulled rank or any other kind of shit. Truth: it had been Kate who brought down that fucking psycho, the Death Artist, though she'd given him the credit—which was the reason he became Chief of Special Homicide, replacing that pain-in-the-ass crew-cut Randy Mead, who was now sitting at some desk job in the police library probably sucking his teeth and growing an ulcer. Yeah, he owed McKinnon, though sometimes he wished he had just retired. Like tonight, when he should have been home hours ago with his feet up watching the game with a cold beer in his hand and his wife, Vonette, beside him.

Instead he was *consulting*—a word he hated since it was just a euphemism for working overtime without overtime pay—on this case that was taking him to the Bronx, which hadn't been his beat for well over a decade. But McNally had asked personally, and when your old chief requests a favor it isn't easy to say no, at least not for Floyd Brown.

The pea-soup-green walls were the same as Floyd remembered, only dingier, though the peeling paint had gotten a lot worse, as if the walls were exfoliating. Who could blame the paint for wanting out of this place?

Timothy McNally met him halfway down the hall.

Floyd thought his old boss looked like he could use a new paint job too, his pallor oddly close to the greenish color of the walls, bags above and below the man's eyes like sacks of crumpled laundry.

McNally whacked Floyd on the back. "Hey, stranger. I gotta have a twisted unsub to get you to visit, huh?"

"Hey, Tim. How's it going?" Floyd tried to smile but he wasn't sure his face muscles were cooperating. He got right to the point. "So this unknown subject—why me?"

The older cop nodded toward the end of the hall. "Come on. I'll show you."

Floyd followed McNally's slow shuffling steps.

"Thought you might have some ideas," said McNally, holding the door open for Floyd.

The bad lighting in the conference room made McNally's skin appear even greener. But Floyd's attention was taken up by the crime scene photos pinned to the bulletin board, two different bodies, both women, so mutilated it was hard to tell what had happened to them.

"This one's in her early twenties, according to the ME," said McNally, tapping one group of photos.

Brown looked closer. The victim's age was hard to tell with all the makeup she was wearing on her blank dead face. "Totally eviscerated. A real fucking mess," said McNally. "Super found her. Freaked. They had to take her to Bellevue, feed her some meds." McNally drew the back of his hand across his mouth, then licked his dry lips. "The other one's also been gutted."

"That why you called me?" asked Brown, shifting his glare to the other photos, these of an older woman, somewhere between thirty and forty, he'd guess. "The similarity to my old case, the Gutter, because—"

"No, no." McNally shook his head vigorously, his jowls and the bags over and under his eyes doing a little cha-cha-cha. "No, that's not it at all."

McNally led him down another corridor, one Brown knew well, toward the evidence room.

"What d'ya think?" McNally gestured at the long metal table. On it were two paintings on slightly sagging unstretched canvas encased in clear plastic. Beside each painting was a number—the same numbers that Floyd had noted under the photos of the two bodies. "These were found at the scenes," said the older cop. "One at each."

Brown narrowed his eyes. The paintings didn't look like much. One was of fruit—apples, bananas, pears—the shapes of the fruit the only thing that identified them because the color was completely off. The banana was purple, the pear orange, the apple blue. The other painting was a street scene, almost entirely black and white except for a pink sky and bright red clouds. Floyd guessed the painter was *experimenting*, though he or she needn't have bothered. To Floyd's untrained eye they looked pretty bad.

"So?" McNally regarded Brown through his hooded eyes.

"I'd say the guy's got a lot to learn."

"I was thinking that you might know something, have an idea. I mean, tell you the truth, if the Death Artist wasn't dead, I'd be thinking maybe he was back in business."

"No, his work was nothing like this. The Death Artist didn't just paint." Brown thought back to the bizarre clues, the collages and postcards that McKinnon had deciphered for the squad, the only way they'd ever have caught that psycho. "He'd never do shit like this." For a moment Brown realized he was insulted that McNally could even think that the Death Artist would do such bad art—as if the Death Artist really had been some kind of artistic genius. He blew air out the side of his mouth.

"You said these were left at the scenes? You sure they didn't belong to the vics?"

"Possible." McNally tugged at his blubbery chin. "But the lab's tellin' us that the paint used in both is the same. Ditto for the canvas. So either the vics took a painting class together"—he snickered—"or they shared art supplies. Pretty fuckin' unlikely, wouldn't you say?"

"Name-brand paint and canvas?" Brown asked.

McNally swiped a sheet of paper off the table. "Uh, lab just says oil paint. Canvas is cotton duck, it says."

Brown took the sheet from McNally's hand. "Generic oil paint and cotton duck. Don't know if that makes a match, Tim." He offered his old boss a sorry look.

McNally's sad-sack face sagged a bit more.

Floyd looked again at the paintings—the banal scene, the fruit, the weird color. They could be the work of the same person, but no way he could be sure. "I'm no art expert."

McNally stopped pulling on his neck, which was now red like the clouds in the one painting. "What about that woman, you know, the one you worked with, from TV? She knows all about this art shit. Maybe she'd take a look."

"I don't know." Brown knew how traumatic the Death Artist case had been for Kate, that now, finally, she had gotten her cushy life back on track. He doubted she'd want to hear from him or have anything to do with tracking another killer—and he couldn't blame her. Still, there were two bodies in the morgue with the same MO and maybe she could tell them something they should be looking for.

"It'd make Tapell real happy," said McNally. "She's coming up for reappointment as chief of police and she don't need no serial killer out there to make her look bad."

"Two murders are no serial, Tim. You know that." Floyd looked again at the two paintings, a grenade going off in his gut. Two eviscerated women, two paintings left at the scenes. It had all the markings of a ritual, of a serial killer. He just didn't want to think so. Maybe he should call Chief Tapell, see what she thought about contacting McKinnon. After all, Tapell and McKinnon were friends—the two of them went all the way back to Astoria, when Tapell was Queens Chief of Police and McKinnon was a cop under her.

McNally frowned. "Two murders in a month. Within blocks of each other. Both vics killed in the same way." The older cop sighed. "But I guess you know best."

Floyd gave him a look. "It's not my jurisdiction."

"Jurisdiction?" McNally repeated the word as though Brown had taken a dump on his feet. "I'm not askin' you to move back to the Bronx. Just help me out here." He slumped into a stiff-backed metal chair. "They're retiring me. Next month. I'd like to go out in style, you know?" He forced a smile. "Don't know what I'm gonna do with myself. Watch TV all day, follow the soaps, right?" He laughed, but there was no cheer in it. "I never did develop no *hobbies*."

Brown took in his old chief's blurred features—the effect of thirty-five years on the force. "Look, I'll talk to Tapell, but I'm not even sure that the chief would want me interfering in another borough. But"—he pinched the bridge of his nose—"I'll see, okay? But no promises."

*   *   *

BAD PAINTER GOOD KILLER

The NYPD has a new psycho on their hands with two murders reported in the Bronx now very possibly linked. The victims, whose names are being temporarily held until families can be notified, were both savagely mutilated. But the most bizarre element in both cases was the oil painting planted by the killer at each scene.

Though the police declined to discuss the details of these paintings, it has been confirmed by an inside source that they were rather ordinary—one a still life of fruit, the other a street scene. No one has yet determined the paintings' particular relevance to the victims or if they contain clues to the murders, though it appears as if Manhattan's elite murder squad has been called in . . .

Floyd Brown crumpled the newspaper in his fist. How the hell these damn reporters got information so quickly, he'd never know. There was no "inside source" as far as he knew, nor had the police intentionally leaked the information, which they did when they wanted to flush out a perp or bring additional witnesses to the surface. Floyd was quite sure that Chief of Police Tapell wanted this kept under wraps until they had more information. Well, too late for that. He figured Tapell was reading this too, probably taking someone's head off. Plus, the reporter had used his special homicide squads' nickname, the "murder squad"—and he had yet to agree they would be a part of it.

Brown scanned his desk, the files of unsolved homicides stacked in the corner like a mini Aztec pyramid, then reached for the phone. Better to call Tapell before she called him.

He was dragging the man by his feet, blood trailing behind like a comet, just visible in the darkness. The body was heavier than he'd anticipated, considering that half the man's guts were ten feet behind him in the middle of the alley.

It had to be discovered soon. Not two days from now, when some street cleaner felt ambitious and went into the alley behind the Manhattan office building, or some crack addict needed a place to shoot up.

He took his time arranging it so that one of the man's legs peeked out of the alleyway just enough to catch a passerby's attention, though they'd probably think it was some homeless person and keep on walking.

Under the jumpsuit, sweat from his armpits was dripping down his sides, and his hands were damp under the gloves.

Somewhere a dog was barking. Odd, he thought, in this part of the city, mainly offices, all shut down for the night. He checked the time. It would be several hours before any of them opened for business.

He unwrapped the still-wet canvas he'd brought with him, and arranged it beside the body. Or should he figure out a way to get it on the alley wall? He wasn't sure about that part. Did it matter? He studied it a minute—a still life of fruit in a blue-striped bowl—then nudged it with his gloved hand a bit closer to the dead man's head.

You know I don't want to hear this, Dominic." The phone felt hot against Tapell's ear. "You're supposed to keep your union members happy, remember? That's why I put you in the job." Clare Tapell regretted the statement the second the words had left her mouth. She sighed into the phone. "Look, Dom, I'm sorry. But I don't need this. Not now. I just can't have a police strike. And it's illegal, remember? Besides, the mayor is threatening to trim the budget, *again,* which sure as hell means less money for police. You just can't let it happen."

The chief of police listened a moment, stared at the framed photos on the walls beside her desk, one of her shaking hands with the mayor, the new conservative mayor, who she was pretty sure did not care for her, a black woman, and a liberal, heading up New York's police force and coming up for reappointment. No, she did not need a strike, something to prove she could not control her people. *Damn it.*

She listened another moment, then reiterated her demands—that the union head stave off even the threat of a police walkout—then spent the next two hours calling every precinct chief in all five boroughs, stroking each of them as best she could, flipping through files to find names of their wives or husbands and children to add that personal touch.

No way Clare Tapell was going to let this job slip through her fingers after one term. She'd fought too hard and too long, and damn it, she'd given up a personal life for it, not that anyone cared about that.

What they cared about was today's report in the *Daily News.* The new statistics were in, and crime had gone up two percent, which had everything to do with a slowing economy and fewer cops, not to mention losing some of her best men and women on 9/11. She was still waiting for that promised federal money to replace them, and it looked as though it was never going to come.

On top of everything, that damn *Post* story.

A serial killer in the Bronx? *Jesus.*

When McNally said the words—*serial killer*—she hadn't thought much of it. The man was a decent cop, a dedicated lifer, for sure, but no genius. But when Brown said it she knew she had to pay attention.

Tapell popped a couple of Rolaids into her mouth.

For the moment she put aside thoughts of federal funding or a police strike or even her reappointment, and called Kate McKinnon Rothstein, though she knew Kate would not appreciate her call.

Tapell squeezed the plastic cap onto the Rolaids container thinking that she knew Kate about as well as she knew anyone. The problem was that Kate knew her too, or rather, things about her—that she would prefer no one knew at all.

THREE

A day off had done her good. Now Kate was anxious to get to Boyd Werther's studio and complete the taped interview for the upcoming installment of *Artists' Lives*. They would have to finish on time if she was to keep her appointment with Floyd Brown. Despite Clare Tapell's assurance that all they wanted from her was an opinion on a couple of paintings, Kate was dreading it. Paintings in a gallery or museum were one thing, in a police station something else entirely.

Kate pushed the thought from her mind and quickened her step.

Mulberry Street felt like a small village waking up just a bit later than the rest of Manhattan: a few trucks and vans delivering wares; shopkeepers pulling open metal grates; window washers sloshing soapy water across glass storefronts; the mostly young, definitely hip residents—women with a strip of exposed gym-toned belly, guys sporting that just-out-of-bed tousled hair that needed an hour of gelling into shape—ambling into one or another of the cool new cafés that dotted the street, cigarettes dangling from the corners of their still young, but otherwise wise mouths. Kate wondered how they could afford the time. Were they artists, musicians, or out-of-work stockbrokers who'd opted for the boho life after the nineties market tumbled? Whatever. Good for them, thought Kate, always amazed when she came down to NoLIta, the area north of Little Italy, at how the city was such a canny chameleon, able to transform neighborhoods seemingly overnight.

Kate's small PBS film crew was completely set up and ready to roll by the time she stepped out of the industrial elevator into Boyd Werther's football field of a studio. With its twelve-foot pressed-tin ceilings, wide-plank floors, and glorious city views, Kate had kidded Boyd that he must have killed someone to have such a grand studio, but she knew better.

Boyd Werther was that rare art world phenomenon, an artist who had been successful throughout his career. First as a cool minimal painter in the seventies, and then, when he'd expanded his artwork and taken up where the abstract expressionist painters of the 1950s had left off, combining the energy and grace of de Kooning's gesture with Mark Rothko's gorgeous color, he had been canonized a "modern master"—his canvases of looping, intertwining color bands compared to such grand and disparate influences as Jackson Pollock's "drip" paintings, the calligraphy of ancient Japanese scrolls, and the Paleolithic cave paintings at Lascaux.

Lately, Kate kept hearing him referred to as the "great white hope." She wasn't sure if people meant Boyd was the keeper of the traditional flame or if it was some sort of put-down, but knowing the art world, Kate assumed the latter. No artist could be successful for forty years and not have people despise him.

Kate hoped Boyd Werther's career was indeed as successful and lucrative as it appeared, since the artist had confided to her that he was currently paying alimony and child support to three—or was it four? Kate could not remember—ex-wives, who had provided him with six or seven offspring, including a toddler in a fancy private preschool—the product of his most recent divorce from a Brazilian beauty.

Kate stepped gingerly between strobe lights and wires to give each of her crew a quick hug.

"Where's Boyd?" she asked.

"Moussing his hair," said Cindy, rolling her eyes.

Kate unfolded her list of final questions for Boyd, whom she'd been interviewing for several weeks. This was the last day of filming and she wanted to make sure she had everything she needed for her show.

This season, Kate's series was simple: Each week a different artist was interviewed about the importance of color. Though the interviews came across as live, they were taped so that Kate could not only edit out the mistakes, but add relevant historical footage, like Kandinsky's pure lyrically colored abstract *Improvisations* of the early 1900s, Josef Albers's intensive color studies, close-ups of impressionist paintings (so she could point out how those painters had optically created color by placing, say, a red beside a yellow to create the sensation of orange in the eye of the beholder), as well as interviews with scientists and color theorists.

Boyd Werther was not only a top-notch colorist, but articulate and entertaining, and Kate was confident she would have a terrific show.

While the TV crew finished setting up, Boyd Werther's ever-present studio assistants—two extraordinarily pretty young women—were floating around the studio picking up brushes and paint rags, answering Boyd's phone, making coffee. Kate assumed they attended to the genius's whims and demands, artful or otherwise.

Boyd Werther strode into the room on bare feet, his studio floors kept clean enough to eat off by those nubile and nimble assistants.

A large man edging toward fat, Werther was decked out in a silky black shirt, half unbuttoned to display his bulky torso, and loose-fitting drawstring pants, cinched below an impressive belly. His hair was long, stylishly unkempt, once black, now streaked with gray. He took Kate's hand, planted a dramatic kiss, then kissed both her cheeks. "Your eyes"—he pulled back and studied her—"are remarkably viridian. Has anyone ever told you that?"

"*Constantly.* The butcher, the man at the deli counter, everyone. It's *so* annoying."

Boyd laughed. "But it's true. They are a pure viridian green. Quite startling."

"Yeah, right," said Kate. "And my hair is the most brilliant burnt sienna, and my lips are what—cadmium-red scarlet? And what else? I must be missing something."

He drew his finger gently along her cheek. "Your skin. A perfect mix of rose madder with an undercoat of Naples yellow mixed with just a dollop of titanium white."

"Oh, brother." Kate rolled her viridian eyes.

Boyd offered up a sexy, confident smile, tugged gently on a thick chain he wore around his neck.

"Interesting shackle you've got there," said Kate.

"This?" He ran his paint-stained fingers under it for better display. "A gift from my first wife. She was Italian, you know. An aristocrat. The piece had been in her family for centuries. Medieval, I believe."

Kate came in for a closer look, admired the handicraft of the interlocking crosslike links. "How come she let you keep it?"

"I remain friends with all my ex-wives—and lovers."

"Can we get started?" said the two cameramen practically in unison. They were obviously immune to the painter's charms.

Kate gave herself a quick once over in one of Boyd's floor-length mirrors, smoothed her slacks and sweater, and arranged herself in one of the two director's chairs that had been set up in the middle of Boyd's studio, with his enormous colorful canvases surrounding them.

The assistant clipped microphones onto Boyd and Kate, and for the next two hours the artist hardly took a breath, gesturing at his paintings, delivering opinions, and making pronouncements.

To her final question—"How important is color to you?"—Boyd said, "It's *everything*. Absolutely everything. The reason I wake up in the morning. One only has to look at my paintings to see that. Really, why bother to paint if you're not going to make use of color, art's most seductive tool? I eat, sleep, and dream color."

"Sounds unhealthy," said Kate, then quick-turned to the cameramen and said, "Cut." She shook her head. "Sorry, Boyd. I couldn't resist. But let me respond to that more respectfully." She nodded at the cameramen to roll again. "I see," she said, more solemnly now. "So what would you say to painters who limit their palette, or use no color at all, simply black and white?"

"Well, Franz Kline got away with black-and-white paintings, but that was in the 1950s. Now, well, it would be a *big* bore. I could never do that. Never. The fact is," said the artist with a nonchalant shrug, "I'd kill myself without color."

"Could you say that again?" one of the cameramen asked. "I want to get a close-up."

"Sure." Boyd Werther sat up straighter in the director's chair, smoothed his silky shirt as the camera dollied in.

"I'd absolutely *kill* myself if I was denied the use of color," he said. "No question."

By the way," said Kate, as Boyd kissed her cheeks good-bye at the freight elevator. "A wise old artist once told me to never say never."

"I imagine you're referring to my statement about never working in black and white."

"I just wouldn't want you to kill yourself," said Kate.

*   *   *

It had been over a year since Kate had been inside the drab tan walls of the Sixth Precinct, and nothing had changed—same fluorescent lighting washing everything in a sickly hue; same smell of bad coffee, perps' lies, cops' ambition, and dreams gone sour turning the air foul, her own bad memories adding to the mix, making it personal.

She nodded at the desk cop, who waved her through. "Brown's waiting for you. You know the way?"

Oh, yes, she remembered.

Kate stared at her hands, at the pearly, not quite clear, polish, and checked her watch.

"I don't think I can do it, Floyd." She pushed her thick hair behind her ears, took a deep breath. She'd already been through it with Clare Tapell, agreed she would take a look. But now that she was here, in Brown's office, with nightmares of the Death Artist crowding everything else out of her psyche, she didn't want any part of it. If Richard were here he'd be screaming NO WAY. But she hadn't spoken to him since he'd called from his office and sounded upset, saying he'd tell her about it when he got back from taking depositions in Boston.

Brown drummed his nails along his desk. "Look, McKinnon, I understand, but it's a favor to me and to Tapell."

Kate nodded, knew she didn't have much choice. But her mind was still fighting it. What the hell was she doing here, now, when she'd finally gotten her life back on track after a year of nightmares and mourning? She wanted to return to her TV series, or Let There Be a Future, to review applicants for the coming term, figure out how and where she was going to get the funds to support a new group of kids. The kind of problems she liked.

"Okay." Kate stood, smoothed her slacks, tried to adjust her mind to the task. It was simple enough. Take a look at a couple of paintings. That much she could handle.

She looked into Brown's dark eyes, and said: "Let's get this over with."

Brown had the siren going, navigating his Chevy Impala through the Bronx streets like a cowboy.

"If you'd mentioned the Bronx I would have said no for sure." Kate stared out the window at tenements and brownstones that reminded her of the street she'd grown up on in Astoria, only shoddier.

"Yeah, I asked if some rookie wouldn't like to personally carry the paintings up to your Park Ave castle, but hey, these days the NYPD is a little short on staff."

"Funny," said Kate with a slight sneer. "And it's Central Park West. Not Park Avenue."

"Yeah," said Brown, smiling. "I know that."

"Been a while since you had someone to abuse, *Detective* Brown?"

"No. But you were always more fun than most. And it's *Chief* Brown."

"Yeah," said Kate, returning Brown's sardonic smile. "I know that."

The Bronx precinct looked a lot worse than the Sixth, even though it was obvious that efforts had been made on their behalfs. The paintings were set up in the precinct's briefing room, with the permanent rows of metal chairs facing a blackboard and bulletin board, and a lectern with a microphone—where all the important meetings took place. There were large black clips attached to the edges of the plastic bags which held the unstretched paintings, pushpins stuck through them to hold them on to the bulletin board alongside the crime scene photos, also pushpinned, which Kate wished they had chosen to put elsewhere—preferably anywhere that she wasn't.

McNally huffed his way into the room. "Sorry." His face was flushed. "No one told me you were here."

Brown made the introductions.

Kate could feel the Bronx chief looking her over, sizing her up. She knew people often assumed from her style and dress, the quality of her speech that she was a product of private-school, summer-home, Mercedes-Benz wealth, when in fact she was simply her own best invention.

On the desk beside the lectern someone had set out a coffee urn along with the ubiquitous stack of Styrofoam cups, Cremora, a dish strewn with packets of sugar and Sweet 'n Low. There were even cookies, Oreos, on a plastic plate.

Kate avoided looking at the crime scene photos, though they were busy imprinting on her brain via her peripheral vision.

But the paintings drew her in. Was it the fact that she'd been spending half her days for the past six months reading everything on color, from Josef Albers's famous *Interaction of Color* to interviewing Ellsworth Kelly, to poring through Mondrian's and Van Doesburg's writings on primary color, even flying to Germany to chat with Gerhard Richter about his color-chart paintings—or was it simply that the color in these awkward paintings was so damn off that it was riveting all by itself? Kate wasn't sure.

"What do you think?" McNally nibbled an Oreo.

Kate moved closer to the still life of fruit. "Well, you could call it *fauve*—the French painters who experimented with color, Matisse, Derain, Dufy—but I don't think so. *Les fauves*—that's French for wild beasts—were trying to structure a painting entirely through color. But this, well, there's nothing connective about the color. It's bold and garish, and certainly wild, but it doesn't add up to anything."

Brown leaned in. "So you think whoever painted it is an amateur?"

"Could be. Maybe he's what the art world calls an *outsider*."

Brown cocked his head. "Meaning?"

"Outsider art. It's the English equivalent of what was originally called *l'art brut,* which the French artist Jean Dubuffet coined in, oh, the late 1940s—it encompasses the untrained, unschooled, and the art of the insane."

"You tellin' me that people care about the art made by a bunch of nut jobs?" McNally shook his head, bewildered.

"Yes, they do," said Kate. "Quite seriously. The French surrealists were influenced by the art of the insane and revered it. Nowadays, lots of people collect it."

McNally shook his head again. "Beats the hell out of me."

Kate plucked her reading glasses out of her bag, came in for a closer inspection, first of the still life and then the street scene. "The edges are interesting, " she said, taking note of the almost perfect one-inch border that ran around the perimeter of both paintings. "He's making his own sort of frame." She regarded the loops and curls of graphite, unintelligible, basically a mass of gray scrawl. "Pencil, I think, mainly scribbles, labor-intensive ones, for sure, but scribbles." She moved closer into the color part of the paintings. "Whoever painted these is really laying into his brush." She pointed out an area of paint that looked scrubbed onto the canvas. "There are individual bristles that have broken off the brush and have stuck into the paint."

McNally flicked Oreo crumbs off his shirt and leaned toward the painting, as did Brown.

"So he's painting them fast and hard?" asked Brown.

"You could say that," said Kate.

McNally squinted at the paintings. "That why the color is so fucked up? 'Cause he's painting them fast?"

"Not necessarily. A forceful, expressionist brush stroke might mean he's working fast and furiously, but a painter can put the color down correctly as quickly as he or she can put it down wrong."

"So it's a choice?" Brown poured a cup of coffee, left it black, and offered it to Kate, who took it not because she wanted lousy cop coffee but because Brown had remembered she drank it black.

"Perhaps." She took a sip. It was even worse than she remembered. "Lots of artists have experimented with color. And there's something about these that remind me—a little—of the German expressionist painter, Kirchner. I'll show you some later."

McNally's face lit up. "So our unsub's a Kraut?"

Kate shook her head, suppressed a grin. "No. What I'm saying is these paintings have a raw quality, an immediacy that *reminds* me of the German painters. It's possible your unsub—or whoever painted these—knows the work of those artists, is trying to emulate them, or—" She shifted her gaze to the street scene. "I don't know. This one's mostly black and white and—"

"Except for the sky," said McNally, proud, as if he were pointing out something that everyone else had missed.

"Right," said Kate, exchanging the briefest look with Brown before going back to the paintings. "I'm really not sure what to say. The work looks unschooled, but there are artists who go for that look intentionally."

"Do you think they're some sort of code?" Brown asked.

"Maybe." An image flashed across Kate's brain—her face pasted over Andrea Mantegna's painting of Saint Sebastian. That was code all right. *The Death Artist.* She leaned back against the lectern, a wave of nausea rising in her throat.

Brown touched her arm. "You okay?"

She was suddenly dying for a smoke after six months without a single puff. "I'm fine. Where was I?" She focused on the paintings. "The ways he's drawn the streets and the fruit are okay. Nothing special; the objects are recognizable, adequate, though there is some distortion. Again, I can't say if that's intentional or not." She pursed her lips and came in close again. "There appear to be suggestions of charcoal beneath the paint, which must be how he starts his paintings. And it looks like a bit of a letter, maybe a *Y* and an *R*." She pointed them out. "See here, and here?"

Kate stood back, took off her glasses, folded her arms across her chest, tried to assess the work coolly. "But what makes these paintings special—though I'm not sure that's the right word for them—is the odd use of color. And I can't figure out what he's trying to accomplish with it because it doesn't really make sense." She turned to McNally. "If you have pictures of these, I'll take them home and see if anything comes to me."

"Got some in my office," he said, turning abruptly out of the room.

A muffled jingle sounded from somewhere inside Brown's clothes.

"Pacemaker?" Kate asked, a wry smile on her lips.

Brown tugged the cellular out of his inside breast pocket, hugged it to his ear. "Brown here." He paused. "Uh-huh. Where? Shit. Who's there? Right. Make sure the tech boys don't destroy the scene until I've seen it."

He clicked off as McNally came chugging back into the room with an envelope for Kate. "Digitals," he said, handing them over.

"What is it?" Kate asked Brown.

"A body. And a painting. In Midtown Manhattan."

Brown maneuvered the Impala through the traffic on the West Side Highway, siren blaring. The Hudson River was flying past Kate's vision, bluish-green brush strokes painted below a steel-gray sky.

But what was it she was feeling? Aside from a nagging desire to smoke a cigarette that would not go away, there was definitely something else. Could it possibly be adrenaline? *Jesus.* Those old cop instincts just kicked in whether she wanted them to or not. But no way she actually wanted to visit a crime scene—a murder scene. Forget it. She rapped her nails against the dashboard.

"You look like you're about to explode," said Brown.

"I'm fine."

"Should I get off at Seventy-ninth to drop you?"

Kate hesitated, tried to fight the words that were already coming out of her mouth. "Why don't you just go where you're going and I'll grab a cab from there."

"No Mercedes today?" There was the slightest sneer on Brown's lips.

Kate offered up her own acerbic smile. "I prefer having you as my driver."

"Funny," said Brown, then gave her a knowing look. "You want to see it, don't you?"

"No." Kate sighed. "I simply don't want to take you out of your way."

Brown threw her a sideways grin. "Uh-huh, sure."

"You said Thirty-ninth Street, right? It's just a block away from Richard's office. It'll give me an excuse to drop in on him."

Brown gave her another dry "Uh-huh."

The police-car radio was crackling with codes and descriptions as Brown cut across West Fortieth.

"You want me to let you out here?" he asked.

"In the middle of the street?"

"Just checking," said Brown, still smirking until he saw the ring of cop cars up ahead and the uniforms keeping passersby from the scene.

Kate checked her watch. Almost four-thirty. Richard would definitely be back from Boston by now, probably even in his office. She should call him, tell him she was close by, maybe they'd go for a bite or a drink. That made a lot more sense than following Brown to a murder scene. But she didn't go for her cellular and when Brown said, "Last chance," she just nodded and he knew what she meant.

Brown had to park on the sidewalk. A dozen cop cars, an EMT van, and an ambulance were crowding the end of the street near the tall buildings at the corner of the Avenue of the Americas, just a few blocks south of the neon and glass and billboards and noise that made up Times Square. He was out fast, gold shield in hand, pushing through the crowd that had gathered and the ring of uniforms.

A beefy guy with a red complexion and a sparse blond mustache flagged him over.

"The vic's way down at the other end of the alley," he said.

"Anyone touch anything?"

The red-faced detective put his hands up as a sign. "Nope. Did what we were told, Chief Brown. Waited for you. Couple of medics and cops are with the body, that's all. Just waiting." He looked over at Kate.

"She's with me," said Brown. "Consults for NYPD."

Kate liked the sound of that, tried her best to look official, tucked her fine leather bag under her arm, stood up straight. *Am I out of my mind?* She took a deep breath, knew the answer to that, but something kept compelling her forward, following Brown.

Brown peered down the alley, but couldn't see anything.

Blond mustache said: "Runs the entire length of the building—right through from Thirty-ninth to Fortieth. The vic, the cops, and the medics are at the end, like I said. According to a guy at the front desk of the Fortieth Street building, the alley used to connect these two buildings— like about thirty years ago." He signaled a uniform over, plucked the guy's flashlight off his belt, handed it to Brown. "You're gonna need this."

Brown turned into the alley, Kate just behind him. But she hesitated. Maybe it was her cop instincts failing her, or her normal human ones kicking in and telling her to forget this folly, or maybe it was something else. She wasn't sure of anything except the chill that had started in her lower back now working its way up her spine, and the tingling in her arms and legs, and a sharp awareness of her own breathing and her mouth gone dry.

Brown glanced over his shoulder. "You sure about this, McKinnon?" *Sure? No, of course not.* But she had to follow, had to see the scene. *Why?*

She had no idea. Just a feeling urging her on.

Brown was waiting.

"Yes," she said.

She would do this, then return to her normal life, call Richard, make him take her for that drink, and everything would be as it was. Naturally she would not be telling Richard what she'd done. He'd absolutely kill her. She flashed on the other night, the two of them in bed, Richard inside her. But instead of warming her it only heightened her anxiety.

The alley was dark, no more than four feet wide, cold. A place the sun never reached. Brown was a few feet ahead of her but already breaking up, becoming a shadow.

Something scampered beside her foot, right up against her fine leather loafers, probably a rat. She maintained her cool, distracted by something less tangible, a buzzing sensation, something she had not felt in over a year; the way she'd felt when the Death Artist was in her brain and she was closing in on him. But that made no sense. The Death Artist was dead.

Brown switched on the flashlight. The brick walls lit up, scarred and decorated with graffiti, the pavement littered with so many beer cans and bottles it looked like a recycling plant gone awry. The air was heavy with garbage, alcohol, and urine.

"Nice smell," Brown said. "Just like Park Avenue, huh?"

Kate ignored the crack. She was thinking about the last time she and Brown were cops together, and how they'd both come close to dying.

She could feel her heart beating fast; Brown whistling a tune as though nothing were wrong, as though they would not eventually come to the end of this dark, dank passageway and find a body.

A *dead* body. So why was it she felt afraid?

She made an involuntary move, her hand inside her jacket, and realized she was reaching for a gun she did not have. She sighed. She was being ridiculous. Ridiculous for coming, and ridiculous for being afraid.

Brown's flashlight was doing the jitterbug as he walked, picking out a patch of wall here, a piece of floor there.

What was that? Something gelatinous at Kate's feet, maybe some rotting food or a dead animal. She didn't know, didn't want to know, but the soles of her shoes had picked up some of it, and were making sticky, smacking sounds with each step she took.

They were halfway down the alleyway, there was light at the other end filtering in like a thick fog. She couldn't really make anything out, or hear much—that buzzing was in her ears, her brain.

"Thought you'd gotten it out of your system, didn't you, McKinnon?"

"What?" Kate could barely understand his words.

"Once a cop, always a cop."

That she heard. And knew he was right, though she hated admitting it. *Damn.* Why hadn't she just called Richard and gone to see him? What the hell was she doing in this dark alleyway in the middle of Manhattan following Brown to a crime scene that had nothing to do with her, when she had vowed never to do anything like this again?

Too late to turn back now. The figures at the end of the tunnel were turning solid, three, no, four of them standing over what looked like a toppled scarecrow.

Kate decided not to look, that when she got to the end of this dark tunnel she would simply step past the group. She didn't need to see it anymore. She must have been testing herself, that's all, needed to see if she could handle the fear after all she'd been through.

Brown's flashlight was picking out the details: three men, one woman, all standing over the scarecrow.

Okay, she'd seen it. More than she needed to. Now she would walk past it, excuse herself to Floyd Brown, go into the light of day and call Richard. Suddenly she could not wait to be out of there.

The woman called out—"Chief Brown"—and the flashlight illuminated her. Kate immediately recognized her—the ME who had examined Elena's body. The image shot through Kate's brain like lightning: the ME huddled over Elena's broken body, gloved hands probing.

Oh, Jesus.

Kate stopped short, leaned against the alley wall, ignored the stench of garbage and alcohol and urine now amplified by death, and took a deep breath. For a moment she thought she might be sick, but no, she was okay. As long as she got out of here she'd be fine.

Brown had met up with the group. They were talking to him, their voices commingling: ". . . white male, totally mutilated." Kate could only see half of what they were checking out, the painting that was on the ground beside the dead man, then one of them handing something to Brown, saying—"His wallet"—and Brown opening it, his flashlight still in his hands, rocking, telegraphing indiscriminate indecent split-second pictures of the scene as he bent over to get a look at the body.

She had to get out of there. Now. But the cops and the ME and Brown were blocking her way.

Oh, God, why did I come here?

She had been stupid, arrogant and stupid. Whatever she had been trying to prove to herself no longer mattered.

She took a few steps, mumbling "Excuse me," pushing past the group, past Brown, who tried to stop her. He touched her arm so gently it couldn't possibly have stopped her, and she knew then—was absolutely certain that something was terribly wrong.

But she didn't stop.

Cool, fresh air was on her face. *Thank God.* She was almost out of there.

"McKinnon. Kate." Brown's voice had gone hoarse.

Her feet were making contact with the normal sidewalk. She was free.

"McKinnon." Brown got a hand around her arm, but Kate pulled out of his grip, would not stop.

What was it she'd seen in that moment that she had dared to look, when the flashlight had arced around that last bit of dark alleyway and the face of the victim had been so clearly illuminated?

"No," she said, not sure what she was saying no to. She had to keep walking, that was all, then she'd be free.

"No," she said again, striding past cops in uniforms and men and women and children who had gathered, and the cars that were honking their horns as she started to sprint down the middle of the traffic-crowded street, running from what she'd seen so that it would not—could not—possibly be true.

But then Brown was beside her and he'd grabbed both her arms and spun her around and looked at her, his brown eyes large and filled with compassion and pity, and she fell against him, and the man's face—the victim's face—the dead man at the end of the alley, the beautiful dead man's face flashed and froze in her mind.

"Oh, God, no," she sobbed into Floyd Brown's clean blue shirt. "Oh, God, please. It can't be. It can't be Richard."

FOUR

How many days has it been?

Kate wasn't sure. Her body felt heavy, leaden, way too much effort to pull herself upright in her bed, where she had been spending most of her time, crying, sobbing, all she seemed capable of doing. Sleep was out of the question; every time she closed her eyes, horror movie scenes of Richard's body in that alleyway started to play.

And then the morgue.

How had she done it, stood there in that frigid room of death with her husband's body on a cold porcelain table, a sheet pulled up to his chin to hide his ruined body, his beautiful body.

Floyd Brown had been beside her the whole time, hand on her arm, just enough human contact to make it possible for her not to turn and run screaming from this living nightmare.

But how had she felt?

Stunned? Yes. Numb? Certainly.

She had tried to look anywhere but at the body: at the walls, the sinks, the black hoses dangling from faucets, the hanging scales—the kind one sees in grocery stores, only these were used to weigh human organs, not tomatoes—the surgical tools, knives, scalpels, scissors, forceps, a Stryker saw to cut through bone, pruning shears.

Kate knew these places, had sat and stood through more autopsies and ID'd more bodies than she had ever wanted to. But that was over; that was history. She was finished with that. She'd paid her dues, hadn't she?

A glimpse of Richard's face, pale, lifeless, and Kate's legs felt like those dangling hoses. Brown must have felt it, or intuited it, seasoned cop that he was. He tightened his grip on her arm, asked, "You okay?"

Okay? No! I'm dying! But Kate had only nodded, taking deep breaths behind the surgical mask, quickly shifting her glance away, eyes focusing on the Dictaphone beside the table, which she knew from experience the medical examiners spoke into, recording details as they worked.

What would this ME say?

White male. Age forty-five. Good physical condition. Six feet, two inches tall.

Kate's eyes crawled along the sheet, the relief map of a beloved and familiar body.

But, my God, he looked so much smaller, so diminished in death, this man, this body that was supposed to be her husband, but couldn't possibly be. No, it just wasn't possible. She refused to believe it.

She squeezed her eyes shut and pictured the beachfront below the dunes of their Hamptons home, the blue blue ocean that stretched out forever, and Richard, backlit by a blazing midday sun, tall and fit, collapsing playfully at her feet, tickling her until she begged him to stop, the sand scratching at her elbows as she pushed him away, the two of them laughing and laughing and laughing as if they were kids—and though she did not feel them, there were tears streaking mascara down her cheeks.

Had she kissed him good-bye before he'd left for Boston?

No, she was asleep.

And he'd never made it to Boston, never made it to the airport.

Had he been killed in his office? The alley was only a block away. He had to have been attacked on his way to or from the office or at the office, and if that was the case, then someone had dragged his body for a block and set it up in that alleyway.

Jesus, what was happening to her—thinking like a cop, now, at a time like this.

Kate stared at Richard's hand, his gold wedding band catching the cool fluorescent light, shocking next to alabaster fingers. A chill rippled through her own fingers, up her arms, snaked its way into her heart, and for a moment the porcelain-and-steel room began to spin until Kate forced herself to study the hand coolly, detached, as though it were nothing more than a perfect anatomical replica of Richard's hand, a piece of art worthy of Michelangelo.

The medical examiner, a youngish man with a sallow complexion and thick glasses, followed her line of vision. "The ring, uh, you can get it later, unless, like, uh, some people prefer them to be buried with it."

Buried with it . . . buried with it . . . buried with it . . .

The words echoed in Kate's brain and somehow kicked off one of those idiotic teen tragedy songs from her youth, a car stuck on the railroad tracks, a girl going back in to find her boyfriend's ring, and dying, "Teen Angel"—which she could not stop, the refrain, *teen angel, teen angel,* playing over and over, absurdly, in her head.

"Can't I have it now?" Kate managed to say, and watched as the ME tugged the ring from her dead husband's finger and placed it in her hand, the precious metal cold, yet burning in her palm.

She looked up at the medical examiner's name tag clipped slightly askew to the lapel of his white lab coat, anything to distract herself: Daniel Markowitz.

"Oh, I'm sorry," Markowitz said. "But, uh, you haven't actually said, I mean, he is, uh, was, uh, your husband, correct?"

"Of course," Floyd Brown barked.

"Yes," Kate whispered, and for the first time allowed herself to take in Richard's face, which was miraculously unscathed, skin smooth, colorless lips slightly parted.

She had devoted the last minutes—or was it hours?—to willing away the truth. But now she looked at her husband's eyes and waited for him to blink, and when he did not she forced herself to stare at the pearly gray-white skin of a face at once so familiar and yet totally alien, closer to a wax-museum dummy than the husband she loved, forced herself to believe that this body was him, was Richard, her husband, and that he was dead and that he would not be coming back to her, and at that moment something deep inside her cracked.

Kate shifted her weight in the bed, brought her fingertips slowly to her eyes to make sure they were open, that in fact she was awake, that this was not a dream, the nightmare she had wished, prayed it was.

The digital radio confirmed the hour and the date; it was true, three full days had passed, and she was still at home, in bed, alive, though she was not sure she could stand the thought of living. She was alive and Richard was dead and nothing had changed and everything had changed.

She breathed in the pillow's scent, Richard's pillowcase, which she had not allowed Lucille—the soft-spoken Jamaican woman who had kept house for the Rothsteins for almost ten years—to change. Something, anything to keep his presence alive, the smell of him, his hair and flesh, and a lingering hint of the English cologne, Skye, which she had bought for him on their honeymoon in London, the bottle's cap a tiny gold coronet. "Here you go, Your Majesty," she'd said, presenting him with the bottle, the two of them laughing when he'd placed the teeny crown on his head.

A few bouquets of flowers dotted the bedroom with color. Even in shock Kate had asked that people make charitable donations in Richard's name rather than send the usual flowers and fruit baskets, which she had no use for, but still they came.

Phone messages had piled up unanswered. Friends had been turned away.

Lucille had brought cups of tea and bowls of chicken soup surrounded by perfect triangles of buttered toast, but Kate barely touched them.

Nola had visited each day, planting herself by Kate's bedside, gabbing about this and that—school, her constant heartburn, anything to distract Kate, God bless her. But it just made Kate feel bad and guilty, that she was the adult who should be consoling Nola, who had also lost Richard, a man who had been like a father to the girl these last few years—and Nola about to have a baby on top of everything else.

Kate hardly recognized herself, this sad, weak woman.

The funeral had been a blur, only days after the murder, the Jews ever-anxious to get bodies into the ground too soon, way too soon for Kate, and so totally unlike the drawn-out Irish-Catholic wakes of her childhood—relatives crowding the McKinnons' Queens row house, cigarette smoke smudging the edges off sadness, alcohol dampening pain.

Kate's memory of her mother's wake was like so many other family parties: her housewife aunts in the kitchen, cooking and sharing recipes (". . . a pinch of sugar in the stewed cabbage, that's all you need, I swear . . ."); and her father's brothers, Mike and Timothy, both cops like her father, in the living room, color television tuned in to any and all possible sports events; the tube's electric hues reflected in the plastic slipcovers that finally came off the brown plaid sofa and matching armchairs—only after her mother was put into the earth—to collect the cigarette burns and beer stains that her mother had correctly feared.

Willie had called Kate close to a dozen times from Germany, where he was painting on a Fulbright Fellowship. God, how she missed that kid, so much more than a protégé, she and Richard having sponsored him all the way through Let There Be a Future starting in the sixth grade. Nowadays, he was not only surviving the art world, but thriving, supporting himself as well as his mother, grandmother, and sister, taking them out of that Bronx housing project where he'd grown up and putting them into an airy garden apartment in a middle-class Queens neighborhood, paid for entirely with the sales from his art. Amazing kid. No, not a kid; a young man.

"I'm coming home," he'd declared.

"No, you're not. You have work to finish for your show."

"I'm finished. The show is less than two weeks away. The paintings have all been shipped."

"Willie. Last week you told me you were still working on watercolors for the show, that you were going to bring them home with you on the plane. So don't lie to me."

"The watercolors don't matter, Kate. I need to be there with you. Right now."

But Kate had held firm. "This is the most important show of your career, Willie. A new gallery for you, and one of the best in New York. You have to finish everything." She took a deep breath, and lied: "I'm doing okay. I'll see you at your show. And you are not to come home one day earlier. You hear me?"

Finally, Willie had agreed, but only because Kate insisted.

It had taken Kate a few hours after the phone call to realize why she had argued so vociferously. The truth was she did not want Willie to see her unglued; for some absurd reason she needed him to go on believing she was a superwoman—his fairy godmother who could cope with anything. Maybe, she thought, if she convinced someone else, it might actually be true.

Richard's mother was doing the official thing, sitting shivah, in her Boca Raton condo, but Kate could not bring herself to go there, to sit with Edie on her airy Florida terrace, to chat and smile bravely. She adored Richard's mother, but no, it just wasn't possible. Not right now.

So what was it she needed to do? Kate played with the sash of her white terry robe, unconsciously plucking out individual strands of straying cotton. She had no idea.

She had never imagined herself like this, immobilized by grief, had always been able to cope, to deal with the most horrific things. Somehow she had survived.

How had she done that?

Kate gazed down at the view through her tall bedroom windows, a strip of faded green treetops, a sort of crew-cut view of Central Park against a gray sky that suited her mood.

A blur in her peripheral version; Kate flinched. "Jesus, you scared me."

Liz Jacobs strode into the room, plopped herself into the overstuffed chair opposite Kate's bed, and took stock of her oldest, dearest friend. "God, you look awful," she said, shaking her head.

"Thanks a lot." Kate narrowed her green eyes in mock anger, though there was no way she could be mad. "How did you get in? I specifically told the doormen *no solicitors*."

"An FBI ID opens a lot of doors, sweetie. And after kissing my boss's fat ass to get away from my Quantico desk for a full day, there is no way I was going to let some stuck-up Central Park West doorman tell me to get lost!" Liz offered a warm smile. "And I'm coming back in a few days, taking my two-week vacation here, in New York."

"To watch over me?"

"No. I needed a break, and I was about to lose my vacation days if I didn't take them. Going to stay with my sister in Brooklyn, do a little catch-up with her and the kids."

"Liar."

Liz squinted at Kate. "Are you eating? You're a stick, which personally pisses me—and every other size-twelve woman—off!"

Kate knew what Liz was doing, trying to kid her out of her misery. It was the way the two women had helped each other through their various tribulations for years—and it was almost working. Kate actually smiled. "I'm really happy to see you."

"And why wouldn't you be?" Liz took another close look at her friend. "Now really, Kate, you're destroying my image of you as the perfect woman—your hair's a mess, no makeup, you're a wreck. By next week you're gonna look like *me*!"

Kate laughed, but seconds later the laughter gave way to tears. "Oh, Liz . . ."

Liz wrapped her arms around Kate and patted her back while she sobbed.

But after a minute Kate pulled away, whipped a couple of tissues from the bedside table, dabbed at her eyes, nose. "Tell me something, Liz. How did I do it? I mean, when Elena died, how did I survive that, because—"

"You worked her case. That's how."

The words hit Kate like ice water thrown in her face. "*What?* You're suggesting I work Richard's case?"

"Forgive me, Kate, but you and I go back a long time—partners on the Astoria force, my divorce, your miscarriages. I think I know you. You are not a passive woman. You're a take-action, kick-ass dame. That's what makes you tick, always has."

Kate took a moment to imagine it, the idea of not only picking up police work again, but actually having the ability to detach enough to pursue her husband's killer.

"You said Floyd Brown wanted you to consult on the case," Liz continued. "Clearly, it was a case he thought you could, and should, be involved in, and Tapell agreed."

"That was before—" Kate swallowed, hard. "Before Richard. It's not just a case now."

"I know that. And believe me, I'm not trying to talk you into anything." Liz rested her hand gently on Kate's arm. "You asked me a question—how did you survive Elena's murder?—and I reminded you. That's all."

Later, in the shower, Liz's question resonated—*work the case*—and while Kate stood naked under jets of hot water she realized that simply the idea itself had made it possible for her to get out of bed, step into the shower, squeeze shampoo into her palms, and lather up her hair, all without crying or thinking about loss and pain, her mind occupied and distracted for the first time since Richard died.

What was it Willie had said after Elena's death—that he had used his painting to overcome his grief, to reconstruct his shattered world?

Kate stepped out of the shower, wrapped a soft white towel around her wet hair, studied her face in the slightly steamy mirror. The woman who stared back at her actually looked different from the woman who had been crying for days, her eyes somewhat more alive now, mouth determined.

Work the case. Was it possible?

Kate plucked a cotton ball from a glass canister, dipped it into aquamarine-colored astringent, drew the liquid across her skin as though stripping away the layers of civility she had painted over the tough young cop from Queens. The face that stared back at her was not quite Kate Rothstein, wife and socialite who gave fabulous dinner parties and worked for charitable organizations. Instead she was getting closer to that younger, grittier homicide detective who could take in the worst possible crime scenes, chase down runaways, and defeat the Death Artist.

Kate nodded at her image, acknowledged an old friend she was damn glad to see.

She could do this. She could be a cop again.

Apparently, Liz knew her better than she knew herself. And why not, after almost twenty years of friendship, though when they'd first met—two rookies, a year on the Astoria force—they had not particularly hit it off. Kate McKinnon, the feisty Irish girl from the family of cops; Liz Jacobs, the brainy Jewish girl whose family had practically disowned her when she'd traded a psych degree at NYU to study police work at John Jay.

It was a case, the disappearance of a sweet-faced eight-year-old boy, Denny Klingman, whose school photo practically broke Kate's heart, and the capture of Malcolm Gormely, a crack-dealing pornographer, pedophile, and possible murderer, that had ultimately brought the two women together.

Gormely was the number one contender in the Klingman disappearance and had evaded the NYPD in Manhattan, Brooklyn, the Bronx, and Staten Island, switching his base of operations from borough to borough whenever he smelled the cops closing in. Now it was suspected he'd set up shop somewhere in Long Island City.

Queens Chief of Police Clare Tapell thought women would be a good addition to the all-male special victims squad. She chose Kate because of her experience in tracking runaways, and paired her with Liz, who was already known as a diligent researcher. Within a day Kate was having a face-to-face with a former prison cellmate of Gormely's, who, in exchange for a five-year reduction on his twenty-year armed-robbery term, informed her of Gormely's predilection for prepubescent boys, preferably blond (Denny Klingman was blond), and the telephone number of a man the feds wanted for child pornography who traded dirty pictures with Malcolm Gormely. Meanwhile, Liz had cross-checked every file on any kid who had gone missing over the past decade, and any MO that even remotely resembled Gormely's (snatching kids in supermarkets while their moms or nannies were preoccupied selecting Birds Eye frozen peas or corn niblets).

The short of it was that Kate made contact with the kiddy pornographer by posing as a buyer, got him into cuffs, and threatened to cut his balls off if he didn't tell her the whereabouts of Gormely's new headquarters. Then she and Liz, fearing that sirens and flashing lights would further endanger little Denny Klingman's life, staked out the deserted rag-and-remnant factory in Long Island City without backup. A few hours and several cups of Dunkin' Donuts coffee and glazed crullers later, they watched Malcolm Gormely leave, then picked the lock, found the nude and terrified Denny Klingman and another eight-year-old boy, both of them blond and cherubic, tied and gagged. Liz brought the kids back to the station while Kate bagged the photo equipment and stash of kiddie porn that almost made her sick, then sat back, lit up a cigarette, and waited for Malcolm Gormely.

Three hours later, when the backup Kate had called arrived on the scene, they needed an ambulance for Gormely. "He resisted arrest" was all Kate had said.

Denny Klingman was returned to his grateful parents. But no one claimed the other boy. Not until Gormely divulged the fact that the kid had been sold to him by the boy's crack-addicted mother for a two-day supply of heroin.

It took two burly cops to hold Kate back when they tracked the woman down and brought her in, and later, after the mother had talked her way around an overwhelmed Child Protective Services Unit, Kate was sorry she hadn't killed the woman when she had the chance. For months that little boy's face had haunted her dreams. Just one more kid she could not save.

At the rather brief Internal Affairs investigation Liz covered for her by testifying that Malcolm Gormely had indeed resisted arrest, that Kate had no choice but to tackle the guy to stop him from escaping—even though she hadn't been there. The fact that Kate had suffered no more than severely lacerated knuckles while the pedophile sustained two black eyes, a shattered cheekbone, several missing teeth, a broken kneecap, and seven fractured fingers was deemed "necessary" by IA. After all, it was reasoned, Kate could have shot him.

After that case, Kate and Liz were heroes and friends forever, though they never spoke about Malcolm Gormely—or the wrath Kate had rained upon him.

Kate crossed her bedroom, bare feet on plush carpets, and opened her spacious walk-in closet. Thinking about Liz, how they had first met and worked together, and what she had done to Malcolm Gormely seemed like another lifetime. She had been an entirely different person then.

Or had she?

Even now she could remember how good it had felt to hurt that guy.

Kate forced the memory away, concentrated on choosing clothes that would feel like cop business, pushing aside the high-end designers, settling for jeans and strong-soled shoes, each selection separating her farther from her normal life.

Her .45 Glock automatic was just where she'd put it a year ago, on the top shelf of her closet, way in the back, behind a stack of old scarves she rarely wore.

Why hadn't she gotten rid of it? She had thought about doing it dozens of times, but hadn't.

Kate wrapped her hand around the weapon, the pistol she'd gotten a year before she'd left the Astoria force, choosing it for its lightweight polymer frame and ergonomic design, reliable trigger pull and pointability, all of which increased the odds of hitting your target.

The pistol felt cool in her hand. She checked the trigger and drop safety before clipping in a magazine. Thirteen rounds. Unlucky number, thought Kate.

She was almost there now. Almost back in the role of cop. Almost not a wife. Almost. But not quite.

Widow.

How could that word possibly apply to her? Other women were widows. Not she.

Kate stopped a moment, taking in the all-white bedroom as though she were looking for something to remind her of who she really was.

Richard's pajama bottoms lay strewn across the bed. She'd been wearing them for days, refusing to give them up, repeatedly telling Lucille never ever to wash them, though she'd impulsively had most of Richard's clothes picked up by Goodwill, had asked Lucille to remove the photos of him, store them away, out of sight. God, the look she'd received for that request. Lucille didn't get it. At first, all she had wanted was oblivion, no images to remind her of him, no memories to haunt her.

She just could not look at them, at anything that reminded her that the man she had lived with and loved for more than a decade was gone.

But now she resurrected one, plucked it out of the drawer, a favorite photo that she'd had on her night table for years. Her fingers lightly skimmed the delicate silver frame, then Richard's smiling face, his hand just above his forehead shielding his eyes from the sun. She rummaged further in the night table, came up with a plastic bag containing his wedding band, heavy gold Rolex watch, and the sterling silver money clip with his initials, RR, engraved, that she'd bought him for his fortieth birthday—his favorite gift from her. She barely remembered tossing the bag into the drawer when she'd come back from the morgue.

Kate ran her fingers over the etched initials. Such an odd memento, a money clip, but one that brought Richard so clearly back to life, "Mr. New York," what she always called him—with just a hint of sarcasm; the way he'd ceremoniously slide it out of his pocket, peel off bills for this and that—restaurants, cabs, coat-check girls—spending cash lavishly, a sport for the poor boy from Brooklyn.

Kate placed the smiling photo of Richard on her dresser, laid the money clip beside it. Yes, Richard would want his money clip with him, she was sure of that.

"I'll get him," Kate whispered as she slipped Richard's wedding band onto the fine gold chain she always wore around her neck. The ring skidded along the chain, coming to rest in the hollow between her collarbones.

Kate looked back at the photo and money clip, felt the coolness of the gold ring against her flesh. It wasn't much, but enough to resurrect his presence, something to keep her heart—or what was left of it—connected while the rest of her detached. A necessity if she was going to work this case—and survive.

She knew what she must do. Find out who did this. And then she would feel . . . Kate rolled the thought around in her mind. *How would she feel?*

No, there wasn't time for that, for her *feelings*. One foot along the path of emotion and she'd be a goner, no help to anyone—not to the cops, not to Richard, certainly not herself.

Just go through the motions.

In the bathroom, Kate stared at herself in the mirror. Makeup. Right. A must. She would not go out and have people pity her. Concealer under her eyes. Mascara. Lip gloss. That was enough, and all she could manage. Then she pulled her thick dark hair straight back off her face, twisted it up, and fastened it with a few pins—a style she rarely wore because Richard had not liked it, and he was right. It did not suit her long nose or the angles of her face, though right now she didn't care.

When she focused on the finished product she hardly recognized herself. Few traces of society woman Kate Rothstein remained, which was good. The work she had ahead of her was no place for the creature of comfort and benevolence she had cultivated.

Funny, thought Kate. She believed that she'd erased the tough cop from Queens, but damn it if she wasn't always there, like that Glock she had not thrown away, waiting.

Kate looped the holster over her shoulder and slipped the Glock in place.

Of course Liz had been right. She needed to do something.

Later there would be time to grieve. Now was the time for action.

He lets his body collapse onto the beat-up couch, feels tears on his cheeks and swipes them away with a fierce gesture. "Baby," he says, annoyed with himself.

Baby, baby, baby don't leave me . . .

Another one of those oldies *she* liked.

"Stop!"

The tune quiets. For the moment.

He paws through boxes and bags on the couch, suddenly starving, pushing aside Oreos, mustard-flavored pretzels, Mr. Peanut Deluxe Party Assortment, and tears the tonguelike metal seal off a column of Pringles, stuffing handfuls of the uniform chips into his mouth, practically choking, his hunger a deep, never-sated void. He is always craving something.

If asked, he would say that it is his work, only his work, his painting, that sustains him; that it is merely frustration, his need to see and know the truth that takes him out of his studio and into a gray world that he would prefer to ignore—a world not nearly as beautiful or wonderful or perfect as the one he strives to create on canvas. It's a shame, really, that's what he'd say, an annoyance and an interruption— no question he'd prefer to be left alone, painting—but then the need starts up and begins to grow inside him, expanding the emptiness until he can no longer stand it, and, work pushed aside, brushes left sodden with paint, canvases unfinished, he is off, the hunt commencing. It's not really a decision, nothing to which he can say yes or no. It's a need, a quest for knowledge, and, yes, a release and satisfaction, he will admit that much.

When he is hunting his hunger abates, sustained by the chase alone. He goes days without food, thinking of nothing else—not eating or sleeping, or bathing—consumed by his need, until he has done it and he has seen what he must see and feel, and then, only then, does the real world intrude again, and the hunger for banal needs like food and drink and sleep return.

It's a process, really, like any other. Only, in his case, deadly.

He sits up, swipes crumbs of broken chips from his lap and thinks, *I am a seeker of the truth.*

Blackened shades shroud the windows, creating luminous skeletal outlines against shadowy walls; overhead fluorescents dim, softening the edges of the long table littered with paint tubes, pastels, and crayons, a beat-up-looking couch, canvases pinned to the gray walls.

So often he imagines he can see those blinking lights, red, green, and blue, the ones she would string up in one dreary tenement after another, but of course it's just an illusion and he knows it. It has been that way since the accident.

He holds a pair of wraparound shades in his fingertips, gently swings them as he moves closer to the canvases.

Was it all a waste of time? These tell him nothing. Absolutely nothing. Hair mashed into gray-black blood, colorless, unexciting. They were so vibrant, weren't they—magenta and violet, wild strawberry, and raspberry?

She wore a raspberry beret—

He tries to remember while the song plays in the back of his brain, but it won't come. It's no good. Nothing is any good. He might as well be dead.

One hundred twenty-three dead and still counting. The plane went down over a cornfield in rural—

"Shhh!"

He looks again at his most recent creations—ones made at the scenes—and is bathed with disappointment, like a baptism gone wrong.

Why can't it ever last? Isn't he entitled to know? Why is he, and he alone, so severely punished?

You're grrrrrrrrrrrreat!

"Am I, Tony?" he whispers into the dim room. He doesn't feel it.

Grrrrrrrrrrrreat!

"Thanks."

It helps having friends like Tony. Someone who knows he is good and smart. Tony has made him feel a lot better, strong enough to pull himself off the couch and get to work.

He squirts several blobs of oil paint onto his palette, lifts one of the several magnifying glasses he owns and stares at the paint, his eyes blinking. He will not allow himself to be frustrated. Right now, he wants to work. And at the moment he is not hungry. Not yet.

N ola Davis struggled to lift herself out of bed. A relatively simple act a few months back, but now, with her beach-ball eight-and-a-half-months-pregnant belly it was like trying to defy gravity.

Had she totally blown it, now, of all times, with a year to go in school and all she had been through to get here?

How stupid was she?

Nola shook her head, shoulder-length dreadlocks brushing the smooth dark brown skin of her cheeks.

Well, it was far too late for self-pity. She had made her choice and would just have to live with it. Hell, she'd survived growing up in a concrete jungle—as wise old Bob Marley had sung in his drugged-out Jamaican patois on one of her favorite CDs.

Nola had a sudden, almost violent urge to pee. If she could run she would have, but a sprightly waddle was about all she could manage.

She flushed, slowly eased herself up, hands under her belly for support as she padded back into the combination bedroom/living room of the Upper West Side studio apartment that Kate was paying for while she finished up her senior year at Barnard—*if* she finished her senior year.

Nola sighed. No way she'd be finishing out the school year, not even the semester, with a baby due in less than a month. She'd just do what she could, take her incompletes, and start up again next fall, which made her feel bad, like an ordinary colored girl who didn't know any better, which she guessed she was though she'd worked hard not to be—ordinary, that is.

She stroked her belly and thought of Kate, who had been great, as always, though Nola suspected she was disappointed by her getting knocked up, even if she'd never shown it.

Nola waddled into the kitchen area and attempted to snare a box of tea bags from a shelf above the sink, though getting onto tiptoes was becoming an effort in her condition. Maybe she *should* move in with Kate and Richard, she thought, straining to get a grip on the Lipton container.

No, not Kate and Richard. Just Kate.

Nola's eyes filled with tears as she lowered herself into a kitchen chair. *How was it possible? Richard dead.*

She just didn't know what to say to Kate, whom she loved so much it hurt sometimes, just babble, anything to keep herself, and Kate, from crying. She had a feeling that if the two of them started, they could cry for a full year straight.

She'd never seen Kate like this, had to admit it scared her. Kate, her mentor, her champion, the woman who could do anything, alone now, and Nola knew she would never admit she needed to be taken care of.

But didn't everyone need taking care of sometimes?

Matt Brownstein, whom Nola had been sleeping with most of last semester, sure as shit didn't know how to take care of anyone, not that she wanted him to take care of her, the arrogant asshole, also a senior at Columbia, studying studio art, painting—who hated using condoms, but when Nola became pregnant insisted she get rid of the baby, that no way he was sticking around for *that*.

Why had she taken up with him in the first place?

Was it because he was a tall lanky white guy with curly hair, and because he was Jewish, just like Richard Rothstein?

Nola tried not to think about it. She stared up at the reproductions of artworks pinned to her wall. Studying art history had been the most amazing thing in her life. And now she'd have to delay her matriculation at the prestigious NYU Art Institute, which Kate had pulled plenty of strings to get her into, not to mention a few months abroad to actually see some of the art she had only seen in reproduction. She hoped Kate hadn't lost faith in her.

She wondered whether, given what had happened, Kate had lost her faith entirely.

Nola tugged a tea bag out of the box and dropped it into a mug. She would have to be strong. For Kate, and for her baby.

But then she pictured Kate, all alone, in that big white bed in that big apartment, and she was crying all over again. Maybe, she thought, it would be a good idea if she did move in.

Work your husband's case? Are you crazy?"

"I have never felt less crazy about anything in my life."

A minute earlier the two women had been embracing, standing in the center of Tapell's One Police Plaza office, the chief attempting in her cool, somewhat awkward manner to soothe her old friend and colleague. But the moment Kate made her request Tapell had taken three steps back. Now she leaned against her desk, glanced at the ceiling and puffed out a sigh. "I'd be a bad friend and an irresponsible administrator if I assigned you to the case, Kate."

"Remind me if I have the facts wrong." Kate folded her arms across her chest. "But weren't you, only days ago, begging me to help out on this case?"

"That was before—"

Kate did not let her finish. "I can still help evaluate the psycho's paintings, and—"

"That's not the part that concerns me and you know it. Come on, Kate. You're too close."

"We've had this conversation before, remember, a little more than a year ago? My being too close, too emotionally involved. And I did the job then, didn't I?"

"At a cost."

"To *me*. Not to you."

"And you're willing to go down that road again?" Tapell shook her head. "Well, I'm not. Sorry, Kate. Not Richard's case."

Kate blinked, attempting to stop her tears.

"Look at you. You can't even hear his name. How on earth do you think you can work his case?"

"That's my problem."

"No, it's my problem, and Brown's, and anyone else's you'd be working with. Cops need to have their feelings in check, and—" Tapell stopped, offered Kate a look that mixed regret with sadness. She certainly did not want to berate her old friend at a time like this. "Look, it's simply not a good idea."

Kate glanced out the window at the complex of government buildings, then back at Tapell. "You've done what you had to do even when it wasn't a good idea. I know that and you know that. I need to do this, Clare and—" She stopped herself from saying the words: *I know the truth about you, Clare, and I'll use it if I have to.*

The air in the room went still, both women replaying a bit of history— Tapell's ascension to chief of police after a cop with a Serpico complex had blown the roof off a cops-on-the-take scandal that had brought down her predecessor. Tapell had been tapped as the replacement because of her squeaky-clean reputation. But Kate knew better. The same shit was going on in Astoria. Not that Tapell condoned it—just that she was an overworked, underpaid civil servant who had chosen to concentrate on bigger issues—cleaning up the bad neighborhoods, getting drug dealers away from the schools. When her name was tossed in the ring she had a choice: come clean and pass up the opportunity of a lifetime, or take the chance to do a greater good, sweep the dirt under the rug, make a few deals, and keep her mouth shut. She'd opted for the latter— and Kate hadn't blamed her.

Kate looked into Tapell's eyes and saw it: the chief knew what she was thinking.

The two women continued to stare at each other, the secret hovering there between them, an odor ready to befoul the air.

Kate thought that if it went on much longer she would surely back down. But she did not stop staring and she held the thought in her mind—*I'm sorry, but I will use this if I have to*—and when Tapell said, "Okay, I'll call Brown," Kate just nodded.

Later, when she was out on the street, she was relieved she hadn't actually spoken the words. She wasn't proud of the fact that she had considered saying the unthinkable, was somewhat ashamed, even a bit shocked, that she had been willing to go so far to get what she wanted. Now she hoped that she was right—that she did have it in her, the ability to work this case and keep her emotions under control, because right now she felt ready to explode.

SIX

Two oversized Andy Warhol silk screens, *Marilyn* and *Mao,* an unlikely duo made compatible by the artist's hand, were on one wall;
a cool large-scale David Hockney print of a swimming pool, palm trees,
and Technicolor-blue sky acted as a faux window featuring a picture-
perfect Beach Boys, Mamas and Papas, California dreamin' vista on the
other; a suite of black-and-white Diane Arbus photos—circus freaks,
suburban couple, *Jewish Giant*—lined up above the comfy leather love
seat Kate had chosen for Richard's office along with the sleek Knoll desk
that appeared to be waiting for him to take his place behind it.

Kate felt numb.

Had she already been so effective in burying her emotions that she
could not even locate them? It was as though she were acting in a play,
and the stage set—"successful, attorney's office"—was missing only one
thing: the lead actor.

But this was a test: Kate was going to prove Tapell wrong. She could
do this.

Her eyes tracked her husband's office one more time: the art on the
walls, his desk and chair. Crime Scene had obviously gone through the
office, but there were no traces of fingerprint powders anywhere.
Probably Richard's secretary, Anne-Marie, had cleaned it all up, efficient
as ever. Richard's desk was cleared of files and papers, which Anne-

Marie had most likely doled out to Richard's associate Andy and to a select number of Richard's lawyer friends.

Kate hadn't given any thought to what she would do with the furniture or the art. Sell them? Probably. She did not think she could possibly have them in the Central Park apartment or the East Hampton summer home without crying every time she saw them.

Kate turned away from the paintings and took in the view from Richard's office window—the glittering glass and steel and blinking neon lights of Times Square with its marquees and Calvin Klein billboards so erotically charged that the colossal-sized young men and women who languished in their skimpy briefs and bras over the city streets would have been arrested, along with their advertiser, only a few decades earlier.

Someone behind her cleared his throat, and Kate turned to find Andy Stokes leaning into the open doorway looking awkward and a bit sheepish, double-breasted jacket open, revealing blue polka-dot suspenders, hands pressed deep into the pockets of his pin-striped pants.

The quintessential preppie, thought Kate, taking in the man's straight blond hair and WASP good looks. Definitely not her type, almost too pretty, though she guessed many women found him attractive.

Andrew Stokes had been brought in about two years ago, when Richard's practice had grown too big too fast and he needed someone to deal with the smaller matters. True, Stokes had already had a succession of jobs, but each firm had been a step up from the last, and Richard believed the young man might thrive under his tutelage, maybe one day even assume the responsibility of partner. But he was wrong—Stokes was simply not partner material, his work uninspired, his self-motivation practically nonexistent. Still, he did what he was told and his boyish good looks and charm seemed to delight many of the clients, particularly the women. If Andrew Stokes had not exactly fulfilled Richard's expectations, he had at least lessened his burden.

"I would have called you after the funeral," said Stokes. "But . . ."

Richard's funeral. Had it been only a couple of days ago? To Kate, it had felt like a movie, something glimpsed or observed: the huge crowd of Manhattan movers and shakers decked out in their best designer black suits and dresses; speeches (not one word of which Kate remembered); Richard's family—the Brooklyn aunts and uncles, his mother up from Florida, who had held Kate's hand throughout the proceedings, a rabbi with an uncanny resemblance to Salman Rushdie, an absurdity Kate had focused on, who had led the mourners in kaddish, the Jewish prayer for the dead.

But what Kate was thinking of right now, what she most remembered and would always remember was the hollow, echoing sound as clods of dirt had been shoveled into her husband's grave, earth and stone hitting wood, and Richard's Uncle Loukie passing her the spade and touching her back gently and saying, "It's okay, darling," and how she had actually done it, driven the spade into the mound of reddish-brown topsoil, scooped it up, and upended it into that dark, shadowy rectangle, thinking—*Where is Richard? Isn't he always beside me at funerals?*—and looking down into that black hole and realizing that he *was* here—and that she was burying him.

"Kate?" Stokes brought her back to the moment.

"Sorry." She managed a weak smile. "Thank you for the flowers, Andy. They were lovely."

"Is there anything I can get you?" He shifted his weight from one foot to the other.

Was he staring at her breasts, or just avoiding her eyes?

"Coffee, or—"

"No. I'm fine. Thanks. Oh, Andy—" Kate dug into her bag for the reason she had come—the bank statement with the attached Post-it that she had discovered in Richard's sports jacket. "Richard obviously meant to give you this."

He gave it a cursory glance. "It's just a bank statement. He must have thought I hadn't seen it."

"Would you normally see the bank statements?" she asked, thinking he probably would not.

"Not necessarily, but—" He glanced at it again. "I'll give this a thorough going-over, make sure there's nothing here Richard thought I should be aware of."

Kate leaned closer to regard the statement along with him. When she had first seen it she wasn't sure what the numbers were, but when she'd looked again, she had clearly seen that the two figures Richard had circled were bank balances. "The balance in that account is almost a million one day and down to six-fifty two days later. Pretty big withdrawal," said Kate.

"Well, gee . . ." Stokes shrugged. "I guess Richard had something he needed to pay for."

"And he hadn't mentioned it, or consulted you?"

A little-boy smile tugged at the corners of Stokes's lips. "Hey, like Richard's the boss, you know. He doesn't have to tell me what he does with his money."

"No—right—of course." Kate stumbled over her words, embarrassment mixing with sadness. "So, what are your plans, Andy?"

"My plans?" He smiled and ran a hand through his hair.

What is he smiling about?

"About what?" he asked.

Kate couldn't decide if he was playing at being a coy little boy or acting the man.

"Your future. I mean, now that—"

"Oh, my future . . ." He looked down at his shoes. "Well, there are a few things to settle up here, and then, well, you know, to be perfectly honest, I hadn't thought about it. I guess I could take some time off, and devote it to my hobby." He stuttered a laugh, almost a giggle. "I'm what *you* might call a Sunday painter."

"Really? I had no idea."

Stokes smiled again and looked away, as though thinking about something else entirely.

"What about the law? I mean, a job. Naturally, there will be a substantial severance package for you, but—"

"Hey, you don't have to worry about me." Stokes swung his arm as if he were striking up a band, and fixed a grin onto his face. "I'll be just grrrrrrreat!"

Kate stared at him, blankly.

"Tony the Tiger, you know?" His grin faded. "Sorry. Just fooling around. Of course I'm not great. How could I be great with—well, with what's happened? I'm really sorry."

Kate could feel her emotions waiting in the wings for their big number, and quickly changed the subject. "Speaking of clients. Do you happen to know who Richard would have been seeing on that—" Kate faltered a moment. "The last day he was here."

"I don't think he was scheduled to see anyone. He was supposed to be taking depositions in Boston."

"But he wasn't scheduled to leave for the airport until later in the day."

"I wasn't in. Had a bit of a head cold. But I'm sure Anne-Marie could tell you if Richard saw anyone. Oh, wait . . ." He shook his head. "Anne-Marie was out that day as well, and the one before that. Her bunionectomy." He made a face.

"I see." Kate plucked the bank statement from Andy's fingers. "I'll speak to Anne-Marie, and give her this on my way out. No need for you to bother."

"It's no bother." He made a try for the statement, but managed only to pinch the air. Kate was already folding it into her pocket.

The bookkeeper, Melanie Mintz, would know," said Richard's longtime secretary, Anne-Marie, a short woman with platinum blond hair who probably tipped the scales at a good two hundred pounds, and considerably more when she fell off the Weight Watchers wagon. Kate had always been happy that she was a great secretary and absolutely never let her husband forget it.

"Did you clean up Richard's office? I mean, after the police had—"

"I, well, yes." The secretary sniffled. "Was that wrong?"

"No," said Kate, working overtime to remain composed.

Anne-Marie dabbed at her eyes with a shredded tissue. She had started crying the minute Kate arrived and was still crying as she wrote the bookkeeper's number on a piece of paper and handed it to Kate. It was soggy. "I don't know what I'm going to do." She wound the tissue into a point and jabbed it first into one nostril, then the other.

"If you're worried about money, I've arranged for severance and I can also—"

"Oh, no, that's not what I meant." She sniffed. "I can easily find another job . . ."

Kate patted the secretary's soft shoulder. "You'll be fine." It felt strange to be the one doing the consoling, but oddly reassuring.

"Anne-Marie, you were out the day . . . the day that Richard . . ."

The secretary choked back her tears. "My foot surgery. If only I'd been here—"

"There's nothing you could have done," said Kate, though she wondered about the circumstances—both Anne-Marie and Andy out of the office, the place empty. But Richard had often worked late into the night, and often alone.

"If only one of us had been here, me or Mr. Stokes." The secretary dabbed at her eyes, and looked toward Stokes's office door. "It wasn't the first time. I mean, lately . . ." She waved her tissue. "Never mind."

"What?"

"It's just that lately Mr. Stokes has missed a few meetings and deadlines—plus the long lunches, well . . ." She raised an eyebrow. "I know Mr. R wasn't happy about it." She reached for a new tissue. "It's really not my place to say anything, but . . ."

Richard rarely discussed his work with Kate, and almost never complained about his employees, though recently he had mentioned Andy's habit of coming in late and leaving early, and Kate knew he was annoyed.

"Did you and Richard ever discuss this?"

"Oh, Mr. R would never say anything like that to me." She leaned closer to Kate and whispered, "But they had a *talk*, you know, Mr. R and Stokes."

Andy's office door sprang open and Anne-Marie let out a little "Ooh!"

"Sorry," said Andy. He glanced up at Kate with that odd little-boy smile on his face. "I thought you'd gone."

"Just catching up with Anne-Marie," said Kate. "But I'm going now."

"Take care," said Andy.

A ndy Stokes quietly shut the door to his office. He had the beginnings of a headache and seeing Kate had not helped.

It was a nightmare. A fucking nightmare. Richard dead, and now . . . *what?*

He looped his fingers under his polka-dot suspenders and tugged on them as on rubber bands while trying to recall that famous Marlene Dietrich line to Orson Welles in *Touch of Evil:* "Your future is all used up." Man, was that ever the truth.

Stokes pulled open his desk drawer. Somewhere in this mess was a bottle of aspirin if Anne-Marie had not been poking around in his things, straightening up, as she always did. But there was no sign of it. He sat back and sighed. It was going to take a lot more than aspirin to make him feel better.

Should he go home? No, his wife would just start nagging, asking why he was not working and then they'd get into one of their fights.

Forget the aspirin. He knew where he wanted to go, could barely contain himself once the idea, the need, had flickered in his brain. He was up before the thought was even complete, stuffing papers into his leather briefcase, his mind in overdrive, cock already hard.

"I'm off," he said to Anne-Marie, who was still sniffling and dabbing at her nose with a tissue. "I've got a meeting."

The secretary eyed him through a shaggy landscape of platinum bangs. "What meeting is that, Mr. Stokes?"

"You know." Why was she always quizzing him? "I'll be back later."

"When?" she asked in between sniffs.

"Later," he said.

K ate had the cabdriver let her out a few blocks north of the precinct. She needed to walk a bit, think a few things through.

The sky was the same dull gray it had been for weeks. Where were those autumn days that New York was famous for—the crisp, clear blue sky, the kind the Flemish painters favored for their pristine landscapes? It was an atypical fall, as though the gods had decided to take away the little color that New York had.

Kate thought back to the conversation with Anne-Marie. Had Richard been planning to let Andy go? The man had obviously been slacking off. And what had Richard said in that talk he'd had with

Stokes? Had he issued a warning, or given him notice? It certainly seemed possible. But would Stokes actually have killed over that?

Kate glanced up at the gray sky. She had no idea. But going to Richard's office had been another test, and she'd passed.

Chelsea was active, people walking with purpose, more than your average sprinkling of leather-clad men and crew-cut women now that the area had become the gay capital of the world, bringing with it a coolness and style that had also made it one of city's most desirable neighborhoods.

Kate passed a couple of chic new restaurants flanking an old bodega that had somehow survived the area's gentrification. It was one of the things she liked best about New York, its diversity and tolerance, certainly its bustle, a place built on generosity and greed, on one man's dreams and so many others' failures, but mainly, she believed, built on confidence—though the city had grown a bit wary since the 9/11 attack, and Kate could not help but look up at the city's icons—the Empire State Building or Statue of Liberty—and worry.

Now she peered down Eighth Avenue and realized this was exactly where she had been on that day that seemed so long ago and yet like yesterday, the day her proud and supposedly impervious city had become a war zone.

Kate had been visiting an elementary school for the foundation when the first tower was struck and had remained in the street with hundreds of others and watched, dazed, as the burning monoliths morphed into gray funnels of smoke and disappeared on that cloudless, painfully beautiful morning.

But it was the sound, the collective gasp and cry that had gone up and out from the crowd that she most remembered; it had chilled her then, as it did now when she looked down the avenue and surveyed the buildings and sky at the city's southern tip where the towers should have been.

For weeks afterward Kate could not pass the fire stations with their makeshift shrines to missing heroes and bouquets of flowers without crying.

But New York had survived. And so would she.

Was it awful to compare her personal loss to the loss of thousands? Probably.

But for Kate, the idea of loss had rarely been abstract, had started early with her mother's death, and again when she'd tended to her father's cancer. Not that she had wanted to be there for the tough guy who had taken out his rage on her. But he was, after all, her father, and she had made her peace with those demons, and so she moved back into the Astoria row house those last awful months, made the meals he could barely eat, changed the bedpans, doled out the painkillers and finally administered the injections to the once fierce tyrant, now unrecognizable, diminished by illness. Who'd have believed he had once been so terrifying?

The Sixth Precinct was only a block away.

Kate pictured the cop cars angle-parked along the street before she saw them, the large double doors she had passed through for the first time just after Elena had died.

And now that Richard had died, she would do it again.

Manhattan's chief of Homicide Special Task Force, Floyd Brown, Jr., leaned back in his ergonomically correct chair, one of the perks he'd received with his new position.

Kate stared at the slightly off-kilter Sierra Club calendar on the bulletin board above Brown's desk beside gruesome crime scene photos of the two butchered Bronx women, and wondered if there had been ones from Richard's crime scene up there with them, if Brown had removed them before she arrived.

For the second time Brown asked, "You absolutely sure, McKinnon?" He continued to call her by her maiden name, which she had insisted upon when they'd last worked together.

Kate glanced at the clock on the wall, the second hand ticking off fractions of the rest of her life, and was transported back thirty years— a similar clock, round, simple, utilitarian, on the wall of a sterile room, and her mother, her beautiful mother, in a hospital bed, looking so frail.

"What's wrong with her?" she had asked her father as they made their way down the hospital corridor, passing patients who roamed the hall-ways looking more lost than sick.

"Your mother's . . . afflicted." It was all he said, jaw clenching, knuckles going white around the small bouquet of flowers he carried, which he'd left on the table beside her mother's bed, not bothering to ask for a vase or pitcher, something to put them in. For weeks afterward Kate wondered about those flowers, if anyone, a nurse, an orderly, had rescued them.

Kate balanced on the edge of the bed, the whole time praying that everything would be okay, though knowing, deep inside, it would not be, that very last time she ever saw her mother.

She stared at that clock counting off the seconds in her head, figuring out how many hours it would be until her twelfth birthday—not quite twenty-four she'd calculated—though there never was a party, not with her father working fourteen-hour shifts at the precinct, and her mother here, which even Kate knew was a special kind of hospital, "for people with problems," her Aunt Patsy had explained.

Her mother would start a sentence and stop, search for words, ask her young daughter, "Where was I?"

"You were telling me to remember one thing, Mom."

"Yes, yes, of course." Her mother fiddled nervously with the plastic bracelet on her wrist, and Kate could hear her father talking to a doctor just outside the half-open door—"We're hoping the treatments will relieve the depression, Mr. McKinnon."

"Don't understand it." Her father didn't bother to whisper. "What's she got to be depressed about?"

The doctor's explanations escaped Kate's twelve-year-old mind, something about the complication of the psyche, though fragments of his description of her mother's treatment—heart rate monitored, anesthetic administered, electric current is fast, seizure lasts approximately twenty seconds, afterward, a headache, then relief . . ."—were burned into her memory.

The idea of it—that they were electrocuting her mother—terrified and haunted her for years. But she also recalled her mother's last words, which she'd never forgotten.

"Remember one thing, Katie."

"Yes, Mama?"

"That . . . that you can do . . . anything." Her mother rested her cold slender fingers on Kate's arm. "What was I saying, sweetie?"

"That I could do anything."

"That's right. *Anything.* But you are the one who will have to do it. No one will take care of you as well as you can take care of yourself, and . . ."

Kate could see her mother straining to focus, to hold on to the thought.

"And . . . no one will care about the things you care about as much as you care. Do you understand?"

She had nodded, though she wasn't quite sure.

"You can do anything, my sweet strong girl."

Now, as Kate continued to stare at the clock on Brown's wall, she recalled those words and knew her mother had been right, had seen it proved over and over again. If you wanted something done, you had better do it yourself.

You can do anything, Katie. But you are the one who will have to do it.

"I can do this," said Kate, focusing on Brown, trying hard to appear in control and unemotional. "You know I can. And I spoke with Tapell about it. She agrees."

Brown knew about Kate's public relationship with New York City's chief of police, a quid pro quo friendship that went all the way back to Kate's days as an Astoria cop, when Clare Tapell was Kate's superior.

But did he know the rest? Kate wondered.

Brown drummed his fingers along the edge of his steel desk. "From my point of view it's not a good idea to work a spouse's case."

Kate leveled Brown with a hard stare. "What would you do if your wife was brutally murdered?"

"I honestly don't know."

"Bullshit! You'd hunt the little scumbag down and rip his fucking heart out!"

Brown almost smiled. The language, so incongruous with the perfectly put together uptown lady, had always surprised and amused him. "Well, I guess if my chief is willing to give you consultant status, I don't exactly have a choice, but"—he sat forward—"you gotta play by the book."

Kate sat up straighter. "Don't I always?"

"Spare me," said Brown. "But you'd better. FBI Manhattan is already coming in on this."

"So soon?"

Brown averted his eyes, said, "Your husband was a high-profile victim, McKinnon—and if all three murders are related, then we're looking at a serial and no way the Bureau is not going to come in."

Kate listened almost too carefully as her brain registered Brown's words: *Your husband was a high-profile victim.*

"Remember Mitch Freeman?"

Kate remembered him all right, good-looking, decent. "FBI shrink. Not a bad guy."

"Well, he's in. But it's not him I'm worried about. It's the special agent in charge they're sending in. Guy named Grange, Marty Grange. Not a fun guy." He gave her a somber look. "I worked with Grange a few years back. He's a stickler. Doesn't take any crap and reports everything back to his FBI cronies."

"Do you think we could somehow use Liz Jacobs as a consultant? She's going to be in town, and she was very helpful with the Death Artist case."

"Unlikely. I'm sure Grange knows you two are amigos. Nothing those guys don't know. And he'll want to run his own show."

Kate straightened herself in the chair. "So what's happened with the cases so far?"

"Not enough," said Brown. "Your basic door-to-door in the Bronx. No witnesses to either crime." He paused a second, seemed to be thinking about his next words before he spoke. "Uh, the night watchman at your husband's building . . ." He paused again.

"Yes," said Kate, flat, unemotional. She had to show him she could handle this. "Go on."

"Night watchman says your husband never signed out—which he would have if he'd left after normal business hours."

"Yes," said Kate, taking a breath. "That would be standard. He would have left by midday, if . . ."

Brown nodded, then shifted back to the other cases. "Statements have been taken all around. Bronx landlady of one vic, Martinez is her name, couldn't give us much. She was pretty shook up. We need a return visit there. Lab's working overtime too, but nothing so far." Brown rubbed his hand over his forehead. "Worries me that we're looking at one of those VW guys."

Kate knew Brown was referring to the serial killer's favorite mode of transport, Volkswagen vans. "So you're thinking he could have come in from Hackensack or Hoboken, stalked, killed, left."

"Maybe," said Brown.

"But Midtown seems riskier," said Kate.

"I agree." Brown continued rubbing his forehead.

"Headache?"

"These sickos *always* give me a headache."

Kate rummaged around in her soft leather bag, came up with a silver pillbox and shook a couple of pills into Brown's waiting palm. "Extra-strength Excedrin."

He washed them down with a quarter inch of brown sludge from a Styrofoam cup that must have been coffee not long ago. "Thanks," he said. "It's a puzzle, I can tell you. No prints. No weapons at the scene."

"So he brought the weapon, along with those paintings. Which means he's organized."

"Seems to be," said Brown. "Lab's going over the paintings with a fine-tooth comb."

"What else?"

"Not a lot, though Tapell's mobilizing the troops. We've got just about every division assisting—Latent, Crime Search, Mobile, General, all the tech services—other than the bomb squad—at our disposal. Scientific is doing workups on blood, seminal fluids—if there are any, though none have appeared, so Sex Crimes isn't involved—not yet. Saliva ID is doing their thing, but nothing there either." He let out a sigh. "Our lab's doing prelims, then everything goes to FBI Manhattan. If they get stuck, they ship everything to Quantico. Of course we're running the unsub's MO through VI-CAP and NCIC."

Kate thought back a moment: *Violent Criminal Apprehension Program and National Crime Information Center.* "The computers find anything?"

"A few things have popped up, but no real match." He sighed again. "Wish I had more to tell you. You know what time means to a homicide investigation."

Brown did not need to explain. The rule of thumb was that the longer it took to get to the bottom of a homicide, the less chance you had of solving it.

"Word coming down from Chief of Police Tapell is that officially you are here to consult on the paintings—"

Kate started in her chair, mouth open, about to speak.

"Relax," said Brown. "I know you, McKinnon, and know you'll be all over the case. Just thought I'd remind you of your *consultant* status."

"I can carry a gun, though, can't I? I've still got a permit."

"Why?" Brown narrowed his eyes. "You looking to shoot someone?"

"I just want to feel safe, able to protect myself."

Brown looked at Kate, then away. "Tapell appears to want you here, so . . ." He plucked a couple of case files from the stack on his desk. "Jackets on the first two vics." He tilted his head at the bloody crime scene photos on the wall behind his desk. "Why don't you acquaint yourself with the scenes. As I said, we could use a rerun up there."

"You want me to start in the Bronx?"

"It's just past your neighborhood, isn't it?"

"Just a bit," said Kate. "And where's . . . Richard's file?"

"You ready to look at that?"

"Yes." Kate hesitated. "No." She stopped, took a deep breath. *Be calm.* "I want to see the file, but I'd rather not see the crime scene photos." Another deep breath. "I was there. I don't need to see them again."

Work Richard's case? Maybe Brown was right, that it was madness.

Brown reached over and laid a hand on her arm. "You don't have to do this, you know."

"That's where you're wrong, Floyd. I *do* have to do this." Kate straightened up, all business now. "Where are the paintings? The ones found at the scenes?"

"Our lab's going over them."

"I want to see them."

"Soon as the lab's done their thing," said Brown.

"By the way. Do you have a statement from Richard's associate, Andrew Stokes? I assume someone's already taken one."

"In the jacket." Brown grabbed another folder off his desk, opening it carefully and removing the envelope that Kate knew must contain the crime scene photos, which he slid into the center drawer of his desk before handing her the folder. "Why?"

"I just had a talk with him and I don't know, but I'd like to keep an eye on him."

"You were already conducting an interview?"

"It wasn't an *interview*," said Kate. "It was a simple conversation, that's all."

Brown locked his dark eyes on hers. "Nothing is a simple conversation if you're going to work with us on this case. You think you can you remember that?"

Kate raised her hands in defense. "Absolutely."

"You'd better," he said. "This Stokes guy, would he want to do your husband harm?"

"I don't know him very well, but—"

"How long did he work for your husband?"

"About two years."

"And you didn't know him?"

"We didn't socialize. I'd see him from time to time at the office, but no, I didn't know him." The bank statement flashed in Kate's mind, and she was about to tell Brown, but something stopped her. Was it that she suspected Richard could have been doing something illegal? She wasn't sure, but wanted to find out before she said anything. "Richard had a talk with him. It's possible Stokes was on notice, about to be fired."

"People have killed for less," said Brown.

"Says he was home with a cold. Has that been checked out?"

Brown tapped a few words into his computer and they both watched as data filled the screen, and Brown scrolled through it. "Here it is. Andrew Stokes's statement." He paused, reading. "Yep. Home with a cold. Wife was there. Building's doorman verified that Stokes had not left the building that day."

"I still say he bears watching," said Kate. "Any possibility of putting a tail on him? The secretary confirmed that Richard was annoyed with him lately, plus the fact that he was probably about to get canned. I know it's not much, but—"

"We need more than a hunch to do that legally, McKinnon."

"How about the fact that he paints for a hobby."

"I thought you didn't know him?"

"Just found out."

"I'll see what I can do. Maybe we can put someone on him." Brown made a note on a legal pad, then looked up. "By the way, I've got you teamed with Nicky Perlmutter. He was in Homicide for five years. I chose him for my squad when I took over. Good guy. Smart. You're gonna like him."

Kate folded her arms across her chest, gave Brown a prove-it-to-me look. "And why's that?"

"Because he's one of the few guys on the force taller than you?"

"Funny," said Kate.

"Perlmutter started up in the Bronx, on foot, so he knows the terrain."

"You're out of the Bronx too," said Kate. "Why don't you work the case with me?"

" 'Cause I'm the boss," said Brown. "And I don't want a partner who's in this for personal reasons."

SEVEN

The lemony-yellow street lamps provide the perfect light. No annoying glare or irritating sun. Others might not find it so, their vision severely limited, details a blur, but for him it provides the ideal mode in which to hunt. He pictures himself as one of those Marvel comics X-Men, imagines looking through special commando night-vision goggles, while everyone else is blind.

There they are, the girls, only a block from the river, on this desolate street, three of them, hanging together on the corner, signaling to slow-moving cars.

He moves swiftly, taking in everything—darkened warehouses, closed-up shops, cars hugging the curbs, men in front seats, eyes closed, girls providing quickie twenty-dollar relief.

He'd like to pull one of those car doors open, slice and dice one of those men. But not now. He is on a mission. He needs to learn. This has to mean something.

He has a jacket on over his shirt, shirttails pulled out to hide the roll of tape that bulges in one pocket, the knives, wrapped in a piece of canvas, in another.

The girls of the night call out to him—"Hey, handsome, how about a date?"—but he keeps moving until he spies a really young one down the end of the street, smoking a cigarette, tugging at her mini as though she were just a little bit ashamed, and he likes that. He slows his pace, lets her have a good look at him.

"Hi, there." Gray puffs of smoke escape her lips as she speaks.

He turns toward her and flashes his smile.

The girl smiles back. She can't believe her good luck. A young guy. And really cute. Not one of the usual slobs.

The street lamp glitters in her hair. Goldenrod, he thinks, and feels a tug in his groin. He knows right away she is the one.

They stand a moment under the streetlight.

"What are you looking for?" she asks.

"Company," he says. *Come and knock on our door—*

"That's me," she says.

"I like your eyes," he says. "They're so blue."

"No, they're—"

He scowls.

"Yeah," she says, thinking, blue, gray, what's the difference? "I bet all the girls tell you how handsome you are."

He grins, shrugs like a little boy.

For a moment she considers giving him a freebie, but thinks better of it, keeps her mouth shut.

"You gotta place?" He looks from her eyes to her hair. *Yellow? Tangerine?* His hard-on is aching, and he needs to know.

She tosses her cigarette to the pavement. "There's a parking lot one block over. Somebody's always left a car open. Lots cheaper than a hotel. Come on."

The lot occupies an entire corner, cars lined up in neat rows, just a few dim overhead lights, not much. For him, perfect. He reaches for a car door handle. She stops him. "Could be alarmed." She creeps from car to car, peering into windows, stops, and says, "This one's got the 'Club' across the wheel. Usually means there won't be an alarm." She tugs and the door opens. "See. Wide open."

"You're pretty smart," he says.

"And you're just pretty."

"You don't think I'm smart?"

The girl leans against the car and looks into his face. She thinks maybe there is something a little weird about this incredibly cute guy. But he smiles again, that little-boy smile, and she looks at his pouty lips, and the bad thoughts melt away and she decides she might even let him kiss her, something she never allows. "It's thirty for a suck. Fifty if you want to fuck me. Up front."

He peels off five ten-dollar bills, and she hands him a condom in exchange.

"You got any kids?" he asks.

"Jesus, why the fuck would you ask me that?"

An image tears across his brain: a gray-fleshed man and woman on a bed. His eyes blink, a vein pulsates in his temple. "Forget it," he says.

"You okay?"

"Me? I'm grrrrrrrreat!" He flashes another one of those Justin Timberlake teen-idol-type smiles. "You're in good hands with Allstate," he says.

She laughs, slides into the backseat of the car and tugs the mini up to her waist.

He drops his jacket onto the ground outside the car before joining her.

The car's interior is dim, to the girl almost black.

He pretends he is undoing his pants while sliding the roll of tape from his pocket.

"Let me help," she says.

He mumbles, "Uh-uh," then pushes her down hard against the seat as he tears the tape with his teeth.

"What the fuck—"

She's a little thing, no more than five-two or -three, maybe a hundred pounds, no match for him. She's kicking and scratching, but it only takes a few seconds to get the tape across her mouth, more around her wrists and ankles.

Her mind is racing: *How can this be happening?* She tries to say something. Impossible.

"Shhh . . ." He pulls on plastic gloves and pats her hair, still wondering about the hue.

Oh, God. This can't be happening. All the creeps she has serviced in her young life and it turns out to be this one, the cute guy. She tries to think clearly, grasps at hope—maybe it's just a game, tries to telegraph with her eyes that she will play.

But then she feels the knife pierce her flesh, a sharp hot-cold flash, and when she looks down sees that blood is spurting out of her chest.

Colors explode before his eyes—red-violet and plum. His erection throbs. He reaches down with one hand and releases it from his pants.

The girl feels the knife moving in and out of her flesh, tries to take in the reality of what is happening to her, and to breathe, but it's like sucking Jell-O through a straw.

He decides it's too cramped in the car to open her up, that he will have to make do with the blood. But it's enough.

The colors intensify—a rainbow—and that's all it takes. He comes against her naked thigh, eyes blinking like a ventriloquist's dummy, and he cries out, naming the colors as they flash before his eyes: "Maroon! Magenta! Mulberry!"

The last word the girl hears him say is *Strawberry,* and she remembers a night, not that long ago, in the remodeled den of her parents' split-level home in Dayton, Ohio: She and her baby sister, Abby—whom she has not spoken to since she ran away—defrosting a packet of strawberries in the microwave and pouring them over vanilla ice cream just before they settled in to watch an episode of *Melrose Place,* which her parents forbade them to watch, but they were out somewhere, who cared, as long as they were out, and now, just before her breathing fails and her heart stops, she hears the theme song from the show playing in her head.

Inside the car, everything has gone a murky, dismal gray, and all he wants is out. He no longer cares about making a painting, the brush having never left his back pocket. It's too late. He can't remember anything. A total waste.

Celebrate the moments of your life . . .

As if.

Another opportunity wasted. He feels nothing but shame and disgust as he plucks his jacket off the ground. It does a good job of hiding his bloodied shirt, though not his pants, which is okay, it's too dark to see the blood against black denim. He peers around the parking lot to see if any other cars are being used in the same way, but it's quiet. He tugs the girl out of the car, leans her body against his, both arms around her waist to keep her upright. She's heavier than expected, the inert body clumsy to maneuver.

He shuffles toward the river, the dead girl's head bouncing on his shoulder. A few cars pass by. No one stops.

He thinks that it wasn't so bad after all. He saw a few things that he would not ordinarily have seen, and though he did not make a painting, he's not left anything behind. It's as if this never happened, like a get-out-of-jail-free card.

At the river's edge he remembers his fifty dollars, gets a hand into the pocket of what is left of her mini, and tugs out a fistful of bills. Then he pitches her body into the river and watches it disappear into the inky-black water.

EIGHT

The detectives' "lounge"—formerly a ten-by-twelve-foot storage bin—had been affectionately referred to as "Graceland" ever since the calendar with the faded color glossy of the King's Memphis estate had been tacked onto the wall beside the vending machines.

Nicky Perlmutter, in loose-fitting khakis and a blue button-down shirt tight across his chest, was leaning against the wall dipping a Lipton tea bag in and out of the mug in his hand. At almost six feet four inches tall, broad-shouldered, and muscular, he would have made an impression even without the apple-red hair, blue eyes, and freckles, but the combination of the Huck Finn face on the strapping thirty-seven-year-old body was disarming.

"McKinnon, right?"

Kate took him in as they shook hands, surprised—he was not at all what she had expected. "How'd you guess?"

"Brown told me to be on the lookout for a tall, beautiful woman."

"Oh, please." Kate actually blushed. "Brown never said that."

"No, but he *did* say you were tall." Perlmutter smiled, which Kate thought made him look about fourteen. "I don't mean that you're *not* beautiful, what I meant was that, uh"—he sputtered—"you know, that *I* added the beautiful part."

"Well then, I guess Brown is right about two things." Kate smiled too. "One, I'm tall, and two, that I'd like you."

A couple of detectives at the far end of the long narrow table were huddled over cups of steaming coffee; one, mid-fifties, balding, and overweight, chewing on an unlit cigarette, the other one, younger, not bad-looking, though he already had that mean, suspicious look that twisted up some cops' faces. They glanced up at Kate and Perlmutter, then looked away, slightly disgusted.

Kate figured the news of her arrival had made its way around the station—news like that always did. And she knew the score—that being police was a fraternity, that the boys were not going to invite her in, certainly not without some significant hazing, which, in this case, they knew was impossible: Kate was Tapell's pal, and close to Brown as well. Bad enough she was a woman, whom the men would not like having around even if they had to pretend they did. Of course the women cops wouldn't like her either. They'd just see her as competition. Kate remembered what that was like when she worked in Astoria. She and Liz had clung to each other like lifelines, just about the only women on the force who got along.

She made a note to have Brown spread the word that she was not after anyone's job or their collars, simply to help catch a psycho, and when that was over she'd go back to her life.

What life? What exactly was there to go back to?

No, she would not allow herself to think like that.

Perlmutter caught a glimpse of the cloud that had suddenly darkened Kate's features. He took hold of her arm. "Let's get out of here," he said.

Zerega Avenue was a wide thoroughfare that might once have been grand, though if that was the case, it had been a very long time ago. Half the tenements and storefronts were boarded up or burned out, and everything was so graffiti-covered that the edges of buildings blurred into one another, creating a kind of urban camouflage. Perlmutter brought the car to a stop alongside a wide ten-story apartment building that looked as though it had been built sometime in the 1920s and not cleaned since.

Inside, the semicircular lobby was big enough to set up a Little League game, though completely devoid of ornamentation, plaster detailing on the ceiling stripped away, walls a combination of flaking paint and grime, pillars the size of redwoods etched with crude initials, names, hearts, and skulls.

"Super's in number one," said Perlmutter.

Kate hadn't seen so much Catholic imagery since her high school days at St. Anne's, and she hadn't missed it. Above every door, crowding the walls, flanking the heavily curtained windows of Rosita Martinez's airless apartment were paintings and objects and reproductions of saints and crucifixes, all smiling beatifically or writhing in pain.

Richard had a passion for the real ones, the Italian version, and Kate always kidded him that it was because he was Jewish, that if he'd been brought up Catholic he wouldn't be able to stomach the stuff.

Martinez was anywhere from forty to fifty, impossible to tell if the lines on her face were caused by age or a hard life, a tiny woman, no more than five feet, with bottle-black hair, and dozens of bangle bracelets on her wrists that created a mini-cacophony when she gestured.

"Oh, such a terrible thing." *Cling. Clang. Clink.* "The worst thing in my life to see." *Clink. Clank.* "The worst thing I have ever to see happen in this building since I become super here—and I seen plenty of bad things." She sighed over the clinking and clanking of her bracelets. "Horrible. I am still taking the pills." Her eyes darted from Kate to Perlmutter. "From the doctor," she added quickly. "I can show you the prescription."

"Not necessary." Kate offered the woman a warm smile. "If I'd gone through what you did, Ms. Martinez, I'd be knocking back handfuls of tranquilizers with Scotch."

Rosita Martinez smiled at Kate. "You are not like the rest of them. The questions they ask. Over and over. As if I don't have it bad enough."

"I can imagine," said Kate, taking the woman by her bangled hand, leading her toward the couch. "You should sit down. Relax. We don't have a whole lot of questions."

Nicky Perlmutter offered the woman one of his Huck Finn smiles, then whipped a small notepad out of his back pocket. "Says you found the body at four P.M. Can you tell us what you were doing in the victim's apartment at that time?"

Rosita Martinez's jaw clamped shut.

Kate threw Perlmutter a look with the slightest tilt of her head, and he understood the message—make yourself scarce. "Could I get a glass of water?" he asked, a nod toward the kitchen.

Rosita Martinez shrugged, and he took off.

"I can imagine how awful it is to have to relive any of this," said Kate, turning to the woman. "But it will help us find out who did it if you can."

The tiny woman took a big breath. "Well, Suzie, she tell me the day before that her hot water, it was not working right. To be honest, this happens many times in this building. I was coming to her apartment to see if there was a problem. That was when I, I—" She crossed herself several times, the bangles striking up an atonal symphony. "When I found her."

"So you saw her the day before," said Kate. "Do you happen to remember what time of day that was?"

"I would see her many times. Her apartment, it is just across the lobby. But that time, the last time, it was at eight or eight-thirty. I know that because she stopped to ask me about the water and I was watching the *American Idol* on the TV." She glanced over at the twenty-seven-inch Magnavox directly opposite the couch with a look of pride, then above it at a garishly painted plastic Jesus and crossed herself.

"You have any idea where Suzie was going at eight or eight-thirty?"

Martinez shrugged as Perlmutter came back into the room sipping water, though he hung back, gave Kate and the witness some space.

"Please." Kate laid her hand over the woman's. "Anything you can tell us is very important if we're going to catch the person who did this horrible thing to Suzie." She caught some sadness in the woman's dark eyes. "You liked her, didn't you?"

"She didn't do anyone harm."

"I'm sure she didn't," said Kate. "Like a lamb to the slaughter, the Good Book says."

"You are a Catholic?" Martinez asked.

"Full-blooded," said Kate, deciding to omit the fact that she had not been inside a church in over twenty years, unless it was to look at art or attend a wedding—or a funeral.

"I knew it!" Rosita Martinez's dark eyes brightened.

"So, do you know where Suzie was headed that night, when you saw her going out?"

"She had one of her . . . dates, you know. Suzie brought men back many times during the night." She was almost whispering. "But is that a reason to die?" She wrapped her fingers around the silver cross at her throat, her eyes on Kate. "Mary Magdalene, she was like that, and she turned out to be a good woman."

"Absolutely," said Kate. "Tell me, Rosita—I hope you don't mind if I call you Rosita—were there any men who were regulars of Suzie's, that you saw here often? You know, on a continual basis."

"A few."

"Can you describe any of them?"

The wrinkles in Martinez's brow deepened with concentration. "There was one man, a businessman, maybe. I say this because he always wore a suit."

"What else can you tell me about him? Tall, short, bald? Anything like that?"

"I remember one time he came into the lobby and I was just leaving to the supermarket because I had no milk and I do not like coffee without the milk, and he was coming in, like I say, and he passed right by me and he was tall." She extended her bangled arm way above her head.

"You have an excellent memory," said Kate. "How old, would you say?"

"I'm not sure. He had one of those baby faces, you know, and good-looking."

"Could you pick him out from a photo?" asked Perlmutter, figuring it was okay to be part of the conversation now.

"*Sí*. Yes. I think so. He was here many times. The first time I see him"—Rosita Martinez clutched her crucifix in her tiny palm—"it was springtime. I think maybe the end of April, a very nice day, the first one after the winter. I was talking to Mr. Diaz, who works on the garbage truck, a nice man, a gentleman—and to have such a job . . ." She clucked. "And Mr. Diaz was saying that it was a lot more easy to collect the garbage when there was no snow and it was not freezing, but that it would be even worse when it was summer and hot and the garbage it would stink and—"

Kate interrupted as gently as possible. "And that's when you saw him for the first time?"

"*Sí.* Yes. He was coming into the building, and he looked nervous with the eyes going all around, and he had a piece of paper, one of those, what do you call them—with the glue on one part?"

"A Post-it?" Kate offered.

"Yes, that was it, a Post-it. It was in his hand, and he kept looking at it and then up at the building, like to check that he was in the right place. And I remember that I wondered who he was, this good-looking man, and who he was coming to see, up here, in the lousy Bronx. So I watched when he went into the building, and I have to tell the truth—I peeked in through the door, and I see that he goes to Suzie's apartment, and I give Mr. Diaz one of those looks—you know, I raise my eyebrows, like you-know-what-this-guy-is-up-to. And now"—she twisted the cross and chain around her throat—"I feel bad that I did that." She glanced up at Kate with some urgency. "You don't think this man, he do this to Suzie?"

"I don't know. But we'll find out." She patted the woman's arm and the bangles played a little jingle. "Oh, by the way, do you know if Suzie painted?"

"Painted?" Rosita Martinez peered up at Kate. "What do you mean, *painted*?"

"You know, made paintings, with oil paint, pictures on canvas?"

"Icons, like Jesus?"

"No, regular pictures. Scenes, or paintings of fruit."

"*Fruit?*" Rosita Martinez shrugged as though the idea of making pictures of fruit was the most absurd thing she had ever heard. "No, I don't think so. I never see any pictures like that in her place."

Kate hadn't thought so, but had to ask. "Were there any other regulars?"

"There was the boyfriend. He stay here many times. Not such a nice one, this boyfriend. But who am I to judge?"

"I'm sure you are an excellent judge of character," said Kate. "Can you tell me what this boyfriend looked like?"

"A black man. Skinny. Tall. With long hair in those clumps, you know."

"Dreadlocks."

"*Sí*. Exactly. And he used a cane, a silvery one, but I do not think he needed it for walking. He did not have a limp. He was a young man. I think the cane it was like a . . . how do you say?"

"A prop? A costume?"

"*Sí*, a prop."

"You have some memory," said Kate. "Doesn't she, Nicky?"

Perlmutter nodded enthusiastically.

"Anything else?" Kate asked. "A tattoo? Any scars?"

"Oh, sweet Jesus. How could I forget? A scar, yes. A bad scar. Like someone had once tried to cut his throat." She brought her hand across her throat dramatically, then crossed herself.

"Would you mind going into the station, looking at some pictures?" Perlmutter asked.

Rosita Martinez eyed Kate, waiting for her approval, and Kate gave the woman's arm a gentle squeeze.

"Okay," she said, patting her hair.

Perlmutter stepped away, called the station and arranged for a car to fetch Rosita Martinez while Kate commended the woman yet again on her memory, then went through a few more questions. By the time the uniforms showed up to take Rosita to the station, she and Kate were chatting like old friends.

"You are a very nice lady," said Rosita Martinez. "And pretty. But a little too skinny. Probably you are always on the diet, *sí*?"

"No," said Kate. "I eat all the time, I swear."

"Good. I will cook for you a delicious meal sometime."

"That would be lovely," said Kate.

"You like fried plantains?" asked Rosita Martinez.

Impressive," said Perlmutter, as he and Kate headed across the lobby toward Suzie White's apartment. "Another ten minutes and that woman was going to adopt you."

"She wanted to talk," said Kate. "And probably no one has given her the time before. Plus, she was scared. I learned a long time ago that all people need to open up is to feel safe."

Feeling safe. Something he had spent a lifetime working on.

Perlmutter peeled a piece of police tape off Suzie White's door. He handed Kate a pair of plastic gloves, slipped a pair on himself, then turned the key in the lock and pushed the door open.

Suzie White's apartment was full of odors, one lying on top of the other: sweat, beer, sex, pizza, garbage, death.

No saints or crosses here. The place was basically one room with a small kitchenette at one end, bathroom off the other, one closet, a big bed up against a wall plastered with pictures clipped from fashion magazines along with ones of long-haired rock stars—Jon Bon Jovi, Steven Tyler, Axl Rose.

The place had been gone over by CSU, and other than the wall of pictures, pretty much stripped. Fingerprint powders—black, white, and silver—dappled the kitchen sink, half-sized refrigerator, the one windowsill, a couple of cheap lamps. The linoleum floor was stained in so many places it was impossible to know which stains were old and what might have been bloodstains.

The bathroom was small and cramped, sink blemished with rust, fingerprint powder on the medicine cabinet giving the mirror a veiled, otherworldly quality. Kate popped it open, found a lipstick, Black Cherry Red, and a cheap mascara brush crusted black.

While she bagged the makeup, Kate had the feeling she was not alone, and turned to see if Perlmutter had followed her in. But there was no one there. It felt like something more than that old cop alarm, something familiar and more recent—a buzzing sensation, as if a high-intensity wire had snapped inside her, sending an electric current through her body, sensitizing her nerve endings and fine-tuning her antenna. It was almost as if the killer were in the room with her right now, leaning over her shoulder, pointing things out, whispering: *Look here, and here.*

"Not much to check," Perlmutter shouted from the other room, and Kate was glad to hear his voice. It was enough to flip the switch and turn off that electric buzz.

"Anything in there?" he asked, as Kate came back into the room.

"No," she said, and found herself being drawn toward the wall of rock stars and models, a shrine to Suzie White's prosaic interests. Kate's eyes floated over Jon Bon Jovi's curly locks and Steven Tyler's toothy grimace, the buzzing back in her brain like a laser. Thumbtacked between two fashion-magazine pictures was one of those photo-booth strips— four consecutive shots of a black man and young white woman crowding together into each small frame, mugging for the camera.

Kate plucked it off the wall. "Could be the boyfriend?" she said, guessing from the man's dreadlocks. "How did CSU miss this?"

"High-risk victim. Low-priority case." Perlmutter frowned.

Kate knew he was right—the murder of a street hooker was never going to be priority.

"Unless she was part of a pattern."

"But CSU wouldn't have known that at the time."

"Right," said Kate. "Maybe Rosita Martinez can ID the guy from the photos." Kate thought a moment. "Though he's probably not our man—not if it's a serial killer. They almost always hunt their own, and he's black." Kate stared at the four laughing faces of Suzie White as she zipped the strip into a plastic bag. There was a sweetness to the girl's face despite all the makeup, and a joy in her smile that had not been killed by her lifestyle.

Kate took a last look around the room, that buzzing sensation now reduced to a low-level hum.

"The other scene's only three blocks from here," said Perlmutter.

It just didn't make sense, thought Kate as she and Perlmutter surveyed the apartment of the second victim, Marsha Stimson—a run-down filth hole in a three-story, otherwise uninhabited tenement on a lonely Bronx side street. *A guy kills two women, two prostitutes in the Bronx, and then moves to Midtown, to . . . Richard. Why?* The pattern seemed totally wrong.

"Not much here," said Perlmutter, surveying the apartment. "Crime Scene has stripped it pretty well."

A wooden dresser, drawers open, contents removed, no blankets or sheets on the queen-size bed, the lumpy mattress naked and bloodstained, an altar to the former resident's sordid life and violent death.

"Were there any witnesses?" Kate asked.

"Nada," said Perlmutter. "Uniforms canvassed the adjacent buildings and the street. No one heard or saw anything. No one on the block claims to know the vic. Maybe she was squatting. The building's slated for demo."

Kate took it all in—the fingerprint powders blanketing objects like dandruff, cracks in the ceiling, dull walls, the almost total lack of adornment in the dim room—and that buzzing sensation started up again. Once again she let it guide her, eyes scanning the walls, landing first on a giveaway-type calendar, REINHOLDT'S FURNITURE STORE, hanging from a thumbtack beside one of those cheap plastic-framed full-length mirrors. Kate pictured Marsha Stimson primping in front of it, and the buzz became a purr. Kate's eyes slid across the dull-beige walls to a Gauguin painting from Tahiti, maybe something the deceased had cut out of a magazine or book, an island scene, greens and blues with half-naked women in between the trees and huts, a paradise. Had Marsha Stimson looked at this and dreamed of faraway places, an escape from her dreary, dismal life?

Kate carefully removed the thumbtack and slipped the reproduction into a baggy.

"Why that?" asked Perlmutter.

Kate stared at the print through the plastic. "I'm just thinking that he may have looked at it, been interested. I mean, because he leaves paintings behind, colorful ones."

"Good point," said Perlmutter. "And Gauguin was one of the great colorists of all time."

"You know about art."

"Nah, not really. But I'm crazy about Gauguin. Sometimes I even dream about running off to the South Seas. But who doesn't, right?"

At the moment it struck Kate as a damn good idea. "The lab can spray the print with ninhydrin, see if anything develops. I know it's a long shot, but maybe the psycho was crazy enough to touch it."

Now the buzz almost seemed to purr "umm hmm," and Kate shivered again.

Kate was thinking it through, aloud, as they headed back to Perlmutter's car. "So the guy stakes out the two victims, waits till they're alone, kills them, and brings along a painting? For what?" She just couldn't figure it. "Marsha Stimson would have been easy to get to—no one else living in that building, but Suzie White was in a big building, her apartment across a wide lobby. There would be lots of possibilities of other people coming and going, of his getting seen or caught. Why would he risk it?"

"Maybe he'd been stalking her, or had a thing for her? It's possible he'd been with her, had picked her up one time and so knew where to find her."

Kate plucked a pack of cigarettes off the dashboard, the ones she'd been avoiding the entire trip up to the Bronx. "You mind?"

"Bad idea," said Perlmutter. "But go ahead. I just keep 'em to give to others—witnesses, suspects. Wouldn't touch 'em myself."

"Uh-oh," said Kate, pushing in the car's lighter. "Am I about to get a lecture on the evils of smoking?"

"Not from me," said Perlmutter. "What I meant was they're stale."

Kate lit one up and coughed. "Oh, awful," she said, but did not put it out. "Damn good thing I don't smoke anymore." She pulled the bitter smoke deep into her lungs, thinking, *Richard is going to kill me for starting up again,* and as the thought registered she could not control the tears that gathered in her eyes.

Perlmutter glanced over. "You okay?"

"Yes." Kate faked a cough. "It's just this stale piece of crap."

"Can't say I didn't warn you."

Kate stared out the car window while she lassoed her emotions. "I'm trying to make sense of it. Two women. Then a man. It's a change in ritual, unless the crimes are not gender-based. Were the women violated?"

"According to the coroner's prelims, there was no vaginal bruising or rape."

Kate did not ask about Richard. She did not want to know. She pulled more tar and nicotine into her lungs. "So what exactly connects the crimes?"

"Umm . . . Gutting the bodies? The paintings?"

"Do you know if the lab's finished with the paintings?"

"Probably with the first two," Perlmutter said. "But the uh, other one, uh—"

Kate breathed in and said, "The one from my husband's crime scene, you mean? It's okay, Perlmutter." She swallowed hard. "Really. Just say it, okay. We're going to have to be honest with each other if this is going to work."

"Right," said Perlmutter. "The painting from your husband's crime scene."

"Right," Kate said, hardly breathing. "Thank you."

"Hey, call me Nicky, please. Perlmutter always makes me think of my father, plus it's gotta be one of the top-ten worst names, right? I used to beg my parents to change it."

"So why don't you?" asked Kate, happy to have the subject changed.

"Nah, too late. I'm used to it. But I'd prefer it if you called me Nicky."

"And call me Kate."

He angled a boyish smile at her, eyes still on the road, though Kate had a feeling he'd been trying to size her up for the past few hours, as though he was thinking about asking her something—or telling her. She wasn't sure. Maybe he'd heard from the few cops who had known about her back in Astoria when she'd gotten a reputation for being cold as ice because she was able to work the roughest cases, look squarely at the nastiest crime scenes. But it had never been true. She was simply a good actor, and right now she was thankful she could still pull it off. The truth was everything affected her, always had. But Kate knew she could not allow the slightest acknowledgment of feeling get to her, that once she did, she'd be a goner. She mashed the cigarette out in the car's ashtray.

"Good idea," Perlmutter said. "Those things will kill you. Sorry. I promised no lectures."

Kate checked her watch. She'd almost forgotten that she had arranged to meet her editor to work on the Boyd Werther tapes, which absolutely had to be finished if the show was going to air as advertised, next week. Her producer at PBS had called a half dozen times to say it was fine to postpone the show, but Kate wanted to pretend everything was normal, wanted to be working every possible minute.

"Can you do me a favor and drop me in Midtown?"

"No problem," said Perlmutter.

"Great. Now here's the hard part—in twenty minutes?"

Perlmutter snorted a laugh. "From *here*?"

"I'm going to be late for an editing session. It's just my silly TV show, but—"

"Hey, I love your show—and it's not silly."

"You watch my show?"

"Where do you think I learned about Gauguin?"

Kate had to smile.

Perlmutter affected a melodramatic voice—"Fasten your seat belts, it's going to be a bumpy night!"—then angled another smile at Kate. "I'll get you there in fifteen if you can tell me where that line is from."

"Piece of cake," said Kate. "*All About Eve.* Bette Davis."

In one quick move Perlmutter snatched the magnetic beacon off the dashboard, stretched his muscled arm out the window, and plunked the light onto the hood of the car. "You won't turn me in for using the beacon, will you?"

"What about the siren?"

Perlmutter flipped the switch.

NINE

The fact that Rothstein's body was found with a painting beside it links this vicious murder of the high-profile Manhattan attorney with two recent murders in the Bronx, though the NYPD has neither confirmed this, nor denied it. The painting at this scene was yet another still life, this one of fruit in a blue-striped bowl—

Leonardo Alberto Martini (né Leo Albert), of Staten Island, stopped reading the story in the *New York Post* at exactly the same place he had stopped the last two times.

A blue-striped bowl—just like the one Leo was holding right now in his shaking paint-stained fingers.

Leo sagged into a chair, the original color of the cracked leather not only faded but masked beneath a multitude of paint smudges and blobs. He was thoroughly disgusted—with himself, his paintings, and his career, or lack thereof, and now this. He might as well commit suicide, as he had so often threatened over the past three decades.

Thirty years ago he'd been on the doorstep to success, the door itself ajar, waiting for him to pass through its portals into bona fide art star status, his work being shown at a top-notch Fifty-seventh Street art gallery specializing in up-and-comers. *Art News* had called him "an artist to keep your eye on . . . an abstract painter of rare sensitivity, a true colorist." Curators were putting his large colorful abstractions in museum exhibitions, and collectors were snatching them up for their living rooms. But then minimal art hit the scene. Decorative color painting was out, and Leo along with it, and after three successive shows failed to sell, the gallery let him go, the curators and collectors stopped visiting his studio, and even fellow artists stayed away, afraid of catching a severe case of failuritis.

He had tried for another gallery, even managed a couple of shows over the next decade, both resounding flops. Nowadays, Leo painted nights and weekends, his weekdays spent at a shitty nine-to-five job feeding Xerox machines.

Leo played with his thinning gray ponytail, weaving wispy hairs in and around his slightly arthritic fingers as he attempted to distract himself with one of the candy-colored abstractions he stubbornly refused to stop making, though his eyes kept drifting away, staring at the impressive stack of hundred-dollar bills he had earned by making that banal little painting. He'd added the blue-striped bowl only because he thought it created a bit of interest, a decorative quality to an otherwise academic picture that he could have produced blindfolded.

Of course, like any artist, he'd painted the still life in his own particular style—how could he not, after forty-plus years of painting?—never using any white paint, allowing instead the unpainted canvas to stand in for the whites, a trick, some said, but he'd gotten the idea from the great French painter Henri Matisse, who often did the same thing. And of course the way he thinned his paint with turpentine and used his variety of foam-tipped brushes or neatly cut squares of sponge so that the paint was sponged-on rather than brushed, which left no brush stroke at all, the watery paint simply absorbed into the canvas—that he liked to claim was his own, even though he knew it had been used by other contemporary painters.

Still, Leo would have (and should have) tossed a painting like that right out the window of the Lower East Side tenement that served as both living quarters and studio, but he needed the money, and no way could he turn down five thousand dollars.

It had sounded like easy money, and, in fact, had been. He'd painted the still life in a couple of hours—an apple, two bananas, in a blue-striped bowl—delivered it, paint still wet, in exchange for the wad of hundreds in a plain manila envelope, more money than he made in a couple of months at his lousy job. Though now, with the bills in a heap on his unmade bed, and that newspaper article describing a still life with a blue-striped bowl screaming at him from across the room, he felt as though he was going to jump right out of his skin.

Leo paced the short distance between his cramped kitchenette and the makeshift art studio he'd set up years ago in what was supposed to be the tiny apartment's living room, back and forth, unable to sit still.

Finally, he slid a crisp hundred off the top of the stack, shoved the rest under his mattress, then tucked the bill into the pocket of his old jean jacket, the one with torn elbows and a couple of missing buttons. He was thinking that maybe he'd stop at the Levi's store on Broadway and pick up a new one before he decided what to do about this problem.

At the door, just about to leave, he turned back into the room and plucked the blue-striped bowl off his paint table. For a moment he considered smashing it, but quickly reconsidered. Better to take it with him, and dispose of it outside.

But a moment later, as he thought it through, he reconsidered once again. If things got out of hand he might need some sort of leverage, and the bowl was exactly that.

Leo scanned the small apartment looking for a safe place to hide it and recalled the TV show he'd watched just the other night where the man had hidden a stash of stolen jewelry in the tank of his toilet, which was exactly where Leo deposited the blue-striped bowl, which dropped to the bottom of the tank and lay there against the rusted chain and black rubber stopper.

W as it simply that she was afraid to go home? Is that why she spent nearly six hours editing the Boyd Werther tape for PBS? And after that had rerouted the cab from Central Park West to take her to the brownstone that housed Let There Be a Future and there spent another hour going through e-mail and phone messages? She still needed to review the applications for next year's program, something she ordinarily loved to do. But she was tired, her mind elsewhere. She would never be able to deal with the foundation, not now, not if she was going to devote her time to police work. She always hated to ask for help, but knew she needed it.

Blair. She'd call Blair.

Blair Sumner fell easily into the category of the Ladies Who Lunch—though Blair ate only lettuce. A mover and shaker among the Park Avenue set (her husband, a client of Richard's, was a ruthless arbitrageur worth zillions), Blair supported the New York Public Library, the Botanical Garden, was active on the boards of the Metropolitan Opera and the Landmarks Preservation Committee, and at least a dozen other worthy organizations.

The past few days, Blair had been attempting to hold Kate's hand, though Kate had refused it.

Now Kate listened to Blair's answering machine, the almost, but not quite English accent that Blair had certainly affected (she hailed from Schenectady). "I'm out and about, but do leave a message. Ta—"

"Blair. It's me—"

"Darling," said Blair, interrupting the machine message. "Thank God. How are you?"

Kate took a deep breath. She did not want to go into how she was feeling or what she was doing. "Fine. I need a favor."

"Name it."

"Fill in for me at Let There Be a Future."

"Of course, darling. As long as they don't expect me to show up before noon. What exactly shall I do?"

"Just go through the files of next season's kids, confer with the director, like that."

"Will do, darling. Oh, wait—"

"Problem?"

"No, no, no. It's just the knee thing, but I'll put it off."

Kate knew what Blair was referring to. The woman had had so much plastic surgery that only last week Kate had kidded her that she was running out of places to fix and Blair had proved her wrong by saying she was having the sagging flesh at her knees tightened. Kate's question—*"How will you walk?"*—received the answer, *"Who cares about walking?"*

"Your knees. How could I forget?"

"Scoff if you will, darling. But wait until you hit my age." She cleared her throat. "Not that you are so much younger than me. But you'll see."

Blair's real age was a well-kept secret. Other than a few pale thread-like scars, her face betrayed no telltale signs of her years on the planet.

"Oh, please," said Kate. "Your knees are better than mine."

"You're just saying that to flatter me, which you needn't. I will gladly pick up the mantle at the foundation. My poor old knees can wait." Blair's tone sobered. "Kate, I want to see you, and I won't take no for an answer. I know you, darling, acting all brave and stoic—"

Kate cut her off. "Yes, Blair. Soon. I promise."

The dinner Kate's housekeeper, Lucille, had prepared was plastic-wrapped, waiting in the fridge, heating instructions on the kitchen counter, but it was way past dinnertime and Kate wasn't hungry. She didn't turn on the lights, getting by with the moonlight that slithered in through the penthouse windows, painting everything in silver and shadow. She did not want to see all the things—bric-a-brac mementos of vacations, photographs, paintings—that she and Richard had collected and loved. But even with the lights out, the place felt too big. She would have to think about selling the apartment, moving into a smaller place, something more *appropriate* for a single woman. Yes, she would have to get used to that idea—of living by herself.

But how to fill the emptiness now?

Maybe Nola would be moving in with her. The thought warmed her briefly. But would that be fair to Nola? After all, Kate had always encouraged the girl to be independent. If Nola wanted to move in, that would be different, but she was not going to drag her in merely to keep her company. Kate refused to be one of those women who could not be alone.

The phone machine's light was flashing, a tiny red beacon in the dark. Seventeen messages. Kate stared at the contraption. *No way.* She couldn't bear the thought of hearing her friends' voices, all well-meaning, of course, but emotionally exhausting. She'd been doing her best to avoid almost everyone. About the only person Kate had forced herself to call was Richard's mother, a one-minute conversation, the same every day:

"How are you, darling?"

"Fine, how's the weather down in Florida, Edie?"

"Good. Why don't you come for a visit?"

"I will. Soon."

"Good."

"Bye."

"Bye."

Not a direct word about Richard or their emotions, the two women treading water, their unspoken agreement: To live in a perpetual state of complete denial.

Kate dumped the folders on the first two murder victims onto the desk beside the answering machine and sagged into a chair. Why had she bothered to bring them home? An old habit: she always thought more clearly away from the station house.

Now she flipped one open, spread the crime scene photos across her desk, overlapping one on top of the other: Suzie White's eviscerated body from every angle—a gruesome Cubist montage.

Is this what she wanted? To have her mind filled with more hideous images that she would never forget?

Kate scooped the photos back into the jacket and glanced down at the newspaper on the floor beside her desk, the one she had avoided reading, the one with the story of Richard's murder.

Why did they have to include her picture? Kate knew these psychos often became obsessed with the newsmen who wrote about them or the cops who chased them—the last thing she wanted to think about right now. She nudged the paper out of view with the tip of her shoe and pushed herself away from the desk.

In the kitchen she grabbed a Diet Coke out of the fridge, popped the top and took a swig—not the best idea if she wanted to sleep tonight, though she wasn't quite ready for the bedroom. She chose the study, flopped into the soft leather armchair, and turned on the TV.

The news. A floater. The Hudson. A young woman, possibly a teen, no ID, the newscaster said, standing in front of a desolate section of the river, uptown somewhere. Had he said the Bronx, or had she imagined it? Probably nothing to do with their case, but now every murder seemed personal.

Kate called the station, got the desk cop. Yes, the Bronx. No, it didn't fit their unsub's MO—no evisceration, no painting anywhere near the scene. The case would stay in the Bronx. "Have a good night."

A good night? Impossible.

Kate exchanged the television for music, aching chords and cry-addled voices—Julia Fordham, Jennifer Warnes, Joan Armatrading, a mix of her favorite female vocalists—following her down the long hallway into her bedroom where she shed her clothes and picked up Richard's pajamas, holding them first to her face, the soft linen against her cheek, the smell of him growing weaker, just the slightest hint now. It would be gone soon. She knew that.

Richard smiled at her from the photo on her dresser, and somehow she managed to smile back. "Hi, honey," she said, her hand, on automatic, going for the ring at her throat, fingers tightening around the gold band.

A quick trip to the kitchen, pushing aside canned goods in the pantry until she found what she was looking for.

Back in the bedroom, Kate placed the two votive candles on either side of Richard's photo, struck a match, breathed in the smell of sulfur as the flames cast golden highlights over the silver frame and Richard's money clip.

My God, she thought, stepping back, observing herself—*Still the Catholic girl from Queens, as superstitious and devout as every one of your Irish aunties.*

Kate had stopped going to church after her father's death, had transferred the little remaining faith she'd had into her work, first as a cop, then her Ph.D., later with the foundation and the kids. Work had become her temple.

But right now she needed a bit more. Something to give herself over to, a force, a spirit, whatever you wanted to call it, and the candles glowing beside Richard's image tapped into something deep inside her from so long ago, and it soothed her.

She pulled Richard's pajamas up over her bare legs, rolled the bottoms up, sat tentatively on her side of the bed, not quite ready to lie down.

She had made it through the day. She had been strong and tough, and had successfully hidden her grief. But she was home now, alone, and could no longer pretend. She glanced over to what had been Richard's side of the bed, blankets neat, pillow smooth, and listened to the music, to Joan Armatrading's deep poignant alto, and the words—*I need you*—and now, finally, allowed herself to cry.

TEN

He squints at the newspapers scattered on his studio floor beside the beat-up couch. How could they have gotten it so wrong? *A still life with a blue-striped bowl?* No way.

And a man? He doesn't remember a man.

Was he hallucinating? Maybe. Sometimes it all seems like a dream.

He flattens his palms against his aching eyes.

He is certain of the others, how and why they had been selected. But not the man. Maybe the newspapers are trying to trick him.

Sometimes you feel like a nut, sometimes you—

He regards the two paintings made of hair and blood that he has tacked to the wall. There have been other such paintings, all of them thrown away in frustration, and of course the ones he had made from the animals, which he could only keep a day or two before they began to stink.

But right now he is sure there would be a third painting if he had done the man, and there is not.

No, he didn't do it. He would have remembered. He isn't crazy.

Sometimes you feel like a nut, sometimes—

"You said it!"

He closes his eyes and pictures the girl standing under the street lamp tugging at her mini, and thinks, yes, it was real, but what did he learn other than the fact that he was not prepared—and that he will have to stick to the indoors? Sure there was a moment, that beautiful moment. But the idea is to make it last—to see if he is right.

He glances over at the other newspaper that tells of the nameless girl found floating in the river, no clues about her—or him. That part is good.

No, it's grrrrrrreat, grrrrrrreat, grrrrrrreat!

"Not now, Tony! I'm trying to think!" he shouts, then apologizes. "Sorry, Tony." He does not want to offend his friend, who has been with him for such a long time. He relies on Tony, as he does on Brenda and Brandon and Dylan and Donna and sometimes Steve, but never David, who he believes might be a little like him and so he despises him.

From his pocket he slides the small high-intensity magnifying glass he always keeps with him; inky-black words march across the newspaper page like giant ants as he scans the stories. He is surprised that they care about those two women. *Who would care about them?*

Maybe, he thinks, they care because of the man—the attorney, a lawyer, it says. A rich man.

He goes over the *Post* story carefully, then switches to the *New York Times,* and studies the small photo whose caption reads: "Richard and Kate Rothstein." He studies the man and the woman, his magnifier fragmenting their already grainy images into abstract patterns of black dots, and feels a tug of familiarity, then slowly reads the story until he comes to a part that interests him—the part about the dead man's wife, an art historian they call her. Hi-stori-an. *His*-story-n. Aren't they making a mistake? After all, she's a woman. Shouldn't it be *her*-story-n?

See, he isn't stupid.

Sometimes you feel like a—

"Shut up!"

He tries to blot out the noise, slides his magnifier back over the paper.

**Ms. McKinnon-Rothstein is best known as an art world fig-
ure, an expert on contemporary art . . .**

He closes his eyes, imagines the art *her-story-n* looking at his paintings, and smiles.

———

Rectangles of smudged morning light streamed through the windows and painted themselves onto the evidence room's dingy tiled floor, illuminating the faded checkerboard pattern, the cracks and dirt.

"This is Special Agent Marty Grange," Floyd Brown said.

Kate put the guy at no more than five feet eight, solid build, starched collar buttoned around a yellow tie causing his thick neck to redden, sleeves rolled up, hugging Popeye-like arms. He stood ramrod-straight, bulky chest out, as if prepared for a military inspection, and narrowed his small dark eyes in Kate's direction. "Heard about you." He cleared his throat. It sounded like a growl.

"All true." Kate linked her hands together and held them out. "Better cuff me now." She added a smile, which the FBI agent did not return.

Perlmutter coughed to conceal a laugh.

Grange's dark eyes laser-beamed in the detective's direction, and Perlmutter froze.

"Agent Grange is from FBI Manhattan," said Brown. "He's just joined us, and will be working the case, as well as liaising with FBI Washington."

Kate said, "Great," like she almost meant it.

Grange's eyes, two opaque black marbles, rolled toward Kate, though she wasn't exactly sure if he was looking at her.

He was.

Agent Marty Grange focused on a spot just to the left of Kate, though he could take her in perfectly, a technique he had developed and used on his personnel as well as suspects, and it worked well. People, he had learned, were unnerved if they could not tell where you were looking.

In less than a minute he had determined that Kate's clothes were expensive, that she was smart, and that she exuded way too much confidence. Of course he had pulled her FBI dossier and knew her history—every case she had ever worked in Astoria, the fact that she'd been expelled from two Catholic high schools, even the names of her elementary school teachers. He'd also pulled files on her father, uncles, all the ones who were cops, and knew details of Kate's mother's suicide that she did not.

Marty Grange's favorite motto was "Knowledge is power."

Grange glanced at Kate again and decided she had another strike against her—*way too good-looking.*

The evidence room of the Sixth Precinct had been readied for the group. The three paintings, encased in clear plastic, lay faceup on a narrow table in the center of the room for viewing from all sides, a card beside each indicating the specific case numbers. The only other item on the table was the magnifying glass Kate had requested. She tugged a book out of her tote and laid it on the table.

Mitch Freeman burst through the door a bit breathless and disheveled, graying sandy hair falling into his eyes, shirtsleeves rolled up, overstuffed briefcase tucked under his arm. "Am I late?"

"Yes," said Agent Grange.

The FBI shrink turned to Kate. "It's good to see you. I mean—" His smile turned into a frown. "I'm really sorry—"

"Good to see you too," said Kate, stopping him. She turned immediately to the paintings, particularly the painting from Richard's scene, which she was seeing for the first time.

My God. This is it. The painting left beside my dying husband.

No. She absolutely could not think like that. She had to detach. Immediately.

It's a painting. That's all. A painting. A painting. A painting.

She could feel Grange watching her. She cleared her throat. "Well, first off—" She was surprised at the calm in her voice. *Yes, I can do this.* "They're totally different. I mean, the Bronx paintings and uh, this one—" A quick breath. "Different—in many ways, some more obvious than others. First, the two Bronx paintings are unstretched, just pieces of loose canvas. But the—" She faltered a moment. How to refer to the painting from Richard's crime scene? ". . . the *Midtown* painting is on a stretcher." Kate held the painting by its plastic-wrapped edges and turned it over for all to see. "Stretcher bars," she said, indicating the wooden rectangle that supported the canvas. "These are store-bought stretchers. You can see they're uniform and stamped with a size. But the artist has cut the canvas himself, and stapled it on. And he's prepared the canvas himself. Notice that the canvas edges are tannish where the gesso has not completely covered it."

"The *what*?" asked Grange.

"The gesso," said Kate. "It's an acrylic mix of titanium white and water that artists use to prep the canvas for paint. You can't use oil paint directly on unprimed canvas or the oil paint will not only bleed through but eventually rot the canvas. The gesso prevents that."

"So we have an artist who knows something about his craft," said Brown.

"Yes," said Kate. "But it's fairly standard." She inspected the gesso more carefully along the edges where it was not covered by paint. "In the past, artists used lead white as a primer, but it's deadly poisonous and not too many use it anymore. I'm assuming this is gesso, but we should have the lab test it to be sure. If it *is* lead white, that would significantly narrow the field."

Perlmutter made a note. "Are there different brands of gesso?"

"I think the main difference between one gesso and another is the amount of water—the cheaper ones add more. But there may be other additives that differentiate the brands. You should check." She exchanged the Midtown painting for one of the Bronx paintings, the still life, and flipped the loose canvas over.

"No stretcher bars, obviously—just a piece of canvas. And this is commercially made canvas that's been preprimed. The artist bought it exactly as it is, ready to paint on. It's cheap stuff."

"Why would an artist go to the trouble of doing it themselves, using that gesso stuff, if they can just buy it ready-made?" asked Grange.

"Because it's a lot better when you do it yourself. You choose your own canvas. Decide how many coats of gesso. Sand it between coats if you want it really smooth. Most professional artists do their own gessoing, or have a studio assistant do it—if they're successful enough to employ one." Kate swapped the Bronx still life for the street scene. "Same thing here. Unstretched and on ready-made, preprimed canvas."

Grange continued his thought. "So why wouldn't our unsub go to the trouble for these two Bronx paintings, just the other one?"

"Excellent question, Agent Grange." Kate stopped a moment, eyes moving from the Bronx paintings to the one from Richard's scene. "I'd have to say . . . because they have *not* been painted by the same person."

"Are you saying there are two different unsubs?" Grange's stony face got stonier.

"What I'm saying is that we have two different *painters*." Kate paced in front of the three crime scene paintings, using the magnifying glass as a pointer. "Aside from the differences with the stretchers and the type of canvas, there are other glaring differences. One, the paint handling." She indicated the Midtown painting. "There are no visible brush strokes here. The paint is thin and has been put on either with very soft brushes, sables, perhaps, maybe even foam brushes or sponges. Whereas in these"—she gestured toward the two Bronx paintings—"the painter is using stiff bristle brushes. The paint is laid on heavily, the brush strokes obvious." She paused briefly while the men studied the paintings. "Of course the most glaring difference is the color. In the Midtown painting the color is realistic. The bananas are yellow. The apple red." She looked from the Midtown still life to the two Bronx paintings. "But in these two the color is totally unrealistic."

Kate plucked the book she had brought with her off the table, *The Art of Ernst Ludwig Kirchner*. She opened it to one of the several pages she had flagged and held up the image for the men to see.

"Kirchner was the first artist who came to mind when I saw the Bronx paintings. You can see the similarity in the use of color." The picture Kate displayed, *Struggles (The Torments of Love),* was bold and wildly colored—a harsh portrait, half black-and-white, half bright blue and blood-red.

"Why the blue face?" asked Brown.

"Kirchner was part of a group of German expressionist painters who called themselves Die Brücke, which means The Bridge. They exaggerated forms and used unrealistic color to portray their innermost feelings. They stressed working at a fever pitch, accepting ugliness and deformity."

"Mission accomplished," said Brown.

"I'm not here to make you like German expressionist painting," said Kate. "I simply wanted to show you a painter who the Bronx unsub brings to mind in his work. They both paint directly, that is, the paint has been put on fast and hard, and they both use unrealistic color. I also wanted you to see that it's not necessarily unusual for artists to experiment with color."

"Could our unsub have seen this German guy's paintings?" Grange asked.

"Yes. There are several in New York museums. But I'm not necessarily saying our unsub is emulating him. Kirchner's paintings have an unschooled look, but he's really a very sophisticated artist." She glanced at the Bronx paintings. "These have the hot, wild color of Kirchner, but they feel unschooled to me. Plus they have the odd framing element, the way the guy has built up a heavy scribble design around the edges that does not exist in the Midtown painting—instead, that one's realistic, sophisticated, and cool. It just can't be the work of the same painter."

"You're sure about that?" asked Grange.

"It's my opinion. But do they look the same to you, Agent Grange?"

Grange did not like the challenge he thought he detected in McKinnon's tone, but he let it go—for now.

Kate leaned closer to the two Bronx paintings and the men followed her, all five heads only millimeters apart. "Notice the bits of charcoal around the forms. You can see them around the clouds in one, the fruit in the other? I think the artist sketches the objects with charcoal first, then paints them in." She shifted to the Midtown painting and their heads followed her. "But there's no charcoal in this painting. No presketching. It looks rather tossed off, like the artist didn't spend a whole lot of time with it, but it's assured. I'd say this painter knows what he's doing." Kate shifted back to the Bronx paintings once again, the heads tagging along. "Whereas these two are . . . raw. I'd have to say these two Bronx paintings are the work of an amateur, an unschooled *outsider,* and the other is painted by a pro."

"Jesus," said Brown. "Are we looking at a copycat?"

Mitch Freeman peered at the paintings over his reading glasses. "Suppose the killer wanted to throw us off, so he painted one painting better than the others, more *assuredly,* as you say?"

"I don't think so," said Kate. "Every painter has his or her own touch. It's like handwriting. Go into a painting class sometime. You'll see twenty students all working from the same still life or model, and every painting, though it's the same subject matter, will look different. The composition will be different, the brush strokes, and certainly the color. No two people see color in the same way. Color is subjective—it's in the eye of the beholder."

"How so?" asked Grange.

"Your shirt, Agent Grange, looks blue because it's absorbing all other colors of light and reflecting *only* the blue back to us. Color is the result of light waves. When you say, 'My shirt is blue,' what you're actually saying is that because of the molecular structure of your shirt's surface, it's absorbing all light rays except the blue ones." Six months ago Kate hardly knew any of this, but her PBS show on color had entailed hours spent with scientists and color theorists, who had given her a crash course in color education. "Your shirt has no color itself. Light is generating the color."

"Do you mean I'm looking at the pink clouds in that painting," said Perlmutter, "but they're not really pink?"

"They're pink because we *perceive* them as pink. But it's all happening in your *brain*. You see, color occurs when light strikes the nerve cells at the back of your eye called rods and cones. The cones are responsible for color. Rods for black and white. The rods and cones respond to the light, which send a message to the optic nerve in our brains, which in turn tells us what color we're looking at."

"So, the guy who did the Bronx paintings, he's screwing around with color," said Perlmutter. "But why?"

"That I can't tell you," said Kate, though something tugged at the back of her mind. "Could be he's experimenting. As I said, he isn't the first painter to play with color for any number of reasons. Emotional resonance? Symbolism?"

"You think the color is symbolic?" asked Brown. "A red sky and pink clouds might mean something?"

"Like Gauguin?" asked Perlmutter, with a good-student smile.

"Could be," said Kate. "Though I'm not sure what. Gauguin used pure, simple color because he was depicting a pure and simple culture— the people he found in Tahiti and Martinique. But in these paintings I don't know what that symbolism would be." She moved back to the

Midtown painting, the still life with the blue-striped bowl, and looked closely again. "I really think this has been painted with foam-tipped brushes, or small pieces of sponge. And notice the white stripes in the bowl are not painted at all, but simply the white canvas." Kate tapped her chin.

"What is it?" asked Brown.

"There's something familiar in the way this is painted, but . . . I don't know." She sighed, and turned back to the Bronx paintings. "There's something else. See here?" She passed the magnifier to Grange. "It's a *Y,* I think. And there—" She directed his hand. "It could be part of an *R,* maybe."

Grange flinched a bit, moved his hand quickly away from hers. "Meaning?"

She took back the magnifying glass and ran it over the Bronx paintings one more time. "Words? Under the paint. We have to get them x-rayed." She moved the glass over the gray edges. "This scribbled border is intriguing. I'm not sure, but this could be words too, written over and over so that they become unintelligible." She squinted. "We have to get enlargements of these areas." She went back to the blue-striped bowl. "I don't see any hint of words here at all, but we should x-ray all three paintings."

"Agreed," said Grange. "I'll ship them to Quantico ASAP."

Kate laid her hand on Grange's arm. "I'd like to have them around, and—well, I hate to say it, but what if we get another? It would be good to have these here for comparison."

Grange stared at Kate's hand, but did not move. "You can x-ray them here, can't you, Brown?"

"Lab's right downstairs. And x-raying is no big deal. We do it all the time. Hernandez, who runs our lab, can get right on it. She already ran prints and fibers on the paintings."

"Anything?" Grange asked.

"No prints, no hairs or fibers other than the vics' in each case. Our nasty unsub—or *unsubs*—wore gloves."

"Okay," said Grange. "We keep the paintings here for a while. But I want all your lab tests and the X-rays copied and sent to Quantico for double-checking."

"No problem," said Brown.

Grange stood, forcing Kate's hand to slide off his arm, which was his intent. Her touch had made it almost impossible for him to concentrate. He paced back and forth in front of the three paintings. "If we're looking at a copycat, two unsubs, two *unknown subjects,* perhaps we'd better divide the investigation." He glanced at Kate, wanted to say: *Okay, you've done your part, you can go home now.* But he'd gotten the word from Tapell. And the word was: *McKinnon stays.* And she would, but only as long as the case was being shared by the Bureau and the NYPD.

Brown didn't much like Grange coming into his territory and taking over, but he knew he had to play the game. "Might be easier, and less costly, if we continue to handle the cases together—until we prove they're different. If that's okay with you."

Grange looked past the edge of Brown's face and said, "Got a point there, Brown," then proceeded to outline how he thought they should proceed with the cases. Kate noticed how Brown pretended to listen, nodding, his brow knit in studied concentration, but she knew Brown would run his elite homicide squad exactly as he wanted while he let Grange think he was playing ball.

After the men had gone, Kate sat by herself for a moment. She felt odd, almost good.

But how could she possibly feel good?

Because she had done it, had functioned, could look at that painting— a clear reminder of her husband's death—and analyze it without collapsing into a heap.

Now she looked again at all three paintings. No way they were the work of the same artist. She was certain of it.

She glanced at the banal Midtown painting—fruit in a blue-striped bowl— that would be forever linked to her husband's death.

Kate did not see herself as a vengeful person, but had to admit that right now it was the reason she got up in the morning, her reason for living—to find the man who had murdered her husband, and make him pay.

One more time she ran the magnifying glass over the surface of the

Midtown still life. What was it about those areas of white canvas and the stained, rather than brushed-on paint, that seemed so familiar?

Y
ou want me to summarize while you look them over?" Hernandez leaned against Floyd Brown's desk, her ample figure straining against the snug lab coat. She was maybe thirty-five, dark brown hair pulled back without much thought, since it was most often hidden under one of those papery plastic bonnets she wore to keep it from contaminating evidence in the crime lab she'd been running for the past four years.

Brown scanned the postmortem files and nodded.

"Okay." She cracked the gum she was chewing. "The first two vics, out of the Bronx, pretty much identical. Stab wounds are fast and deep. Heart and lungs pierced. They wouldn't have lived long. At least three different knives used. If you look at the last page, you'll see I'm suggesting a short hunting knife, a thin stiletto, and definitely another, heavier serrated number for cutting through ribs. Very efficient work. Your unsub came prepared."

"Overkill, for sure."

"No question. He opened them up as if he was searching for something." She cracked her gum and Brown gave her a look, which she ignored. "But there are no signs of torture. No bite marks. No obvious trophies taken. Nipples, labia, all there." She paused, cracked her gum a few times, unconsciously. "I'd say he played around with them once they were opened up, but the organs are all intact. He didn't take anything home for supper."

Brown blew air out of his mouth. "What about Rothstein?"

"If you look at the suggested weapons on page three . . ." She waited a moment, chewing loudly while Brown found it. "One weapon only—switchblade, I'm guessing. The vic was slit twice—horizontally and vertically, up from the pubis to just under the sternum, where the bone stopped the blade, then yanked out—" She mimed the moves with jerking arm and hand movements. ". . . then sliced across the midsection like a big plus sign. Fairly clean wounds, deep enough to cut through skin and muscle. But the heart and lungs were never penetrated." She hesitated a moment. "Way it looks to me is his lower intestines fell out as he was dragged through the alley."

"Jesus Christ." Brown stared at the photos clipped to the file, Richard Rothstein's naked body broken into abstract details of bruised, wounded flesh.

"From the body temps I got from the ME, who took them at the scene, plus the fact that rigor was just setting in"—Hernandez was chewing her gum with a ferocious intensity—"I'd have to say that the vic was alive, possibly for a while, in that alley."

"Listen to me, Hernandez." Brown took hold of her wrist. "Under no circumstances is McKinnon to see or hear about this. You got that?"

"Wouldn't be my job to tell her. That's up to you." Hernandez wriggled her hand out of his grip. "Tapell's got copies. But it's up to *you* who gets any others." She punctuated the statement with a loud gum pop.

"Right," he said softly. The idea that McKinnon's husband lay dying, slowly, in that goddamn alleyway made Brown feel sick. He'd gotten to know Richard a bit during the Death Artist case, and afterward, when Kate had invited Brown and his wife, Vonette, out to dinner and to their home a few times, and he had liked the brash and charming Brooklyn-born lawyer.

"If you look at page two, you'll see that both Bronx vics had tape across their mouths, hands, and feet. We managed to pull a few hairs and fibers from the inside of the tape. Most of the fibers were from each vic's apartment. Same is true of the hairs—came from the victims. But we also got a couple fibers and hairs that don't match either vic. So most likely they belong to your unsub. We put the fibers through spectrometry and gas chromatography so they can be matched to clothing and anything you might find in a crib. Evidence ran the hair samples through their system, but so far, no match. But there too we can test for a match once you bring someone in. I attached the evidence results and reports at the back."

"Nice work," said Brown. Now all they had to do was find a suspect. No matter how good the forensics, if there was no suspect to match to the findings, it didn't mean squat. "Any tape used on Rothstein?"

"No. He was knocked out, probably hit with a gun barrel, from the size and shape of the bruise on the back of his head, which would have rendered him unconscious. For a while. Then he was cut. I didn't find any defensive wounds on his hands, so he was probably out when he was sliced."

"Small blessing," said Brown. He thought a minute. "But why cut him if you've got a gun?"

"Your guess," said Hernandez.

"Any prints?"

"No way to dust in that alleyway. Place was a sty. Crime Scene did his office, but nothing other than the vic's and his staff's prints came up. Your unsub wore gloves."

Brown closed the file on Richard Rothstein. He'd heard enough for the moment. "What about the Bronx? Any prints there?"

"Lots of half-prints and smudges, both scenes. And the ninhydrin produced a couple of gloved prints on that Gauguin picture that McKinnon brought in, which must be your unsub, as I doubt the vic wore gloves around the house."

"A gloved print doesn't do us much good," said Brown.

"No, but there could be some sweat on the print, like if he touched his face, maybe. Not a hundred percent sure, but it's being tested for DNA. Could be something there—if we're lucky."

"How long for the DNA?" Brown asked.

"A few days."

"Anything else?"

"There were scuffs and tears on the front and tops of Rothstein's shoes, which means he was dragged facedown—which would also account for the intestinal leakage in the alleyway."

"Can someone actually live with half their guts spilled out?" Brown had to ask.

"Until the blood loss is too great. Though the trauma would most likely have put him in shock and comatized him."

"Thank God," said Brown. This much he might pass on to McKinnon if he could ever figure out a way to say it.

"Yeah," said Hernandez, thinking that sometimes, particularly when she was out of her lab, away from the microscopes and spectrographs and petri dishes, and dealing with the living, she really hated her job. "I gotta get back," she said.

"Right. Thanks."

Brown linked his fingers behind his head and sat back in his chair. This much was clear: No question they were looking at two different MOs.

The Bronx victims were stabbed and gutted; Rothstein, knocked out first with a gun, then stabbed. Someone was obviously capitalizing on the Bronx murders, playing copycat, the painting added to seal the deal. McKinnon had been right about the paintings being different. Though whoever had murdered Richard Rothstein did not know what the Bronx paintings looked like, simply that an oil painting—a still life and a cityscape, thanks to the ever-hungry press—had been found at the crime scenes.

Brown made a few notes, summarizing the two cases and their differences while leaving out the part about Rothstein's being alive in that alleyway. He would pass his summary on to the detectives, then speak with the chief of operations and with Tapell and ask to have more detectives assigned. It was the last thing anyone wanted to hear with the mayor cutting funds daily and the entire NYPD overworked, exhausted, and pissed off.

Brown rubbed both temples with his fingers, a headache setting in. If McKinnon were there, he'd be asking for a couple of Excedrin.

He knew what the operations chief and Tapell were going to say—that Homicide would have to double up on cases, stay on top of everything, that the cases were already costing the NYPD and the city more than they could afford in manpower, and that it was his job to get results— no matter how short of staff.

Another thing he knew: That there was no way McKinnon was going to stay away from her husband's case. The woman was like a dog with a bone. And she'd been right about Brown too—if anyone ever did anything to his wife or daughter, he *would* rip their heart out.

ELEVEN

He peers across the dimly lit room to the pictures he has cut from his books, some bought, others stolen, thumbtacked to the wall. His little shrine of greats: a horrific Francis Bacon, the central form, a man, surrounded by a flayed body, muscle, bone, and viscera stretched and exposed; de Kooning's *Woman I,* all breasts and teeth and wild brush strokes, a document of what the artist must have done, he believes, to a woman, which both chills and excites him; three Soutines: *Carcass of Beef, Flayed Beef,* and *Side of Beef and Calf's Head,* wild bloodbaths that he presumes were the painter's fantasies. He has no idea that Soutine based the series on Rembrandt's classical *The Slaughtered Ox* of 1655, hanging in the Louvre, in Paris.

He tries to remember them from before, when things were different, when he was different, before the accident, when he'd first seen all of these works in an exhibition called Expressionist Painting, at the museum on Fifth Avenue. What interested him then was the way all of the artists had approximated flesh with pigment. All day he had looked and lingered, wanting so badly to touch the thickly painted surfaces, or lick them, though he didn't dare—he could feel the guard's eyes on his back. But then, on his way out, when he spotted the exhibition catalog with its cover picture of Soutine's *Carcass of Beef,* he had to have it, and slid it under his shirt and walked as naturally as possible out the front doors and down the enormous staircase, the whole time holding his breath while that raw Soutine image burned against his flesh, and into his heart.

Now he tries to recall the exact coloration of the Soutine painting. Was it mostly scarlet and maroon, with touches of melon and cerise? He considers bringing the reproduction with him next time, to check it out, but it's too precious to carry around, he couldn't risk that.

He glances back at the wall, toward the corner, where the light is bad, at one more picture that he both loves and detests, another Francis Bacon, *Two Figures,* from 1953, a painting in black and white and gray, which remains unchanged for him, which is why he loves it, but which evokes the most horrific day of his life and brings the accident back all too vividly. He keeps the reproduction on his wall, somewhat apart from the others, in the corner, where the light is dim, and it is almost lost to the shadows.

The painting—so much like his memory, it is uncanny—depicts two gray figures on a white bed against a black wall in a violent, sexual frenzy. Of course he has no idea that Bacon borrowed the image from a black-and-white photograph made in 1887 by Eadward Muybridge, of two men wrestling nude. Perhaps if he knew this fact he would be even more drawn to the painting; might even think the artist clairvoyant for transforming the two men into what looks, to him, like an event from his life.

He looks away from the reproductions, rubs his eyes, and sets the magnifying glass back over that *New York Times* article, which mentions the wife, Kate, and her TV show, and though it's been a long time—he stopped watching after the accident—he has to admit that aside from his crayons, the television was his best buddy, always on when she was there and even when she was not.

He thinks it might be nice to have a TV again to keep him company, plus he could watch her, Katherine McKinnon, Kate, the art *her-story-n,* and hear what she has to say. Yes, a television would be a really good idea, and he still has most of the money he took off the women, and more that he's earned and saved over the years.

He steadies the magnifier above the newspaper over Kate's face. He feels like he knows her, or should, and thinks he will make it his business to do just that. "What do you think, Tony?"

She's grrrrrrrrreat!

"You bet," he says, and reads a bit more. It says the man, Richard Rothstein, lived on Central Park West, in one of the best buildings, the San Remo.

If the man lived there, then obviously the art *her-story-n* lives there too. Maybe he should visit her?

He stares back at the art *her-story-n*. In the photo she appears to have really nice hair. He shuts his eyes, tries to remember, then simply assigns it a color: *Tumbleweed? Mahogany? Sepia?* He decides on a mix of tumbleweed and copper, and spends a while trying to imagine it, what it would feel like, how the tumbleweed and copper strands would shimmer as they slid through his fingers, and he is instantly hard, and holding that thought in his mind works his hand into his pants and struggles to see the colors in his mind's eye, as he comes.

Quieter now, he retrieves a pencil and tiny sharpener and hones the lead to a fine point, then starts to create the frame of his last finished painting, something he always does—his *signature*.

For almost two hours he works on only one edge of the painting, writing and writing and writing, over and over and over, until he has created a band of dense graphite.

This, for him, is the easy part, the gravy, no concentration necessary, no test, no eyestrain, merely a repetitive act that calms and soothes him, that brings to each painting a private part of him, and his world; the frames, as it were, make him feel safe, bordering each of his paintings, holding them in, his friends embracing his images.

When he finally finishes the edge he puts the painting aside and studies the two other canvases he's got on the wall, loosely tacked. One is not much more than a charcoal sketch of the still life of fruit he's set up on a stand to work from, simple outlines of objects that he has drawn onto unstretched white canvas. Inside the apple shape, he's written the word red; inside the pear shape, green. Just to be sure. The other canvas, of a city street, is a bit more advanced, parts of the charcoal shapes of apartment buildings with windows and garbage cans and lampposts already filled in with paint. In the half of the garbage can that is unpainted one can make out where he had written the word *silver,* though the painted half is a shocking pinkish red.

It's grrrrrrrrrrrrrrrrrreat!

"Thanks, Tony."

There is nothing like a friend, he thinks, an old friend.

He shuffles to his paint table, magnifier in hand, runs it over the numerous tubes of paint with their labels peeled off. The same is true of the pastels. No labels. Only the crayons still wear their thin paper skins.

It's a test, you see. Always a test.

Testing testing testing . . .

He scans the crayons beside the naked paint tubes, selects the blue crayon he is after, sets the magnifying glass aside, and brings the crayon very close to his face and squints before placing it in the center of the glass palette. Then he squirts out small samples of oil paint from various tubes until the blue crayon is surrounded with dozens of possibilities— small blobs of infinite color and variety.

Testing testing testing . . .

Which one is it?

He dips the edge of a paintbrush into one of the blobs, brings it close to his eyes for inspection, then lowers it to his mouth, tip of his tongue flicking paint-soaked bristles ever so lightly, taste buds exploding like a small nuclear reactor as he loops his tongue over lips and inside his mouth—oily linseed, acidic resins, caustic turpentine, and chemical compound pigment mixing with his saliva.

Mmmm . . . blue. He believes he can actually taste the blue sky that he remembers only vaguely, or the ocean.

He stares at the name "cerulean" on the crayon's wrapper, moving the crayon beside this blob of oil, then that one, the one he has tasted and decides, yes, absolutely, that is the one—the right color blue—chooses a clean brush, dips it into the blob of pigment and starts painting in the sky part of the city scene where the word *cerulean* has been written.

Testing testing testing . . .

He seems quite pleased with his choice, a smile breaking across his face. He loves to work, to paint, alone in this small building, really not much more than one room with a bathroom, attached to Pablo's Towing Station on a remote street in Long Island City. He pays no rent; Pablo is happy to have him around on off-hours, likes the idea that someone is here with a light on to scare away potential burglars.

While he works he wonders again about that dead man. Are the newspapers fucking with him? And he has a thought: *Why not fuck with them?*

He lets the idea bounce around in his brain, and though it's not so easy to concentrate with all the bits of songs and ads and jingles and announcers' voices—*Today it will be mostly sunny with a high of seventy*—*Girls Just Wanna Have Fu-un*—*Coke is it!*—he comes up with a plan. He doesn't have to bring one of his own paintings. It's the experience—the learning and memorizing—that he is after, right? Of course.

He considers the plan, how to go about it—and how it will throw them off. Naturally, he does not want to be caught. He needs to do what he does. Anyone can see that.

He thinks and plans while he paints, and finally the fully realized concept comes to him like the sun breaking through periwinkle clouds, bright yellow beams sparking in his brain—he will bring someone else's painting! How smart is that?

"Brilliant," he says in a high falsetto voice.

"Thanks, Donna," he answers in his own voice.

Man, is he ever lucky to have friends like Donna and Tony to give him confidence.

He continues to paint in the area of sky where he has previously written the word *cerulean* with a furious back-and-forth stroke, bristles flaking off the brush, fueled by his idea until the entire sky is bright bright green, then stands back, snatches the cerulean crayon off the table and holds it against the painted sky, and squints so hard the tiny muscles around his eyes begin to ache.

He believes he got it right this time, though there is still a slightly nagging feeling that he could be wrong.

It's Crrrrrrraaaaaaaazzzzy Eddie—

The announcer's voice is screaming in his head, but he has learned how to think over and under the jingles, ads, songs, and voices, and continues to concentrate on his plan. He has to figure out how and where to buy a painting.

And then, if he has enough money, he is definitely going to buy himself a brand-new television. To watch her.

TWELVE

Back in her home office, Kate tacked up the photographs of the three paintings from the crime scenes to the corkboard wall just above her desk. There was no question in her mind that they had not been painted by the same person—the two Bronx pictures with their bizarre color were nothing like the painting left at Richard's crime scene.

Richard's crime scene.

The words, so absurd no matter how many times she heard them or said them. Kate felt tears gathering behind her lids and quickly reached for the pack of Marlboros she had finally bought. She wasn't sure if it was the act of smoking or the hit of nicotine that did the trick, but the deadly habit seemed to steady her.

Now she stared at the crime scene paintings through a gauzy veil of smoke.

What was it about that still life with the blue-striped bowl that continued to nag at her? Something to do with the way it had been painted and those naked patches of white canvas. Where had she seen white canvas used like that before?

Down the hall, in her library, Kate scanned the shelves crammed with hundreds of art books, hoping something would jog her memory. The two lowest shelves were filled with books devoted entirely to the research she'd done for her PBS series on color. Was there something in there that might help?

She skimmed the Albers book, and found nothing. Kandinsky. Nothing. Ellsworth Kelly, Gerhard Richter, Boyd Werther. Nothing. Nothing. Nothing. Then the books on color theory. Again, nothing. Her frustration mounting, Kate scooped up an armful of exhibition catalogs, some of them going back over forty years, spread them out on the floor, and began to go through them slowly. It was almost an hour before she came across the one called *Coloration,* from 1973, and the two plates of paintings by Leonardo Alberto Martini—lyrical abstractions made up of wavy color bands with intermittent stripes of white.

If her memory had not completely failed her, those stripes were not white paint, but unpainted canvas, a trademark of a once admired painter whom she had studied, albeit briefly, in graduate school—one of those artists who had had his fifteen minutes of fame and then had precipitously fallen through the art world cracks.

Kate flipped to the front of the catalog, skimmed the essay, her eyes flitting over words and sentences until she found what she was looking for, the curator's description of the paintings:

Martini's use of bare canvas instead of white paint allows light to filter into his paintings almost magically. By laying in the paint with his foam-tipped brushes or pieces of neatly cut sponges so that the paint soaks into the canvas, the artist eschews brush stroke or mark, and allows the color to live, breathe, and speak for itself.

Kate's body was tingling. This was it, the painting technique she had been trying so hard to remember—a description that fit the still life with the blue-striped bowl perfectly.

But if she was right, what was a painting by Leonardo Alberto Martini doing at Richard's crime scene?

Kate's hands were shaking as she checked the statistics on the artists in the back of the catalog. Martini's birth date put his age at just past sixty. Was he still painting? Exhibiting? Living in New York? Even living at all? Kate hadn't seen a show, or read about his work in years. Of course she knew that many artists disappeared from the art world's radar screen, though most continued to paint, eking out a living with carpentry jobs or adjunct teaching, anything that would pay their expenses and support their art habit. Real artists needed to create their work whether or not the art world paid attention, and Kate had always regarded Martini as a real artist—even if he had only briefly been a successful one.

Back in her office, fingers trembling a bit on the computer keys, Kate checked the Art Index, a site that kept records of exhibitions and artists. There was no record of Martini dying, or any record of an exhibition in the past twenty years—no address, no telephone number, no gallery representation.

Why would a has-been artist want to murder Richard?

It made no sense.

Kate hurried down the penthouse hallway into the kitchen, pulled open drawers until she found the Manhattan telephone directory, practically tearing several of its thin pages, impatient to get to the name Martini. There were over two dozen, but no Leonardo or Leo, four with the initial L, three of them on the Upper East Side (an unlikely address for a starving artist), and one on East Tenth. Kate called them all, eliminating each in turn, saving Tenth Street for last.

But when she punched the number into her cellular and an answering machine with one of those generic messages engaged, she immediately hung up. If it was Leonardo, and he was involved in the murder, what could she say that would not scare him off?

Besides, a bit more confidence that the still life with the blue-striped bowl had been painted by the artist would help her make a case for a search warrant—and she knew just the man to help her.

Leonardo Martini." Merton Sharfstein held the photo of the still life with the blue-striped bowl below his beaklike nose and squinted over his half-glasses. "There's a name I haven't heard in some time."

"But you've sold his work, haven't you, Mert?"

"In the seventies, a few paintings, yes." He continued to scrutinize the photo.

Mert Sharfstein had been a mentor to Kate, educating her on the ins and outs of the art world when she'd first started frequenting his posh Madison Avenue gallery as an art history student pursuing her Ph.D. more than a decade ago, and there were few people in the art world Kate respected more. Sharfstein had studied art history with all the greats, and now ran one of the city's most admired and successful galleries, where he showed an eclectic mix of late-nineteenth-century and post-war modern masters, high-end objets d'art (Ming dynasty vases, sixteenth-century tapestries), as well as blue-chip contemporary art. His eye for quality and authenticity was esteemed not only in art circles, but at Interpol as well, which had, on more than one occasion, employed him on cases of international art theft and fraud.

"So what do you think?" Kate's eyes darted from the painting to the art dealer, back and forth.

"It's difficult to be absolutely certain in a photograph, but it appears to be sponged-on pigment and bare canvas used as white." Mert ran his magnifying glass over the picture. "It certainly has the hallmarks of Martini's painting style—though the subject matter is entirely different." The little man peered over his magnifier at Kate. "What's this about?"

"If I told you, I'm afraid I'd have to kill you."

"Very funny." Mert's eyebrows raised. "Don't tell me you're doing police work again, Kate. I mean, after the last time, I wouldn't think—"

"Mert, darling. Please. Don't think." Kate pecked him on the cheek, and laid the photos of the two Bronx paintings onto his Biedermeier desk. "What about these?"

"*Outsider art?* Sorry, my dear, but I have no patience for this sort of stuff, especially now that it's being taken so seriously, competing with real art at Christie's and Sotheby's." He sighed. "Can you imagine paying hundreds of thousands of dollars for a sculpture made out of beer-bottle caps by some toothless backwoods hooligan when you could buy any number of exquisite drawings by a modern master for the same amount of money? Chills me to the bone." He mimed a shiver. "These aren't *yours,* are they?"

"No," said Kate. "They belong to a . . . friend."

"Well, I hope so." Mert peered over his half-glasses. "I didn't think you and Richard bought any of that tripe." He stopped, a somber look coloring his features. "Richard had the most exquisite taste in art."

"Yes," said Kate, feeling an emotional rush that she could not afford. She quickly returned to the subject. "Is there anyone you would recommend I show them to?"

"The Department of Sanitation, perhaps?"

"Seriously."

"Well, you could try one of the *merchants* who deal in this stuff." He plucked the glasses off his beak and peered at the ceiling. "There's that little *shop* that's recently relocated to Chelsea, the Gallery of Outsider Art, though, if you ask me, it's not nearly outside enough—perhaps New Jersey would be best—and naturally I have never, nor will I ever, step foot inside it."

Kate angled the Mercedes up the ramp. It was Richard's pride and joy, though she had grown to love it, spoiled by its elegance and comfort, ease of steering, subtle leather—a talisman, bringing back her husband all too vividly. She handed the keys to the attendant, hurried down the ramp and onto the street.

Tenth Avenue and Twenty-first Street. Heart of the Chelsea art scene—an area Kate knew well.

Five years ago it was car dealers, enormous warehouses, and the occasional strip joint, the mostly deserted streets dotted with hookers of all ages and indiscriminate gender: young girls and boys, African American transsexuals in wigs and hot pants that sported telltale bulges of surgeries yet to come—a veritable potpourri for the sexual adventurer; all of that now history.

The art galleries cometh.

Rough concrete floors. Sky-high ceilings. Hudson River views to die for. Fancy boutiques and restaurants. Slums converted to condos. Dog walkers. Tourists. Culture-vultures. Art lovers.

Kate glanced up at the low clouds that stubbornly refused to lift, then across the wide avenue at the black-and-silver New York icon, the Empire Diner, and felt a wrenching pang. How many times had she and Richard collapsed into one of the booths, exhausted from an afternoon of intense gallery hopping? No way she could possibly go there now, sit alone, sip coffee, pretend Richard were with her.

She walked another block, crossed Twenty-third Street, glanced up at the large corner wraparound windows of Kempner Fine Arts, where she had purchased the Warhol and Diebenkorn prints for Richard's office; then just past it, at the Red Cat Restaurant, where Jimmy, the colorful, always attentive owner, would bring them on-the-house martinis, Kate's vodka, Richard's gin. Kate looked away, peered across Tenth Avenue at Bottino, yet another of the watering holes she and Richard had haunted, mainly the bar, when they were in the mood to meet and greet the art world denizens who seemed to live in the restaurant's front room. Damn it, everywhere she looked, ghosts beckoned, igniting memories, shared conversations, foods they had eaten, wines they had sampled—all of them tearing at her heart.

Tears were threatening. Another minute and she would be blubbering in the street. Kate quickened her step, practically running until she saw it, Herbert Bloom's Gallery of Outsider Art.

Bloom's gallery was the direct opposite of the spacious, minimal white cubes of the area's contemporary galleries. A tiny space crowded with all sorts of primitive-looking paintings and drawings, double and triple hung, covering most of the walls, with more oddly handcrafted objects and knickknacks perched on sculpture stands and windowsills, crowding a desktop, others stacked along the baseboard.

A short man with huge glasses that dwarfed his face was engaged in a lively discussion with one of those well-groomed New York women of a certain age, the two of them bent over what looked like a small house either whittled or made entirely of finely put together pieces of jagged wood.

"You won't find a better example of tramp art anywhere in the world," Bloom said, making a grand sweeping gesture above the small piece, as if bestowing a benediction.

"Yes, it's quite exquisite." The woman lightly tapped the sides of her meticulously lacquered hair, which did not move. "Let me think about it."

"Well, don't think too long," he said, removing the huge red-framed glasses that would give Elton John a pang of envy. He offered the prospective patron a sober look. "The market for outsider art is heating up as we speak."

"Yes, I know. It's just that my husband, well . . . I'll let you know," she said, and turned out of the gallery.

The dealer's face fell. Husbands. Always a problem. But he perked up a bit when he spied Kate perusing his wares. "See anything you like?"

"Lots," said Kate. "But I wonder, could you tell me something about these?" She laid the photos of the Bronx paintings onto the dealer's crowded desk.

"Oh, well—" His face fell. "*I* never sold them."

"I know that. I simply wanted your expert opinion."

He smiled at that. "Are they yours?"

"Um, yes. I purchased them at the Puck Building's Outsider Art Fair a couple of seasons ago. I'd love to contact the artist, possibly buy another, but I'm such a ninny, I can't remember who sold them to me. It's embarrassing."

"Not at all." Bloom leaned toward the pictures, a bit more interested. "I'm afraid I don't recognize the artist. Who did you say these were by?"

"That's the other problem. They're unsigned and I don't know what I've done with the provenance."

"*Provenance?* That's hardly a word we use in the outsider market." He peered at Kate. "Wait a minute . . . You're that woman on Public TV, aren't you?"

"Guilty as charged."

"I knew you looked familiar. I thought you were heavily into high art, modernism?"

"I am, but I like outsider art too. In fact, I'm hoping to build a first-rate collection."

Bloom licked his lips. "I can certainly help you there. But . . ." He eyeballed the Bronx pictures through his thick specs. "I'm afraid these are not ringing any bells. And you know, a woman of your taste should be collecting blue-chip outsiders like Henry Darger and Martin Ramirez."

"Eventually," said Kate. "But can you tell me a bit more about these first?" She tapped the pictures. "Would you agree they're the work of a genuine *outsider*?"

"Looks it. But who can be sure? Nowadays there's a never-ending debate about what *outsider* even means. Is it the work of some urban eccentric or a rural recluse—or just someone with a serious mental problem who likes to paint? That's what the serious collectors are into these days— the truly *deranged* geniuses." He corkscrewed his finger beside his temple. "Now, your artist here, well, the color is certainly bizarre, and there is a weird quality to the borders—what is it? Some sort of code? His inner ramblings?"

Kate peered along with him. "Actually, I don't know." But it reminded her to find out.

"Too bad it's not obsessive doodles of naked little girls—or boys. Not that work has to be perverse to be outsider art, but it helps. Everyone is striving for that unschooled look now that outsider is such a desirable label. Do you believe there are students with art degrees from Yale making paintings with a brush between their toes in an attempt to look *primitive*?" He made quotation-mark signs with his fingers. "Absurd. The true outsider artist lives largely by his or her own rules, knows nothing about the art world or the system." Bloom's tone turned serious. "These are culturally isolated individuals, living on the fringe of society—and often quite disturbed." His words resonated.

Living by their own rules . . . culturally isolated . . . on the fringe of society . . . disturbed.

"I've just taken on the work of a young woman, well, not exactly," said Bloom. "She's a hermaphrodite who chooses to live as female but refuses to have the operation to remove her male genitalia. She told me she has grown too fond of it, likes to occasionally bend it into her vagina and poke it around in there." His eyebrows made arcing circles above his glasses. "She lives in a tiny little house in the middle of rural Kentucky that her granddaddy left her and makes the most extraordinary drawings with a ballpoint pen of—well, let me show you." Bloom slid open a drawer of a metal flat file. "Here, have a look."

From the distance of a few feet Kate thought she was looking at nothing more than drawings of circles and lines, tightly packed abstract doodles that obsessively covered the entire piece of paper—not totally unlike the borders in the Bronx paintings.

"Look closely," Bloom urged.

In close-up, the circles and lines turned out to be a mass of intertwined penises and vaginas. "Oh," said Kate.

"Oh, indeed," said Bloom. "She—or *he*—has produced one of these drawings every week for the past ten years. Each one in blue ballpoint pen. They take a full week, ten hours of concentrated work each day—which I know to be true, as I spent a most unsettling week watching her draw one. To put it in your modernist terminology—the work is surreal, but not surrealist in the art historical sense." He removed his Elton specs and looked squarely at Kate. "The artist has no knowledge of surrealism. In fact, no knowledge of art, period. She rarely leaves her little Kentucky cottage."

No knowledge of art. The idea resonated. A self-trained artist. Obsessed.

"How does she feed herself?" Kate honestly wanted to know.

"A neighbor shops for her once a week, though I never saw her eat anything but the occasional Slim Jim. She weighs, oh, I would guess . . . no more than a hundred pounds, is almost six feet tall with long shiny red hair and a wonderfully silky mustache." Bloom paused. "I'm sending a photographer to Kentucky. I want a huge portrait of her for my show, which opens next month. I couldn't convince her to come to New York, though I tried. I think she'd be the new *it* girl—or boy." He grinned. "But seriously, the imagery in these drawings is obviously so very close to her, or his, heart. It's all about her—his *predicament*." He glanced back at the Bronx pictures. "Now, if you could furnish me with some terrifically bizarre backstory for your odd-color painter, you know . . . he or she has been institutionalized for the past twenty years and makes these paintings while communing with the spirit of a dead dog . . ." He laughed. "Well, I exaggerate, but you get my drift. It would help give them *meaning,* which might interest a serious collector so that I could sell them for you and then we could get started on putting together your outsider collection."

Kate peered closely at the borders of the Bronx pictures again, but the doodles did not suddenly become penises or vaginas, or anything, for that matter. "Thank you," she said. "You've been very helpful. And I'll be back." She gathered the Bronx pictures before Bloom could convince her to write out a check for one of the hermaphrodite's drawings, though she considered it. They were definitely haunting.

Those low clouds were still hovering as Kate made her way back to the station, Bloom's words echoing in her head: *Living by their own rules. Culturally isolated. On the fringe of society. Disturbed.*

The art dealer could have been describing a sociopath.

The hermaphrodite made art of male and female genitalia—subject matter, as Bloom had said, *close to her heart.*

So why did the *Bronx painter*—as Kate was starting to call him—use wild, inaccurate color? What *meaning* did the paintings hold for him?

Kate stared past the traffic and passersby, lost in thought. She believed that every artist was searching for something, often trying to understand the world more clearly through their artwork. So what was it the Bronx painter was trying to understand?

Certainly, he wanted the public to see what he did. Why else bring a painting to a murder scene and leave it behind? But was it left as some sort of gift, an offering to the dead—or did he leave the paintings behind because they had served their purpose, which was . . . *what?*

He has been standing outside, across the street from the familiar old stone building on West Fifty-seventh Street, a place he knows well. He aches to go inside, to see all the people at their easels, but knows better. Later, someone might remember him. And so he watches them come and go: students and teachers, young and old, white, black, Asian, Latin, some with large newsprint pads tucked under arms, others with paint boxes, and he despises every one of them.

He thinks back to when he was a boy, the chalk drawings he would create on the sidewalk, and the way they would get attention, occasionally someone giving him a dollar simply for the enjoyment of viewing his artwork. Then there were the others, mostly scared-looking middle-aged men in whom he recognized a need, whom he would smile at and allow to take him places—bus-station toilets, hotel rooms, and pay him for the kind of sex he was, by then, quite used to; only this money was not for her, this money he saved so that one day he could pay for art classes, and while they were doing whatever disgusting things they did to him he simply imagined himself here, in this building, and it was worth it.

Behind his sunglasses there are tears gathering in his eyes because if it had not been for the accident, he too could have been one of these students with paint-stained jeans, but the thought simply reinforces his resolve, and the little bit of emotion he felt a moment ago vanishes like smoke.

He has brought a small pad and a thick graphite pencil so that he will not look out of place, makes a rough sketch of the large old building itself, stopping every so often to look up and check someone out, to decide: Is she the one, or he? This one? Maybe that one? And finally has narrowed it down—either the pretty girl with light hair, or the guy whose hair is dark. Both carry paint boxes, which is what got them into the semifinals. But what sealed their fate was that each of them smiled at him. Who will win the contest is still a question. He'd love to do them both—*Double your pleasure, double your fun*—but that would be too much, at least for now.

Yesterday, when he started his quest, the girl was carrying a canvas and he cadged a peek at it—a still life—and was very pleased, because the painting would work perfectly. But he worries that it will not be so easy to get her to go with him. Girls, he knows, can be difficult. Whereas boys, a certain kind of boy, a kind he knows well, are easy, and this dark-haired boy, who is slender and graceful, with paint splotches on his jeans, is one of those kind. He could see it in the boy's smile, which lasted too long.

Sunday Monday Happy Days—

He stares up at the art school and thinks about how much he misses working in his studio. But this is important. It will make it possible for him to continue to work and it is worth the sacrifice.

He has sacrificed plenty in his life. No one knows how much he has sacrificed. And suffered.

One time he told Dylan about some of it because he knew that Dylan had it rough too, and he was sure he'd understand. Naturally, Tony knows, but Tony would never tell anyone. "Right, Tony?"

You're grrrrrrrreat! Grrrrrrrreat! Grrrrrrrreat!

"Thanks," he whispers. He's glad Tony is here with him, keeping him company. He's not sure where Dylan and Kelly and Brenda and Brandon are. Maybe over at Steve's, having one of their pool parties. But he doesn't hate them for that. They've been good friends to him and they are entitled to have a fun time.

The dark clouds have erased the tops of New York's tallest skyscrapers and he is thankful. Still, he keeps his wraparound shades in place, which he hopes both the light-haired girl and dark-haired boy find mysterious and sexy.

The girl went inside the old stone building about three hours ago, which, if she is on the same schedule as yesterday, means she will be out any minute. He checks his watch, looks up, and *bingo!* There she is right on time, skipping down the stone steps, paint box in hand.

God, he's smart.

You're grrrrrrrrrreat!

"Shhh, Tony. She's coming."

He knows that she has seen him, but does not look up from the drawing he is doing, furiously filling in an area of the page with his thick graphite pencil, and then, when she is right beside him, and he can feel her and smell her, he continues to keep his head down, working.

You deserve a break today . . .

"Wouldn't it be a lot easier without the shades?" the girl says. "Especially since there's like, no sun today."

"Without *what*?" he says, though he's heard her perfectly.

"The shades. Without the *shades*."

"Oh," he says. "I like seeing the world this way."

"Through rose-colored glasses?"

Rose-colored. Are they? He takes them off, and squints at them. *No, they're brown.* At least he always thought so.

"Your eyes are nice," she says. "You shouldn't hide them."

He flashes his teen-idol smile, concentrates on not blinking or squinting, thinks: *What luck to be handsome. How handy.*

He has practiced and cataloged his gestures—smiles, tilts of the head, a tug of the earlobe—mostly from TV, and knows how to use them, these convincing portrayals of charm and sanity. He traces a finger along his smooth, practically hairless chin, then with his fingertips takes turns ever so lightly tapping his full, almost feminine lips, the feature that most often elicits a reaction—*so pouty, pretty, sexy*—and hopes she will notice, though at that moment his mind is playing a reel of smudged pornographic scenes: dark alleys, claustrophobic booths, public rest rooms, hotels, all blurred memories without feeling. Never any feeling.

"Hey, you with me?"

"What? Oh, sure." Another fast, practiced smile. "What's it like?" He nods toward the building, at the Art Students League.

"Oh, it's okay, I guess." She shrugs.

He isn't going to get any descriptions of art student camaraderie he used to dream about from her.

"You wanna get a coffee?" He slips the shades back into place, and sings, "You deserve a break today . . ."

She completes the tune: ". . . at McDonald's!"

"Wow!" he says.

She laughs, shifts her weight from one foot to the other, breasts doing a little rumba under her tight cotton top.

"I'd really like to." She takes in his heartthrob good looks, and sighs. "But I gotta get home or my roommate will like, totally kill me."

"Really?" he asks, dead serious. "Do you think so?"

"You slay me," the girl says, and laughs again. "Another time?" She tugs the pencil slowly out of his fingers and writes her telephone number on the back of his pad. "I'm Annie. Call me," she says, and lopes off down the street. She turns back once and throws him a sexy smile, but he doesn't bother to return it because he has just noticed the dark-haired boy coming out of the League, and this is his chance and he does not want to blow it.

What do you think, Tony? Is he the one?

Yeah. He's grrrrrrreat!

The dark-haired boy stops on the bottom step, sets his paint box down, gets a cigarette between his lips and takes a long time lighting it. Then he leans back against the wall and lets the smoke drift out of his mouth slowly. It's a pose that cries out for music, one of those girl groups that she liked so much, another oldie, the Shirelles or the Chiffons, with their oohs and aahs, and strings and heartbreak. *"Will you still love me tomorrow . . ."*

Clearly the guy is posing it for him. He'd burst out laughing if it were not so important.

After a minute, the boy drops his cigarette and crushes it under his heel, then runs a hand through his longish dark hair, picks up his paint box and sprints across the street, dodging cars and taxis as if he were in a movie chase scene, and stops, catching his breath, just beside him, leans in close, the smell of tobacco on his breath. "Nice drawing, man."

"Thanks."

"What'd you do to your hand?" says the boy, taking in the jagged, purplish welt.

"Oh." He tugs his shirt over his scarred wrist. "I did it a long time ago . . . when I was, uh . . . sharpening a pencil with a razor." He takes off his wraparound sunglasses because everyone, not just that girl, has always said he has nice eyes, for whatever that's worth—the irony could make him laugh, or cry. He can never get the emotions quite right. But he wants to distract the boy from the scar, get back on track, and smiles, trying very hard not to squint. He can see it's worked because the boy's smile has broadened and gone a little dreamy too.

"You like that place?" He nods toward the school.

"Yeah, it's cool."

"You an artist?"

"Trying to be." The guy bites his lower lip, nervous, or maybe flirting." What about you?"

"I *am* an artist," he says.

"Oh, cool. Where do you show?"

Show? The word throws him for a moment, then he thinks it through and comes up with an answer. "Museums."

"Wow. That's cool." The guy just stands there, doing the same thing the light-haired girl did, shifting weight from one foot to the other.

Go for it. Remember, you're grrrrrrrreat!

"You live around here?"

"I, uh, have a place downtown, the East Village. All I can afford until I'm showing my work in museums, like you." He laughs a nervous girlish laugh.

"You paint there?"

"Paint. Live. You name it. It's cool."

He picks up the guy's lingo. "Cool," he says. "You live alone?"

"Yep." Another nervous giggle. "Ummm . . . You wanna go there?"

"Grrrrrreat!" he says.

The guy giggles. "Tony the Tiger?"

"You *know* him?"

"Who doesn't?"

"You *really* know Tony?"

The dark-haired guy giggles, says. "You're funny."

He puts his wraparound shades back on, and smiles.

THIRTEEN

While Brown did a little background check on Leonardo Martini, Kate watched through the interrogation room's one-way glass as Nicky Perlmutter finished up with Lamar Black—Suzie White's boyfriend. With priors for drugs, petty larceny, and prostitution, the man had not been hard to find. Currently, he was draped around a wooden chair, one arm looped through the rungs holding a cigarette he puffed on like a joint, the other under his knee, which he'd pulled up to use as a chin rest. He was trying to act cool, but Kate thought he looked beaten, eyes weary, jaw muscles quivering. According to Brown, Perlmutter had been at him for a couple of hours.

"Says he has no idea who could have done this to his 'little Suzie,' that they were in *love,*" said Perlmutter, shutting the interrogation room door behind him. He looked a bit worn himself, lips dry, eyes bloodshot. "Could be telling the truth. Got all choked up when I stuck that photo-booth picture in his face. Swears he was in a pool hall till the morning hours the night Suzie White got cut up."

Kate stared through the glass at Lamar Black, his head tilted back, fluorescent light illuminating an angry crescent of raised flesh that stretched from his left earlobe to the right one. The scar Rosita Martinez mentioned. "What else?"

"He says Suzie White was a runaway. Can't remember where from.

Bumfuck, USA. Maybe we can locate her family. Black says she used to work the Midtown streets for some wise-guy pimp, an *I-talian,* to quote him. He thinks organized crime, but who knows? Suzie made a break for it after the wise guy beat her up. Came to Black through one of the girls in his stable, though that girl has since taken a powder, so we can't talk to her."

"Somebody should go up to the Bronx and speak to his girls."

"Already in progress," said Perlmutter.

"Doesn't really make sense that he'd have murdered her. Why kill your investment?" Kate cadged another look at Black, who was hunched over now, head in his hands. "And I can't see him as our painterly unsub."

"Probably not. But he doesn't know that. All Lamar knows is with his jacket we could put him away if we felt like it."

"He know the other vic, Marsha Stimson?"

"Says no. But maybe one of his girls did."

"What about the regular client that Rosita Martinez mentioned?"

"Says Suzie saw a guy once or twice a week—someone she used to do in Midtown who continued to see her in the Bronx. Says the guy knew Suzie's wise-guy I-talian, and threatened to snitch on her if she didn't see him when he wanted."

"Description?"

"Says he only saw the guy maybe once or twice, and from a distance. Youngish, good-looking."

"And Suzie never said anything about him?"

"Said the guy liked her to bark."

"Make sure the detectives ask the girls about barkers." Kate rolled her eyes. "Could be he's still doing business with Lamar's girls. Might be a good idea to put a little surveillance on them."

Permutter nodded. "Guy has to trek all the way up to the Bronx to get laid? Sounds pretty desperate."

"Or pretty obsessed," said Kate.

L ooks like you've missed him," said Brown. He turned his computer screen so Kate and Perlmutter could read it for themselves.

LEONARDO ALBERTO MARTINI. DECEASED.

"Jesus. When?" asked Kate.

"Day before yesterday. Killed himself."

Kate did a double take. "This is way too much coincidence. Do you know if Crime Scene has been through his place?"

Brown plucked a sheet out of a brand-new folder on his desk. "Yes. And no. Apparently they didn't do much. Not much of a report here. Suicide. That's it. Took the body. 'Investigation pending,' it says." He handed it to her.

"I've got to get over there and see Martini's paintings," said Kate. "Right away. Can you call ahead? Make sure we can get in?"

Brown said, "Will do," but Kate had already turned out of the door.

Kate and Perlmutter each pulled on a pair of latex gloves as they stepped into the apartment.

The air in the room was stale, with an overlay of something fruity and foul. Martini had lain dead, the back of his head blown off from the revolver he'd supposedly stuck into his mouth, for a day and a half until his friend, Remy Fortensky—whose phone calls about why Martini had not shown up for their weekly dinner had gone unanswered—insisted that the superintendent get a key and open Martini's door.

The uniforms who had been called to the scene—a pair of rookies straight out of the Academy—assumed suicide and contaminated the scene by traipsing around the apartment touching just about everything. The paramedics who followed zipped Martini into a body bag and hoisted the body out of the apartment before Crime Scene had arrived, so the tech team had not hung around for very long.

In death, Leonardo Martini had received as much attention as he had gotten in life.

According to his friend Remy Fortensky, Martini was depressed about being constantly broke, his no-point art career, and was drinking too much. To everyone it looked clear-cut: Has-been artist kills self. Case closed.

"This the way the NYPD operates these days?" said Kate, once more reviewing the sketchy police report.

"Overworked and demoralized—the new musical now playing at your local NYPD precinct."

In Leonardo Martini's ad hoc studio, canvases were stacked up one on top of the other, crowding the room. Two large paintings that appeared to be in progress—abstractions of swirling colorful stripes against large areas of unpainted white canvas—were hanging on the walls.

Perlmutter tilted his head and squinted at the paintings. "What do you make of them?"

"Nothing revolutionary, but good."

"Something spare and really nice about them." He went in for a closer look. "The way those bands of color just loop and slide over the surface."

"You'd make a decent art critic," said Kate.

"Yeah, sure." The brawny detective's freckled cheeks turned pink.

Beside the two paintings was a table covered with jars and tools, mangled oil-paint tubes, and a large tin of turpentine; on the floor, a roll of unprimed cotton canvas and a gallon can of gesso.

Kate took a closer look at the paint table, noted the cut squares of paint-stained sponge and foam-tipped brushes Martini used to paint with rather than ordinary bristle brushes. Kate plucked a piece of sponge off the table and held it up. "This is why the paint seems to be part of the canvas, as opposed to lying on top of it. Martini sponges the paint into the surface."

"Is that common?"

"Not necessarily, but it's been done before. By painters like Morris Louis and Helen Frankenthaler."

"I've seen some of her paintings at the Museum of Modern Art. Big paintings with washy areas of color, right?"

Kate nodded while unscrewing the lid off one of the small glass baby-food jars in which the artist had mixed the colors he was using in his current paintings. The pungent smell of turpentine filled her nostrils. She tilted the jar onto the palette. Bright blue paint liquefied with enough turpentine to make it appear to be watercolor streamed onto the palette, ready for sponging.

"It's the blue he used for those stripes, there," said Perlmutter, pointing at one of the large abstract paintings on the wall.

Kate stared up at the paintings. A similarity between the way they were painted and the still life with the blue-striped bowl was undeniable. "And maybe for another painting with stripes too." She replaced the lid and bagged it.

She was moving slowly, taking everything in, but her mind was racing. *Had Martini been involved in Richard's murder—and then killed himself over the guilt?*

From behind her, she heard Perlmutter mutter, "Holy shit," and turned to see the detective standing in the tiny alcove that served as Martini's bedroom, mattress suspended above the bed by one muscular arm. With his free hand, he was scooping up stacks of bills. "All hundreds," he said. "Must be about four or five grand here."

"That's a lot of cash for a starving artist," said Kate.

"Maybe he's been saving it for years. Could be one of those guys who doesn't trust banks."

"Maybe," said Kate. "But all hundreds? And didn't Martini's friend say the guy was complaining about being broke?"

For the next two hours Kate and Perlmutter searched every inch of the apartment, going through Martini's chest of drawers, ransacking his Fruit of the Loom underwear, rummaging through the pockets of every item of clothing that hung in his one small closet. Back in the studio, Kate bagged some of the artist's oil paint and a few of the sponges to see if they could establish more of a link with the crime scene painting of the blue-striped bowl, then Perlmutter called for a van to fetch the stuff and bring it all into the lab.

"Give me a minute," he said. "I've got to use the facilities."

Kate lit a cigarette, adding her smoke to the stale air, glanced at Martini's half-completed paintings on the wall and the dozens of old ones stacked up. All of this dedication to making art that no one cared about was depressing.

"Place is falling apart," said Perlmutter, coming out of the bathroom. "Toilet won't even flush."

"Hold on," said Kate, turning into the bathroom. She had been through the medicine cabinet, bagged Martini's razor and toothbrush, wiped out his stall shower, and bagged the gunk in the drain, hoping that maybe they would find a hair here and one in that damn crime scene still life that would match—but there was one place in the bathroom she hadn't looked.

Kate slipped on a new pair of gloves, knocked the toilet seat down, and gently raised the porcelain back of the tank.

No. I said on your knees, barking."

"Barking?"

"Yes. Barking. Like a dog, you know?"

"Can't I do it on the bed? I don't wanna ruin my stockings."

"So take them off."

"I thought you liked them on."

"I do." Jesus. Why couldn't she just do what he asked? He pulled a blanket off the bed and tossed it to the floor. "Kneel on this."

"So you want me like on my knees and sitting up, or like down on all fours?"

His head was starting to throb. "On all fours. And *barking,* for Christ's sake. How fucking hard is that!?"

"All right. You don't have to yell. I get it."

The girl seemed to be taking forever, first spreading the blanket, then getting into position, then finally managing a pip-squeak "Arf." She smiled and did a few more: "Arf, arf, arf."

"Is that the best you can do?"

"I'm barking, ain't I? You want me to growl too?" The girl was thinking she'd like to bite him maybe, and that she wasn't getting paid nearly enough for this shit, that she had thought this one was going to be easy, maybe even a little fun, the guy being so cute and all. But man, was she ever wrong. "I can growl pretty good."

"Like who? Tony the fucking Tiger? I want you to *bark.* Like you *mean* it." Oh, man, how Suzie could bark. Really howl. Just the thought of her on her hands and knees baying away got him hard. He'd have to keep her image in his mind or he'd never be able to get it on with this dopey slut who wasn't worth the forty bucks for her services, plus another fifty for the Bronx transient hotel. He knew when he chose her that it was only because she was young and reminded him of Suzie, and worked a few streets from where Suzie had worked once she'd moved up to the Bronx, but no way she could replace his Suzie, who would let him come to her place and could bark up a storm while he fucked her in the ass. She was worth the hundred, easy. She was special. He'd have paid double if Suzie had asked, which she wouldn't because she was fair, and because, deep down, he believed, she cared for him.

He looked over at the hooker. Pathetic, the way she was straightening the blanket, again.

This wasn't working. He was only half hard and still worried about everything. The idea that he could be caught and sent to jail, and now even his wife, his ever-loyal Noreen, threatening to leave him. Noreen. God, if she knew the half of it. Well, fuck her. Good riddance. She would never do the barking thing, no matter how many times he'd begged her over the years. "Fuck you, Noreen!"

"My name's not Noreen, mister."

"Was I talking to you?" He flopped back onto the crummy bed, glanced up at the naked lightbulb, and was momentarily blinded. He squeezed his eyes shut and stars danced against a black backdrop.

What was he doing here anyway? He pictured himself against a bright blue ocean, and sighed out loud. How had he gotten to this point, fallen so low? He felt dirty and worthless. He looked down at the girl on all fours and let out a bitter laugh.

"What's so funny?" the girl asked, still fooling with the blanket.

"Nothing." He felt like killing her, smashing her head against the floor, watching the blood and brains—if she had any—spill out.

It seemed such a long time ago, all that promise, the dreams—dashed, dead or dying. He should kill himself. He should have done it long ago. Before this all started spiraling out of control.

He peered down at the hooker. This wasn't helping him forget and that's what he wanted, needed—to forget. And he was tired. Too tired to do anything. "Just get out," he said.

"What?"

"GET OUT." He crumpled a couple of twenties and tossed them across the room.

The girl scrambled after them on her hands and knees, and he sat up to watch. "That's it," he said. "Run, doggie, run!" He charged off the bed, mounted the girl, jerking his semi-limp dick, attempting to work himself into an erection. "Now bark!"

"This is gonna cost you another twenty," the girl said, looking over his shoulder.

"Just bark, damn it! BARK!!!"

FOURTEEN

It's great you could be here, Liz." Kate leaned against the brick wall of the Sixth Precinct and fumbled in her bag for her Marlboros. She was happy to be out of the airless conference room.

"I'm in town, aren't I? Might as well do some work. It was no big deal. Called in a few Quantico favors. But I'm not a field agent, Kate. I doubt they're gonna let me sit in again—and I don't think Agent Grange appreciated my being here."

"You see the way that guy looks at me?"

"That's the way he looks at everybody. It's part of the Bureau job description—paranoia and intimidation. Truthfully? I think he sort of likes you."

"Oh, please. You're delusional."

"And don't think I didn't catch your little tricks, hand on his arm, the smile."

"Hey, I'm desperate. The guy obviously wants me off the case."

"It's not up to him. Not unless the Bureau totally takes over," said Liz. "And you've done good work. Finding the blue-striped bowl that Martini used as a model pretty much proves the guy did the painting."

"But not the murder." Kate struck a match and lit up. "There's no motive. Martini was an artist his whole life, Liz, eking out a crummy living to support his painting." Kate couldn't believe she was finding excuses for the man the squad thought might have murdered her husband, but something in her gut was telling her they were looking for easy solutions. "I just don't see it."

"Could there be a connection between Richard and Martini? Richard collected art and the guy was a painter."

"I'd have known if there was." The question ticked off that damn year-old vision: Finding Richard's cuff link at a crime scene, and how he had lied to her about it.

Would I have known?

"Richard was into blue-chip artists or young up-and-comers. Leonardo Martini was neither." Kate dragged on her cigarette, stared up at the gray clouds, and sighed.

Liz rested her hand on Kate's shoulder. "You okay?"

Kate turned on a too-bright smile. "Sure."

"You don't have to try so hard. It's me, remember?"

"You want to take a walk or something?"

"Love to, but I promised my sister I'd watch the baby." Liz kissed her cheek, started down the brown stone steps, then turned back. "And throw that damn cigarette away."

Kate crushed the Marlboro under her heel and made a mental note to buy a box of Nicorette as she watched her friend disappear down the street.

Now what? Perlmutter needed a couple of hours to write up an old case before they were meeting at the copy shop where Leonardo Martini had worked.

Go home? That would only make her more tense—and lonely. She needed a break, and a place to think.

The New Museum of Contemporary Art, brainchild of a curator who had once worked at one of the big uptown museums, had, over its twenty-five-year life span, matured into a full-fledged institution, with its own set of curators, a history of ground-breaking exhibitions, and even a hip little bookstore.

Kate was still thinking about Leonardo Martini and the blue-striped bowl she'd found hidden in the tank of his toilet as she mounted the stairs to the museum's second floor and spied the perfectly round, flesh-colored orb just slightly smaller than a bowling ball, magically suspended in a corner of the wall.

Kate read the wall label: APPROXIMATELY FIFTEEN HUNDRED PIECES OF CHEWED BUBBLE GUM—and smiled.

The artist, Tom Friedman, as literal sculpture-maker, thought Kate, only this time not working with clay or plaster, but with ordinary bubble gum, which he chewed, then molded. Odd, funny, and in its own way rather beautiful.

Kate smiled again when she observed a fluffy white mass hovering on the floor and noted it was made by separating a pillow's stuffing strand by strand. Artists were constantly inventing and reinventing what art could be. It reminded Kate of Martini's naked white canvas stripes, and the fact that she was certain he had painted the still life found at Richard's crime scene.

But why?

No matter what Kate said, the squad now wanted to believe it was possible that Martini had painted all three paintings. She pictured Marty Grange and his ever-present agents, Marcusa, who never spoke, and Sobieski, a cocky crew cut, thinking they had their man. But they were grasping at straws. Kate was certain of it. Someone had paid Martini to paint that still life, which, to Kate's mind, explained the five thousand dollars found under the starving artist's mattress.

Kate was still considering Martini's involvement as she approached a white pedestal with apparently nothing on it until she spotted the tiny brown sphere no bigger than a Tic Tac. This time, she did not have to read the wall text. She knew what it was—a perfectly molded piece of the artist's shit. She'd seen a similar piece before, in a group exhibition, where a viewer, unaware that the pedestal had anything on it, used it as a seat, and when he stood up, the piece of shit had disappeared. Kate wondered at the time if it had somehow crawled into his pants to find a familiar home.

Kate laughed. She loved the idea of artists' using unconventional materials. But that laughter was cut short when she thought about the Bronx psycho and his very unconventional approach to painting. Exactly what was it he was trying to convey?

Kate turned a corner, and there, on the floor, was a life-size figure made of colored construction paper, a self-portrait, the artist's vision of himself splayed and torn apart, viscera exposed, in a pool of paper blood, a fantastic tour de force, amazing in its detail, and possibly, to some viewers, hilarious. But not to Kate, not now.

That was it. She'd had enough.

The Seventh Street Copy Shop was a long narrow alleyway; the whir and whine of a dozen Xerox machines going at once creating a din while two employees manned the machines, slipping reams of paper into them as if it were feeding time at the zoo.

At the front counter, a middle-aged woman with a portfolio under her arm was tapping her foot repeatedly, a teen clutching a batch of comic books loaded up with Post-its rapped his fingers along the edge of the counter, a young bookish-looking woman with a mountain of loose man-uscript pages tried to balance the stack while checking her wristwatch—none of which had the slightest effect on the kid at the front desk, who moved at his own narcoleptic pace.

Nicky Perlmutter squeezed his massive frame between them, and they let loose with a collective assortment of scowls, frowns, and "There's a line here . . . we've been waiting . . ." He placed his NYPD gold shield onto the counter, said—"The owner here?"—and they all shut up.

The counter kid did a slo-mo pivot and scanned the work area behind him. "Must be . . . in the . . . back room." The words oozed out of him like unctuous tar. He might as well have been toking a reefer, he was so obviously stoned. Kate exchanged a look with Perlmutter, who turned back to the kid. "Here's the plan," he said. "Go get your boss and bring him here or we go back there and look for ourselves. You got that—or is the weed making it a little hard for you to understand what I'm saying?"

The kid twitched, and picked up the phone.

A muscular young guy in jeans, muscle-T, and sunglasses emerged from a door at the back of the shop and strutted toward them, his heavy black boots adding a staccato beat to the clatter of the Xerox machines. He gave Perlmutter's badge a cursory glance, folded his muscled arms across his inflated chest, and said, "Wassup?"

"Leonardo Martini," said Kate. "He worked here?"

Mr. Muscle painted a sad clown face over his features and said, "Goddamn shame."

"So you've heard," said Kate.

"Was in the papers," he said. "I shoulda' known. It wasn't like Leo to not show up, not call. He was a real conscientious guy."

Kate strained to hear him over the racket. "Are you the owner here?"

"That's me. Angelo Baldoni."

"What's with the shades?" asked Perlmutter.

He tilted his chin toward the bank of lights that covered most of the ceiling and bathed the room in a harsh blue-white glare. "Those damn neons, y'know, they bother the hell outta me."

"Fluorescents," said Kate.

"Whatever." Baldoni shrugged.

"How long had Martini worked for you?" Perlmutter aped Baldoni's pose, muscled arms folded across his broad chest.

"About two years, he—"

"What?" Kate cupped her ear. "The machines. I can't— Is there somewhere else we can talk?"

Baldoni lifted a section of the counter, gestured for Kate and Perlmutter to follow him as he strutted past the Xerox machines and into a back room.

Two guys, late teens, maybe early twenties, both with cigarettes in their mouths, one dangling from the corner of his lips à la James Dean, the other blowing smoke rings, big boys like Baldoni, with that stayed-too-long-at-the-gym look, had their feet up on a long table littered with beer cans and ashtrays.

Baldoni nodded at the door and their heels hit the floor in unison. They cut out without a word.

"Sit," said Baldoni. "Sorry about the mess."

"They work here?" asked Perlmutter, eyeing the guys as they left. "Because if they knew Martini, I'd like to—"

"No, no. They're friends of mine is all. They couldn't tell you anything about Leo." He reached down and wrapped his fingers around a small barbell and started doing curls. "Leo hung by himself, far as

I know. A loner, y'know. I didn't know too much about his life. I didn't even know the guy was a artist till I seen it in the paper." He switched hands and continued curling. "Leo was a good worker, though. Here every day. Quiet as a mouse. Did whatever he was asked."

"Such as?" asked Kate.

Baldoni stopped the barbell in mid-curl. "Huh?"

"Like what sorta things didja ask him t'do?" said Kate, slipping into her old Queen's cadence. Perlmutter eyed her and tried not to smile.

"Copyin', bindin'. What else is there?" Baldoni's lips twisted away from his teeth; Kate wasn't sure it qualified as a smile. "It's a fuckin' copy shop, right? Sorry. Didn't mean to offend."

"No fuckin' problem," said Kate, and they both laughed. "Hey, Angelo. Where you from?"

"Kissena Boulevard, Queens."

"No way," said Kate, with a flip of her hair. She was glad she'd worn it down and glad she'd worn a sweater. "Me, I'm from Astoria. Grew up on a Hundred Twenty-first."

"No shit." He pointed his barbell at her. "You know Johnny Rotelli?"

"Musta missed him," said Kate, flashing a smile. "I'm guessin' I'm a little older than you and your buds."

"Lookin' good, though." Baldoni seemed to be assessing her from behind his shades. "You sure don't look like no cop t'me."

"What can I tell ya'," said Kate. "When I was startin' out there was no openings at the White House. That bitch Monica Lewinsky got my job."

Angelo Baldoni hooted.

"So, uh, did Leo seem depressed to you?" asked Kate. "Any sign that he mighta been contemplating suicide?"

"Y'know, now that I think of it, he was real mopey." He painted that sad clown face back on, mouth cast down, lower lip out, like a baby. "Guess I shoulda paid more attention, but, hey, I'm no shrink, y'know." He plunked the barbell onto the floor.

"Of course not. How could you know?" Kate offered him a sympathetic look.

"Right. Like I said before, Leo was a loner, and I don't pry. The guy was quiet as a mouse."

"Hey, Nicky," said Kate. "How's your stomach doing? Still givin' you trouble?"

"What?" Perlmutter's face went blank.

Kate kicked him lightly under the table.

"Oh, yeah, my gut. It's been killing me all day," he said to Baldoni. "Think I ate something rotten." He swallowed like he was ready to barf. "You have a john here?"

Baldoni lifted his chin toward a door in the corner. "Be my guest."

Perlmutter hoofed over to the bathroom as if he were on a serious mission.

Kate waited till Perlmutter shut himself into the bathroom, then leaned in close to Baldoni. "You never know about those mousy guys," she whispered. "Me? I tend to go for the strong silent type."

"Oh, yeah?"

"Yeah. Do you really need those shades?"

Baldoni peeled them off, and blinked slowly. His eyes were deep blue fringed with thick lashes, a striking, almost feminine feature.

His secret weapon, thought Kate. Whip off the shades, bat the eyes, paralyze the girls. "Anyone ever tell you you've got beautiful eyes?"

Baldoni looked down like a shy little boy, then winked and put the shades back in place.

Kate tossed her hair like a forties movie star. "I've got this *thing*, for muscles."

Baldoni flexed a biceps about the size of a cantaloupe.

"Amazing," said Kate, and knew she was going to hate herself in the morning.

"Hey, I eat my Wheaties. Breakfast of champions." He beamed a grin, took a deep breath and pumped up his pecs.

"Wow," said Kate. "Was he any good?" Her fingertips grazed Baldoni's rock-hard chest, as if by accident, as she pushed her hair away from her face.

"What? Who?"

"Leo? As a painter, I mean?"

"Didn't look like anything t'me," he said. "But what do I know? Modern art. It's all horseshit, right?"

"Believe it," said Kate, sitting back with a smile.

N ice kick," said Perlmutter, rubbing his ankle as they got into his Crown Victoria. "You just ruined my dancing career."

"Sorry, but I wanted a moment alone with Mr. Baldoni."

"And?" Perlmutter steered the car onto University Place.

"He didn't know Martini was a painter, right?"

"Right."

"Well, while you were in the bathroom he said Martini's paintings didn't look like much to him."

"How'd you get that bit of info?"

"I've got my ways."

"I'll bet." Perlmutter grinned. "I enjoyed your married-to-the-mob impersonation."

"That was the *real* me," said Kate. "I worked damn hard to lose it. Wake me in the middle of the night, I sound like Carmela Soprano."

Perlmutter laughed. "Those young thugs in the back room," he said, shifting into a serious gear. "Could be Baldoni is running a little more than a copy shop. They seemed like errand boys to me—and not for pizza and soda. I'll eat my shoe if that guy is clean."

"Cocktail sauce or salsa?"

"Salsa," said Perlmutter. "And you know, that name, Baldoni—it keeps nagging at me."

"Suppose Baldoni had Martini make a painting to cover up a murder, and then Baldoni doesn't want him around anymore, so he stages a suicide."

"Possible."

Kate was quiet a moment, thinking it through. *Martini creates a painting to be used at Richard's murder scene. But why?* She stared blankly at the stores and apartment buildings blurring past the car window. *To make it look like Richard was just the unlucky victim of a serial killer.* The copycat theory that they had all previously assumed to be the case. *But why Richard? Why would anyone want Richard dead?* What had her husband been involved in that would get him killed—and possibly by a professional?

My God, Richard. What have you done?

Perlmutter took his eyes off the traffic, glanced over, could see that something had gotten under Kate's skin. He wanted to tell her how sorry he was about her husband, how he understood about loss and pain, but he could also see she was trying hard to maintain her composure and he respected that. "Okay," he said. "Here's one for you. Who played Michelle Pfeiffer's husband in *Married to the Mob*?"

"What? Oh. That's easy," she said, thinking, *God bless you, Nicky Perlmutter.* "Alec Baldwin."

It took Floyd Brown less than five minutes to fill them in on the fact that Angelo Baldoni was the nephew of Giulio Lombardi, deceased, who had been a major player for one of the five families, more commonly referred to as the Mafia, and less than that to pull up Baldoni's record, which included breaking and entering, assault, and suspicion of murder—more than once—which the feds were trying, unsuccessfully, to make stick.

"We're not going to get much out of Baldoni if he's connected to organized crime," said Perlmutter.

"No," said Brown. "But I'll send a couple of uniforms to bring him in for questioning. Can't hurt to annoy him. And maybe Marty Grange would like a go at him."

Richard, the victim of a mob hit? Was it possible? The idea that she could just have been talking to the man behind Richard's murder chilled her.

"You with us, McKinnon?"

Kate forced herself to focus. "Yes."

"Good, because those X-rays of the paintings are ready and waiting."

FIFTEEN

The colors are swirling, a spectrum sparking in his eyes and brain like firecrackers igniting.

He pushes the knife in a little deeper and the dark-haired boy's eyes—which he now sees are a cool Pacific blue—widen with shock before he doubles over, his erection going limp.

He catches him before he falls, balances the boy's nude body by the knife that he has jabbed into his gut, and twists the blade without really looking, distracted by the room, the boy's artwork on the walls—mostly nudes and still-life paintings that have been made in classes at the League, he assumes—all of them coming to life in full Technicolor magnificence.

He is nude too, having allowed the boy to fondle him, though, until this moment, he could not get hard. But now he is excited, hard, and tries not to be overcome by the stunning streams of scarlet and plum that are pouring out of the boy's belly, over his hand, and puddling around his bare feet. He looks up and takes in the shimmering cornflower-blue walls of the apartment.

Where to look first? His tender eyes dart here, there, alighting on the boy's blue denim jeans tossed to the floor, a cerise shirt on a chair painted bright fuchsia—all of it thrilling. But he cannot allow himself to linger on those insignificant things. He has to make use of his limited time.

Stick to the plan. Choose a painting.

He considers shoving his erection into the boy's open mouth but notices the scarlet at his feet going slightly pink, and knows that he cannot waste the time.

Another twist of the knife; that sometimes helps.

Sure enough, the intensity of that pinkish red ratchets up a notch closer to vermilion, as blue-violet sausagelike links of intestine tumble from the boy's split abdomen onto the floor, and over his toes.

He thinks it looks so much like one of the Soutine Carcass paintings or the Francis Bacon he has pinned to his wall that he is almost overwhelmed. He dips his hand into the boy's blood and paints his erection bright red.

Instantly, he is back in a memory . . .

Squalid room. Torn drawings. Blood-red phallus.

The music has already started, and he sees that tilted floor, feels a sense of nausea, and hears her screams.

He stares at the cornflower-blue walls until their absolute splendor drowns the memory away in a sea of color and he once again knows where he is, feels his muscles straining against the dead boy suspended on his arm, and sees all of the other delicious colors—tickle-me-pink flesh and royal-purple organs. All he needs is the gentlest tug and instantly he comes.

Now he can get back to work.

Grrrrrrrrrrreat!

Oh, Tony is here. "Hi," he whispers. "Can't talk now. I've gotta choose a painting."

On one wall are two painted nudes, flesh-toned figures with hints of burnt sienna, but a figure, he decides, is wrong, is too different. Another wall has several paintings, another nude, this one more rose-colored than flesh, and a landscape done in shamrock and sea greens. Also wrong. But beside the landscape is a smallish still life with a mint-green vase on a navy-blue cloth with three razzmatazz-red apples, and it is just what he is looking for.

He takes a minute to lock the color into his visual memory—*testing, testing, testing*—and when he is certain he has memorized it, he lets the boy's slender lifeless body drop to the floor with a thud. He strides across the room and smears his bloodstained hand across one of the boy's unfinished canvases.

That's grrrrrrrrreat!

"Thanks, Tony."

Later, when the color has faded, he looks around at all the paintings—including the still life of apples and a vase that he has chosen—and decides the boy's paintings are mediocre, and hopes they will not embarrass him.

The aesthetic part is over.

He takes a long time cleaning up. Several hours to spray and wipe every surface in the small apartment. He's in no hurry. The boy told him no one would disturb them.

Afterward, he enjoys a long shower, then cleans out the trap, goes over the bathroom with Fantastic and folds the towel he has used into his backpack.

He tugs the wallet from the back pocket of the blue jeans that the boy had tossed onto the floor and slips it into his backpack. Then decides he'd better take the jeans too.

He looks again at the boy's painting, squints to see any trace of that mint green–colored vase, but now it's pale gray. That's okay. He remembers, and that makes it worth it.

He takes the boy's painting, and his own creation, the one made from the boy's blood, and wraps them together neatly. It's funny, he thinks, that he had at one time actually considered *buying* a painting for his plan. *How dumb was that?*

"You're so smart," he says aloud, in a high falsetto voice.

"Thanks, Donna," he answers. "Have you been here long?"

His Donna-voice says: "Long enough."

"What do you think?"

"I think you're grrrrrrrrrreat!"

"Not you, Tony. Donna."

But Donna has vanished; sometimes his friends do that.

With the two carefully wrapped paintings under his arm, the knife, spray bottle of Fantastic, bath towel, and jeans crammed into his backpack, he circles the dead body on the floor and the spreading pool of blood that now appears inky black.

He attempts to recollect the color of the boy's hair. Was it really black, or was there a hint of mahogany?

Shit. He's already forgotten.

Words," said Kate. She held the X-rays of the paintings up to the light. "Colors. That *Y* I saw that was still visible in the finished painting is the beginning of the word *yellow*. And there's *red,* and *blue* and *green*. And *wild watermelon,* and *magic mint*?" I don't quite get those. But I guess they could be colors too. And *mulberry* could be another. But *razzmatazz*? What's that?" She exchanged the X-ray for a large photograph of scrawled, just barely discernible writing. "Blowup of the painting's border?"

Brown nodded. "Blown up four hundred percent."

"These are words too." She tilted the photo one way, then another. "Handwriting, sort of. Childlike. But names, I think. Look . . ." She held them up for the others to see. "I think that says Tony, doesn't it, over and over, so that it's become a blur, but it is Tony, right? And . . ." She peered at the photos, masses of gray squiggles, just barely intelligible. "I think maybe . . . um, Don or Dot, and is that Bren . . . Brenda, or . . ." She passed them around. "What do you think?"

"Tony, for sure," said Perlmutter. "And maybe . . . Dyan, no, Dyl, maybe it's Dylan. You know, like Bob Dylan, or Dylan Thomas."

"Who's Dylan Thomas?" Grange asked, looking from Agent Marcusa to Agent Sobieski. They both shrugged.

"Poet," said Perlmutter.

Grange made a face like how-the-hell-am-I-supposed-to-know-that?

"Yeah, looks like Brad or Brenda, or something like that," said Brown. "And yeah, Dyl-something."

"Victims?" said Grange, studying the odd photos.

"Doesn't jibe with the vics' names we've turned up," said Brown.

"Could be ones we haven't found yet, or prospective ones," said Grange.

"Maybe," said Kate. "But it's the same names in both paintings' borders." She compared photos from each painting's framing edge. "See, they're the same."

"What about family?" said Brown. "Friends?"

"If he's a true psychopath," said Freeman, "he's not going to have many friends. These characters don't form lasting bonds."

Obsessive doodling. Writing words and sentences over and over again.

"This kind of thing often shows up in outsider art," said Kate. "Particularly the art of the insane."

"Right," said Freeman. "Repetition is often soothing to schizophrenics."

"You ever read Dr. Kurt Ernst?"

"German psychiatrist, expert on art of the insane. Required reading," said Freeman.

"I met him when he wrote a catalog essay for the Drawing Center's show on art of the insane. He's also an art historian. And he's coming to New York. In fact, he might already be here." Kate glanced back at the images. "I'd like him to have a look at the paintings, and I doubt I'll have to twist his arm. He stays with my friend who runs the Drawing Center. I'll call."

"Do it," said Brown.

Perlmutter picked up one of the other X-rays. "It's like a plan for the painting."

"Except that he doesn't follow it." Kate held the X-ray just above a full-scale, full-color reproduction of the actual painting. "Look, he's written *yellow,* but painted blue on top of it. And in the sky and clouds area where he's written *sky blue* he's painted it red and pink."

"The guy's all over the place," said Brown. "He's organized. Brings the weapon—and the paintings. He doesn't go in for torture, so he's not a sadistic killer—but he eviscerates the bodies like a madman, which feels out of control and *disorganized.*"

"These guys live in elaborately concocted fantasy worlds," said Freeman. "We just don't happen to know what his fantasy world is—not yet. But it's somewhere in the ritual."

"Something to do with going after hookers?" asked Perlmutter.

"Could be a part of it," said Freeman. "It's hard to profile the guy until we know what's driving him. And so many of these guys have more than one profile."

"I think the key is in these paintings," said Kate. "What do they represent to him?"

"An offering to the victim?" said Freeman.

"Maybe." Kate started to pace, unconsciously fanning herself with the X-ray. "He brings the paintings with him, we know that, but then leaves them behind. So he either *wants* them to be found or doesn't *care* if they're found, right?"

"Right," said Freeman. "Go on."

Kate stopped fanning herself and stood still. "I've been thinking it's more like he's done with them. That he's brought them with him for some sort of purpose, and then, when that part is over, he no longer cares about the paintings."

"So we have to figure out what's so important to him in these paintings in the first place," said Freeman. "And then why they become *unimportant*."

"Yes, I think so." Kate laid the X-ray back over the painting reproduction and studied it. "He writes in the names of colors, but then fills in the area with a totally different color."

"Doesn't make much sense," said Brown.

"No," said Kate. "But there are artists who have done that sort of thing for conceptual reasons."

"Conceptual?" asked Agent Sobieski.

"Conceptual artists pose questions to the nature of art," said Kate.

"Meaning?" asked Grange.

"Well, a conceptual artist illustrates *ideas*." Kate shut her eyes a minute, then opened them. "Okay, perfect example: The painter Jasper Johns, who is not really a conceptual artist, but uses some conceptual notions in his work, and—wait a minute." She looked again at the X-rays, the words. "This is sort of uncanny, because our unsub is doing something *just* like Jasper Johns."

"What do you mean?" asked Brown.

"Well, Jasper Johns made a series of paintings where he covered whole areas with heavily brushed-on paint, say yellow paint, and then on top of that he stenciled the word *yellow*."

"And that means . . . what?" asked Grange.

"Johns is pointing out the difference between the *word* yellow and the *color* yellow. Also, that there are two different ways we see or describe something—through a word or an image. In this case the word *yellow* versus an expanse of yellow color. You get what I'm saying?" She looked at the men to see if they were following her. "And Jasper Johns has also done the opposite—which looks just like what our unsub painter has done—painted in, let's say, an expanse of yellow paint and then stenciled over it the word *blue*. So that he denies the reality of what you are seeing."

"So the viewer looks at yellow, but *reads* blue," said Freeman.

"Right," said Kate.

"To make the viewer think about what the word *blue* really means? Is that it?" asked Perlmutter.

"Exactly," said Kate. "He's making you *think* about color—about how artists use color in both real and unreal ways. Color can be descriptive, or naturalistic, versus, let's say, abstract."

"And that's what our unsub is doing?" asked Brown. "Playing with us about the word he's written and the color he's actually painted?"

"Maybe." Kate thought a moment. "But he hides the words *under* the paint, so unless, like us, you have an X-ray of the painting, how would you *know* he's playing with you? Plus, I don't know if he's sophisticated enough to be teasing us with such high-art notions." She looked again at the Bronx paintings. "It's totally perplexing. On the one hand, the work feels amateurish, what the art world calls outsider art, and those obsessive, scribbled borders seem to confirm that. But that would mean the entire conceptual thing would be something he'd be unfamiliar with. And if he was an art world player I'd know his work, which I don't, nor does anyone else I've talked to. And yet . . . this is so close to Jasper Johns's paintings, I wonder if he's seen Johns's work? If he's emulating the guy?" Kate stared at the images, lost in thought.

"What?" asked Brown.

Kate raised the X-rays up to the light. *"Wild watermelon* and *razzmatazz.* Those words mean anything to any of you?"

None of the men had the slightest idea.

"So the X-rays don't tell us much." Brown rubbed his temples.

"Maybe they do," said Kate, reaching into her bag, tossing Brown her pillbox. "But we just don't know what it is yet."

SIXTEEN

Did she actually feel happy? Was that possible? Kate had been certain she would never feel that particular emotion again. And yet, watching the moving men stack Nola's two canvas suitcases and cardboard cartons in the large guest room, the one just beside the room Kate and Richard had originally planned as a nursery—bassinette, crib, and changing table already installed—was giving her a kind of pleasure she had been resigned to let go.

Kate smiled warmly at Nola, hoping to hang on to the feeling, though the words in those damn paintings kept flashing, and she could not stop thinking about Leonardo Martini's convenient suicide, or those obsessively scribbled borders, and the art of the insane. "Do you like the bed where it is?" she asked, working hard to stay in the moment.

Nola had decided to move in after she'd tumbled off a step stool in her cramped apartment, and Kate had hired the moving men, gotten Nola's studio apartment listed with Columbia housing, and purchased the baby furniture within hours, before Nola could change her mind. Now she nervously shifted the bassinette a foot to the left, the changing table to the right.

"Kate. Relax. Please. You're making me nervous."

Relax. Was that possible? She didn't think so. "You hungry?"

"Starved."

"Good." Kate led the way down the hall, ignoring the gruesome crime scene pictures flashing in her brain, trying, for Nola's sake, to act as if she was okay. In the pantry, she pushed canned goods aside. "I know Lucille stashed some Mallomars in here. I was thinking we'd stay in tonight and I'd cook."

"*You?* You must mean order-in-cook, right?"

Kate laughed, somewhat forced. "Believe it or not, I can cook." She poured Nola a glass of milk, then slid the Mallomars onto the long oak counter, watched, delighted, as Nola tore into them. Maybe it *was* possible to forget—for a while. She leaned onto the counter. God, she was tired; tired of the energy it took to distance herself so that she could work the case; tired of fueling the rage that she needed to keep going.

"You sure you're okay? You don't seem it," said Nola.

Kate peered at the young woman. "Are you a witch, or what?"

"I'd choose perceptive." She returned Kate's stare. "So?"

"So . . . I'm coping." Isn't that what she had always done? Her mother's suicide, father's cancer, Elena's death, runaways, homicides. "If you'd asked me a few days ago, I'd have said no, I was *not* okay—that I couldn't even imagine going on with my life, but . . . This is what one does, right? Just . . . go on." Kate turned away, wiped invisible cookie crumbs from her fingers into the sink, tears collecting in her eyes, though she tried to ignore them. "I guess I've gotten pretty good at burying my emotions . . . at denial." An image of that dark alley flickered in the back recesses of her mind.

"Nothing wrong with that. I think I dreamed away the bad parts of my life." Nola thought about her brother Niles dying, then her mother. "Sometimes the truth is just too hard."

"Yes." Kate rested her hand over Nola's. She suddenly had the feeling that something was about to go wrong. But why now, at this particular moment—the first time in over a week that she'd felt anything but miserable? She tried to shake it off, but Nola caught it.

"What?"

"Nothing. It's just . . . everything, I guess." For the briefest moment there was another face in her mind, that of her former protégée—a young woman not unlike Nola, whom Kate had been unable to protect.

She slid her arm around Nola's shoulder. "I'm glad you're here," she said, and she was. So why wouldn't that nagging, awful feeling leave her alone?

"Me too," said Nola. "Come on. Let's watch your show."

The black shades are drawn, the tiny screen shimmering into the dark room. He's a bit disappointed at first—the show isn't nearly so good as cartoons or that Xena show he watched yesterday, but he sure does like her, the art *her-story-n,* Kate.

He has that feeling again, just for a moment, that he actually knows her. Is it because of the way she smiles at him, or gives him a serious look as if she were aware of him watching?

He squints at the TV screen, believes he is right, that they do know each other, are somehow psychically or even physically connected, maybe from a former life. But no matter—it will come to him. Sometimes he has trouble remembering things, thinks it is because of what they did to him.

The taste of rubber in his mouth. He shudders, looks back at the TV, at the art *her-story-n.* Soon he hopes they will be good friends. She might even become his new best friend, though he wouldn't want Tony to know that, or Brenda or Brandon, or Donna, especially, who can get really jealous. He would never want to hurt their feelings because that's the kind of friend he is.

So far he wouldn't want to be friends with any of the artists on the show, though she seems to like them, the way she listens as though she cares. It makes him think she is a very good person.

He's even taking a few notes, like when she showed that big painting with all the wooden crosses and plastic dolls attached to it and said that the artist, WLK Hand, was one of the great young artists of his generation, and though he didn't understand why, he'd like to know why *she* thinks that, and so he's written down the date of WLK Hand's exhibition and the name of the gallery, Vincent Petrycoff, and thinks that maybe he'll go and see for himself.

The artists she interviews say things like—"chromatic," and "complementary and tertiary colors," and "warm versus cool"—in very serious voices, and it reminds him of the times when he would sneak into the Art Students League and listen to the teachers, or some of the art books he has managed to read.

A painting flashes on the screen—a big painting comprised of horizontal bands with words stenciled into and onto the painted surface—*yellow* and *blue* and *red*—and the art *her-story-n* says, "Notice how the artist Jasper Johns *illustrates* color with words," and he jerks to attention.

My God, she knows him!

"Tony," he shouts. "Come here! Listen to this! She *knows* him! *Jasper Johns!*"

He thinks back, remembers that day, the moment, in the bookstore, when he turned the page, not expecting anything, and there they were, those paintings! He'd chosen the book purely for the artist's name, which interested him, but then seeing those paintings with the words, so like his own paintings, how amazing was that?

Now he lifts the book on the top of the stack beside his paint table—a place of honor, where he keeps it because he so often refers to it. It gives him faith and confidence that there is someone who thinks like he does. He flips pages until he finds the particular painting that was just on the screen, *By the Sea*, 1961. He never could figure out why the artist called it that, because no matter how hard he looks, he cannot see even a hint of the sea. It must be some kind of joke. But the words are clear—*red, yellow, blue*—and then, in the lowest quadrant, it's like the artist has merged all the words on top of one another so they are impossible to read and yet he can read them all at once. He figures that the artist, his blood brother, his idol, must have gotten confused or angry and painted all the words over and over one another like that, and it makes his heart ache with love for him, and he wishes he could tell him that it's okay, that he understands his frustration.

He hurries back to the couch, to the television show, and to Kate, who is saying "Thank you and good night," and feels depressed that it is over so soon, and that there is nothing more about his soul mate, and then something even more amazing happens, but it is so fast that he isn't sure it actually occurred.

Can it be? He squints at the screen. *Did I really see it?*

And then it happens again.

Her hair, chestnut.

Oh my God!

Just a flicker that burns bright and dies in an instant, but he sees it for sure this time—her hair, in color. He did not imagine it.

He leans forward, nerve endings tingling, and rubs his eyes, which are so tired from staying up all night and working all day on his paintings and then watching too much TV. Are they playing tricks on him?

"Join me next week," says Kate. "When my guest will be . . ." But her hair's gone black again and now there is some older guy, barefoot, sitting in a really big studio surrounded by huge gray paintings, and the guy is talking to her, the art *her-story-n,* saying something about how color is "everything," and he wishes he could reach into the TV set and grab the guy around the throat and squeeze until—

There it is again! My God! Her hair *is* chestnut, and her eyes are blue!

He stares at the screen, but the moment has faded.

He falls back against the beat-up cushions of his beat-up couch, breathing hard. *What's going on?*

How can he possibly wait until her next show? He thinks about what just happened—her chestnut hair and blue eyes, then shuts off the TV and sits surrounded by the semidarkness that envelops him like the embraces he has always wanted and never received, and concentrates on her, the art *her-story-n*—and her beautiful, miraculous chestnut hair and blue blue eyes.

He snatches up a handful of crayons, thinks that maybe he will see them as he used to, but no, nothing.

A memory: His first box of crayons. It was from their wrappers that he first began to understand the concept of words—*red, yellow, blue, green*—and from Holly, the fifteen-year-old girl who lived with them for a while, who would sit with him sometimes, sniffing Duco Cement glue and reading the names off the crayon labels, particularly the exotic-sounding ones she liked the best—*wild watermelon, hot chartreuse,* and *hot magenta*—and wait until he repeated them, then clap her hands and tell him how smart he was when he was right.

He smiles until he remembers finding Holly on their bathroom floor with a needle in her arm and foam bubbling out of her mouth.

But he doesn't want to think about the past. He wants to focus on the present. And the future.

He thinks about last night. Up in the Bronx. When he was selecting the next one. What patience he had, watching her all night, getting in and out of cars, then following her in the very early morning hours, when it wasn't quite light. He could have taken her then, but that wasn't the plan. He'll be back. With the boy's painting. That's the plan.

He glances up, his eyes perfectly adjusted to the dim light, focusing on the painting he made at the dark-haired boy's apartment. How vibrant it had been, bright painful scarlet and sad dark plum; how much it had resembled the Soutines and Francis Bacon and de Kooning paintings—like innards and guts themselves—though they don't look it anymore. Maybe next time, when he watches her show, it will happen again—the miracle—and he'll look at all his wonderful reproductions and see them as they were; as they are.

He reaches out and runs his fingers over the black TV screen, picking up electric static and pictures her, the art *her-story-n,* then coils his body into a fetal position, sticks his thumb into his mouth, and like a baby with a bottle begins to make soft sucking noises.

Kate was quoting the color theorist Johannes Itten when a Jasper Johns painting she had used to illustrate a point flashed onto the screen. She'd almost forgotten. Now it brought back the image of those two Bronx paintings. But a moment later Josef Albers's *Homage to the Square* painting of concentric green squares replaced it.

"Hey, that's one of the paintings I chose for you," said Nola. "I even found Albers's notes on the green pigments he used and mixed. Let's see . . . viridian, phthalocyanine green, and I think Hooker's green—no question my favorite paint name, ever."

Kate looked at Nola. "What did you just say about Albers?"

"You mean about the way he mixed the various greens?"

"No, the color names?"

"You mean viridian, phthalocyanine, and Hooker's green?"

"Yes." What was it she was trying to get at? *Phthalocyanine green. Viridian.* The serious, technical names manufacturers gave to oil paints.

That was it. They didn't give their pigments names like wild watermelon or raspberry. "Wild watermelon," said Kate aloud.

"Excuse me?"

"Wild watermelon. I was just wondering where I'd find a color with that name. Maybe on one of those little swatches that interior decorators use?"

"Crayolas," said Nola.

"Crayolas? Like crayons, you mean?"

"Yeah. I pretty much know most of those names by heart." Nola closed her eyes. "Sky blue, goldenrod, mulberry."

"And wild watermelon?"

"I think that was in the box of seventy-two colors—along with hot magenta, blizzard blue, and razzmatazz." Nola shook her head. "No, actually I think razzmatazz came out a little later, in the box of eighty colors."

Razzmatazz. The word flickered in Kate's memory. "What's razzmatazz?"

"Kind of a red-violet, sort of what Alizarin crimson is to oil paint."

Crayon names. What on earth did that mean? Were they dealing with a kid?

Kate stared at the TV screen, her face reduced to color pixels, mouth moving. Lost in thought, she had stopped listening to what she was saying.

SEVENTEEN

Kate crossed her legs, and Mitch Freeman's eyes followed them. "Crayola color names?"

"The words under the paint," said Kate. "Grange is faxing Quantico to see what Cryptology makes of it. But I'm wondering what you think." She glanced into Freeman's blue-gray eyes, then quickly away, took in his small FBI Manhattan office, bookshelves sagging, psychiatric journals and more books stacked on the floor, the place a bit disheveled, somewhat like the FBI shrink himself, but comforting.

"My first thought? Arrested development."

"Almost as if we're dealing with a kid," said Kate.

"Or just immature, stunted, someone beyond adult rules and conventions."

The words of Herbert Bloom, the owner of the Gallery of Outsider Art, resonated in Kate's brain: *Living by their own rules, culturally isolated, disturbed.*

"Here's a question for you." Freeman slid his reading glasses into place. "Does the fact that he uses crayon names mean we're looking for an amateur?"

"Not necessarily. There are mature artists who use crayons in their drawings and paintings, but"—Kate paused, pushed her hair behind her ears—"I don't know any who write the names of the colors in before they paint them. That's what seems amateurish, why I keep labeling him an *outsider*."

"And an exhibitionist. After all, he leaves his paintings behind for everyone to see."

"Maybe."

"You don't agree?"

"All artists want to show their work publicly. It doesn't necessarily make them exhibitionists." Kate's fingernails were tapping out something that sounded like John Philip Sousa. "But this guy definitely wants attention, and wants us to know he's an artist."

"He's looking for some sort of approval, and possibly recognition," said Freeman.

"Right." Kate stopped tapping a moment, an idea forming in her mind, perhaps a way to get to this guy.

"So what have we got?" Freeman sat back in his chair and ticked off points on his fingers. "One, he eviscerates the bodies. Two, he's obsessed with art. Three, he brings his paintings to crime scenes. Four, he writes and identifies everything with those Crayola names. Five—"

"Hold on. The fact that this guy needs to identify everything, why is that?"

"Obsessive-compulsive?"

"Possibly. But I was thinking it's almost like he doesn't know. That little kid thing again." Kate shook her head. "Damn. I feel we're missing something basic, but . . . what?"

"Don't think so hard. You'll get it." Freeman sat forward. "We just have to figure out what's driving him."

"It's got to be in those paintings." Kate glanced at her watch. "Come on. Dr. Ernst is on his way."

He jerks awake, wipes away a bit of spittle that he has drooled onto his chin while he slept. It's time. He can feel it. The way Coke is it and Tom knows Jerry, and how Jessica always solves the crime.

He puts some drops in his eyes. He has to take care of them, now more than ever—with the miracle beginning.

For such a long time all he thought about was closing his eyes.

Forever. Of dying. But now there is something to live for and it's all thanks to her, the art *her-story-n*.

He glances at the newspaper: the San Remo, on Central Park West. Where the art *her-story-n* lives. How nice of them to provide the information.

He knows Central Park well, has spent some time there, earned a little cash on its less traveled paths.

He should go again. See where she lives. See if he is right about her hair color. But how will he know for sure, unless . . .

No! He kicks the paper away, disgusted at himself, at his thoughts. He can't even consider that. Not yet.

He closes his eyes. Just thinking of her, the art *her-story-n,* has made him hard, the need beginning to gnaw away at his insides—and he knows what that means: It's just a matter of time. But right now another girl is waiting and he has to get ready.

He cuts a rectangle out of a roll of primed artist's canvas. Gets his knives ready. Spends time sharpening the serrated one that tends to get dull really easily after cutting through ribs. While he prepares, he chants, "It's all about the work—the work, the work, the work," scuttling around the room as he harvests his tools, chanting as he wraps the knives inside the rectangle of canvas: "The work, the work, the work, the work." He checks the bottle of chloral hydrate, lifts a roll of wide silver duct tape off his paint table and places the two items gingerly beside the knives and canvas. "The work, the work, the work, the work." He selects a couple of long-handled bristle brushes, then stops chanting and stares at the still-life painting he stole from the dark-haired boy, the painting with the mint-green vase on the navy-blue cloth with the three razzmatazz-red apples. He remembers it all perfectly.

He strikes a pose and flexes his impressive biceps. He's been using the weights that Pablo has stored in his place for almost a year now and they have made a big difference. He can no longer afford to be weak.

It was different when it was a frog or mouse or a rat or even a cat. They were easy.

He thinks back.

White room. Doctors. Nurse screaming. The mouse, the one he had killed, cut practically in half with his dull-edged dinner knife. Not so easy. But it worked—the colors. Beautiful. That's when he knew.

An old image—*knife in; black changing to red*—flashes in his brain.

Yes, he remembers it. How could he forget? The first sign of what was to be. Not that he'd recognized it at the time. It was later, after the accident, when he killed the mouse that he remembered, and knew for sure.

Then he went after the cat. A mistake. He'd never use a cat again. It almost took his eye out, which would have been—what was the word that artist had used on the TV show? *Counterproductive.*

He slips on a pair of latex gloves and steps into the one-piece jumpsuit that makes him look like a garage mechanic. Then he slides the brushes, tape, knock-out drops, and knives into the coverall's deep inner pockets, and in one fast stroke zips it up from his crotch to his neck, then wraps his hands around Pablo's barbells and hoists them above his head, his hands trembling slightly, the veins in his muscled arms throbbing.

He is getting better, stronger, and though he is often disappointed and drowning in dark and loathsome feelings, feels filthy and overcome by a desperate hunger, and for absolutely no reason that he can imagine pictures himself alone in a dim room with only the television's flickering synthetic light and all the bits of songs and ads and hollow disconnected voices for company, he can forget them when he is working, and right now he absolutely refuses to think about any of that because he knows it is . . . *counterproductive.*

With the rolled-up canvas and knives in his pockets he feels confident. She is waiting for him. And this time will be the best time. He will see and remember everything.

Dr. Kurt Ernst, tall and reedy, though slightly stooped by age, seventy or more, white haired, thin skin mottled with brownish spots across a broad forehead, was unable to mask his excitement, hands fluttering, adjusting and readjusting his wireless glasses up and down his nose as he moved from one painting to the next.

It was not every day he had the opportunity to see the work of a living homicidal maniac.

Brown had joined Kate and Freeman in the evidence room, where the psycho's paintings, bagged and numbered, but perfectly visible through the plastic, were tacked to the bulletin board.

"The color in them is rather ferocious, but simultaneously childlike," Ernst said, attempting to answer the questions they'd posed. "Of course there is no correlation between mental age and actual chronological age. Your killer could be as young as sixteen or seventeen or substantially older." Ernst's English was a bit formal, slightly accented. "The immature quality in the artwork reflects only the state of his mind's development." He stared at the paintings. "This mix of obsessive doodles with bizarre color is not something I have observed before. Naturally every illness produces its own manifestations." He came in for a close-up, bony nose practically grazing the painting's plastic covering. "Of course the obsessive doodling that occurs in the borders is something one often associates with the work of schizophrenics."

"The repetition," said Freeman, anxious to share his expertise with someone he had studied in the classroom. "And you would make that diagnosis, schizophrenia?"

Ernst peered over his glasses at Freeman. "Yes, schizophrenia is the likely diagnosis, though one can never be absolutely certain." He tilted his angular face at one of the paintings. "Have you deciphered these doodles?"

"They're names," said Kate.

"And have you identified them? That is, are they fictional, or . . . known names. Say, names in the news?"

"Just names," said Freeman.

"They are never *just* names." Ernst lanced a stare at the FBI shrink. "These names have significance. To him. What are the names?"

"We're fairly sure we've identified Tony," said Kate. "Maybe Brenda and possibly Dylan."

"But they're not any of the victims' names," said Freeman, anxious to offer something to restore his image.

"They could be names of loved ones," said Ernst. "Though it is unlikely he has had many loved ones. More likely they are fantasy figures. Often, the mentally ill incorporate their fantasy life into their art." He turned back to the bagged paintings. "But the images themselves are so standard, as if this man is trying to be a real, that is, an academic, painter. Don't you agree, Katherine?"

Kate nodded.

"So you have here a mix in the work . . . in this man: the desire to make a good and standard kind of art and the obsessive scribbling so often seen in the art of the insane." Ernst regarded Kate. "I know you have seen the Prinzhorn collection."

"Just the sampling they showed at the Drawing Center, but I studied Prinzhorn at the Institute." Kate tried to recollect the many drawings and paintings she had seen from the famed psychiatrist's collection, both in person and in the catalog of the work she knew was now housed in Heidelberg—possibly the world's largest collection of art of the insane. Prinzhorn, she remembered, had culled the work from psychiatric hospitals sometime in the late 1800s until around 1933.

"I mention this because Hans Prinzhorn drew comparisons between the art of the insane and the contemporary artist. He believed there were strong connections, such as the way many contemporary artists attempt to tap into their psyches. Of course with the contemporary artist this is a conscious effort, whereas the madman, he or she has no such choice."

"Prinzhorn intended the comparison between insane art and contemporary art as a positive thing, didn't he?" asked Kate.

"Yes," said Ernst. "Though it was used quite perversely by the time Prinzhorn had finished compiling his collection."

"The Nazis," said Kate.

"The Nazis, exactly," said Ernst.

"Degenerate Art," said Kate.

Ernst offered her a sad smile. "You have been studying, Katherine."

Kate blushed slightly. "Not lately, but of course I remember Degenerate Art from school. The Nazi's intent was to draw parallels between the art of the insane and such great artists as Max Beckmann, Egon Schiele, Paul Klee, and groups of modern artists like the futurists, dadaists, expressionists, and members of the German Bauhaus."

"Excuse my ignorance," said Brown. "But I don't know what you're talking about."

"Forgive me, Detective," said Ernst. "Degenerate Art was an enormous exhibition organized by the Nazis that traveled all around the Reich. It began in 1937, in Munich, and from there went to practically every major town and city in Germany. It finally, thankfully, came to an end in 1941. It was enormously popular, and drew huge crowds. And, unfortunately, did its job."

"Which was?" asked Brown.

"To reinforce the layman's conventional fears that modern art was obviously made by madmen." Ernst pulled his reading glasses off and shook his head. "The Nazis' aim was to place the troublesome avant-garde artists in the same arena as the mentally ill."

"So that they could argue euthanasia for those artists," said Kate. "Just as they were planning to do to the insane."

"Precisely," said Ernst. "And many artists who did not flee the Reich were, in fact, sent to camps where several of them perished."

A moment of silence passed.

Brown glanced at the paintings tacked to the walls. "I doubt you'd get an argument from most people if the state urged euthanasia for our psycho."

Ernst regarded Brown coolly. "But what if your *psycho* is acting out totally delusional fantasies, does not even know what he is doing, Detective?"

"Well then, Doctor, let me ask you this," said Brown. "Would you say we are looking for someone insane—or a rational killer?"

Ernst slid his glasses back up his nose and peered at the paintings once again. "Frankly, Detective, I don't see *anything* rational in these paintings."

Y ou're real pretty."

The girl does a little pirouette on her stilettos, and giggles. "Not half as pretty as you, baby."

He digs his hands into his pockets, shrugs, kicks one shoe against the other, a pose he has borrowed from Opie, that kid on Mayberry, or was it from a cartoon? He can't remember. But it doesn't matter. She's bought the act. Sweet little boy in a man's body.

"What's with the shades?" she asks. "You a movie star, or something? Afraid someone might recognize you?"

"Oh, these." He lifts them off—it's night, dark, safe—and tries out his look, a way to mask the squinting, a sort of a wink-thing he's been working on, very 007. "Stirred, not shaken," he says in a deep voice.

She laughs. "Wow, what lashes you've got. Too bad you're not a girl."

He's heard that before, doesn't much care for it, but he won't let it upset him, not now. He sets the shades back in place, asks, "How much?"

"Depends on what you want."

"Well . . ." He peers over the sunglasses and offers another 007 wink. "If you've got a place, I'd sure like to go there."

"It'll cost you."

"I've got a hundred."

"Fine," she says, "but I need it up front."

He reaches for the bills folded in his coverall pocket.

"What's that?"

"Oh. This?" He tugs out a paintbrush. "I'm an artist."

"Really?" she says, without much enthusiasm.

"Maybe I'll paint you someday. I mean, with your carnation-pink skin and goldenrod hair, you like, inspire me."

"Yeah, sure," she says, laughing. "But for the record? My hair color? It's called Frost. Platinum, you know. But what the fuck, you like goldenrod, goldenrod it is."

"Yeah, I like goldenrod. A lot. I also like sunglow and laser lemon."

"Wow. You really are an artist, huh?" She touches her bleached-out hair. "But I guess I should tell you now so you won't be disappointed. I'm not a natural blonde."

"I guess that means I get two colors for the price of one—goldenrod *and* chestnut. That's grrrrrrrrreat!"

The girl trills a laugh.

EIGHTEEN

Floyd Brown raced down the station house corridor. "Call Perlmutter," he shouted to a uniform attempting to keep pace with him. "And tell him to meet me."

Outside, the sky was gray, threatening rain.

Brown slammed the beacon onto the hood of his car and turned the ignition key. *Damn.* A year past retirement, chief of Manhattan's Special Homicide Squad, and still dragging his ass up to the Bronx, his old stomping ground, a place he had never wanted to be in the first place.

Brown backed the Impala out of its angled spot, switched on the siren, adrenaline coursing through his veins almost as fast as he was feeding gas into the engine.

Another murder. Another painting. That's what McNally had said.

There was no getting around it now. This would do it for sure. Full-scale mobilization. More cops. More agents. More pressure from the mayor's office. Brown was certain Tapell would be holding a press conference. She was probably writing her speech right now.

Kate sat beside Perlmutter as he raced the Crown Victoria up to the scene, cars on either side of them blurring while bits and pieces of old cases played in her mind's eye like fragments of a silent movie: Ruby Pringle, her very last case, heels crunching in the gravel around the dumpster, the young girl's discarded body, blue eyes with flat black irises staring up at her; Ruby's face replaced by those sweet blond boys in Long Island City, bound and gagged, bruises on their naked flesh morphing into the autopsy scar peeking out of a stark white sheet covering Richard's body, until the whiteness went gray and Kate realized she was staring blindly at the clouds through the windshield and there were tears on her cheeks, which she swiped away, but not before Perlmutter had seen them.

"You okay?"

"I'm fine." Kate readjusted her vision, regarded the boats in the Hudson, quick studies, sketches, really, blurring past the window.

It was just getting dark when Perlmutter pulled the Crown Victoria beside a couple of Crime Scene vans. It had begun to drizzle and the street lamps painted the rain a sour lemony hue; every few seconds the police car beacons sprayed the street, tenements, and crowd of bystanders bright red; shrill screeching sirens provided the sound track. A scene of almost cinematic beauty. Life imitating art.

"How do they always know?" Perlmutter said to Kate as they passed a couple of newsmen setting up cameras and lights.

Floyd Brown was standing outside the building; Marty Grange, nearby, huddled with Sobieski and Marcusa.

"What's it look like?" asked Perlmutter.

"Our boy, for sure," said Brown.

Marty Grange, skin cast in citrus-yellow from the streetlights, glanced over at Kate, then Brown, a look on his face that said: *What the hell is she doing here?*

"Freeman's inside," said Brown. "Wanted to see one of the crime scenes firsthand, thought maybe it'd help him narrow the profile. Tapell's here too." He sighed. "Go have a look."

Kate and Perlmutter exchanged their shoes for gauze booties, then slipped into lab gowns and plastic gloves. Gold shield in front of his face, Perlmutter made his way past a ring of uniforms and detectives into a tiny foyer, where one of the Crime Scene crew was dusting and a photographer was shooting pictures of bloody handprints on the wall, Kate just behind him. They followed the handprints down a hallway where more techies were dusting and bagging.

Perlmutter was moving faster than Kate, who had slowed down, studying the blood on the wall and floors, reconstructing the scene in her mind, her heart pumping. She turned the corner into the living room. Detectives, couple of uniforms, the tech team, Perlmutter across the room now with Bronx Chief McNally, who was leaning toward Chief of Police Tapell, all of them whispering as if they were in church.

Mitch Freeman was crouched beside them, alternating peeks at the body and the painting—another still life, set up on a cheap metal folding chair. The way he was squinting and swallowing every few seconds, Kate thought he looked like he was fighting hard not to be sick.

Perlmutter seemed to sense it, leaned over, patted the FBI shrink's shoulder.

Near the center of the room lay a woman—or what was left of her—naked except for torn fishnets down around her ankles and bangle bracelets on her wrists. Kate had difficulty identifying much else about her, torso and abdomen split open, an almost perfect circle of dark blood surrounding the body, as if it were floating in black-cherry aspic.

Every few seconds the photographer's strobe bleached the scene a stark shocking white and Kate flinched.

"Looks like this one gave him a run for his money," said Perlmutter, coming across the room. "Crime Scene says she was probably attacked just inside the door, stabbed, but fought, made a run down the hall and was killed in here."

"Yes," said Kate. She had been picturing it from the first bloody handprint she'd seen, every move, the horror movie playing in her mind, the hunter and his prey, that buzzing sensation in the back of her mind humming along.

"Not a break-in," said Brown. "Vic either let him in or brought him home."

A medical examiner hovering over the dead body pulled a thermometer out of a wound while another technician scraped under the victim's fingernails.

Kate turned away. She'd seen more than enough.

Brown nodded solemnly at her, then to one of the Crime Scene guys, who had been huddled over the body. "Any ID?" he asked.

"Name's Mona Johnson. Obvious street pros." The guy handed over a driver's license. One set of gloved fingers to another. "Wallet was on the floor," he said. "Empty except for the Pennsylvania driver's permit."

Brown glanced at the tiny photo, a sweet young face, nothing like the broken painted doll lying on the floor. He noted the birth date, did the math: seventeen.

"No cash in the wallet," said the cop. "Or on the vic. ME is guestimating this went down sometime last night, late, probably toward morning."

Chief of Police Tapell signaled Brown over. "I've scheduled a press conference," she said. Her deep brown skin had lost a little color, was edging toward gray.

"From the look of it, the press have already gotten the story," said Brown.

Tapell pulled at the flesh of her neck. "At least I can reassure the citizens of Manhattan and Queens. The psycho seems to favor the Bronx."

"For now," said Brown.

"Don't even say that." Tapell shot him a look with tired eyes. "You finish up here. We'll speak later. I've gotta talk to the mayor."

Kate avoided looking at the dead girl, her eyes focused on the painting, a still life, nothing spectacular, no shrill color this time.

Behind her, the body was being bagged and tagged for the morgue.

"Look at this," said Kate, signaling Brown and the others over. She pointed at the lower right corner of the painting. "Initials. M.L."

"Jesus," said Brown. "The psycho is signing them?"

"Someone signed it," said Kate. "But not our psycho. This isn't one of his paintings. It's totally different—on a stretcher, no pencil border, and the color is totally normal."

"Could it be another one of Martini's paintings?" asked Grange.

"This is nothing like Martini's work. This one's strictly academic."

"Didn't Dr. Ernst say that was what our unsub was striving for—a good academic painting?" asked Perlmutter.

"Yes. But he hasn't pulled it off before, and I don't think he suddenly could," said Kate. "This painting has been built up slowly, not like Martini, who painted thin, or our Bronx unsub, who paints heavy and directly."

"Meaning?" asked Grange.

Kate slipped her reading glasses on for a closer look. "It's been built up from an underpainting, an old-fashioned technique, one the Italian painters used for centuries. The painter covers the entire canvas with a wash, pigment mixed with a lot of turpentine, usually a burnt sienna or burnt umber—which leaves a stain on the canvas that can be drawn into with a darker sienna or umber, and wiped out with a rag dipped in more turp to create the light areas."

"Sounds complicated," said Perlmutter, inspecting the canvas.

"Just slow. Once the light and darks are dry, the painter simply adds the color on top. Look here." Everyone leaned in. "There are several places where it's still just brownish underpainting—where the artist hasn't put on any real color yet."

"So it's unfinished?" asked Perlmutter.

"Could be," said Kate.

"M.L.," said Brown. "Those initials mean anything to you?"

Kate tried to run them through her art-historical-Rolodex-brain, but came up blank. "No, nothing. But I'm tired."

"So, where do we find the people who teach this underpainting technique?" asked Grange.

"The more traditional art schools." Kate thought a minute. "Parsons, the Studio School, maybe the Art Students League on Fifty-seventh Street. That place has been around since the beginning of time."

NINETEEN

Michelle Lawrence, School of Visual Arts.

Marilyn Lincoln, the Studio School.

Mark Landau, the Art Students League.

Michelle Lawrence and Marilyn Lincoln were questioned by detectives who interrupted art classes, leading each of the young women into similar hallways reeking of turpentine and linseed oil.

Neither of them had recently given away or sold a painting, nor did they recognize the painting left at the latest crime scene the detectives showed them, nor was either of the young women considered a real suspect, as the cops were fairly certain they were looking for a man.

When questioned about boyfriends, Michelle Lawrence started to cry about a recent breakup from her Advanced Painting instructor, Harvey Blittenberg, a man more than three times her age, who was subsequently queried but released when he produced his teaching schedule (mostly night classes), none of which he had missed except when he was in the sack with Michelle and, more recently, after their breakup, in bed with yet another young woman student, who vouched for him. One of the detectives asked what the hell a man of sixty-plus was doing carrying on with his twenty-year-old students, and Blittenberg answered, "Why not?" adding, "God bless Viagra." As Harvey Blittenberg was overweight and balding, the detectives didn't get it; but then, neither detective had ever been a young woman art student in thrall to an older artist teacher—despite the fact that the guy's art career had been pronounced DOA nearly two decades earlier.

According to Mario Fiorelli, the Oil Techniques instructor at the Art Students League, Mark Landau had missed his last two classes. Fiorelli, a seventy-four-year-old native of Orvieto, Italy, trained in the age-old technique of Florentine underpainting—which he had been proudly passing on to his students—was surprised that Landau had not shown up or called, as Landau was, in his words, "a conscientious *studente* and a very pleasant and quiet young man."

Fiorelli identified the painting from the Mona Johnson crime scene as almost certainly a painting made in his class, and very probably the work of Mark Landau.

Within hours, troops were assembled, a squadron of SWAT-trained cops decked out in Kevlar vests and polystyrene hoods. The police were not taking any chances. If Mark Landau was their man, they had to act fast—shock and awe the prescription of the day.

Now, with guns and clubs and Mace and gas, the cops went into formation—three cops at the front entrance, three at the rear fire escape, weapons ready—while the SWAT team leader, a short burly man with iron-heeled combat boots, kicked down the door of Mark Landau's East Village apartment.

A moon landing, that's what it reminded Kate of.

Landau's body was on a slab at the morgue, and Crime Scene had already gone over his place. The Special Crime Scene Unit had been dispatched, and though Brown's murder squad was exhausted, they were all hanging around to see what, if anything, might turn up.

Now Kate and the squad were huddled in the hallway outside of Landau's apartment, all of them crowding around a monitor, angling for a view of the small screen.

Inside, technicians in protective suits and hoods to guard against the UV light from the cathode-ray camera were scoping out the place in search of human fluids that neither the eye nor the normal crime scene chemicals might detect, the camera transmitting its findings directly to the monitor in the hall, its blue light floating over floors and walls, every so often sending up a white flare that would alert one of the suited technicians to scrape a sample for the lab.

When the technicians emerged a half hour later, Kate's eyes were stinging from staring at the screen.

The technician pulled off his hood and goggles. "Plenty of samples," he said. "Might all belong to the vic. But if we're lucky, your unsub is a secretor. We'll freeze 'em up and see what we get, but it'll take a few days."

"We'll need those results to go to Quantico," said Grange, pulling on gloves, and bagging his shoes. He turned to his agents, Marcusa and Sobieski. "Follow up on that."

They nodded in unison.

Kate pulled on gloves too, as did Brown and Perlmutter.

Grange turned toward Kate but spoke to Brown. "Why is she here?"

Kate looked past Grange, at Brown, and answered the question: "*She* is here to examine the victim's paintings."

Grange scowled and thumped into the apartment.

Landau's small apartment was dark, dust motes dancing drunkenly in the air, walls crowded with paintings, more stacked against baseboards, one on an easel.

Kate took in the half-finished still life on the easel. "There's the same kind of underpainting here as in the crime scene painting," she said to Brown. "Let's bag one to be sure."

The room was warm, but Kate was shivering. She moved from one painting to another, careful to step around dark bloodstains on the floor.

They had all viewed photos of the crime scene, the butchery performed on Mark Landau's body. But it was his face that lingered in Kate's mind, sweet, young, like so many runaways she'd chased after back in Astoria. She was thinking that right now what she wanted most was to find the creep who had done this and do him some damage. Funny, she thought, what it took to galvanize her; what it took to make her want to catch this creep as much as she wanted to find the person responsible for Richard's murder—an equation she hadn't ever thought possible. A kid. That's what it took. It was always the kids that got to her.

"Have Landau's classmates at the Art Students League been checked out?" asked Perlmutter.

"Doubtful he'd hunt someone so close," said Grange. "Doesn't jibe with the MO. More likely, the killer's a stranger who ingratiated himself with the victim. Came back with him to his apartment, killed him, took the painting."

"Detectives from General have been interviewing every kid and instructor," said Brown. "One girl from Landau's class says she talked to a guy who was outside the building that day, sketching. Girl says the guy wasn't a regular. She'd never seen him before."

"Description?" asked Perlmutter.

Brown referred to his notes. "Twenties. good-looking. Her exact words: 'So cute.' " Brown frowned. "They put her together with a sketch artist, but she couldn't decide if his face was long or round, and no distinguishing characteristics, except that he was wearing sunglasses."

"Anyone else see this guy?"

"So far, no," said Brown.

Kate said: "So the killer steals one of Landau's paintings to use at one of his crime scenes and to throw us off."

"Almost worked—and it certainly wasted our time. Means our unsub is aware of us now, playing with us." Gloom clouded Brown's features. "The really sick ones always like an audience."

"But why kill the kid?" asked Kate, trying to keep the emotion out of her voice. "Couldn't he have gotten a painting without killing him?"

"Sure, he could," said Brown. "But he likes the killing part. Needs it too."

Kate thought about that, an idea forming.

"According to the coroner's prelims"—Perlmutter referred to his notes—"time of death is sometime after Landau's last class at the League. So it's a good guess the killer picked him up near the school."

"*Chose* him, more likely," said Brown. "He got himself a victim and a painting all rolled into a neat package."

"Poor kid," said Perlmutter.

Agent Sobieski shrugged his cocky shoulders, and said, "One less faggot."

Brown trained his eyes on him, said, "That was inappropriate." He glanced at Perlmutter, then quickly away. But Kate caught it.

"Sort of reduces your chances for a date this Saturday night, doesn't it, Sobieski?" she said.

The guy's face turned red, but he didn't say anything.

Nicky Perlmutter stripped off his latex gloves as though he'd been contaminated by the scene, and stalked out of the room.

W hy would she do that? Try to hurt him?
      Come on, baby, make it hurt so good . . .
Didn't she understand that he needed to know? Maybe he should have waited until they were in bed and she was more vulnerable. But he couldn't. The walk to her place had gotten him too excited.

He stands in the small bathroom, stares into the cracked mirror above the small two-faucet sink, runs his fingers oh-so-tenderly over the scratches on his face. The mirror's jagged fissure bisects his face—divides his forehead, zigzags through an eye, along the right side of his nose, over his lips—to create two faces from one.

He blinks at his fractured face, the diagonal scratches along his left cheekbone, which he imagines to be shocking pink or maybe wild strawberry, and begins to probe, pick at them with his fingernails, gouging deeper, opening wounds so that now slender rivulets of blood follow the contours of his face—down his cheek, rounding his jaw, splattering like ruby raindrops onto the chipped porcelain sink.

For a moment he actually saw it: a flash of maroon. *Oh, God! Yes!*

But seconds later, when he looks again, the sink is merely covered with ebony droplets, his cheek streaked with gray. He turns the cold-water tap, stares as inky whirlpools swirl around the basin and down the drain.

Still, it was a sign.

He glances up at his bisected face in the cracked mirror, throws icy water on his bleeding cheek, which only now has begun to throb.

He replays the chase in his mind. No way she could escape him, not with the lights out. Her feebly groping her way down the hall, while he was fast and sure, his night vision sharp.

He flexes a muscle, checks it in the mirror, the swelling flesh, veins that run through it, thinks he can detect the slightest trace of apricot, or maybe a hint of tickle-me-pink just under the pale gray.

Oh yeah, things are changing. *Ch-ch-ch-ch-changes . . .*

He thinks of the girl's hair. Definitely goldenrod. Maybe he should have tried to paint her. But he did, in a way.

This time had been good. He saw. He learned. Had not forgotten. He checked the painting at the right moment and saw that he had remembered it perfectly—the mint-green vase on a navy-blue cloth with three razzmatazz-red apples. Exactly as he'd seen it the first time in the boy's apartment.

Even now, when he gazes at the piece of canvas that he has tacked to the wall, his most recent painting, he swears there is a magenta hue just visible in the wild finger painting he had created with the girl's blood— and it all began with her, the art *her-story-n,* Kate, with her chestnut hair and blue blue eyes.

The Donna-voice says, "I don't think her eyes are blue. I think they're green."

"You're wrong, Donna. They're blue. They have to be."

Are they? Aren't they? He tries to remember. He once knew, didn't he?

Maybe he's just tired. He lays his head onto the arm of the beat-up couch to rest, but a song clicks in. *Wake me up before you go-go . . .*

No way he can sleep.

He needs to work awhile, paint, no matter how tired he is, because he wants to impress her.

He selects one of his older, recently finished paintings, a still life, checks to see if the paint has dried, then gets his pencils and sharpener ready and starts to write the familiar names over and over, Brenda, Brandon, Donna, Dylan, and Tony, and then, without even realizing he is doing it, he starts a new name—Katherine McKinnon Rothstein—a bit crudely at first, but soon it flows—*Katherine McKinnon Rothstein, Katherine McKinnon Rothstein, Katherine McKinnon Rothstein*—until, like the other names, it becomes nothing more than a scribble, a blur, written over and over itself, the pencil point wearing down often, the only time he stops is to sharpen it, while he writes her name again and again, creating a lovely graphite gray border for his painting. It makes sense that she should be part of the work, and while he scribbles, an idea comes to him—a way to let her know. *Yes. She has to know. Has to remember.*

With his pencil he draws the tiniest pictures into the few open spaces in his painting, and puts it aside, certain now that Kate will know him.

After he finishes he switches on the TV, and is happy to see Ricki Lake and cheers along with her audience at some fat girl who is on stage with Ricki next to some hulking guy with pimples on his face, who is crying. But it starts to make him sad and he switches to cartoons.

His eyelids begin to droop, fatigue finally settling in. He folds himself into a corner of the couch, and there, spotlit in the tender luminescent glow of the TV screen, thumb in his mouth, legs curled under him, he looks like nothing more than a sad scared little boy with scarlet scratches on his cheek. He giggles at the cartoons, prays the miracle will happen again so that he can see them in color, thinks about Central Park and the famous landmark building, the San Remo. Soon he must see if he remembers correctly—if the art *her-story-n*'s eyes are blue or green.

TWENTY

Brown plunked an assortment of folders onto the conference table, waited until the others were seated. There were dark circles under his eyes. "We've just topped a hundred in the call-ins and drop-ins claiming to be our Bronx unsub. Unfortunately, none of them had the details right." He sighed. "As for the recent vic, Landau, no fluid links yet. Lab's trying to work up a DNA from the scraping samples."

"If your lab doesn't come up with something ASAP, I'm gonna push for Quantico to take over completely," said Grange. He looked over at his agents, Marcusa and Sobieski, who were leaning against the back wall, quietly taking notes.

"Fine." Brown was in no mood to buck up against the agent. He distributed papers around the conference table. "Medical examiner's report on our dead artist, Leonardo Martini." He waited until everyone was with him—Kate, Perlmutter, Grange. "Bruises on the neck indicate fingers digging into flesh like someone held Martini by the throat."

"While they stuck the gun in his mouth?" said Perlmutter.

"Possible," said Brown. "There was more bruising, bleeding under the skin, on Martini's lower back, possibly a couple of kidney punches." He flipped a page. "No record of Martini owning a gun, or at least he hadn't registered the one found in his hand. ME is calling it suspicious."

Brown flipped another page. "Check out Toxicology, page three. Traces of Valium and chloral hydrate in Martini's system. Not enough to cause bodily injury, but enough to sedate him. No pill vial was found in Martini's medicine cabinet and no prescription on record at his local CVS. Add that to the two point one alcohol count in his bloodstream and it would have been difficult for the guy to fight anyone off."

"So we know two things," said Grange. "One, that Martini did the Midtown painting, and two, that he was probably murdered."

"Maybe for doing that painting," said Kate. "We've got a down-and-out artist, right? Someone—and I'm guessing, but let's say shady Mr. Baldoni, his employer at the copy shop—comes to him with an innocent-enough request: paint a painting. Martini's happy to do it. He needs the cash. But later, he finds out what the painting was used for and he's no longer so happy."

"And it wouldn't have been difficult for him to find out," said Perlmutter. "The painting was described in the newspapers."

"Right," said Kate, trying to catch Perlmutter's eye. He hadn't given her a direct look since they had been at Mark Landau's East Village apartment. She turned back to Grange. "Okay, so now Martini thinks he can get even more money, so he tries blackmailing Baldoni, and whammo, that's the end of him."

"Your boys get a lead on Angelo Baldoni yet?" Brown asked Grange.

"Nada. Complete disappearing act. Copy shop's closed down. Home address is sketchy. Guy moved around a lot. Naturally, did not pay his taxes like a good boy." Grange turned to Kate. "Just out of curiosity. There any reason you can think of why a guy with mob connections, a suspected hit man, would want your husband dead? You see why I gotta ask."

Grange's words hit her like the flu, but Kate took a deep breath, straightened in her chair, and locked her gaze on Grange. "As you may or may not know, Mr. Grange . . . Excuse me, *Agent* Grange, Richard was a man of considerable influence, and therefore not without enemies. He also worked for the mayor's office—the previous mayor—pro bono, assisting in a variety of capacities, and often conferring with the DA's office. I suspect there were plenty of disgruntled felons who would have been very happy to see him . . ." She swallowed. "Dead." Kate's heart was racing, but she kept her eyes glued to Grange. She was trying hard to believe her own words.

Grange's tone was flat. "We should get a list together of possible felons who might be pissed off enough to kill your husband." He turned to his agents, said, "Get on that." Sobieski continued taking notes, carefully avoiding everyone's eyes. Grange said to Brown, "Maybe it's better if your squad concentrates on the Bronx psycho and we handle the Midtown case from here on in."

Kate should have expected this, the Midtown case, Richard's case, being taken away from them, the feds taking over. She just wished she hadn't helped by giving them ammunition.

Brown looked at Kate, then Grange. "Can't do that. Chief of Police Tapell wants us on it—at least for now."

For the life of him Grange could not understand why the NYPD chief wanted McKinnon on this case so badly, but he made a mental note to find out. "Okay," he said. "But anything to do with Baldoni, you refer to me and my agents."

Brown nodded, reached for another folder, slid out a series of black-and-white photos, and laid them onto the conference table. "Courtesy of Special Investigation and a telephoto lens. Looks like you were right, McKinnon, about having a tail put on Stokes."

The photos, marked with the date and time, showed Stokes leaving his Midtown office building, hailing a cab, picking up a hooker in the Bronx, taking her to a transient hotel, and coming out a half hour later.

Perlmutter plucked the photo of Stokes going into the transient hotel off the table and squinted at it. "Street sign says Zerega Avenue."

"Home to our first vic, Suzie White," said Brown.

Kate's mind was spinning. *Andy Stokes, Richard's assistant, in the Bronx with a hooker? Was there a connection between the two cases?* She had another thought: If the two cases were connected, then Grange would not be able to keep her off Richard's case. "We've got to show these pictures to Rosita Martinez. Maybe the landlady can ID Stokes as the guy who was seeing Suzie White on a regular basis."

"And don't forget Lamar Black," said Perlmutter. "Let's see if Stokes rings any bells with him."

"Don't much care for a pimp's opinion," said Grange.

"Fine," said Brown. "You don't have to talk to him."

"What about Stokes?" asked Perlmutter.

"Sent uniforms the minute I saw these pictures. Not home. Not at the office. Secretary hasn't seen him since yesterday, and his wife says he didn't come home last night. Says she was about to report him missing."

Kate's thoughts continued to race: *Stokes and Suzie White? Angelo Baldoni? Were they connected?*

"Anyone check out the hooker?" asked Perlmutter, tapping the surveillance photo.

"We'll find her," said Brown.

"I'm trying to remember if Andy Stokes has a country place, you know, a weekend house, somewhere he might hide out?" said Kate.

Brown checked some notes. "According to his wife, they sold their place in Bridgehampton six months ago. No replacement. Just the apartment on East Seventy-second." Brown turned to Kate. "Maybe if you talked to her, woman-to-woman, wife-to-wife, sort of thing?"

He didn't have to ask. Kate had decided that was her next move. She was already up, heading toward the door.

"Anything you get from the wife you report back to me," said Brown. "You got that?"

"Sure," said Kate. "But I wouldn't count on a whole lot. I hardly know Noreen Stokes."

G range laid one of his beefy mitts on Brown's arm. "Hold on a sec." He watched the door shut behind Kate, waited another minute for Perlmutter to leave.

"What?" said Brown. He did not like the look in the agent's dark eyes.

Grange nodded at Marcusa and Sobieski, indicated the door, hesitated another moment until they were gone. "Something we gotta talk about."

"Yeah?"

"It's not like I want to be a turd in the punch bowl, or anything, but . . . if Rothstein's murder *was* a hit, you know the procedure. First place you look, the spouse."

Laughter sputtered out of Floyd Brown's mouth. *"McKinnon?"* He waved the comment off with a dismissive hand. "You don't know what you're talking about."

Grange's features hardened. "You think you know everything about that marriage? You know, say, if Rothstein was banging his secretary and McKinnon found out, or—"

"I know McKinnon. And I knew her husband. You're way off base."

Grange sighed. "Look, there's nothing I'd like better than for you to be right. All I'm suggesting is we check it out—phone records, talk to a few friends—"

"Forget it," said Brown.

"Sorry. But it's my job *not* to forget it. It's my job, and *your* job, to check out everything." Grange's dark eyes looked like black marbles. "You know, I didn't have to say anything to you. I don't need your permission. I'm trying to work with you."

Oh sure you are. Brown took a deep breath and let it out slowly. "You mind telling me why McKinnon would want to cut off her money supply?"

"How about life insurance? Rothstein had a five-mil policy."

"I guarantee you Rothstein was worth more to McKinnon alive."

"Maybe," said Grange. "But there could be extenuating circumstances, like I said—another woman, another man, maybe they hated each other, for all you know."

"McKinnon is here helping us with the case, for Christ's sake. You want to tell me why would she do that?"

Grange trained his marble eyes on Brown. "Could be perceived as the perfect cover."

"I *asked* her to come on board."

"The way I heard it, you asked her to consult on the Bronx case, and that was *before* her husband was killed."

Brown sucked in air. "McKinnon was the first to point out that the painting found at her husband's crime scene was different, that it was *not* the work of our unsub. Why would she do that when she had the perfect cover for her husband's murder by simply leaving it alone? If McKinnon came on the case to keep an eye on things, or keep us off track, she could have lied, she could have said all three paintings were the work of the same painter and left it at that."

"McKinnon's a clever woman."

"Meaning?"

"Meaning she's clever is all." Grange's lips tightened. "It does not please me to have to do this, but everything and everyone has to be checked out."

"When it makes sense."

"I'm simply doing my job." Grange tapped Baldoni's file. "We have a suspect linked to organized crime—a man the federal government believes may be responsible for at least a half dozen contract murders."

"Mob murders," said Brown. "Not wives and husbands hiring him to kill their spouses."

"Well, we don't really know why Richard Rothstein was murdered, do we?" Grange folded his thick hands calmly in front of him. "But I intend to find out."

TWENTY-ONE

The Stokeses' apartment had an uninspired decorator look, taupe ultrasuede on the couch and dining room chairs, a lighter version for the curtains, an almost identical shade picked up in the rugs, and a slightly paler taupe on the walls, which were dotted with pastel-colored landscape paintings, American impressionist, not first-rate, but Kate recognized a few of the second-tier names, and knew they had been far from cheap.

Andy and Noreen Stokes lived in one of those semi-fancy Upper East Side high-rise buildings between Madison and Park; like their art collection, it was not exactly A-one, but pricey. Kate took in the view from the fortieth floor, mostly buildings, a tiny swatch of Central Park, but plenty of sky, which came at a premium in Manhattan. She was a bit surprised—she didn't think Andy Stokes earned enough money to support the lifestyle.

On a smaller wall, dividing the living room from the dining, were a half dozen landscape and still-life paintings. Kate went over for a closer look. The drawing wasn't very good, the color a bit garish.

"Andrew's hobby," said Noreen.

Kate looked again. The color was off, but not as extreme as the Bronx paintings. Still, they made her uncomfortable. "You have no idea where Andy might be?" she asked.

"No. I've called all of his friends. I really can't imagine. I even tried the hospitals." Noreen Stokes wore a floor-length pinkish-taupe robe that matched the room so well her head and hands seemed detached. She was a small, plain woman with fine brown hair and skin so translucent that the purplish network of veins at her temples and beneath her eyes showed through, giving her a fragile, almost breakable look. "I'm *terribly* worried," she added, though there was little emotion in her voice.

If it were Richard who was missing, thought Kate, she'd be pacing and smoking, barely coherent. The thought stopped her cold: Richard *was* missing. She suddenly envied Noreen Stokes with an absent husband who could reappear. "Do you mind if I sit down?" she asked.

Noreen Stokes gestured toward the taupe couch. "Can I get you anything?"

"If it were later in the day I'd be begging for a tall Scotch, but no thanks." Kate forced a laugh, which helped fortify the charade of well-being she was playing. "Forgive me for asking, but has Andy ever done something like this before? Disappear, I mean?"

Noreen Stokes looked at Kate, one of those purple veins throbbing beneath her eye, lips slightly parted, about to speak, but she stopped, folded herself into an armchair, and sat very still. "No," she said. "Of course not."

Kate studied the woman's face, wondering how this rather plain, fragile woman had ended up with Andy Stokes, who, by superficial standards, must have been considered a catch. "I'm sorry, I didn't know Andy well. I'm afraid I had very little to do with Richard's business. He didn't like me interfering. Men and work—boys with their toys, you know."

"I suppose you're right about that." Noreen Stokes found a loose thread at the sleeve of her robe and wove it around one of her fingers.

"I mean, my God, trying to get anything out of Richard, well . . ." Kate felt the strain in her performance, but was trying to find a way, any way, to bond with the woman. "I can't tell you how many times I'd awaken at three in the morning, discover he wasn't home, frantically call his office, and he'd be like, 'Oh, sorry, I guess I lost track of the time.'" Kate sighed deeply to mask the pain of talking about Richard. "Do they ever think of *us?*" she added.

"Andrew would often stay away . . . for days, but—" Noreen Stokes stopped abruptly, catching herself, that loose thread now so tightly wrapped it was turning her index finger white.

"I thought you said he hadn't disappeared before?"

"That's not . . . what I meant. He stayed away, that is, he'd go off on a trip and . . . forget to call . . . like you said." She appeared to be holding her breath.

"I see," said Kate. "Did Andy say if he was happy working for Richard?"

"Why do you ask that?"

Kate sighed, suddenly exhausted, no longer able to play games. "Look, Noreen, I'm just trying to figure out what happened to my husband. The same as you are."

Noreen Stokes slowly began to unwind the thread from her tortured finger. "Andy hasn't had a particularly easy time with his chosen profession. I often wonder if perhaps he's gone into the wrong field entirely. I suppose he was happy enough at your husband's firm. I know he certainly preferred it over that stuffy place, Smith, Henderson, and—"

"Tighton?" Kate tried to remember what it was Richard had called the place.

"Yes, that's it."

"Richard had a problem with that firm too, so I'm not surprised if Andy did." Kate offered her a warm smile.

"Really? Well, Andy wasn't there very long. I'm afraid that my husband has had a succession of jobs, but—it's old news, the jobs. This couldn't possibly be of any help to you. Andrew said I shouldn't say—" Noreen stopped, slid her hands, which were shaking, underneath her thighs.

"Say *what?* Look, Noreen, anything you can tell me that might help find your husband could be helpful." She locked eyes with the woman. "You do want to find him, don't you?"

"What a thing to say." Noreen sat up straighter, posture rigid as an Egyptian statue, the only part of her moving that purplish vein pulsating under her eye.

Kate waited, but clearly Noreen Stokes wasn't talking. The air in the room thickened; the ticking of the antique clock on the wall grew louder; the smell of Noreen's gardenia perfume was almost overwhelming. Kate suddenly wanted out. "Well, then. If there's nothing else you can tell me, I should be going."

"Yes," said Noreen Stokes, sitting perfectly still. "You should."

O utside, the temperature had turned colder, letting New Yorkers know what winter had in store for them.

Kate leaned against a mailbox, taking deep breaths of the cool, damp air. Playing the role, talking about Richard, had taken a toll. She pulled out a Marlboro.

Oh, Richard. Tell me what happened. Please.

Just across the street was a tiny bistro she and Richard had frequented and the sight of it made her heart ache. *A missing husband.* Noreen Stokes had no idea how lucky she was. Kate watched the wind tear her cigarette smoke into small gray rags, and tried to concentrate on what had just transpired, if she had learned anything. One thing for sure: Noreen Stokes was lying. The woman knew where her husband was, Kate was certain of it. Would it make sense to take her down to the station, try to intimidate her into giving him up? Kate had the urge to race right back up to the fortieth floor and drag Noreen out—but she knew that wouldn't work. A decade as a cop had taught her to read people as well as any therapist, and the way she was reading Noreen Stokes was that this was a woman who was going to continue to lie for her husband.

Kate pictured Noreen Stokes winding that thread around her finger, and replayed the conversation.

Andrew would often stay away for days . . . Perhaps gone into the wrong field . . . He didn't stay very long at his last job . . .

His last job.

T he small bronze plaque beside the door was discreet, not much larger than a man's ID bracelet: Smith, Henderson, Jenkins & Tighton.

The reception area looked like an Old World men's club, all dark wood and leather with a hint of expensive tobacco in the air, which Kate assumed had been pumped into the room, or perhaps simply oozed out of the pores of the aging Yalies who worked here.

"Mr. Smith's secretary will be out to fetch you in a moment." The receptionist's accent was pure Katharine Hepburn. "Do have a seat."

Kate melted into one of the plush leather couches. She was exhausted. If she shut her eyes she thought she could be asleep in a minute. She forced herself to peruse the newspapers and magazines arranged on a low oak table— *Forbes, Business Week, American Law Journal*—and was just reaching for *The Wall Street Journal,* anything to keep awake, when Mr. Smith's secretary, another Brit, or trying to be, this one in her sixties with starched gray hair and a matching suit buttoned to her throat, fetched her. Kate followed the suit through a succession of hallways painted a cool pewter, decorated with hunting scenes and antique political cartoons. Now Kate remembered how Richard had always referred to one of the oldest, most distinguished firms in the city—Smith, Henderson, Jenkins and *Tight Ass.*

Chase Smith, closing in on seventy, tall, distinguished, gray, obviously hand-tailored shirt showing off the fact that he was fit, gave Kate a handshake that left her fingers tingling.

"Terribly sorry about your husband," he said, chin jutting, teeth clenched in perfect Locust Valley lockjaw. "He was a credit to the bar."

"Yes. Thank you." Kate couldn't tell if there was any irony in the man's statement, but probably not—she didn't know many WASPs who *did* irony.

"You mentioned over the phone that you wanted to speak about Andrew Stokes," he said, getting right to the point. "And I just spoke with Chief Brown, as you suggested." Smith indicated a small leather love seat behind Kate, waited until she was seated, then folded himself into the matching leather chair behind his desk.

"Can you tell me why Andrew Stokes left your firm?" asked Kate, equally to the point.

"We were forced to let him go. Stokes became, shall we say, a tad too chummy with one of his clients."

"An affair?"

"Oh, no, that's not what I meant." Smith stroked his tightly set jaw as if it ached. "Our firm was court-appointed to defend a Mr. Giulio Lombardi. Not exactly our kind of client."

Kate nodded. *Giulio Lombardi. Angelo Baldoni's uncle.* "I know the name."

"Yes, in his own way, Mr. Lombardi is famous, or should I say *infamous*." Smith ran his hands up and down his suspenders. "I'm certain you know how it is with court appointments, not much one can do about them, though naturally none of us wanted to touch the case. I must admit that we may have foisted the case off on Stokes because he was relatively new here, and because, well, truthfully, he hadn't shown much talent. But he surprised us. He actually did quite well. He got Lombardi off. We were all rather amazed, thought perhaps we had underrated Stokes. But getting a client off is one thing, fraternizing is quite another."

"Fraternizing?"

Smith's tight jaw twitched. "It appeared that Stokes had struck up a friendship with Lombardi. One of our associates saw the two of them in a Midtown bar on more than one occasion, drinking and laughing. Most inappropriate. And this was weeks after the case. At first, we let it go, hoping it was a celebration for winning the case, but I have to confess I asked the associate to keep an eye on Stokes. One can't be too careful, you understand."

"Absolutely. I couldn't agree with you more," said Kate, who had developed a severe case of lockjaw herself.

Smith smiled, teeth clenched. "Well, the associate reported back that Stokes and Lombardi continued to meet, often in the company of"—he cleared his throat—"a certain kind of woman, if you know what I mean." His eyes slid off Kate's and looked away. "The point is, our firm was appointed to represent the one case only, and that should have been that. We certainly did not want Lombardi as a client."

"And you made your position clear?"

"I certainly did, though Stokes actually had the gall to argue with me. Can you believe it? He felt that Lombardi would be a profitable client, said that he was courting the man. Naturally, I explained this was not something we desired, and I assumed Stokes understood me. But I was mistaken. This friendship apparently continued." He sniffed. "I'm certain you can appreciate that we could not allow this to go on. We have a reputation here." He sat up tall and proud, and Kate waited for the Yale cheer.

"Indeed you do."

"I'm afraid we had no choice but to let Stokes go. A law firm, particularly one with a clientele like ours, cannot be too careful. For one of our attorneys to be fraternizing with such a person was simply out of the question."

"How did Stokes take the dismissal?"

"Well, what could he do?" Smith seemed to consider something for a moment, then whispered, "There was something else that came out about Stokes, and—"

"Yes?"

"Well, it turned out that we were not the only ones checking up on him." Smith spread his hands onto his desk and leaned forward. "There was a detective, a private eye, if you will, on his tail as well. A man named, um . . ." Smith closed his eyes a moment. "Baume."

"Like the watch?"

"Yes."

Kate glanced at the sleek stainless-steel number on her wrist, a Baume et Mercier *Linea*. Richard had presented her with the exclusive Geneva company's *Gala* on her last birthday—a white-gold-and-diamonds number, which she knew cost a small fortune. She'd exchanged it for the more modest *Linea* at a fifth of the price and had Richard donate the remainder of the money to Let There Be a Future, where it could actually do something other than spell out the time in diamonds—an embarrassment no matter how you looked at it. Kate rested her hand on Smith's for a brief moment and looked into his pale blue eyes. "Do you happen to know who hired the private investigator, Mr. Smith?"

"Oh, yes," said Smith. "It was the wife. Andrew Stokes's wife."

Lamar Black had no intention of getting involved, that much was for sure.

First off, the guy was a fucking loser. Second, Lamar worried about those supposed wise-guy connections. Look what happened to Suzie, his sweet-as-sugar-honey-bun Suzie. Lamar felt a wave of sadness, but it was soon replaced by hunger. He hadn't eaten any breakfast and was anxious to sink his teeth into a couple of Sausage and Egg McMuffins, which he would, right after he got to the ATM machine.

Talk about pathetic. Lamar pictured that fucked-up white dude back in his crib, curled up on the couch like a baby, all strung out. Lamar had been very generous, mixed in a nice amount of smack with the usual cocaine.

He'd been supplying the guy with cocaine on a weekly basis for over a year—which he hadn't bothered to tell those cops. But why would he? He wasn't a fool, and they weren't offering anything in ex-change. But supplying a little coke was one thing, and having Suzie's regular hang with him in his crib was just too fucking weird. And what did he really know about the guy other than the fact that he was into whores and drugs? Nothing. Hell, the guy could have killed Suzie easy as one of them I-talians. Maybe this pathetic act was just that, an act.

A little time to get his money together, that's what the dude had come to Lamar asking, talking jive-talk like he was a goddamn brother.

Hey, man, like can I crash with you? Just a couple a nights is all, bro, till I get my shit together.

Lamar almost laughed in his face—until he realized how he could make it work for him. Yeah, he'd help him get his shit together, all right, just like he was doing right now. The coke-smack combo was going to keep him out of it while Lamar emptied his bank account. According to Mr. Blabbermouth, there was like three, four grand in his account, which he was planning to empty, then split to some desert island or some such shit because the cops were after him, all of which he'd spilled to Lamar in a rush when he was begging to hole up with him, promising Lamar a *percentage* of the money if he helped him out. Yeah, a percent-age sounded good to Lamar, like maybe a hundred percent. After all, if the guy had killed his sweet Suzie, it was only fair.

One stupid man, thought Lamar, dipping the guy's card into the ATM slot, punching in the code, VIRGIN, which hadn't been hard to get out of him—a taste of coke and that dude was talking like there was no switch between his brain and his mouth.

Lamar laughed again. But when the ATM machine said that all he could take out of the checking account at one time was five hundred dollars, Lamar's laugh died and he had to hold back from kicking the shit out of the goddamn machine.

Lamar took a breath. He'd hold on to the card, that's all, get another five hundred tomorrow, and the day after that, until the money ran out. For the moment the five hundred dollars in crisp twenties would have to do.

Lamar fingered the bills, worried for a moment about those I-talian wise guys and the police. No way he was going to go back to his place. Better to stay away a few days, maybe even a week. By then, Suzie's regular would be arrested or gone, maybe even dead.

Lamar threw his head back and hooted a laugh, the thick purplish scar stretched taut across his neck. He slipped the crisp twenties into his pocket and made his way toward the golden arches on the corner, those Egg McMuffins beckoning.

TWENTY-TWO

Kate was chewing two pieces of Nicorette at once, her jaw beginning to ache.

She'd considered a real conversation with the woman, had dialed the number twice, but hung up both times when Noreen Stokes answered. After all, what was there to say?

Now she waited. Hovered across the street from the Stokeses' apartment building, drizzling rain chilling her bones. Noreen Stokes had been lying. A woman who had once hired a private detective to trail her hubby? Oh, she'd know where he was, all right. Noreen Stokes, the long-suffering wife. No matter how much shit she'd taken from her man, she was covering for him, Kate was sure of it.

What was it with some women? If Richard had pulled half the crap that Andy Stokes had, Kate was certain she'd have dumped him in a minute.

Or would she?

And exactly what sort of crap *had* Richard pulled?

Kate glanced across at the Stokeses' apartment building. She had no idea.

Had she too been blinded by love?

"Richard . . ." She whispered his name under her breath, an old memory gnawing away at her—the last time there had been missing money, and Richard lying. But it had all been a mistake, a terrible mistake, and Richard had promised, sworn, he'd never lie to her again, and she had believed him. Oh, God, how she wanted to believe him.

Richard, please. Tell me what's going on.

Her cell phone was ringing and Kate recognized the flashing number, Floyd Brown. *Shit. Not now.* She could not talk to him until she knew what was going on. She needed to have all the facts. Before the cops had them.

The Nicorette had lost its flavor. Kate wrapped the wad inside a tissue and popped a fresh piece. She could feel the drug. It brought back the old days, on a stakeout, huddled in a police car for hours, smoking one cigarette after another, drinking bad coffee, her ass going numb. Right now, she missed all three—the cigarette, the car, and the coffee. Oh, yeah, and the authority. Brown would kill her if he knew she was here, stalking Noreen Stokes, hoping the woman would lead her to Andy.

She pictured FBI Agent Marty Grange sitting across from her in the conference room, giving her that suspicious look, and here she was proving him right.

Her phone rang. Brown. Again. She should tell him what she was doing, but she didn't answer. She would talk to him later. When she knew.

When she knew . . . *what?*

Kate stared down at the sidewalk, and her wet shoes. *Go home. You know better. Leave it alone.* But she did not move. She couldn't think straight. How could she, on three hours of nightmare-riddled nonsleep. It was too much to ask of her—to be rational. She just knew that she could not allow Andy Stokes to disappear, to take what he might know about Richard's murder with him. She had made a promise, a vow, to Richard, and to herself, and she would see it through no matter what the truth turned out to be. She had to know—and she had to know first. She was entitled to that, wasn't she?

Kate glanced up at the high-rise building as if she could see inside the Stokeses' apartment, the secrets it contained, and wondered what she might find out.

For a moment she prayed that Noreen Stokes would never come out of that damn building.

Noreen Stokes pushed the stacks of carefully folded sweater sets aside, tugged out the jewelry box she kept hidden at the back of her dresser, and laid it on her bed. It had been years since it held any jewelry; the pearl necklace, plain gold earrings, even her diamond engagement ring long ago sold, or pawned, accompanied by Andy's usual promises of bigger and better ones when times improved, which they never did.

But that was okay with Noreen. Jewels had never much interested her. She had not expected much out of life, a midwestern girl with a degree in library science.

Noreen yanked out the upper partition of the velvet-lined box, her mind replaying her first glimpse of the boyishly handsome Andrew Stokes, who had come up to the library desk and smiled that smile of his; and later, when they were on their first date, she could not believe that a man like Andrew Stokes would even pay attention to her, and then, only a few dates later, propose marriage. When she asked him why he wanted to marry her he'd said because she made him feel safe, and though it was not exactly the answer Noreen had hoped for, she took comfort in it. Her banker father and librarian mother couldn't quite figure it out either until, less than a year into the marriage, Andy started hitting them up for loans, which they supplied—for a while.

Inside the jewelry box, Noreen collected the cash she had been secreting away once she'd realized that her dashing husband was not quite the breadwinner she had hoped. In ten years she had managed to save more than twenty thousand dollars.

She'd almost left him. More than once. His unexplained disappearances. The drinking. Drugs. And after that detective had given her the bad news—and the photos—of Andrew with those women. But all that was in the past. Andrew needed her again, had begged her forgiveness and confessed his sins—for the third or fourth time since they were married—but had also confessed his undying love, and that's what counted. He had seen where he had gone wrong, promised to reform, begged for another chance. They would run away together, he said; start a new life, he said. And though voices were telling Noreen to beware, she could not remember feeling this happy since the day she had first seen Andrew Stokeses' dazzling smile, and nothing was going to ruin it—and this time *she* was holding all the cards.

Noreen stacked the bills, bound them with rubber bands, and placed them neatly into a small carry-on, carefully concealing them under several changes of clean underwear, a blouse, a light sweater, a bathing suit, and sandals—enough to get her through a few days, then added a few necessities for Andy.

Her heart beat fast. She had never in her life done anything like this, anything so . . . exciting. She was running away with Andy, her handsome scoundrel husband. She had taken care of everything. Put the co-op apartment on the market, opened an off-shore account for the funds, booked a room in a "small, charming, off-the-beaten track" (according to the guidebook) hotel in Guadalajara, the tickets waiting for them at JFK. By tomorrow they would be walking on a secluded Mexican beach hand in hand.

Noreen slipped their passports into her pocket, wrapped a beige scarf over her hair and tied it beneath her chin. She wished she owned a beret or a fedora, something like Ingrid Bergman wore in *Casablanca,* or Faye Dunaway in *Bonnie and Clyde.* She wanted to look as dangerous and glamorous as she felt.

She pictured her sad scared husband hiding way up in the Bronx, and how she would come to his rescue and how indebted he would always be.

She tried to imagine what the hotel room she had booked in Guadalajara would look like. She hoped it would be nice, because this time, she thought, if Andy wanted her to, she would definitely bark.

On the northeast corner of Seventy-second Street and Park Avenue, a young man in a nondescript gray jacket and a cap that shaded half his face was huddled in the shadow of a double-parked FedEx van just beside a navy-blue Chevy Malibu. He had been in this spot for almost two hours; the light but constant drizzle had soaked his shoes, and his feet were starting to go numb. He shifted his weight from one foot to the other, considered getting into the car, but did not. Another young man was sitting in the driver's seat of the Malibu, waiting for him to give the order.

He sneaked a peek at the Stokeses' apartment building, then at Kate, unwrapped two sticks of Doublemint and folded the gum into his mouth, the stupid jingle playing on automatic in the back of his head: *Double your pleasure, double your fun.*

Damn, his feet were cold. He leaned past the FedEx truck and caught a glimpse of Kate looking up at the apartment building, waiting, just like him. He shook out his legs and imagined what he'd like to do to her, but as the fantasy was kicking in he saw Noreen Stokes come out of her apartment building, and the doorman opening the door of a waiting taxicab, and the cab taking off.

Seconds later, he watched Kate do exactly the same thing, then he slid into the Malibu as easily as a snake through grass.

N ow that the drugs had totally worn off, Andy Stokes felt shaky, skin itchy, gut burning. He leaned over Lamar's cracked, moldy toilet and gagged up a thin rope of bile, then gripped the sink and pulled himself up until he was staring into the mirror. Thinning blond hair sticking out in all directions. Pasty skin. Bloodshot eyes.

Just a bad fucking dream, man.

He ran a hand through the once golden hair. "Hey, Golden Boy, where've you been hiding?" He frowned and turned away. Maybe it *was* just a bad dream. Stokes gagged again, his insides empty of everything but failure and disgust. *Damn.* It wasn't his fault. Anyone could see that, couldn't they? He really wasn't a bad guy. They were just . . . urges, needs. He didn't have a choice.

A dream? No. A nightmare. Like right now, coming back to the conscious world and realizing that Lamar had not only deserted him, but stolen his wallet.

He plucked a rusting double-edged razor off Lamar's moldy sink and held it over his wrists. *What the hell, just do it already, end it all, do the world a favor.* But he couldn't. Hell, he couldn't do anything.

Then he remembered that Noreen was coming to get him out of this mess. He'd get out of the country. Leave all the damage behind. Start over. Noreen was going to save him because he'd told her how much he loved her; how much he needed her.

Stokes wheezed a laugh. Good old Noreen. Reliable, trustworthy, loyal. Dependable as a fucking puppy—though not as cute.

He gazed up at the small photo of Suzie White that Lamar had thumbtacked beside the bathroom mirror, grabbed it off the wall, tore it to pieces, dropped them into the toilet and flushed.

From halfway down the treeless Bronx street, Kate watched Noreen get out of the cab and disappear into a building that was possibly the winner in the worst tenement contest, brickfacing pitted, upper-story windows boarded up, front door plastered with papers.

Kate scanned the surroundings: Two black kids, preteens up past their bedtime, ambled down the street, headphones hugging their ears, absurdly baggy pants riding so low they threatened to fall off; one all-night deli, neon sign blinking like it was close to burning out.

The drizzle had progressed to rain, and it was working Kate's nerves, playing an out-of-sync jazz tune on the idling taxi's metal roof. She took several deep breaths, and let the air out slowly. She could wait. Any minute Noreen would be back out, Andy by her side.

Brown was going to kill her. No doubt about that. She'd have to figure out what to say, what lie to create. Not that Brown would buy it. But that was later. Right now all she could think of was Andy Stokes, getting him to tell her what was going on—and what had happened.

Kate stared at the tenement door. Another minute passed like an hour. One more minute, that was all she was going to give them.

She patted the .45 automatic strapped under her jacket. Yes, it was there, confirming that this was real, that it was not an awful nightmare in which her husband had been murdered and she was tracking his associate to some fleabag tenement in the Bronx to find out why.

If only . . .

The corner of her eye saw a streak, dark blue, a car racing by, then abruptly stopping, breaks screeching. Seconds later, a man, cap low on

his forehead, strutting toward the building's entrance, something familiar about his hulking body language, though Kate had no time to figure
it out, just a feeling in her gut: *This is bad.*

She had to call Brown.

"You're *where?*" His voice crackled through the cell phone.

"Just off Zerega, on a Hundred Forty-seventh. I followed Noreen
Stokes and—"

"I told you to let me know. Jesus Christ—"

"There wasn't time. I was with her one minute, then the next thing I
knew she was taking a cab and—"

"And this was how long ago? Damn it. Never mind. I'll have McNally
call cars in the area, ASAP. And you stay put, hear me?"

Kate closed her phone without signing off. She'd heard him all right,
but how could she *stay put?* Her adrenaline was making her twitch.
She'd come this far to find out the truth about her husband and was not
about to stop now. She slapped a fifty into the driver's hand, asked him
to wait, then bolted out of the cab, releasing the safety on her Glock.

Kate was just at the entrance when she heard the three shots and a
woman screaming.

She wrenched the tenement door open, took a cautious step into a
dim gray hallway, dropped to a crouch, and froze. She peered up the
staircase into the dark, a persistent beat of footsteps growing louder,
echoing over and under a woman's spine-chilling screams, and then, in
what seemed like seconds, the darkness became a shadow that became
a form that became a man who was rushing toward her, gun in hand.

Kate's first bullet caught him in the shoulder. He lurched to the side,
then righted himself, arm outstretched, light glinting off the gun barrel,
still aimed at her head.

Another shot. Then another. The Glock kicked back in Kate's hand.
One more shot. No way she was taking a chance. She had seen good
cops die because they were playing fair, firing off warning shots, wound-
ing a suspect rather than going for the kill.

The man tumbled forward down the last part of the staircase, landed
at her feet, gun still gripped in his hand.

The screams from above had stopped.

It was quiet now except for the ringing in her ears.

Kate took a step forward. In the dim hallway light it was impossible to tell if the man was breathing. She kicked the gun out of his hand, laid her weapon against his temple just to be sure, bent over, tried to locate a pulse in his neck, felt nothing, then reached around and slid her hand inside his jacket in search of a heartbeat. Her fingers came away soaked with blood.

She rolled Angelo Baldoni's body over. His eyes, with their long lashes, were open, blood still pumping from his chest, shoulder, and gut.

There were sirens in the distance.

Kate stepped over Baldoni and started up the staircase.

The first landing had a boarded-up door. Kate continued past it, taking the stairs quickly, closing in on a sound like pigeons cooing.

Through the open doorway, Kate saw them, Andy and Noreen Stokes, a modern-day *Pietà*—Stokes was cradled in his wife's arms while she gently rocked him, humming; his loose limbs dangling like a doll's, blood trickling out of a hole in the center of his forehead, painting his face with a clownlike stripe of intense scarlet.

There was blood on Noreen's chest, and Kate wasn't sure if it was because she had been shot or if it had come from Andy's wounds.

But moments later, when the police arrived, and they had to tear her away from her husband's body, Noreen realized that something was wrong, and tapped her chest, fingers exploring the hole the bullet had made in her blouse, and then, only then, did Noreen Stokes pitch forward into Kate's arms.

TWENTY-THREE

Yes, *sí.* That is Suzie's businessman." Rosita Martinez returned the crime scene photos to Floyd Brown, pushed the bottle-black curls off her face, and angled a look at Kate, who was leaning against the wall. "Was this Suzie's fault?"

Brown said, "Thanks for coming in," but Martinez continued to stare at Kate.

"No," Kate said softly. "An officer will see you home Rosita, and thanks."

Brown waited until the door to his office shut behind Martinez, then flattened his palms onto his desk, and looked directly at Kate. "Not good."

Kate returned a stare composed of one part defiance and four parts exhaustion—six straight hours with Internal Affairs.

"You just couldn't call in, could you?"

"I did call."

"After the fact."

"I'm sorry."

"Me too."

"How is Noreen Stokes doing?"

"Took a bullet in the lung. And her husband shot in the head right in front of her. She's still in shock. But she'll be okay. You must have scared Baldoni when you came into the building or he'd have finished her off."

"See, I did do something right."

"Not everyone would agree."

Kate ignored the crack. "So what do you think? Stokes owed Baldoni, couldn't pay, so Baldoni kills him?"

"Looks like it. We know Baldoni's history—the organized crime connections, his uncle, the loan-sharking, contract hits." Brown sighed. "Now we've got the Organized Crime Bureau coming in to nose around."

"I think there has to be something else," said Kate. "What about the Martini painting found at Richard's crime scene?"

"Don't know how we can prove that now that both parties are dead." Brown leveled a cold stare in Kate's direction. "Crime Scene found pieces of a photo floating in the toilet, appears to be our first dead hooker, Suzie White. Not sure who put it there, Lamar Black or Andy Stokes. We've got an APB out on Black, who's gone missing. Have a lot of questions for that guy. Like what the hell was Stokes doing in his apartment, for one?" Brown massaged his temples. "The way I'm figuring it, your husband got in the way, maybe tried to intervene on Stokes's behalf, or it could've been a case of mistaken identity. Killer thinks Richard is Stokes."

It was a chilling idea. One Kate had already imagined.

"But the mistaken-identity concept only works if Baldoni never met Stokes—and that seems unlikely if Stokes had borrowed money from him, right?

Brown rolled the idea around. "Could be that Baldoni farmed out the Stokes hit. Particularly if he had done money business with the guy, he might not want to handle the job himself. Too much of a link. Then the contract man confuses Richard for Stokes."

Could it be that simple? The idea that her husband had been murdered by mistake was both horrifying and a relief—but Kate wanted to believe it.

"Since the Organized Crime Bureau wants in, we might as well hand that over to them, see what they can come up with—contract killers Baldoni might have used. Oh, and the ME has a hair from Martini's shirt collar that didn't belong to him. If it turns out to belong to Baldoni, then he's pretty much a lock for the murder.

"I'd like to work on that. Anything that will get at the truth—"

"You must be kidding?"

"Not at all."

"You're *out,* McKinnon. I can't say it any simpler than that."

"Look, I know I fucked up, but—"

"Save it." Brown put a hand up to stop her. "I don't know what the hell you thought you were doing—what you could possibly have been thinking."

"Okay, so I wasn't thinking, so I broke a few rules—"

"A *few.* You want me to get the manual out, read you the first *ten*?"

"Look, I had to know what was going on. I just thought maybe—"

"No, you had it right the first time—you *weren't* thinking."

"I just . . . I had to know. I was worried that . . ." Kate stopped. She did not want to bullshit Brown. "I did it for Richard. I, I made a vow, a promise that I'd—" She waved a hand in front of her face. "Oh, forget it. It doesn't matter."

"You're right, it doesn't." Brown softened his tone. "Look, I *do* understand. If it were up to me, I'd keep you on, *maybe.* But Grange is not going to allow it, no way. And he wields a big stick."

"No doubt compensation for a small dick."

"Not funny," said Brown.

"Wasn't trying to be," said Kate. "Look, Baldoni was coming at me with a fucking revolver in his hand. Another few seconds and I'd have been dead. Would that have made Grange happier?"

"Probably."

"IA accepted my version. Why won't Grange?"

"Because he doesn't have to. He's not IA, not even NYPD, remember? Grange has got a real hard-on for you, excuse my French. He's got this crazy notion that you set Stokes up, that you purposely led Angelo Baldoni to him."

"Why would I do that?"

"Because Grange thinks"—Brown hesitated—"you're covering up Richard's murder."

"Wha—" Kate choked on the word. "You're not serious? If there is anyone who wants the truth, who really *needs* to know who did this to Richard, it's *me*. Why would I want to cover up Richard's murder?"

Brown rubbed a hand across his forehead. "You would if you had something to do with it—if you had hired someone to kill Richard, and Grange thinks—"

The laughter spewed out so fast, Kate couldn't contain it, but it died just as quickly. "Wait a minute. You're serious."

"No. But Grange is. You know rule number one in a homicide: Check out the spouse." Brown sighed. "Look at it from Grange's point of view. You're working your husband's case. You find a lead—your husband's business partner. You interview the wife. You get some piece of information that you obviously don't want to share and—"

"That's not true, I simply wanted—"

"Let me finish. You don't call for backup. You follow the wife, who leads you to the husband, who may know something about Richard's murder. You're followed by a known hit man, who probably killed the artist who made the painting found at your husband's crime scene. The hit man shoots your husband's partner, and then *you* kill *him*. No one left to tell tales. That's the way Grange sees it—that you helped get rid of anyone who knew the truth about your husband's murder."

"Jesus Christ. Don't you think I wish there *was* someone around to tell tales?"

"It doesn't matter what *I* think." Brown frowned. "Grange has also turned up the fact that Richard had a five-million-dollar life insurance policy, which doesn't help matters."

"You think that money means anything to me? My God, my husband is dead, and—" Kate was up fast, tears building behind her lids, and no way she wanted Brown to see them. "I don't have to sit here for this horseshit."

Brown snagged her by the wrist. "Hey, I'm laying myself on the line telling you this."

Kate sagged back into the chair, Brown's words sinking in, all of them true—she had accomplished the exact opposite of what she'd set out to do.

"Look," said Brown. "The good news is that Grange has absolutely no proof. All he can do at this point is use it to keep you off the case."

"Yeah, great news."

"My gut tells me that deep down he knows it's bullshit, but he didn't like you being here in the first place, a woman, a civilian, and since you've already made your contribution—interpreting the psycho's paintings—as far as he's concerned, we no longer need you." Brown laid his hand over hers for a brief moment, then went back to rubbing his temples "You could use the break, McKinnon. Go on vacation, or something. Let's not give Agent Grange anything else to work with, okay?"

Kate dug out her pillbox, deposited a couple of Excedrin into Brown's open palm. "And what about our little psycho painter?"

"What about him?"

"You may not believe me, but I'm as committed to that case as I am to Richard's."

"Sorry," said Brown, downing the Excedrin. "Not anymore you're not."

Kate hurried down the hall, gray-green walls a blur, passing uniforms and detectives, all of them staring at her, or so she thought, some offering pitying looks—*poor thing, husband involved with the mob, got himself killed*—others unable to hide pleasure from the knowledge that the uptown lady had screwed up.

The omnipresent clouds seemed even more oppressive than usual, bearing down on Kate as she turned out of the precinct.

Consequences. She knew there would be consequences. But not this. To be off the case. Her head ached. She needed a couple of Excedrin herself, and to sleep. Just to sleep. But how would she do that, now, after she had totally fucked up?

She thought about going back to Tapell. But if Tapell went to bat for her this time, everyone would know something was up. And no way she would expose the chief.

It was just too late.

Kate."

Mitch Freeman touched her arm, gently stopping her, or she would surely have kept going. She did not want to talk to the FBI shrink, or anyone. Not now.

"Hey—" The corners of his mouth turned up, almost a smile, then down.

"So you know, huh? That I'm off."

Freeman pushed the hair off his forehead, nodded. "Have time for a cup of coffee?"

Kate sighed. She did not want to talk; she wanted to talk forever. "All the time in the world apparently."

They walked a few blocks, neither of them speaking.

At Ninth Avenue they chose an almost authentic-looking French café, settled themselves around a small table. Freeman ordered for both of them, café au lait, almond croissants, and though Kate was not hungry she didn't bother to stop him, her will on sabbatical.

"You look tired," said Freeman. "Are you sleeping?"

"Not much. Ambien helps."

"Ah, one of the hypnotics."

"Hypnotics?"

"Yes, that's how the drug is classified—as a hypnotic. Unlike the old-fashioned narcotics, which knocked you out, Ambien puts you into a state, but you have to go with it, lie down, close your eyes, allow yourself to believe in sleep, then you will."

Kate wasn't sure she did believe in sleep—not anymore.

"But don't take Ambien if you do not have a solid seven or eight hours ahead of you or you could end up with 'traveler's amnesia.' "

"Which is?"

"Named for the folks who pop sleeping pills on an airplane and are awakened a few hours later to deplane while the drug is still in their system. Not good. You're awake, but in a sleep state." Freeman peered over his glasses at Kate. "You're more open to suggestion, almost like hypnosis. And later, you wouldn't remember it."

"Well, I won't be taking Ambien except to get a full night's sleep. I promise."

Freeman smiled, then got serious again. "And don't ever increase the dosage. Hypnotics work with the natural brain chemical known as GABA, a neurotransmitter. Neurotransmitters control communication among neighboring brain cells by increasing or descreasing their electrical activity."

Sounds complicated."

"Let's just say that sleeping aids, while they are a boon to millions of insomniacs, can cause not only memory problems but changes in normal behavior if not taken as prescribed."

"You've got my word, doctor." Kate crossed her heart.

They were both quiet a moment.

"You know, you could have been killed," Freeman said, after the waitress had deposited their bowl-sized mugs of coffee.

"I wasn't thinking about me."

"Maybe it's time you did."

Kate raised the bowl with both hands, felt the heat on her face. "It doesn't worry me."

"What doesn't?" Freeman's warm blue eyes were on hers.

"Are you trying to psychoanalyze me, Doctor?"

"Just a little." Freeman almost smiled. "So what . . . exactly . . . doesn't worry you?"

"What happens . . . to me."

"That's not something a psychiatrist likes to hear."

"I'm not your patient, Mitch."

"I know that, but . . ." Freeman looked down at his croissant, then up. "Sorry, I can't help myself."

"What would you like me to say? That I'm sorry I followed Noreen Stokes? That I'm sorry Andy Stokes is dead? That Baldoni is dead too? Well, I *am* sorry. I'm sorry for . . ." Kate took a deep breath, worked hard at holding back tears. "For failing."

"Whom did you fail?"

"Never mind. It doesn't matter."

Freeman tried to catch her eye, but she looked away. "It's not your fault that Richard died, Kate."

"I know that."

"Do you?"

Did she know that? It seemed that so many people she loved had died and there was nothing she could have done to prevent it.

"Things happen, Kate. Terrible things beyond our control, and—"

"But I *can* control it, I mean, I should, I need to, I—"

"But you *can't*. None of us can control fate."

Fate. The word resonated in her mind. What was *her* fate? "I know you're trying to be nice, Mitch, but please, just stop, okay? All I said was I didn't care what happened to me. Is that so bad?"

"Suicidal tendencies? Yes, I think that's bad. You obviously put your-self in harm's way."

"I was chasing answers, that's all."

"Without regard for your own safety." Freeman eyed her across the small table. "You're going to have to make a decision you know."

"About . . . ?"

Freeman held her glance. "About whether you want to live or die."

Kate heard the words and came up with an answer: No, she did not care if she lived or died. "Please stop analyzing me, okay?"

"Okay," said Freeman. "But why don't you go away for a while? Give yourself time to grieve."

Kate stared into her coffee. *Grieve for what?* For her failure to get an-swers; for a husband whom she possibly never knew, for his death, her loss? What exactly? Kate arranged her features into a cool mask. "Well, it looks like I will be getting away. Early retirement, I guess you could call it." She forced a smile, but Freeman did not return it.

Antiseptic smells failed to mask the odor of human waste and disease, doors ajar, split-second glimpses of the sick and recovering, some, the lucky ones, with visitors trying to entertain them, others left alone in their beds, waiting for overworked nurses who might never get to them.

No place Kate liked less than a hospital. She headed quickly down the corridor, not quite sure why she felt compelled to visit Noreen Stokes or what she would say. What propelled her—guilt, or her nagging desire to find the shred of the truth that kept eluding her? Probably both. Plus the fact that she would be denied police access if she waited even a couple of hours longer.

Just as Kate had anticipated, a uniform was posted at the door. After all, Noreen Stokes had been witness to a mob murder.

Kate flashed her temporary shield, thankful Brown had forgotten to take it back.

The uniform gave Kate a perfunctory glance as she pushed through the door.

The blinds were drawn, the fluorescents casting a sickly greenish tint over everything.

Noreen Stokes was half propped up in bed, arms on top of the sheet that was pulled up to her neck, IV in one arm snaking up to a pole with a dangling bag of clear liquid, half empty, her pale skin only a shade darker than the sheet.

She turned her head as Kate entered, eyes registering surprise, then squeezed them shut, as if the act would make Kate disappear.

Kate edged a bit closer to the bed. "How are you doing?"

Noreen did not answer, but her lids twitched, and Kate was once again struck by the network of veins under her translucent skin, even more noticeable now, the delicate skin like a veil.

"I'm sorry."

Noreen's eyes blinked open like a doll's. "Are you?"

"Yes."

"You lead a man to kill my husband and you're . . . *sorry?*" Her voice was little more than a hoarse whisper, but filled with loathing.

"Baldoni was following *you,* not me, Noreen." Kate hoped what she said was true. She wasn't entirely sure.

"That's your way of saying you're sorry?"

"I simply wanted to talk, Noreen. To you, and Andy. I just wanted— I needed to get a few answers, to find out what happened."

"What *happened?* I'll tell you what happened. Your husband condemned Andy to death, and *you* helped execute him."

"That's not true, I—"

"You asked me for answers. Well, I'll give them to you." Noreen

Stokes inhaled a breath, her fragile hand, black and blue from the IV's needle, twitched on the sheet. "Your husband racked up debts, terrible debts. He put the firm in jeopardy. Andy was only trying to help . . ." She took another breath, her face almost colorless except for the purplish veins pulsing beneath her almost transparent flesh. "Baldoni owed Andy a favor because Andy had successfully defended his uncle. So Baldoni got Richard the money he needed to keep the firm from crumbling."

Kate listened to the words as if they were a foreign language that she had to interpret: *Richard so in debt that he turned to mobsters?*

"Richard promised to pay it all back, but he didn't. He knew the consequences—"

That word again: *consequences . . .*

"—but he didn't heed them. And now . . . now they're both dead."

"Richard wouldn't have, he . . . How do you know this?"

"Andy told me everything. How Richard came to him, begging, and Andy just wanted to help." Noreen took a deep breath. "After Richard was killed, Andy knew he'd be next. Naturally he couldn't come up with the money. He had to get away." Her eyes caught Kate's, angry, sad. "It wasn't enough that your husband got himself killed, you had to make sure Andy went with him. You didn't want the truth."

"I did." Thoughts were buzzing inside Kate's brain like mosquitoes. Had she really wanted the truth? "You're wrong. None of what you're saying is true. Richard would have told me—"

"Andy told me not to listen to you, not to speak to you. That you'd only defend your husband—that you would believe him no matter what."

Would she? Did she still? Kate's fingers unconsciously slid along the gold chain at her neck until they found Richard's wedding band. She tried to focus her thoughts. "Did Andy know a young woman named Suzie White?"

"Who?"

"She was murdered, and—"

"Now you're saying that Andy was a murderer."

"I didn't say that. I simply asked if he knew her."

"How would I know that?"

"I know this isn't easy, Noreen, for either of us, but the apartment where Andy was staying, it belonged to a man named Lamar Black, a drug dealer, and a pimp, and Suzie White worked for him, for Black. She was a prostitute. And I think Andy knew her."

"How dare you." The words came out flat and hard.

"I'm sorry. But you once hired a detective . . ." Kate hesitated. She knew these statements would sting. ". . . to follow your husband, and—"

Noreen Stokes began to take fast gulps of air.

"According to the medical examiner, Andy had heroin and cocaine in his system, and—"

Noreen Stokes jerked up in the bed so fast her IV went flying, blood spurting from her hand, the IV tube whipping around like a snake spitting pale liquid poison. "Get out! Get out of here!"

"I just want the truth, Noreen. Don't you?"

"The *truth*? You don't want to know the truth. Just get out." She grabbed hold of the nurses' call button and pressed it over and over.

"Noreen—"

"Get out!"

Kate was about to speak when a nurse bolted into the room, the uniform just behind her. He got a hand around Kate's arm and led her out. When she looked back from the hall, through the half-open door, a nurse was trying to find a decent vein in Noreen's bruised hand, and except for the rise and fall of Noreen's chest, the woman was lying so still she could have been dead.

TWENTY-FOUR

He's got a bag of Cheese Doodles, two packages of Hostess Twinkies, a liter-sized plastic bottle of Coke, all spread out in front of him, ready. He has been waiting, thinking about this for days in between painting, so much that no matter how many drops he puts in his eyes, they sting. Six new paintings that he thinks are really good, several brushes scrubbed almost to shreds in the process, a dozen pencils worn down to stubs creating his frames, writing the names over and over, excited this time by the new addition. He's ready to show them to her. But how? And where?

"Hey, Tony, it's about to start. Donna, you gonna watch? C'mon. Hurry!" He calls out into the dark, nods and smiles as his friends curl onto the couch with him, believes he can feel the warmth of their bodies surround him. "What about Brandon and Brenda?"

"Brandon's working, and Brenda *says* she's got a headache," he says in his falsetto Donna-voice, "but I think she's lying because she's jealous."

"Girls," he whispers, elbowing an imaginary Tony the Tiger.

"They're grrrrrrrrrreat."

"Yeah, sure. Sometimes."

He leans forward, plays with the rabbit ears to adjust the picture. "Okay, everybody. Shut up." He twitches with excitement.

Titles and credits are replaced by buildings, cafés, and stores as the camera follows a handsome heavyset man ambling down the street. A street sign: MULBERRY STREET. *Oh, just like the color.* He writes the name in his sketchbook with a bold black marker. Now the man comes to a door, then a close-up of keys in the lock, and a quick cut as the man tugs an old metal gate across a large industrial elevator. A view from below of the elevator ascending. Another cut—a huge studio filled with paintings, light streaming in from enormous windows. The picture goes black for a split second, then Kate's face fills the screen, and he is overjoyed to see not only that he was right, that her hair *is* chestnut and her eyes blue, but that it is still happening, this most amazing of miracles. "See, Donna? What did I tell you?"

"Yeah," he answers in his Donna-voice, though in his mind the debate continues: Kate's eyes may *not* be blue; he can't remember, always gets it wrong; but what does Donna know; why is she right and he wrong? No, he's right; no, she's right. "Shut up!"

"Tonight," says Kate, "a rare treat. A visit with one of the art world's best-known and most accomplished painters, Boyd Werther." The camera pans the artist's impressive studio, first a long, wide shot of the huge colorful canvases leaning against paint-splattered walls, then traveling along the floor through a maze of turpentine cans, bottles of varnish and oil, the occasional housepainter's brush resting on an open tin of thick paint, a few oil tubes scattered about as though they have been dropped or flung in some moment of creative fury, when in fact the artist's assistants had carefully arranged everything according to the artist's detailed instruction just moments before Kate's TV crew arrived. Now the camera moves in close, creeps up and down the surface of one painting, then another, while Kate's disembodied voice provides commentary. "*Art News* has said that Boyd Werther's paintings mix the refinement of Japanese scrollwork with the energy of abstract expressionism."

He strains to see what she is talking about, but to him they are just simple abstractions, and then the screen goes gray. Everything gray. No more chestnut hair, the color totally gone now, as if it has leached out the bottom of the set. He checks the floor just beneath it, half expects to see puddles of actual color lying there. Is it because of those awful paintings?

"Tony, do you get those paintings?"

"They're grrrrrrrrrreat!"

Are they? He can't imagine why Tony thinks so, though lately he's begun to suspect that Tony says the same thing about everything.

In between Werther's abstractions, other pictures flash on the screen—a Kandinsky *Improvisation,* fragments of wall paintings from the caves at Lascaux—nothing familiar to him—while Kate continues to narrate: ". . . all of these influences come together in Werther's work . . ."

He grabs handfuls of Cheese Doodles, fingers picking up acidic orange dye that he cannot see, excitement and frustration merging as he stuffs them into his mouth, chomps and chews as if he were gnawing away at every word the art *her-story-n* offers.

New scene: Kate, seated in the studio with the handsome heavyset man who now wears loose-fitting clothes that look like pajamas, the large canvases arranged around them. Kate says, "I'm here with New York artist Boyd Werther in his NoLIta studio . . ."

With his bold black marker he writes "No Lee Ta" just below where he has written "Mulberry Street," in his sketchbook.

Kate talks. Werther talks more. Paintings flash on the small screen. Soon the Cheese Doodles are gone and he is tearing open the Hostess Twinkies and trying to memorize the conversation, words like *deconstruction,* and statements such as "formal versus antiformal," and "modern versus postmodern," his brain reeling from all the new information, and only once is he rewarded with a flash of brilliant green—Kate's sweater—either forest or pine green, he isn't sure and it's gone so quickly, and then Boyd Werther is scratching his big belly, and saying: "Why bother to paint if you're not going to make use of color, its most seductive tool?"

"Yes, yes," he says to the screen. "I agree. And I want to."

"A painter who doesn't know his color is wasting his time."

"But I'm *trying* to learn." He leans even closer to the small screen. "Really I am."

"As for me," says Werther, "I eat, sleep, and dream color."

Dream color. Yes, he has dreamed in color. Hasn't he? Or is that gone too? He can't recall. He holds his head, which has begun to ache. A wave of nausea tagging along with the pain, and an image—a man and woman on a bed, the flash of a knife, red to black, black to red.

The artist is gesturing at the large canvases leaning against the studio walls. "Look what color, real color, can achieve. A miracle, no?"

A miracle. Yes. "Please." He squints at the TV screen, sees nothing but gray paintings, shouts—"Where the fuck is *my* miracle?!"— and as the camera switches to Kate, he receives it, his miracle, Kate's luscious hair shimmering golden brown, her green sweater as precious as jade. Now he understands. *It's her. Only she can deliver the miracle.*

He flicks his tongue against the TV screen, believes he can actually taste the refreshing minty flavor of her green sweater.

"Watch," says the artist, and pulling himself out of his chair, he struts toward a large table littered with tubes of oil and containers of pigment. He holds up a glass jar filled with dark powder. The camera zooms in for a close-up.

"It looks black, doesn't it?"

"Yes, yes," he says, sitting on the edge of the sofa, face only inches from the screen, rapt.

Werther uncaps the jar and spills an anthill of powder onto his glass palette. "Raw pigment," he says. "Paint before it is paint." Now he unscrews the cap of a metal tin, adding droplets of a slightly unctuous liquid to the pigment. "Linseed oil," he says. And with a flat palette knife begins to mix until the two form a thick sparkling paste. Werther plucks a brush out of a coffee can, dips it into the newly mixed oil paint and lays a long stroke of paint across a blank canvas. "Like magic, isn't it?" he says. "Phthalo blue."

Blue? He doesn't think so. It still looks black.

"Of course the raw pigment and linseed should be ground with a mortar and pestle, for an ideal blend," says Werther assuming his seat beside Kate. "But you can see how the pigment comes alive with the oil."

"Indeed," says Kate. "Beautiful."

Is it? Why?

"Oil painting is such an old technique," says Werther. "But for me, numero uno."

"Yes," says Kate, assuming a professorial tone as the camera focuses on her. "It was invented by the Dutch, possibly the great Master of Flémalle, or the brothers Hubert and Jan van Eyck, sometime in the early- or mid-fourteen hundreds. Oil paint allowed for smoother tones and subtle blending, which painters before them could not achieve with their quick-drying egg temperas or labor-intensive frescoes."

"Painting's greatest achievement," says Werther.

"So, what would you say to painters who limit their palette, or use no color at all, simply black and white?" asks Kate.

"I'd say why bother? Look at Franz Kline. He's already done it—and as good as it's ever going to be done. Nowadays, it's just a big bore. I'd never do that. Never. Fact is," says Werther, "I'd kill myself without color."

The words play over and over in his mind: *Kill myself without color . . . Kill myself without color . . . Kill myself without color . . .*

The screen pans Werther's paint table.

Oh, how he wants to learn—to mix his own color like the artist just did, to improve, to understand everything.

He wants the artist to teach him.

"Next time," says Kate. "A rare treat. The Rothko Chapel, in Houston, one of the great testimonies to art." She smiles warmly. "And don't forget to see the WLK Hand show opening at the Vincent Petrycoff Gallery in Chelsea." One last smile before her face fades and the credits begin to roll.

In his sketchbook, where he has written "No Lee Ta" and "Mulberry Street," he writes, "WLK Hand, Vin-Sent Petreecof gallery, Chel-see," then pulls himself up from the couch and checks to make sure that his paintings are dry, his hands trembling with excitement as he covers each one loosely with plastic, then tapes them all together. From the back wall, he carefully removes a few of the pictures from his pantheon of greats—the Francis Bacon of the gray couple, one of Soutine's *Carcass* paintings, and a Jasper Johns. He has decided that he would like the artist's opinion on them. And if it works out well, he might even consider giving them to him as a gift, a token of mutual respect.

He stops a moment to consider what else, goes through his backpack, notes his usual supplies, and removes his brushes. There will be plenty there he can use.

A conversation: artist-to-artist. He trembles with excitement.

Now, with the New York City subway map spread out in front of him, he runs his magnifying glass over it until he finds Mulberry Street and a subway stop close by. He shuts his eyes, replays the beginning of the show, the man ambling down the street, some of the stores he passed, the door he came to with his keys, and sees it perfectly—the numbers on the door, 302.

TWENTY-FIVE

Nola insisted they watch *Artists' Lives,* though Kate was hardly in the mood, the day playing and replaying in her mind; first the conversations with Brown and Freeman, then Noreen Stokes lying in that hospital bed accusing—everything mixing in her head, competing for her attention, the interview with Boyd Werther now just images on a small screen, not nearly enough to distract her. Still, she managed to make small talk with Nola, to smile, to say everything was fine, until Nola finally went to bed. Then she poured herself a tall glass of Johnnie Walker and tried to make some sense of it, and think what, if anything, she could do about the situation.

Kate tapped on the penthouse stereo system, kept the music low, a favorite Julia Fordham CD she had not been able to listen to since Richard died, so many of the songs about love and loss or a kind of happiness that she thought she might never have again. But she was singing along now, whispering, really, with one of her favorite cuts, "Missing Man," before she even realized it, the lyrics sighing into the room, soaking into the walls, the rug, Kate's aching heart. She realized the song had been in her head for days, "Missing Man," a mantra for Richard, her missing man.

She tiptoed down the darkened hall, peeked into Nola's bedroom, listened a minute until she heard the reassuring slow steady breaths of sleep. She leaned against the doorjamb as moonlight slivered in from a window and illuminated Nola's beautiful face. She wanted to rush to the girl, stroke her brow, hug her and protect her, promise to keep her and her baby safe forever.

But how could she make that promise? She felt incapable of protecting anyone.

She closed the door quietly, headed back to the living room and a refill on her Scotch, still trying to sort out what she knew and what she didn't, Julia Fordham's gorgeous voice and tender lyrics trailing after her.

A call to Richard's accountant had confirmed that the law firm's finances were in trouble due to large, unexplained withdrawals of cash in the week just before Richard's death. The accountant had called Richard, concerned, but the meeting to discuss it never happened, scheduled for the day just after Richard's murder.

Had Richard been withdrawing money to pay off loan sharks? But couldn't he just have easily paid them from his personal funds? The accountant had assured Kate that their personal assets were fine. It didn't make sense. And if Richard *had* been paying off the debt—which Noreen Stokes said he hadn't—then why would they have killed him?

Kate paced around the perimeter of the living room, her eyes sliding over art and objects that no longer meant anything to her. She would exchange all of it for the truth in half a second.

According to Noreen Stokes, it was all Richard's fault. But the woman blamed Kate for Andy's death—naturally she wanted to be hurtful. Would she lie when it no longer mattered? Maybe Noreen didn't know her husband had been lying to her; maybe this was simply the truth according to Andrew Stokes—a man who had been lying to his wife for years; a man who frequented prostitutes, who knew Lamar Black well enough to be holed up in the pimp's apartment, who fraternized with known mobsters like Giulio Lombardi.

Kate reached for the phone, started punching in Floyd Brown's home number to wake him up, tell him he absolutely had to reinstate her, had to pursue this, had to let her help him find the truth.

But how would they do that? Stokes was dead. Baldoni was dead. Richard was dead. The thought rippled through her.

Richard, dead. Yes, that much was true; whether it was a case of mistaken identity or an intentional hit, it didn't make much difference. He was gone. And so were the men who could give her the answers.

Kate gazed out the window at the night sky, then down at the park, inky smudges of landscape illuminated by street lamps.

In the bathroom, she shook an Ambien into her palm. Probably a mistake on top of the Scotch, but the thought of another sleepless night was unbearable. Mitch Freeman may have had a point. And Brown too. Maybe she should get away. Yeah, she thought, to the Betty Ford Clinic.

A hand on her breast, slowly caressing her nipple, then down, between her legs. Back arched, body pressed against his. Lips at his neck, a whiff of citrus.

His fingers softly stroking, perfect. He knows her. He kisses her lips, parts them gently with his tongue.

She can taste him. So familiar.

Legs apart as he moves on top of her.

So why doesn't she feel anything? She whispers his name, *Richard,* lifts her hips to meet his and the bedroom dissolves, replaced by the alleyway, which is darker than she remembered, longer too, interminable, shoes sticking to the ground as if she were walking on wet tar, the sliver of light at the other end growing smaller, not larger. She spreads her arms to touch the walls and her hands sink into something soft rather than hard, viscous and warm, like intestines.

Kate gasps, trapped, the light at the end of the alley gone as if someone had suddenly flipped off the switch. Total darkness. Black.

She staggers along like a drunk, shoes dragging through muck, hands dripping with viscera, blind.

But when the darkness gives way and she can see again, the body at the end of the alleyway is Leonardo Martini, and the man standing over him wielding the knife is Richard, who stabs Martini over and over and over, blood gushing from the artist's wounds like a fountain, coursing through the alleyway, and swirling around her shoes.

Red.

Kate stares at the color until it goes slightly pink and becomes the clouds in the Bronx psycho's painting, and then the painting comes to life around her, and she is walking past tangerine-colored tenements and razzmatazz-colored garbage cans, and there is Richard painting everything these absurd colors.

"Nice, huh?"

"No," says Kate. "It's nuts."

"You don't like it?"

"Why did you kill him?"

"Who?"

"Martini."

"Had to," says Richard, painting the sidewalk with broad stripes of tickle-me-pink. "He knew too much."

"Like the movie," says Nicky Perlmutter, who has suddenly appeared. "You know, *The Man Who Knew Too Much*. Alfred Hitchcock?" He sings out in a deep bass: "Que será, será!"

"Stop it," says Kate. "This is serious."

"Of course it is," says Nicky, who continues to sing.

The candy-colored world fades and Kate is in a hallway, flaking paint, flickering yellow light, and there are footsteps, like a dull heartbeat, echoing. A scream, and Angelo Baldoni is right there, in her face, grinning, gun in her gut. He pulls the trigger and she stumbles back, falling, falling, falling through the dark, back into the alleyway, with Richard. Two Richards—one lifeless, slumped against the alley floor, the other alive and busy working on a small painting, which he finishes and leans against the alley wall. "Good, huh?"

"Not bad," says Kate, staring at the painting with the blue-striped bowl. "But what are you doing?"

"Faking my death. That's okay, isn't it honey?"

"Sure. But . . . why?"

"Gotta go, sweetie. See ya." He smiles as his living self dissolves into smoke, and, like some animated cartoon ghost, snakes itself into the dead Richard lying on the ground.

"No, Richard. Wait! Please. Tell me what this is all about."

The dead Richard's head comes alive, looks up at her and says— "Shhhh, it's a secret"—and the alley goes dark.

Now a stark white room. Walls, floor. But when Kate looks up, there is no ceiling. Gray clouds race across a pale blue sky, as if she were inside a painting by the French surrealist René Magritte. In front of her is a white table. On it a body, Richard's. Daniel Markowitz, ME, is tugging at the ring on his finger.

"It won't come off," he says, his features contorted with frustration. He picks up a Stryker saw. "This ought to do it."

"No. Wait." Kate snatches the saw from his hand. "Let me," she says, and starts sawing away at the finger, separating the digit from the hand, blood spurting, painting everything in deep, rich vermilion.

Kate tugged herself out of the dream, half conscious, half caught in the nightmare, the hideous image of sawing off Richard's finger clinging to the recesses of her brain. She checked to be sure she was awake, her hand going for Richard's wedding band on the chain around her neck, then pulled herself out of bed, anxious to be as conscious as possible.

Other mornings her dreams had been sweet, with her and Richard together, and she had tried so hard to hold on to them before the real world intruded. But this nightmare had been far worse than the real world, and she wanted to forget it as soon as possible—though it lingered. Why had she condemned Richard in her dream, her subconscious making him a cheat and a murderer?

Kate stripped off Richard's pajamas, crushed them down into the wicker hamper. She no longer wanted to wear them, no longer wanted to be reminded of him every minute. *Or did she?* She had no idea. She plucked them up out of the hamper—one last time—and held them to her face. His scent was gone.

From her dresser top she grasped the silver-framed photo and stared into Richard's laughing face. Was he mocking her? Lying to her all this time? What had he been involved in? Why was he killed? Kate wanted to know so badly, and did not want to know at all.

"What happened, Richard?"

But Richard only continued to smile, shielding his eyes from the sun, the photograph betraying nothing more than stopped time, a moment that would never exist again.

Kate regarded the burned-out votive candles, glass blackened by smoke, wicks withered and embedded in flat amoebas of dirtied wax. She turned the framed photo facedown onto her dresser.

Freeman was right. She should get away. To think. Or not to think. She couldn't even decide that. Her TV crew was down in Houston, getting ready to film the last episode of her show. They could film the chapel without her, but why not join them? Nola wasn't due for a few weeks, and Lucille could look after her for the couple of days Kate was gone. Get out of her apartment, out of New York City. A good idea. And Houston held no memories waiting to ambush her—she had never been there with Richard.

Before the sun rose, everything was booked—plane tickets, hotel. In another hour she could call her friend who worked at the famous chapel.

Kate tugged a small suitcase from the closet, laid it on her bed, and started packing.

The Rothko Chapel. A place of worship based purely on color. Art as religion; religion as art. There was a time she had truly believed that possible. But now, she hardly believed in anything.

TWENTY-SIX

Boyd Werther dragged the gate across the industrial elevator, thinking this was a big fucking pain, that he'd had two major studio visits today—curators from London's Tate Modern and the new director of the Whitney Museum—and he was in no mood for another, particularly with some needy, insistent kid who must have buzzed his loft about a dozen times saying he was a friend of Kate McKinnon's, and just after his assistants had left. Now he'd have to deal with him alone, at least until Victoria got back to pack up his drawings. She'd be his excuse to tell the kid to get going, if he was still around. But okay, he was a friend of McKinnon's, so he'd give him a few words of wisdom about his work, which the kid had actually brought with him, and he could stand five minutes of the kid fawning over him and his work. The kid gave him a sweet, shy smile. Damn handsome, thought Werther.

"So how do you know Kate McKinnon?" he asked as they rode up in the elevator.

"Oh, I've known her a while. She was my, uh . . . teacher."

"At Columbia? Art history?"

"Yeah, and we're like, good friends."

"And she told you to look me up, huh?"

"Yeah. She said you'd look at my work and give me some good ideas. I won't stay too long."

Damn right. Werther stepped out of the elevator and led the kid into his loft.

Immediately, the kid was unwrapping his paintings, spreading them across the studio floor. Werther stifled a groan. They were worse than he'd imagined. Garish color, unsophisticated, clumsy. What the hell was he going to say about this crap? He was really going to let McKinnon have it. Plus, the kid wasn't even looking at *his* work, which pissed him off. He expected, and was used to, a certain amount of attention, especially from young artists on the make.

The kid finished arranging his canvases on the floor, stood back, hands on his narrow hips. "So what do you think?"

"Well . . ." Werther stroked his chin, took in the crude still-life paintings and cityscapes, the eccentric color. "First of all, why don't you take off the shades so you can see better."

"Oh. I forgot." He removed his sunglasses, and blinked.

Werther looked into the kid's eyes. He didn't think he'd ever seen anyone who looked so sad, so in pain. "You okay?"

"Yeah. I'm grrrrrrrrrrreat!"

"Just that you're blinking, and I thought maybe—"

"Nah, that's nothing. I've got a . . . condition."

Yeah, thought Werther, regarding the paintings, a condition, all right, it's called *no talent.*

"So, what do you think?"

Jesus, this kid was like a puppy, so fucking needy. "They're, uh, interesting."

"How do you mean?"

Oh, fuck. "Well, the way you use color, for one. It's . . . unusual."

"Is it?" The kid squinted at his work. "I don't see *why*?" An edge in his voice.

"Well, you've got to admit it's not standard. I mean, you've got purple clouds and blue apples. Been looking at the fauves?"

The young man stared at his paintings as hard as he could. What was the artist talking about? He'd gotten the color right, he knew he had. "I think you're wrong about that."

"About the fauves?"

"No."

"Not the fauves? So what then, the German expressionists?"

"No." His head was starting to ache a bit and the music had started up along with a few jingles.

"I don't know what they're teaching you kids in art school today."

"I didn't go to art school."

"I thought Kate was your teacher, at Columbia."

"I took a night class, that's all." He blinked as if blinded by a flash bulb, then quickly offered up a studied, suggestive smile.

Werther took a good look at him, full lips and fine bone structure, almost too pretty, but there was definitely something off too. "Maybe we should do this another time."

"No. This is the right time. This is it! Coke is it! The real thing."

"Excuse me?"

"Wait a minute." He yanked the papers out of his backpack. "These are for you. A gift."

Werther looked at them, a bunch of prints, all obviously torn from books, the edges frayed—Francis Bacon, Jasper Johns, a Soutine. "Oh. Thanks."

"They're grrrrrrrrreat, aren't they!"

"Well, Johns is very good, and the Soutine is interesting, though a bit overheated for my taste. But Francis Bacon, well . . ." He held the reproduction at an arm's length, wrinkled up his nose. "I just can't get into him at all."

Can't get into him . . . Can't get into him . . . The artist's words were echoing in his brain along with the songs and ads and jingles. "Why not?"

Werther shrugged. "Who knows?" He handed the prints back. "You should hang on to these. They obviously mean more to you than me."

"You don't like them?"

"They're fine. But I have plenty of art books and reproductions. Plus I own a Johns painting."

"What do you mean?"

"I mean, I bought a Jasper Johns painting. I *own* it."

"Can I see it?"

"It's not here. It's in my home. This is only my studio." Werther was really growing impatient. "You know, I should be getting there; home, I mean."

"But we've hardly started. You haven't taught me anything."

"Look." Werther sighed. "We can do this another time, okay?" *Like, never.* "I'm tired. Long day, you know."

"Just a couple of minutes. Then I'll go. Okay?" He looked up at Werther with those sad blinking eyes.

Werther glanced at his watch. Five minutes, that was all he was going to give him. "Okay."

"Grrrrrrrrreat!" The young man pointed to one of his paintings lying on the floor, a street scene. "What do you think of that one?"

"It's . . . fine. Very nicely . . . constructed." Werther wanted to say it sucked, but he also wanted the kid out.

"How do you mean?"

"Your composition, the way you set it up on the canvas. Very nice." It was all he could come up with.

The kid smiled. "And what about the color?"

"The color?"

"Yeah, the color?"

"Well, there is no color."

"Of course there is. Are you crazy, or something?" *Sometimes you feel like a nut!*

"Well, if you mean, the gradation of tone, or—"

"No, the *color.*"

"But it's entirely black and white."

"You're lying." Panic was starting to overtake him, nerve endings tingling. "Are you just teasing me?"

"Why would I do that?"

"Because . . ." He didn't know why the artist would be so cruel to him. He snatched the loose black-and-white canvas off the floor and brought it close to his face. "There's lots of color." His blinking eyes were starting to tear. "You have to be wrong."

This is getting too fucking weird. Time to get him out. "Look, I've got to get going."

"Where?"

"Home."

"One last question. *Please.*"

Werther sighed heavily. "Yes?"

"Okay. So it's black and white, but it's good, right?"

"Yes. It's fine. I think it's very nice."

"Nice?" The kid stared at him, those sad eyes blinking wildly. "You don't think it's nice. You think black and white is *boring.* You think any artist who doesn't use color is *wasting his time.*"

"What are you talking about?"

"I saw you, heard what you said about black and white. Boring, you said."

"Oh." Werther laughed. "You mean on TV, on Kate's show."

"That's right."

"Why don't you pack those up," Werther said, indicating the paintings. "We'll talk another time."

"I'm *trying* to learn. Really I am."

"Sure," said Werther, hearing the plaintive note in the kid's voice. *What a case.* He couldn't wait to give Kate McKinnon a piece of his mind. If she even knew this kid, which he was beginning to doubt. He watched the kid scoop up his paintings. Were those tears on his cheeks? *Jesus.* "Listen, it doesn't matter what I think."

The kid wiped the tears off his cheeks, and Werther turned away.

When Boyd Werther next opened his eyes his head was aching, and when he tried to move he realized he could not. He struggled against the duct tape that held his broad chest strapped to the chair, and when he looked down he could see there was more tape wound around his wrists and ankles. How long had he been unconscious? He had no idea. The last thing he remembered was watching the kid packing up his paintings and crying. No, that wasn't the last thing. There was the hand coming across his face from behind, and the chemical smell, and he remembered trying to fight the kid off, but then the room had started to spin.

The kid was rubbing his arm where a bruise was already setting in. "You hurt me, you know."

"What the fuck is going on?"

The kid blinked, and glanced to his side. "Hey, Tony, get the lights, would you?" He waited, squinting, shielding his eyes from the studio's spotlights, then after a moment strutted toward the wall, found the switch, and the room went dim. "Gotta do everything myself, I guess. Thanks *a lot,* Tony."

Boyd Werther glanced at the empty space beside the young man. "I said, what the fuck is going on, what do you want?"

"I—I want you to help me."

"Fuck you! Get me out of this. Now! Are you fucking crazy!" Werther struggled against the tape and the chair jumped a bit.

The kid got behind him, started making a circle, wrapping more duct tape around Werther and the chair, connecting it all to a heat pipe.

"What are you doing?" Werther told himself to be calm. "Just tell me what you want, okay? I'm sure we can work this out."

"Shhh . . ." The young man tilted his head to the side like a dog, as if listening for something. "What? No, Tony. Not now! Sorry. What was it you asked?"

"I, uh, asked what you *want.*"

"Oh. Conversation."

"Conversation?"

"Uh-huh."

Boyd Werther felt panic rising from his gut, bile in the back of his throat like he was going to be sick. But no, he had to keep it together, this was just a kid, he could handle him, get out of this absurd situation. "I told you before, we can talk, anytime."

"No, you wanted me out."

"I was tired, that's all."

"You didn't like them. The gods." He pointed to the prints scattered on the floor—Francis Bacon, Johns, Soutine.

"That's not so. I told you, I *own* a Jasper Johns painting."

"He's . . . afflicted, you know?"

"Who?"

"Jasper Johns."

What the hell is this lunatic talking about? "Really?"

"That's right."

Werther couldn't see his watch, but knew that his assistant, Victoria, would be back soon. *Keep him talking.* "Uh, how old are you, twenty-two, -three?"

"Why?" The kid, in dark silhouette, seemed larger now, moving around the studio, muttering. The question threw him; he'd never known his real age.

"I—I was just wondering, I mean, you're young, and . . ." Werther was figuring it out as he spoke. "I, uh, always wanted a . . . son, someone I could mentor."

The dark silhouette stopped moving. "Mentor?"

"Yes, you know. Someone to help, to show the ropes. In your case, help you with your . . . your artwork."

"You'd really do that?"

"Absolutely. I'd like to."

"Gee, that's grrrrrrrrrrrrrreat! You can't beat the real thing, you know. I mean, you're in good hands with Allstate!" The kid stopped and laid a hand on Werther's shoulder. "Let's play a game. I'll point to an area of your painting and you'll tell me the color."

"It's going to be difficult with the lights out." Werther remembered the kid squinting in the bright lights earlier.

The dark silhouette backed up, flipped a switch and the room was bright again. "I'm doing this for you, the lights. I wouldn't want to be . . . counterproductive." He was blinking like crazy. He put a hand up to shield his eyes. One of the spotlights was glinting off the heavy silver chain at Werther's neck.

"What's that?"

"What?"

"On your neck."

"Oh. A chain, that's all. Very old. Rare. It's medieval."

"I've read about that. The Middle Ages, right?"

"Right. It was a gift." Werther thought back to the moment when his beautiful first wife fastened it around his neck after they had made love. Any other time he'd have smiled. "I wear it for good luck." A thought: "Hey, why don't you have it? It will bring you luck."

"Wow, that's so nice of you." The kid leaned in and for a moment Werther thought about sinking his teeth into the kid's forearm, then saw a thick, jagged scar on the wrist and just couldn't do it.

The young man held the chain in his hands, admired it for a minute, then fastened it around his neck. "That was real nice of you. I won't forget it either."

"Don't mention it." Werther forced himself to smile.

"Okay. The game. It's just to teach me about color, okay?"

"Okay."

He faced one of Werther's huge abstractions, pointed a finger at an area of intense yellow. "What color is this?"

"Yellow."

"Yellow? Are you *sure*?" He listed toward another area, and pointed. "What's this?"

"It's, uh, red."

The kid squinted at it. "Don't fuck with me."

"But it is. Can't you see that?"

"Of course I can see it!"

"Okay. Okay. Sure. Sure you can." Werther's heart was pounding against the tight duct tape. He didn't know what to say, didn't get the game. Why was the kid asking him about the color? "Your eyes. Is there a problem?"

"Like what?"

"I don't know. But . . . you seem to have trouble . . . seeing the color correctly."

The kid came right into his face, spitting out the words: *"No—I— Don't."*

"Okay. Fine. You don't."

The kid darted over to Werther's six-foot-long paint table, half the surface covered with a glass palette, small mounds of dried paint around the perimeter, dozens of oil tubes lined up beside jars of raw pigment. He took a moment to survey the tubes, unscrewed one of the caps, brought it over to the artist, shoved it under his nose, paint oozing out of the opening. "This it? That red over there?" He nodded toward the painting.

Werther stared at dark green oil paint, not knowing what to say.

"Is it?"

"Well, uh, no."

"You telling me this *isn't* red?"

"Uh, look at the label."

The young man brought the tube within inches of his eyes, but without his magnifying glass it was hopeless, impossible for him to focus on what was clearly printed on the label: PHTHALOCYANINE GREEN. He touched his tongue to the oil. "Tastes like red," he said. "You try it." He placed the tube against Werther's tightly closed mouth, dark briny green smearing across the man's lips.

"Right," Werther mumbled, a bit of linseed oil and pigment leaching between his closed lips. "I was mistaken."

The young man pivoted back toward one of Werther's large paintings and in one fast stroke squeezed the tube of green paint across the canvas, then stood back to assess it. "Doesn't really match," he said, blinking and frowning, seeing that the tones were, in fact, different. "Maybe you're right." He turned back to the artist. "But this isn't going to work if you lie to me. That's just counterproductive. I thought you were going to be . . . what was it you said?"

"A mentor?"

"Yeah, a mentor."

Werther quietly watched the thick noodle of green paint ooze and drip down the surface of his finished painting, ruining it.

"What about here? What's this color?" The kid pointed at an area of deep orange in Werther's painting.

Werther took a breath, inhaling the smeared oil paint on his lips along with it. "That's orange. A mix of uh, cadmium red medium and lemon yellow, with a little titanium white."

The young man squinted hard at the area, which, to him, looked like a medium brownish-gray. "Show me."

Werther squirmed against his restraints. "How can I?"

The young man scurried back to the paint table, started scooping up paint tubes into his arms like babies.

"It moves."

"What does?"

"The paint table. It moves. It's on wheels."

"Oh, cool." He slid the table beside the artist. "You got a magnifying glass?"

"Yes. Over there." Werther pointed with his chin at a desk across the room.

"Why do you use one? Are you *afflicted*?"

"I, uh, use it to look at slides of paintings."

"Oh," he said, disappointed. He ran the magnifying glass over Werther's tubes of expensive oil color, selected cadmium red medium, lemon yellow, and titanium white. He unscrewed the caps, squeezed dollops of paint onto the palette, swirled one of the artist's thick bristle brushes through all three colors, mixing, his eyes blinking the whole time. "How's this?" he asked, staring at what appeared to him as nothing more than brownish-gray glop.

Werther stared at the sad, handsome kid. He could not believe this was happening, nor imagine what it was about. "You, uh, need a bit more of the yellow."

The young man's eyes blinked and darted between the blobs of paint he'd squeezed onto the palette.

"That's the one on the right," said Werther, almost a whisper, as though he knew the assistance would not be well received.

"I know that!" He added more yellow into the mix, then painted a swatch of the newly blended color over the area Werther had identified as orange and stood back for another assessment. He could tell that at least tonally they matched. "I guess you're telling the truth."

"Why would I lie?"

"Everybody lies." He pointed with the brush at another area—a wide band of color that ran the length of the painting, top to bottom. "Is this orange too, teacher—I mean, mentor?"

"No, it's . . . pink."

The young man dragged the brush of orange paint across the pink. To his eyes the two colors matched perfectly.

"You trying to trick me?"

"No."

"But it is orange, right?"

"Okay."

"Okay, what?"

"Okay, you're right. They're both orange, like you say."

He turned away from the artist—"Tony, is it orange or pink?"—then turned back and roared—"It's grrrrrrrrreat!" Then in his normal voice said: "Tony could be lying. He does that." A turn to the left. "Who's lying, Donna?" His voice ratcheted up several octaves. "They're both lying!" The young man spun around toward Werther. "How can you be a mentor if you lie to me?"

Werther didn't know what to say, nervously licked his lips, tasted the paint as the kid came toward him, paintbrush aimed like a gun. "I, I guess I was wrong. No, you were wrong. I mean—"

"*I'm* wrong." Eyes blinking, wildly. "*I'm* wrong?" Volume rising: "You think I'm *stupid*?"

"No, no. Not at all."

"But then, why would I be wrong?" He flicked his tongue against the tip of the paintbrush. "It tastes orange to me."

"Yes, yes. Of course. It's orange. You're right." Werther's heart was pounding.

The young man moved a step closer, laid the brush against the artist's mouth. "Taste it."

Werther mumbled through lips pressed tightly shut. "Mmm . . . yes. Orange."

"*Taste it!*" The kid dug his fingers into Werther's cheeks, pressed until the artist's jaw muscles gave way and his mouth opened, than shoved the brush in. "*Can you taste it?* Orange! Right? *Orange!*" He jerked the brush out of Werther's mouth.

Werther gasped and spit out flecks of oily paint.

"It *is* orange, right? You can taste it, right?"

"Y-yes."

The kid scooped a palette scraper off the artist's paint table, nothing more than a straight razor in a holder, spun toward the artist's largest canvas, and zip! A slice to the left, then right, top, bottom; within seconds a six-figure artwork destroyed, canvas hanging from the wooden stretcher bars like rags, a few pieces dropping to the floor. The young man gathered up remnants of canvas, sniffed at them, then brought them toward Werther. "What color is this?"

"It's . . . it's . . ." The taste of oil, resin, and pigment was still in Werther's mouth, making him queasy.

"I'll give you a hint. It's my *favorite* color."

"R-really?"

"Yeah. So tell me. What is it?'

"Uh . . . raw sienna."

"No, it's not." He leaned over the artist. "It's razzmatazz."

"Razzmatazz? I don't know what that—"

Blinking like mad, face going red. "You call yourself an artist and you don't know *razzmatazz*?"

"Explain it to me. Please." Werther felt paint slide down the back of his throat, acidic, burning.

"You tell me. You're the one who knows everything about color."

"No . . . I . . . I don't."

"But you said you did."

"No. Never."

"You did."

"When?"

"On TV. Remember?"

"No, I—"

"Yes. You know everything, but you won't teach me."

"I will. *I swear.* I'll be your mentor, like I said. Take the tape off me and let me really teach you. We can be friends."

"Friends?" The kid's face went blank a moment. "Donna, Dylan, what do you think?" He appeared to be listening, eyes blinking madly, head cocked. "Yeah, I agree."

"What?"

The young man smiled sadly for a moment, leaning toward Werther's bound hands with the palette scraper poised above them. "They think you're lying."

"Who?"

"My friends."

"I'm not."

The young man regarded his own paintings stacked neatly on the floor, the black-and-white cityscape on top. "I know what you think, that black and white is *boring,* that *I'm* boring. Donna says you're lying to make me feel bad. And Donna always knows." He picked up the black-and-white painting from the floor. "*You* say it's only black and white, but Donna says it's got lots of color, beautiful color." He snared a jar of raw pigment off the paint table, unscrewed the cap and emptied it over Werther's head, instantly turning the artist into a member of the Blue Man Group. "You look good." He laughed. "You're all magic mint. And now . . ." He stood back, assessing Werther as one would a work of art, and whipped a tube of paint off the table, crushed it in his palm, bright red paint squirting all over Boyd Werther's face and chest. "So what color is that, huh?"

"It's . . . red."

"Liar!"

"No, I—"

"You don't know green when you see it? *You?* Who sleeps, dreams, and eats color!" He snatched up another tube, gripped Werther's chin until the artist's jaw muscles opened, crammed the tube of paint into the artist's mouth and squeezed it dry, tossed it to the floor, grabbed another, squeezed, and another, and another, a veritable rainbow of colors spewing from Werther's mouth, dripping over his chin, onto his shirt, and into his lap.

Werther was gagging, but still breathing when the idea hit the kid—that he was about to lose a rare opportunity, and with a genuine artist. He let go of Werther's jaw, scrambled through his backpack while the artist gasped and sputtered for breath, then turned back and with one fast stroke slit Werther's belly wide open, and in that instant the room exploded around him with the most magnificent and luscious color he had ever seen, ever imagined—fuchsia and salmon and razzmatazz—and he scooped up handfuls of bloody entrails that spilled over the artist's legs and raced from one of Werther's huge canvases to another, smudging and drawing, swirling the stuff in big broad strokes.

It took a long, agonizing time for Boyd Werther to die. He watched, unable to speak as the crazed young man scooted between his bleeding body and the canvas, dipping his hands into his open belly, using his blood and guts to create a painting, which, just before his vision failed, he realized looked very much like the Soutine print, *Carcass of Beef,* which lay on the floor beside his feet.

The young man was getting tired running back and forth, wanted more of the precious medium at his disposal, plucked a coffee can from the paint table, held it under the blood that poured out of the artist's gut, then snatched a brush off the artist's palette and went carefully from painting to painting, writing and identifying everything, until the gorgeous scarlet blood started turning pink and all the color in the room began to pale, and then, just then, as the room was fading to a wan gray, he heard the gate of the industrial elevator slam shut, and turned, his hands like raw steaks, out in front of him, dripping, and went for his knife as the front door of Boyd Werther's studio swung open.

TWENTY-SEVEN

The humid Texas air coiled itself around her like a cocoon the moment the airport's automatic doors had shut, but Kate's brain was still buzzing. She had not been able to relax the entire flight from New York, thoughts of Richard, the withdrawn funds, Noreen Stokes's accusations, all of it refusing to quit, especially that rainy Bronx night, and all the senseless bloodshed. Kate kept replaying the moment when Angelo Baldoni was coming toward her, his gun aimed at her, and recalled that for a brief moment she had thought—yes, shoot me, do it, have it over, it's fine, that she would be happy to join her husband. And yet she had been the one who fired the fatal shots. Perhaps Mitch Freeman was wrong after all. Perhaps some small part of her wanted to live.

A honking horn interrupted Kate's thoughts, and she was relieved to see her friend waving from a car window.

Marianne Egbert, curator at the Rothko Chapel, had been a friend since they'd met at New York's famed Art Institute, both returning students—Marianne after a bad marriage and worse divorce, Kate after ten years on the Astoria force.

"It feels like August," said Kate, as she got into the car.

"You're in Texaaasss, honey chile," Marianne drawled, then got quiet, and when she next spoke her tone was completely serious. "How are you doing?"

"I've been better." Kate sighed. "But listen, I'm here for all of one day and one night, and if it's okay with you I just want to forget my life, okay?" She leaned back against the padded leather headrest.

"Your crew is all set for tomorrow. Sorry we can't give them more than a couple of hours, but it's the best we can do."

"Not a problem," said Kate. "All they need to do is pan the room and the paintings, film me walking around for a few minutes. I can add what I need in a voice-over once I'm home. Truthfully, I could have done it all at home, but I needed a break. Any chance of me getting a few minutes in the chapel alone?"

"Why don't you go before your crew arrives," said the curator. "I think there's gotta be some really good karma floating around in there. His Holiness the Dalai Lama and six or seven other religious leaders were just in there praying for world peace."

"Hope it works," said Kate.

Marianne peeled away from the curb and merged into the stream of traffic. "Come on. Let me buy you a Texas-sized margarita."

"I'll take two," said Kate.

Clare Tapell rubbed her tired eyes and stared at the eccentric downtown skyline through the windows of her One Police Plaza office. The meeting with the mayor had not gone well. Clearly, this case could ruin her.

A madman eviscerating hookers was one thing, and horrible, no question. But an innocent kid, an art student, and now a world-famous artist and his assistant—clearly, this could not continue.

"Do your job." The mayor's words.

His meaning had been clear. If she did not do her job, she might be out of one. And with her reappointment only months away, the mayor could use this case as an excuse to get rid of her if he wanted to—and she knew he did.

Lately the press hadn't been kind to Chief Tapell. There was criticism of her plan to merge a few stations to cut costs, and that small but unpleasant scandal only six months ago—two Upper West Side cops running drugs out of their precinct's evidence room—and now the threats of a citywide police strike.

Damn it, she needed this case resolved, and not in a few weeks.

Tapell sighed, looked away from the window and back at the prelims on Boyd Werther's murder. All indicators pointed to the painterly unsub. She noted the fact that there had been no break-in, that Werther had obviously let his attacker in, which either meant he knew him, or that his assailant had not posed a threat. *Why was that?*

An artist murdered—and not just any artist. An artist Kate McKinnon knew. *Was that a coincidence?* No question Kate had to have a look at this. *Kate.*

Tapell had to admit she was not unhappy that Kate had screwed up and been thrown off the case. She'd half expected her to come begging, or threatening to be reinstated. But Kate hadn't done that.

So now what?

Tapell laced her fingers together and stared out the window.

Would Kate really have blown the whistle? Tapell couldn't be sure. Funny, she thought, how life so often played tricks on you. Kate hadn't even asked, and now she was going to have to put her back on the case.

The Houston sky was a mix of clouds and sun, not as hot this morning, as Kate pulled herself out of the cab, head aching. Two margaritas? More like four over the course of the evening, when she'd poured her heart out to her old friend. The drinks had seemed like a good idea. At the time.

Kate gulped the last of her second Starbucks coffee, found a trash bin, dumped the cup, and headed toward the Rothko Chapel.

She'd been here years ago as a student, with a crowd of art history majors who had annoyed the hell out of her with all their talk, dissecting the paintings, the building, and a lecturer who kept up a steady stream of dates and facts: commissioned by the wealthy Texas art patrons Dominique and John de Menil; the names of the various architects, including Philip Johnson, who had resigned because the artist was so difficult; the project begun in 1965, completed in 1971, a year after the artist's death; Rothko's fee of $250,000, a ton of money for an artist at the time. All of it was still fresh in her mind, though during this visit there would be no one saying it out loud to disturb her.

Kate made her way past the reflecting pool and Barnett Newman's twenty-six-foot steel balancing act of a sculpture, *Broken Obelisk,* as the pale red facade of the chapel came into view, offering little explanation of its contents or purpose—no signs, no steps, no windows, no religious symbols of any kind. Though conceived as a Roman Catholic chapel, it had become a site for all religions, described by its patron as a "universal sanctuary."

The guard was waiting for her; glanced at his clipboard and then at the driver's license Kate offered as ID. He smiled. "You got the chapel all to yourself. Ms. Egbert said she'd see ya'll after the taping." He tugged one of the heavy black wooden doors open. "You've got about a half hour before the TV crew comes in," he said, taking a seat beside the doors that led into the actual chapel, which Kate pushed through and let close behind her.

Silent.

Womblike.

Enigmatic.

Kate walked swiftly, eyes on her feet, not wanting to see anything until she was in the center of the room, then looked up, and allowed the octagonal space to embrace her.

The fourteen large paintings that covered the walls did a slow dance, moving forward, then back, deep dark maroons and blacks, playing a sly game of hide-and-seek. Kate could almost feel them breathing. When she focused on the paintings in front of her, the ones behind petitioned for attention; to the right and left, more of Rothko's enormous works filled every part of her vision—canvases begging for interpretation where none seemed possible, shadowy rectangles empty of image and explanation. Endless black. One minute inviting. The next forbidding. A promise. An abyss.

Kate swayed a bit, took a deep breath, felt trapped, eyes searching shadowy surfaces that offered no answers and certainly no consolation.

Is that what she was looking for, consolation? But for what? Exactly what was it she was searching for?

Answers, of course. For a husband who had left without good-bye, without explanation.

Kate's eyes slid over murky maroons, fell into mottled blacks.

Was Richard responsible for his own death, or simply a victim? She peered into the ebony slabs and wondered if his murder would remain as remote and mystifying as these paintings.

Oh, Richard.

Kate glanced up at the skylight as if asking the heavens, and through the metal baffle could see banks of clouds rushing past as if on a mission, then back at the paintings, impenetrable, holding on to their secrets, the artist having stripped the work of subject matter, of almost everything.

Here were the most sophisticated works of art, paintings that operated in the absence of all color, objects for meditation, vessels to fall into, to reflect. Mark Rothko, a difficult, remote, and dedicated artist, had chosen not to seduce the viewer with gorgeous color, but instead to take it away, leave you on your own to confront yourself in these monoliths of despair.

Those fast-moving clouds were passing over the skylight, illuminating and dimming the room as if God were playing with a light switch, painted black surfaces opaque one moment, smoky veils the next. Kate looked up, and at that moment the clouds parted—a blast of sunlight. She was momentarily blinded, then blinking, the paintings flipping back and forth—black, white, positive, negative—while other paintings winked in her mind, the total opposite of Rothko's: brash color, words like a map beneath them. Kate shut her eyes and when she opened them for a split second, the chapel was stark white again—as if she were blind.

Blind. Yes. Of course. He's blind.

But was that possible? That the killer was blind? If that was true, how could he commit his heinous crimes or paint at all? No, that wasn't it. Kate blinked again, and when her vision returned she was staring into one of Rothko's colorless black voids, and then she had it: He wasn't blind. He was color blind. Of course. The screwed-up color, the words—red, green, wild watermelon, razzmatazz—written beneath the colored areas like a guide, each painting obviously some kind of test for himself.

How simple. That's whom they were looking for—a color-blind painter.

The sun retreated, grays returning to solid blacks, veils becoming vaults, secrets sucked back into the void.

Color blind, thought Kate, staring into one of Rothko's hollow black paintings.

She was trying to think it through when her cell phone broke the chapel's silence.

Thank God no one else was there.

How odd, thought Kate, recognizing the number, that Brown should be calling her just when she wanted to call him.

"I can't really talk," she said, whispering. "I'm in a chapel, in Houston."

"Texas?"

"Last time I checked."

"Why? Never mind. Doesn't matter. When are you coming back?"

"Later. Today. Why?"

"I need you here, at the station."

"I thought I was out."

"You are. Well, you *were*." Brown took a breath. "But something's happened."

TWENTY-EIGHT

Boyd Werther's memorial service was an art world event—artists, dealers, curators, and collectors out in full force, endless speeches and praise for a man Kate knew most envied for his fame and fortune, all of them decked out in their high-priced black duds. Kate didn't hear much of what was said, the thought that somehow she might have led the killer to Werther weighing heavily on her conscience.

She could not stop thinking about the emergency squad meeting she'd attended just before the service, or get the crime scene photos of Boyd Werther's studio out of her mind. But it was not the horrific pictures of Werther that kept replaying; it was the ones of the killer's paintings lined up neatly on one wall as if he were giving himself a one-man show. But for whose eyes? Had he set it up for Werther—or the police who he knew would be cleaning up the mess? Kate wasn't sure.

Especially after the newest revelation: her own name among the scribbled borders of the psycho's paintings. That had been a shock. What possible connection could he have to her? Kate had no idea other than the fact that the newspapers had played up her involvment in the case. Freeman believed the psycho might have been watching her on TV, and Kate knew it was a possibility—the interview she had done with Werther had aired only a few days ago. The thought of this creep holed up somewhere, watching her and writing her name over and over chilled her.

Blair Sumner elbowed Kate as another artist took to the podium and began to praise the dead artist.

"Was he really such a saint?" Blair whispered.

Kate took a moment before she answered. "No, but—" The pictures of Werther—sliced, covered with blood and paint—sparked in her mind. "He was very respected," she said softly.

"Diplomat," said Blair.

According to Freeman, the killer's ritual was changing; something must have triggered the attack on Werther, and then his assistant; plus he hadn't bothered to clean up, had left saliva on the paintbrushes that could easily be tested for DNA. Not that the cops had anything to compare it to. Not yet. But why so sloppy? Did he want to be caught?

Grange was in Washington enlisting more agents, while Tapell was busy manning the local troops. Now, practically every division of the NYPD would be involved in the hunt.

Kate glanced up at the podium, a young woman trying hard to control her tears. "I was Boyd's assistant for the past two years."

The other assistant, thought Kate. The lucky one.

"Boyd Werther taught me so much. To be completely obsessed with your artwork, to be focused and fixated on every detail."

Obsessed. Fixated. The words triggered the earlier squad meeting, which replayed in Kate's mind.

"I don't think Werther was necessarily the obsession," said Freeman.

"Who then?" asked Perlmutter.

Freeman looked at Kate. "Sorry, but your name is in his paintings, and he chose an artist you know. It doesn't take much for these guys to fixate. Sometimes it's as simple as someone they pass in the street, and sometimes it's Jodie Foster. You are, after all, a minor celebrity."

Kate shivered and Blair stroked her arm. "You okay, darling?"

"Fine," she said, though she was lying. Crime scene photos of Werther's slashed paintings, names of colors that the psycho had painted on them, some right, many wrong, flickered in her brain.

Identification. That's what it was all about. Kate was sure of it and had told the squad. Color blind. They were looking for someone color blind. Kate could almost imagine the psycho's game, quizzing Werther about color, disputing the answers, finally killing the man in a rage.

Werther's lucky assistant covered her mouth as she began to cry, and Kate was reminded of another new addition to the psycho's paintings—crude, tiny pencil drawings of faces with tape across the mouth drawn into empty spaces. Freeman had suggested they might be self-portraits.

Is he mute as well as color blind?

"Kate?" Blair was tapping her on the shoulder. "Kate."

"What?"

"It's over, darling."

"Oh." Kate hadn't seen or heard any speakers after the assistant, nor could she remember the girl leaving the podium.

"I'm worried about you," said Blair, taking her arm. "Shall we go?"

"I'd like to hang around a few minutes. Out of respect for Boyd."

There was a spread of wine and cheese, like an art opening, but Kate had no appetite, and after a few minutes she was sorry she hadn't left with Blair. She was eager to get going when Vincent Petrycoff, Boyd Werther's art dealer, snagged her.

"You wouldn't consider parting with one of those two large Werthers you have in East Hampton, would you?"

The shock must have registered on Kate's face.

"Sorry if that sounds crass. I'm only asking because, as you know, all the new work was destroyed by the lunatic who killed poor Boyd, and so . . . um . . . there's a shortage of uh, new work—"

"I have no intention of selling those paintings." Kate glared at the art dealer.

Ramona Gross, head of Contemporary Art at one of New York's leading auction houses, leaned in. "Awful," she said, dramatically closing heavily shadowed lids and pursing her scarlet lips. "I mean, why destroy the man's paintings? Who did *they* offend?"

"Me," sneered a twenty-something conceptual artist lately getting a lot of attention for her nude underwater performances. "Color-field painting? I mean, come on. Painting is like, dead."

"No more dead than an Esther Williams movie," said Petrycoff.

Enough. Kate did not bother with good-byes, but hurried out of the chapel, anxious to get to her next appointment.

The crime scene photos of Werther's studio continued to flash through her mind-—particularly the way the psycho had brutalized both the artist and his work, yet took the time to line up his own paintings like a neat little exhibition.

Of course. That was it. What he wanted. Why hadn't she thought of it earlier? He wanted his own exhibition. Now she wondered if she could provide him with one. Would the squad go for it?

Kate checked her watch as the taxicab headed east. She didn't want to be late for her appointment. If she was right about the psycho, and he was color blind, she wanted to know all about it.

Professor Abraham Brillstein was a small stooped man with a large pointy nose, thinning gray hair slicked back, exposing gaps of pale white scalp, reddish-brown eyes magnified to the size of golf balls through Coke-bottle-thick glasses. Once the head of Mount Sinai Neurology, as well as having his own lucrative private practice, Brillstein had given it all up for research after a trip to Guam where he and a team of neurologists had gone to study a Parkinson-like disease called lytico-bodig, which in turn had led him on a pilgrimage to a remote group of Pacific islands, one of whose populations had an overabundance of color blindness. There, he'd discovered a lifelong obsession.

Kate took in the man's office, windowless and gray, the perfect cell for someone studying lack of color.

Brillstein held up a half-finished glass of orange juice. "Imagine if this looked like nothing more than brown sludge. Bet you wouldn't want to drink it, would you?"

"No," said Kate, and she meant it.

"Think about it—gray roast beef; black tomato juice; black, tannish-brown bananas. Even musical tones can be translated by the brain so that music itself can become nothing more than a depressing, colorless experience." He finished the glass of juice in a gulp, Adam's apple bobbing in his thin, ropy neck.

"And all of that is possible?" asked Kate.

"In cases of complete cerebral achromatopsia, yes." He locked her in his magnified glare.

"Translation, please?"

"Sorry." Brillstein rapped a pencil against the edge of a desk crowded with stacks of papers, dozens of folders, small mounds of half-bent and tangled paper clips. "I am referring to an extreme form of color blindness that occurs because of an event—be it a disease or an accident. You see, most color blindness is congenital. You're born with it. Not at all uncommon, particularly in men. Of course there are degrees of severity." He started counting off on his slightly arthritic fingers. "You've got your anomalous trichromacy, the most common form of color blindness, where the subject may have some trouble discriminating between colors but still sees them. Then there is your red-green color blindness, deuteranomaly, which affects approximately five out of every hundred men, and protanomaly, which is referred to as 'red-weakness,' which affects about one out of a hundred. To a protanomalous viewer, any redness in color is perceived more weakly. A red traffic light could easily be mistaken for a yellow or amber one."

"That could make crossing the street risky business," said Kate.

"Indeed." Brillstein pushed his glasses up the bridge of his nose and his eyes jumped another ten percent in magnification. "But complete achromatopsia, well, that is rare, and very severe, affecting oh, one person in say, thirty or forty *thousand*. It's all a question of cones, you see."

"The cones are what decode color in our eyes, as opposed to the rods, right?"

"Yes." Brillstein smiled. "The rods, which do not provide color vision, are located at the periphery of the retina. The cones, our color receptors, are at the retina's center. Cones come in three varieties, red, blue, and green, though I am speaking quite simply here."

"I appreciate that," said Kate, trying to take it all in, watching the little man exchange his pencil for a paper clip, which he started bending out of shape. "The thing is, Dr. Brillstein, we've got a suspect who paints, but his color is all wrong, and he labels the colors incorrectly, and—"

"Oh, so you don't actually *know* the subject?" Brillstein looked up from his fidgeting, his huge, distorted eyes on Kate.

"Unfortunately not."

"Then how do you know he's color blind?"

"Well, I don't." Kate plucked a paper clip off his desk and joined the doctor in his game of restless sculpting. "I just *feel* it. I realize that must sound absurd to a doctor, a scientist, but—"

"Not at all." Brillstein smiled at her warmly. "Fact is that half of what a researcher does is go on instinct. Eventually one hopes that one's instincts pay off, but we would never get anywhere without instinct and hypothesis and, as you say, a feeling." Another smile. "So, please, tell me everything you know, why you have this *feeling,* anything that might help me understand what led you to this deduction."

For the next twenty minutes Kate explained the oddly colored paintings, the repeated labeling, Boyd Werther's murder scene and the labeling there, her experience in the Rothko Chapel, everything she could think of, complete with the crime scene photos of the psycho's paintings and Boyd Werther's studio that she'd brought along. "Again," she said, summing it up, "I may be shooting in the dark here—no pun intended, Doctor—but the way this guy seems to be groping to learn about color is what struck me and led me to the idea that he's color blind."

Brillstein removed his thick glasses and rubbed his surprisingly small eyes. "Not a bad hypothesis at all, my dear."

"Well, then, suppose I'm right, that he is color blind. Completely. What can you tell me?"

The doctor replaced his glasses, ran a hand over his slick balding pate. "Well, first of all, that he most likely suffered an accident—something that interrupted the neural path between his eye and the brain. Some sort of brain damage."

Kate thought about that a moment. "And would that affect his behavior?"

"Absolutely. I mean, if your world suddenly went gray, I'm certain it would affect your behavior, would it not?"

"Yes, but I meant, more . . . pathologically."

"Hmmmm . . ." Brillstein starting bending another paper clip. "I'm afraid I can't tell you that, but . . . you are talking about an artist, a painter. Think about it—bad enough to lose your ability to see color if you are, say, a businessman, but an artist, one whose entire life is wrapped up in color, well . . ." He shook his head. "It would be devastating, no?"

"Yes." Kate stared at the gray walls, trying to imagine a colorless world.

"Color-blind people, the ones who are born color blind, are usually quite well adjusted because they have never known a world of color," said Brillstein. "But for a cerebral achromatope, one who has lost that sense completely, well, that is something else entirely. He will always remain aware of the fact that he's lost something incredibly precious, that he has lost color." Brillstein sighed. "Imagine if suddenly everything you were used to seeing in color—the green grass, flowers, the blue sky—were all suddenly drained of color, simply dreary shades of gray."

"Like a black-and-white movie?"

"Not nearly so good, or clear. With complete color blindness, visual acuity is also quite impaired." Brillstein thought a moment. "I know of one case, a young woman painter, who had a motorcycle accident that rendered her completely color blind. Eventually she committed suicide. Her life was simply no longer bearable." Brillstein removed his glasses and glanced up at the ceiling, then shook his head.

"What?"

"I was reminded of something, but . . ." He replaced his glasses. "I can't think of what." He shrugged and smiled sadly. "I'm getting old. What do they call it, a senior moment?"

"I have them all the time," said Kate. "Listen, if it does come to you—whatever it is—would you call me? The NYPD are a bit stymied on this one."

"Of course," said Brillstein. "Where was I? Oh, yes. The loss of color. What can I say, for the totally color blind life can be not only difficult but . . . very sad."

Kate tried to imagine the bright sandy beach below her East Hampton home, the glittering blue-green ocean devoid of color. But the thought only brought another sense of loss—that she would never again walk along that particularly beautiful stretch of beach with Richard. She quickly shifted gears. "What else? I mean, what else can you tell me about total color blindness?"

"Like what?"

Kate thought a moment. "Is there anything we should be looking for? I mean, how would someone with this condition act?"

"Act. Ah, yes, I see. Well, for starters, he'd be wearing sunglasses—and I mean all the time. Dark amber-colored sunglasses, probably the wraparound kind, to block as much light as possible."

Sunglasses. The guy loitering across the street from the Art Students League the day Mark Landau was murdered.

"Why is that?"

"Achromatopes are extremely light-sensitive. At high levels of light, his vision would severely decrease. And in bright light, well, an achromatope is practically blind." Brillstein opened his magnified reddish eyes to underscore the point. "Coping with light sensitivity is a terrible problem for achromatopes. Of course the opposite is also true, that he would be quite comfortable in dim light—much more so than you and me. And there are other small compensations, a sensitivity to outlines and borders, say."

Kate thought of the heavily outlined forms in the psycho's paintings, and the gray borders.

"Oh, and there is the incessant squinting and blinking. Even with sunglasses, achromatopes are so light-sensitive that they are constantly blinking and squinting in an attempt to shield their eyes from light."

"You said earlier that it's caused by an accident, a blow to the brain, and, what did you call it—a disruption of the pathway between the eye and brain?"

"Exactly." Brillstein smiled at Kate, the good student.

"So then the condition could be corrected by fixing that pathway, yes? Surgically, perhaps, so that the patient could see color again?"

"Oh, no." Brillstein's magnified eyes widened slowly behind his glasses. "I am afraid that a cerebral achromatope is doomed to a life completely devoid of color. The condition is completely incurable."

TWENTY-NINE

He struts around the darkened studio like a victorious soldier. He has never felt so powerful. Is it because he drank the artist's blood from his cupped hands that he feels the artist has become a part of him? He's never done that before, but this time, well, it just felt right, special. He didn't need or want gloves, nothing to separate him from the act. He is no longer afraid of being caught. He is stronger and smarter than any of them.

But then a memory, a feeling, an unexplained sensation of suffocation overcomes him, and the grunts and groans have started at the back of his mind, accompanied by music and jingles.

He shudders.

Those doctors always wanted him to talk about it.

Tell us what happened. Was there some sort of accident?

But he wouldn't tell them. It was his secret. His to harbor; a deep, festering sore to cultivate, to feed.

One time he weakened, told that woman doctor some of the stuff that had happened to him—*just for the fun of it! Just for the taste of it!*—and he saw tears in her eyes and wanted to cry along with her, but he did not, would not, could not, and then told her he'd made it all up, to make a fool of her. They thought he was stupid. But he showed them, didn't he, left them a little something to remember him by. A picture flickers in the back of his mind: a name tag on a white uniform, which turns a brilliant and beautiful red, and a name, Belinda.

Another memory . . . The taste of rubber in his mouth. Counting backward. Goop on his temples. Head splitting. Jaw aching. Arms and legs weak and sore. And then the pictures, the noise, even his friends—Tony and Dylan and Brenda and Donna—would disappear. Where would they go? He was so lonely waiting for them to return, which they did, finally, bringing all the racket along with them, but it was worth it to have his friends back.

He doesn't want to think about that now, presses his fingertips into his temples until the pain brings him back to the moment, and the memories dissipate. He would prefer to remember his most recent work. Phantom color, like an amputated limb, flashes in his brain, and he believes it is all happening in front of his eyes rather than behind them.

How amazing it was, two of them, back to back. *Double your pleasure* . . . Perfect timing. The girl arriving at precisely the right moment—just as everything was starting to fade—so that he could keep it going longer than ever before, and the colors—*oh, the colors*—how they shimmered and glowed, the chromatic intensity like nothing he'd ever seen.

She witnessed his power, how well he had identified everything, and agreed with everything he had written onto the artist's canvases. For a moment, he had considered taking the girl home with him to keep around his studio and help him the way she had helped the artist, who was no longer going to need her help, but he was afraid that Donna and Brenda wouldn't like it, and the girl did seem a little jumpy and nervous and screamed and cried, and who needed that?

"Not me," he says, then shuts his aching eyes and pictures the art *herstory-n* viewing his work lined up on the wall in the artist's studio and how impressed she will be. It's all for her now. She's the one. *You can't beat the real thing!* She is his savior. Has always been there for him. Maybe she will even tell Jasper Johns, which would be so grrrrrrrrrreat, and then the three of them could get together and talk about art and maybe have a drink the way people do in the movies. It all makes sense: The artist's studio being on Mulberry Street, which was clearly an omen, because mulberry was his second-favorite color in the box of sixty-four colors.

He glances at his hands, notes a slight blush of flesh tone and knows why: The artist's scarlet crimson raspberry magenta mulberry cerise razzmatazz blood runs through his veins.

He turns on the TV and flips channels until he finds something comforting and familiar, *The Flintstones,* is keenly aware of Fred and Wilma against a multicolored prehistoric landscape, and wanting to believe so badly tries another channel, and yes, Xena's hair is a lustrous blue-black, but then it fades and he remembers those first days after the accident when he wanted to die.

But not now.

Killing the artist made him feel alive, and close to her, to Kate, the art *her-story-n*—and now he wants to feel even closer.

T he minute Kate saw Willie, she was crying, a combination of happiness and all the sorrow she'd been trying to tamp down for the past two weeks since Richard had died brought to the surface. Willie, whom she had known and loved since she and Richard had adopted his sixth-grade class through Let There Be a Future; Willie, the smart and talented little boy who had grown up to become the successful artist; Willie, who was almost like a son to her.

"Oh, God, I'm sorry. Really I am. It's just that I'm so glad to see you." Kate hugged him and he hugged her back, and he cried too, and they clung to each other for what seemed like a long time, until Kate broke the hold and pulled back. "You look great," she said, sniffling. "More mature, I think."

"But no taller," said Willie, as Kate laid her arm on top of his shoulder and led him down the hall.

"Hey, kiddo, don't think life up here at six feet is a picnic. I am sure I've recounted, in detail, the horrors of being a five-foot-eleven girl in the ninth grade. Not pretty." She swiped tears off her cheeks and plopped a filter into the coffeemaker. "Trust me, you're perfect just as you are."

Willie smiled one of his dazzling smiles, and Kate felt her heart opening up again.

"It's good to be back. Too many of those tall Aryan types in Germany.

Of course they're all *so* nice to me," said Willie. "It's sort of getting on my nerves."

"A week in New York will take care of that. I wish you were staying longer."

"I would, but I've got like a dozen talks to give in Berlin and Frankfurt. They really make you work for these fellowships. Very annoying."

Kate regarded Willie, the grown man, successful artist, and thought back to the little boy she'd first met and she could not stop her eyes from clouding.

"You okay?" He laid his hand on her arm.

"I will be. So, your show," she said, shifting gears quickly. "I can't wait to see your new paintings."

"I'm terrified. Petrycoff. What a trip that guy is."

"It's the best gallery in New York."

"A lot to live up to."

"I'm not worried."

"That makes one of us." Willie smiled, then frowned. "I can't get over what happened. Boyd Werther, I mean."

Crime scene photos flipped through Kate's mind like a deck of cards. "It's horrible," she said. "I still can't believe it." Lately, there were so many things she had trouble believing.

"How's Petrycoff dealing with it?"

"Too busy thinking about doubling the price of a Werther canvas to think about it." Kate frowned. "I shouldn't say that. Everybody grieves in their own way." Grieving. Something she might have to consider herself.

"Only if you're human. And Petrycoff, well . . ."

Kate managed a laugh. "When can I see your new paintings?"

"We're installing tomorrow. Come by the gallery. Get a preview."

"I'm there."

"So where's Nola? She e-mailed me that she's a whale."

"At a doctor's appointment. She'll be back. She's dying to see you."

"I can't wait to see her too. Can't believe she's having a kid."

"I've gotten used to it," said Kate.

After they had coffee Willie had to get going, a meeting with the *Art in America* writer who was doing a story about his new work, and Kate did not cry again until she closed the apartment door behind him.

When the phone rang she let the answering machine pick it up until she heard it was Dr. Brillstein.

"It came to me," he said. "What I'd been trying to remember. A case study. A color-blind boy, a teen, who'd been institutionalized for a spell, back in the mid-nineties. One of the therapists, a Dr. Margo Schiller, who worked with him, wrote a paper about the experience for a psychiatric journal. I can fax it to you, if you'd like. I think you will find it quite fascinating."

Moments later, Kate was collecting the pages from her fax machine. She settled onto the couch, riveted from the very first line: *Tony T, a patient at the Pilgrim State Psychiatric Center, is completely color blind.*

Kate skipped over the more technical psychiatric lingo and concentrated on the therapist's notes from the time of treatment, scattered throughout the text.

Subject suffers from extreme delusional paranoia, possibly dual or more personalities. Speaks to, and takes advice from, imaginary friends . . .

It appears that patient Tony T has moved from killing insects to rodents. Believes that the act of killing restores his normal vision.

A chill shuddered through Kate's body. Could he be the one? There was nothing about whether or not this patient was cured—or even alive.

D r. Margo Schiller was not at all what Kate expected, a pretty woman in her late forties, maybe early fifties, sparkling eyes lined with kohl and hair to match, a light, sweet voice that bordered on the babyish. She showed Kate into a room with one huge window that offered an airy vista from lower Fifth Avenue up to the Empire State Building.

"Tony T," said Kate, after they'd gone through a few preliminaries. "I realize this is confidential information, but I'm wondering if you could divulge what the T stood for?"

"The police tried to discover his name, later, after he'd gone missing. He never supplied one other than Tony the Tiger, and obviously that wasn't his name."

Tony the Tiger. Tony. One of the names in the psycho's scribbled borders.

"He used to say he *borrowed* it," Dr. Schiller continued. "He told me once that he didn't remember his real name, but it was always hard to tell whether he was lying or telling the truth. I'm not sure he even knew. He often broke off in mid-sentence. I am quite certain he heard voices, had aural hallucinations."

"Like David Berkowitz, the Son of Sam?"

"Perhaps. It's always difficult to know. As a therapist one attempts to glean the truth from a patient, but he was an extremely difficult one to reach."

"What about his childhood?"

Dr. Schiller offered a paradoxical smile. "He claimed he was an orphan, that he'd been abandoned as a baby and grew up on the street. But on one occasion he broke down and recounted a most horrendous childhood, acts of appalling abuse, absolutely chilling. The next day he said he'd made it all up, that one of his *friends* had told him to do it." She hooked quotation marks around the word *friends* with her fingers. "I could never tell if he was playing me. But I believed the story of his abusive childhood had been a true one, and that when he remembered it he had to immediately deny it had ever happened to him—the memories were simply too painful."

Kate nodded. She'd known way too many child-abuse cases, both as a cop and working for Let There Be a Future. "How old was he when you worked with him?"

"I'm not sure. We had no family history. I would guess he was twelve or thirteen, possibly a bit older. It's difficult to say. He changed his birthday and age every few weeks. In some ways he was like a little child. But in other ways . . . very mature." Dr. Schiller stared out the window as though she were looking into the past. "He had the most startling blue eyes, but they were . . . dead." She turned back to Kate. "I saw him twice a week for almost a year, but as I said, it was difficult to know him. He was very clever, I can tell you that, though uneducated. Charming one minute, withdrawn and moody the next. And quite . . . beautiful. An asset of which he was keenly aware." She raised a dark-penciled eyebrow. "He often flirted with me in a way that was extremely inappropriate. Many abused children become overly sexualized. That is, they learn to use their allure, to use sex to get what they want." The doctor sighed. "I think on some level he just wanted approval, some kind, any kind of love—though I doubt he could accept genuine love or affection. He had an extremely damaged, though needy, ego. A true sociopath, I believed at the time." She took a few small breaths. "There was something both frightening and tragic about him. He never mixed, a complete loner, and when he did not know he was being observed you could see his lips moving, and sometimes hear him speaking in different voices."

"The imaginary friends."

"I think so, though he would never talk about them when asked."

Kate was taking copious notes. "And he was color blind."

"Totally. He was sent to us by physicians who treated him after he'd been in some kind of accident, a head injury."

"You wouldn't remember any of the doctors' names, would you?"

"As a matter of fact, I do. One, that is, Dr. Warren Weinberg. He's a friend of mine, which is why Tony T was referred to me. Warren treated him at Roosevelt Hospital."

"And he thought Tony T should be in a mental hospital?" The words *mental hospital,* brought up memories that Kate did not want to think about.

"Warren, Dr. Weinberg, found him to have extreme mood swings from depression to extreme hostility, and he would not disclose what had happened to him. Nor did he ever tell me, or any of the other therapists at the center. The accident that caused his color blindness remained a mystery." She shook her head. "Warren thought we might be able to get him to deal with the fact of his color blindness, of which he was in complete denial, though he was clearly afflicted in the way any cerebral achromatope would be—limited vision, extreme sensitivity to sunlight. He wore sunglasses all the time, though he pretended they were simply a part of his costume, a way to look cool. He was always trying to prove that he wasn't color blind, saying things like, oh, what a beautiful pink blouse you're wearing, but he'd often be wrong. If you corrected him he'd become incensed, furious. Once, with an orderly who had taunted him about his condition, he had to be restrained because he lashed out so violently."

"Did you treat him the entire time he was at Pilgrim State?"

"Pilgrim Psychiatric Center. Yes, as I said, for almost a year."

"They're one and the same, aren't they?"

"I can see by the look on your face, Ms. McKinnon, that you know something of the facility's history. I'll admit it has had its share of controversy, but it is not the same place it was thirty or forty years ago."

"Good to hear," said Kate. "From your paper, Doctor, it was unclear whether or not Tony T responded to treatment."

"I wish I could tell you he did." She shook her head. "Unfortunately, he was quite resistant to most psychotropic medications." Schiller ran her hands over the arms of her chair. "I'm not necessarily a proponent of ECT, but it was not entirely up to me—there were several other doctors seeing him, and they believed it would be beneficial."

"ECT?"

"Electroshock therapy."

Of course. How could she forget? "I didn't know it was used anymore."

"Oh, yes. ECT is quite respectable these days. There are over one hundred thousand patients being treated with ECT as we speak. I realize the public has formed its views from movies like *One Flew over the Cuckoo's Nest,* but it's not at all the barbaric method they used in the old days."

Kate had not formed her opinion through movies, though she did not want to discuss it with Dr. Schiller, despite the fact that the woman was intelligent and compassionate.

"I can assure you that ECT has come a long way from Nurse Ratchett," said Schiller. "Patients are no longer shackled to gurneys, and they receive anesthetics and muscle relaxers, their heart rates are carefully monitored. It's really quite civilized."

"A jolt of electricity to the brain?" Kate let go of a breath, and her bad memories along with it. "Sorry, but it still sounds barbaric to me."

"Well, you're not entirely alone in that belief." Schiller sighed. "As I said, I'm not exactly a fan of ECT, though many consider it a clean and efficient way to help a severely depressed or suicidal patient when medication fails."

"And Tony T, did he respond?"

"Well, it appeared to quiet the voices and subdue his rage, at least temporarily, but it didn't last. I can't say it was successful, no."

"And he disappeared?"

"Yes."

"He just walked out?"

"He was not put in Pilgrim Psychiatric Center as a criminal, Ms. McKinnon. Tony T had committed no crime. Not yet." She took a small quick breath. "There were plans to move him to another, more secure facility, but he disappeared before that ever happened. Believe me, he would certainly not have been released on his own. For one thing, he was still a minor." Dr. Schiller shifted her weight in her chair and demurely pulled her skirt over her knees. "After he vanished there was simply no way to trace him. We had no records. No birth certificate. No relatives that we knew, or that he ever spoke of."

"You mentioned the police tried to find him."

"Unsuccessfully. The only records we had were dental, but the police never found anyone who matched."

"Why were the police involved?"

"They would have been involved simply to find him, but it was more complicated than that." Schiller ran a hand through her jet hair, and Kate noticed it was trembling. "A nurse was found murdered the day before he disappeared, horribly mutilated. We had no proof that it was Tony T, but he was the only patient missing—and the killer was never found."

"You wouldn't by any chance remember the nurse's name?"

Schiller tapped her coral fingertips against her chin. "I think it was Linda or, no . . . Belinda—I'm certain the psychiatric center would have her name on record. I'm sorry. I can't remember. It's been ten years."

"Actually you seem to remember quite a bit."

She looked into Kate's eyes. "Some patients you never forget."

"Dr. Schiller, I told you when I called about the case that has the homicide squad stymied—and why your article so interested me."

"Yes."

"I hope I can depend on your discretion."

"It's the foundation of my profession, Ms. McKinnon, and I uphold it."

"I have an idea, a way to possibly flush out our suspect, and I'd like your professional opinion."

"Of course. If I can help."

"I was thinking that we might give him a show, an exhibition of his paintings. We have several that have been left at his crime scenes."

The doctor ran her tongue over her matching coral-colored lipstick. "If you are asking me if the patient I knew, though I can't say I ever *knew* him, would be susceptible to such a plan, I would think yes. It would be a temptation few—sane or disturbed—could resist." She locked her eyes on Kate. "But the ones most susceptible, like Tony T, have such brutally damaged egos, they're often equally paranoid. He would be suspicious. Not to mention, dangerous."

"Yes." Kate rapped her pen against her notepad. "Of course I have no way of knowing that the suspect we are after is the same teenager you were treating, but do you think he could still be alive?" Kate did the math. If he was twelve or thirteen when he entered Pilgrim State, he'd be thirteen or fourteen when he escaped, making him twenty-three or -four now.

"I have no idea, but . . ." Dr. Schiller glanced back out the window, and sighed. "I would say his survival skills were extremely keen. They would have to have been, considering the abuse he'd already sustained." The therapist rubbed at her arms as if chilled.

Kate thought a moment. "You mentioned that he was always trying to guess at colors?"

"Yes. Though, as I said, he was usually wrong. And he'd use names like . . ." Dr. Schiller glanced up at the ceiling and shut her eyes. "Um, magic mint or mulberry, or . . ."

"Razzmatazz?" asked Kate.

"Yes," said the therapist. "Exactly."

D r. Warren Weinberg picked a blob of tuna salad off his white lab jacket. "This is what happens when you eat and talk, right?" He offered Kate a bemused smile.

"Believe me," said Kate. "I don't have a single blouse without a food stain. I'm sorry to be taking up your time, Doctor."

"I don't have any time, so you couldn't possibly be taking it up." He laid the sandwich onto his desk, and sighed. "Twenty patients a day to make enough money from those damn HMOs just to keep my office doors open, plus my nights at Roosevelt—"

"That's where you treated him, right, at Roosevelt Hospital?"

"Yes. I don't have the records—anything over a year old goes onto microfilm—but I remember him. An unusual case. I had never come across a case of cerebral achromatopsia before—or since. Quite astonishing, really. Total loss of all color sensation." He closed his eyes a moment. "I was manning the emergency room the night he came in. What a mess. Looked like he'd been in one hell of a brawl." He picked at the stain left by the tuna. "We did the usual, cleaned him up, a few stitches, I can't remember that part precisely."

"What part do you remember—precisely?"

"That we might have sent him home, but he lashed out at a candy striper, a volunteer, sweet girl really, just trying to be nice, distract him while I finished up with his stitches. She said something to him about my blue shirt, that it was unusual for a doctor to be wearing a blue shirt and he went totally ballistic, said it was gray, and she, innocently said, 'No, it's blue,' and he went ape-shit—forgive me—and started swinging at her like a crazy man. I mean, up until that moment we had no idea that his injuries had caused any sort of neural damage."

"And your shirt, it was blue?"

"Bright blue," said Weinberg. "We decided to keep him around for a few days, administer a few tests. That's when we saw what had happened— something had crushed the pathway from the vision center of his brain, rendering him completely color blind. Though he denied it. He was in a severe depression. Even attempted suicide. Slit a wrist." The doctor pursed his lips.

"Would he have a scar?"

"Oh, yes. A thick one. He used a pair of scissors. Not very neat." He reached for the tuna sandwich, but stopped. "There were other scars, other than the one on his wrist, and not self-inflicted. We did a complete physical and I can tell you that kid had been beaten, and raped, many times, probably from a very young age."

Kate winced. "Did you get a family history, any story about the abuse?"

"Not a word. He claimed he had no family, that he remembered nothing—nothing about the accident, not his name, nothing. Complete amnesia. It could have been caused by the blow to his head, but we were never sure. We shipped him off to Pilgrim State. What could we do? There was no adult to claim him, nowhere for him to go. He never told us his age, but he was just a kid, about thirteen, I'd guess, though it was hard to tell." Dr. Weinberg leaned back in his chair, stared into space a moment. "He was both young for his age, and . . . old, you know what I mean? Childlike, but cunning, and something too old and too wise about him." The doctor shook his head.

Just what Dr. Schiller had said.

"There was something off about him, and clearly it wasn't just because of that blow to his head."

"Could you describe him?"

"It's been a long time, but . . ." Weinberg closed his eyes again. "Tall for his age, and thin. Light hair. Big blue eyes. He looked like one of those teen idols, you know, almost too good-looking, in a feminine sort of way." The doctor sat forward and regarded Kate with an expression of concern. "You know, I've thought about him once or twice, and wondered if he survived."

Kate distributed Schiller's article from the psychiatric journal and updated the squad on her meetings with Drs. Schiller, Weinberg, and Brillstein. She finished up with the murder of the nurse the day before Tony T disappeared from the psychiatric facility, then handed each of them another set of papers. "National Crime Information Center's report on Belinda MacConnell, RN," she said. "Murdered and eviscerated in a manner disturbingly similar to our unsub's ritual."

"So how do we find a man who has no record of ever existing?" said Tapell.

"FBI can do a search," said Grange.

"I doubt you'll find anything," said Kate. "Not if it's the same young man. Pilgrim State never got a history. Neither did the police."

"How then?" asked Tapell.

"I've been thinking about that." Kate regarded the chief of police, then the others. "Suppose we make him come to us."

"How?" asked Grange.

Kate displayed a crime scene photo from Boyd Werther's studio—the psycho's paintings lined up in a neat row. "I think he's telling us what he wants—his own one-man show. And we can provide it. We have his paintings."

"I don't know," said Tapell. She was thinking about the mayor, how he kept asking her when she was going to catch this guy, as if she could simply say, "Okay, there's the killer, hanging out on the corner of Lexington and Thirty-first; go get 'im boys"—like she was Wyatt Earp. Tapell sighed. She had better become Wyatt Earp or some other legendary lawman, and soon, or she'd be out of a job, or worse, back in Astoria.

"What then?" asked Kate. "We wait for the next body?"

"It's a risk," said Brown.

"Everything's a risk," said Kate.

"And what if he doesn't fall for it?" said Grange.

"Then we haven't lost anything, have we?"

"Except precious NYPD man-hours," said Tapell. "And taxpayers' dollars." *Which I have to answer for,* she thought, but did not say.

"Look, Clare. Nothing comes with a guarantee. You know that." Kate pushed her hair behind her ears and noticed that Grange's eyes took in the move and then quickly focused on something beside her.

Freeman, who had been quietly listening, finally spoke. "It could flush him out, a show of his work."

"That's what Dr. Schiller seemed to think," said Kate. "Let me play the two-minute tape I made for PBS." She hit the lights and they all stared at her face on the screen, the short announcement of time, location, and dates accompanied by an image of the unsub's paintings.

"You did this *without* authorization?" said Grange.

"All I have done, Agent Grange, is make a tape and a few phone calls. Whether this will be put into action is not up to me."

"Where would we do this?" asked Brown.

"I've spoken to Herbert Bloom. He has a gallery in Chelsea. He'll let us use it for two or three days. It's not a big space, no back door; only egress is from the street."

"It's still a full-scale operation," said Brown. "We can't go into this without a dozen men inside the gallery, outside, as well."

"Plus agents," said Grange. "Though I'm not saying I agree. Not yet."

"That's at least two dozen cops over a two- or three-day period." Tapell was trying to calculate the cost in her head. "And why several days?"

Kate popped the video out of the VCR. "Simply to give him enough time to catch the promo, time to decide he absolutely needs to see the show. If we're lucky he'll show up on day one."

"Big *if*," said Tapell, though she seemed to be considering it.

"It's completely unorthodox," said Brown. "And if the press got a hold of it . . ."

"Well, we wouldn't send out a press release," said Kate.

"Since when do they need one?" said Brown.

Tapell was up, pacing. "I'm not saying I agree to this. But Floyd, *if* we were to do it, how long would you need to mobilize the troops?"

"Most of Homicide and half of General has been on standby for the past week. A couple of phone calls, a few meetings. That's all." He turned to Kate. "What about the gallery?"

"You're talking a few hours to tack the paintings up on a wall."

There was a sudden quickening beat to the air—Grange on his cell, Brown making notes, Tapell pacing back and forth—a collective heart racing that was almost palpable.

"I need to talk to the mayor," said Tapell, heading quickly toward the door.

"It might just work," said Brown.

Tapell turned back. "It had better."

THIRTY

Liz sat back against the couch, glanced around at all the art and precious objects in Kate's living room. "It's been good to have a little time off from Quantico, I can tell you that, see my sister, her kid, and you—though I haven't seen enough of you."

Kate offered her old friend and partner a wan smile. "The case. Cases, I should say. Sorry. It's been a full-time job."

"I thought you'd been retired."

"I thought so too." Kate sighed. "I just met with the squad, filled them in on what I was telling you—about the psychiatrist and the doctor."

"The disturbed, color-blind teen."

"Yes. Pilgrim State verified he vanished without a trace, and NCIC provided the stats on the murdered nurse. The MO is just like our unsub's."

"So you think it's your guy."

"Could be," said Kate. She stood up, sat, then stood again. "Listen, I've got an hour or so before I head down to see Willie. How about a walk?"

Outside the San Remo, there wasn't a hint of blue sky. Low clouds hung over the city, a relentless gray.

Liz looped her arm through Kate's. "You know, I've never seen Strawberry Fields."

"It's just across the street, opposite the Dakota, where John and Yoko lived." Kate indicated the pseudo-Gothic monolith that hovered on the corner of Seventy-second Street. "Come on."

The park was quiet, the path winding into Strawberry Fields overhung with trees.

"Here we are," said Kate, pointing to the mosaic circle on the ground, the word IMAGINE in the center. "Originally Yoko Ono put an ad in the *Times* requesting gifts from all over the world, and from what I understand, almost immediately they started pouring in—Moroccan benches, French fountains. But the Parks Department returned them and Yoko came up with a simpler plan of an international garden."

Liz stared down at the mosaic. It was strewn with coins and photos, a bouquet of flowers past their prime.

"People paying their respects," said Kate, and felt a wave of sadness and grief. "Come on," she said. "I'll show you a really special, very quiet part of the park."

Is it real? Is this happening? Or is it just his eyes playing tricks on him? He lifts his sunglasses and rubs his eyes. He can hardly believe it.

The art *her-story-n*. In living color. Chestnut hair blowing in the breeze. He feels as if he might die, and right now, that would be fine.

The last time he stood outside her building he thought perhaps he had invented her, that she was a figment of his imagination. But no. She is real.

"Look, Tony," he whispers. "It's her."

He watches as she crosses the street with the other woman, his heart beating fast.

Kate chose a path that followed along the lake, which today was a deep, opaque green. It was quiet and still, just a few boaters out on the lake.

"You'd never know you were in the middle of Manhattan," said Liz.

"Olmsted's genius," said Kate, referring to Central Park's original designer, Frederick Law Olmsted.

"Did the squad go for it, the idea of giving your unsub a show?"

"It's being considered," said Kate. "And I'm hoping they try it. Action is better than inaction." What she had been doing for two weeks: moving, constantly moving.

Kate took a few steps onto a small bridge, stopped a moment for Liz to take in the scene.

"Weird," said Liz, staring down at the perfectly still water covered with algae so thick the pond glowed an intense yellow-green, gorgeous and sickly. They crossed over and followed a path practically hidden by trees.

"This is it, the place I wanted you to see, the Ramble." Though as Kate looked around, taking in the dark trees and secluded path, she wasn't sure it had been such a good idea. There wasn't another person in sight.

He knows the area well, has his preferred spots among the trees and hills, but his favorite is somewhat inaccessible—one needs to climb a fence— though it never stopped him, or the hungry men who paid for his services.

He hovers above the art *her-story-n* and the other woman sheltered by the trees and shrubs. She gestures and talks, and though he cannot make out her words, her tone is instantly recognizable from her TV show. He would like to charge down the path, touch her, hold her awhile, explain to her what she has done—given him the ability to see color, and to go on living.

Oh, God, how he loves her.

A flash—a face. That other face. Her face. Love? Hate? What is it he feels?

Hold her. Caress her. Hurt her. Fuck her! Kill her!

No. Not her. Who then? Which her? Which one? His mind, like a radio station, is losing reception, all static.

Relief. That's what he needs.

Kate led Liz on a path that cut through a series of large rocks that felt almost prehistoric.

"I've taped a promo for the exhibition that PBS will air every hour once we give them the word," said Kate.

"You think he's watching?"

Kate hesitated a moment. Had she seen something move in the trees, the slightest hint of flesh among all the deep green foliage? She popped a piece of Nicorette into her mouth. "Well, the theory is he's been watching my show. That's how he knew about Boyd Werther." Kate shivered. Was it simply thinking of Boyd—or being in the Ramble, where the shadows had added a chill to the fall air?

"I don't think I've ever seen you chew gum. Even in the old days, before you were a *lady*."

"Funny," said Kate. "It's Nicorette. And I can't stop. I'm thinking about going on the patch to get off the gum."

Liz laughed, then looked around at their deserted surroundings. "You know, it's sort of creepy in here. I haven't seen a single person since we came over that bridge."

"That's what makes it special," said Kate. "Though I wouldn't recommend walking it alone." Another chill, and that buzzing sensation. "You know, it's getting to me too. Maybe this wasn't such a good idea. Come on. If we head up this way, we'll be at Belvedere Castle. There are always people there."

No. She can't be leaving. Not yet. He has to—what? Speak to her? Ask her questions? *Have you driven a Ford lately? Do you really want to hurt me?* Tell her things? *I want my MTV! You're in good hands with Allstate.*

Concentrate. Which way were they headed? Belvedere Castle? Must be.

But how will he contain himself?

The fence is no problem, easy for him to scale, the staircase, carved out of rock, dark and cold. He knows where it ends—the barricaded cave. He takes the steps quickly, a fifteen-step descent into hell. How many times has he been here? A dozen? A hundred? The perfect place for twenty-dollar trysts, so many, he's lost count.

At the bottom of the steps he unzips, frees his erection.

A collage of faces and images—Kate's face, her face, the nameless faces of those he has killed, and colors, dazzling, imaginary colors— skitter through his brain.

That's it. Zip up. Get moving.

A castle is calling.

Kate stood on the stone terrace perched atop Vista Rock and looked out over Turtle Pond, dark green reeds and murky water, forbidding.

"Nice," said Liz. "But lonely."

There were twenty or so people, tourists, thought Kate, not really looking at them, a couple of kids tossing pebbles over the terrace.

Lonely: the word resonated. She had no idea if she felt lonely or not; she hadn't taken the time to figure it out. Is that why she was unable to shake the creepy feeling she continued to have?

"We should get going," she said.

The children are infuriating him, the way their parents dote, and their shrill laughter.

He stands among them, two couples speaking a language he cannot understand. He wonders if it is some sort of code, if they are aliens. No matter, they offer camouflage. The art *her-story-n* cannot see him. Though he sees her clearly, and the other woman, who looks oddly familiar. Why? He can't figure it out. Not now. He's too excited.

Kate stares at the water.

She looks sad. He wonders why.

What's she got to be sad about?

He sticks close to the tourists, shifting with them, remaining hidden, and then, when he thinks he might actually do it—approach her and ask some simple questions—*How did you do it, turn the color on? Was it magic?*—she moves away and starts down the path.

He follows, staying off the path, hanging back, watching them, two slightly blurry figures among the trees.

When he catches sight of her, the trees flash bright green; when she disappears, they go black.

Oh, yes. She's got the power.

She's the one! Coke is it!

At the edge of the park the two women hug, and then Kate hails a cab.

Hidden by those green-black trees, he hesitates a moment, adrenaline pulsing through his veins, and when he sees her shut the cab door, he sprints down the path and imitates her gesture.

A moment later he is closing himself into a cab of his own. He stares at the meter clicking off dollars and cents as inky gray-brown trees of Central Park blur past the windows. Only a bit of color. But enough to give him hope. He can't lose her. Not now.

"Where're you headed?" the driver asks.

"Could you like, uh, follow that cab," he says. "It's my . . . friend."

He's never done this before, feels as if he's in a spy movie. "Stirred, not shaken," he mumbles to himself.

W as it simply the idea of giving the killer his own exhibition that had gotten under her skin? Kate wasn't sure. She glanced out the taxi's windows at the neon lights of Times Square, artificial color shimmering. What would it be like if all the movie marquees and ads were nothing more than dull gray?

She leaned back against the seat and closed her eyes.

The fact that her name was now in his paintings crawled into her psyche like a parasitic worm. Damn, why did she always end up chasing felons or having them chase her? Was it simply that she got too close— or that she touched something in them?

Kate thought back to all the atrocities she had witnessed, all the ugliness a cop had to see on a daily basis—the reason she had gotten out the first time. Not to mention the shitty pay and the nagging suspicions that eventually got to every cop—that all human beings were liars and cheats and possibly worse, all of that spilling into your private life, if you managed to have one.

The Ramble. Why had it so unnerved her? Was it just the case, Richard's death, everything that had happened? Central Park was usually one of her favorite places. Kate closed her eyes again, thought back to her first date with Richard—an opera in the park. Three weeks and six dates later, the two of them in a pizzeria down the block from her Astoria precinct, where he had proposed. Man, how she had jumped at the chance to get out and start a new life; how much she had loved him, their future stretching out in front of them like the ocean's horizon on the clearest day of the year.

And it had turned out well—even better than expected—and it wasn't the money or the privilege, though surely that hadn't hurt. Of course it wasn't perfect. But what marriage was? She wasn't perfect, that was for sure. She could be moody and withdrawn, and Richard could be selfish and immature, a spendthrift, though that spending spoke of his generosity, she'd always thought, particularly in regard to her. The idea brought her back to the money missing from Richard's firm. It just didn't make sense. Kate still believed Richard would have told her. Their life together hadn't been a lie, had it?

It wasn't a lie, was it, Richard?

The city blurred past the taxi's window.

Their marriage may not have been perfect, but they had loved each other, that much she knew—and trusted each other. It was the reason she was willing to pursue this, to risk everything to prove she was right, to prove that Richard was a good and decent man—that their life together had not been a lie.

But how would she do that now?

People were *doing* the galleries, as it's called—artists, collectors, tourists, and voyeurs, all darting back and forth across the wide Chelsea street, hugging jackets and sweaters to their bodies, wondering who had stolen the usually bright fall sun.

Kate was happy for the distraction, particularly a preview of Willie's paintings, though she could not stop thinking about Boyd Werther's murder or questioning the wisdom of giving the psycho his own exhibition.

As she crossed the street, she checked her watch, and wondered if Nola was already at the gallery. She pictured Willie's last exhibition and paintings, the way he orchestrated his large complex pieces that integrated painting and mixed media as well as abstraction and representation, and was so lost in thought that she suddenly found herself part of a tour group of suburban woman that filled the entire sidewalk, all of them chattering.

"Ow," said a blonde groomed to museum perfection—lacquered hair, flawless makeup, Chanel suit with all its neat brass buckles and chains, similar ones on her matching loafers, which Kate had just stepped on.

"Sorry," said Kate.

The blonde frowned, then lit up. "Oh. My. God. You're Katherine McKinnon."

Instant surround sound, a dozen women speaking at once—"I *adore* your show!" "It's fabulous!" "*You're* fabulous!"—and enough perfume to fix Lady Macbeth's hand problem permanently.

Kate smiled and muttered "Thank you, thank you," finally disentangling herself, though their perfume hung around her like smog for another block. She was still enjoying her brush with minor celebrity when someone passed by, and though it was just a fleeting image, it registered— young man, tall, wraparound sunglasses. Kate turned for another look, caught a glimpse of his profile, then a young woman coming out of the gallery met him, and they kissed.

No, it couldn't possibly be the antisocial loner Dr. Schiller had described.

Or could it be? Schiller had also said he was a charmer, capable of deceit. Kate watched the young couple head down the street hand in hand, and shook off another chill. It was just his shades that did it, that's all. Innocuous enough. Though she wondered if sunglasses would be forever setting off an alarm? It was absurd, of course. She was wearing them herself.

How beautiful, her hair a bit more copper than he realized, blouse a deep plum. It's all working.

He watches from across the wide street, sees her staring at a young couple holding hands, and imagines splitting them open, their guts spilling onto the pavement, a cornucopia of scrumptious color. He practically swoons.

A moment later, she is gone, the gallery door shutting behind her.

Does he dare follow? *Just for the fun of it!* No. Too risky. He'll wait.

Occupy himself with fantasies of this group of women who are now passing—not at all like the women he has known in his life—all of them so well-groomed, smelling delicious, chattering and gesturing, a few of them glancing over, offering a smile.

Betcha can't eat just one!

The Vincent Petrycoff Gallery occupied half a block of prime Chelsea real estate. No windowed front to peer into; the whitewashed cinderblock facade spoke of privacy, an inner sanctum devoted to the art of looking with no distractions.

Kate followed a couple of art handlers past a discreet sign taped to the doors: INSTALLATION IN PROGRESS.

Inside, the exhibition space was the size of a gymnasium, ceilings so expansive Kate couldn't even guess at the height, dismantled wooden crates and bubble wrap littering the floor, gallery assistants on ladders, patching and sanding, touching up mars and nicks with brushes dipped in pristine white paint.

Nola was already there, observing Willie, who stood in the center of the room like a ringmaster directing the installers: Move a painting a few inches to the left or right, switch this painting with that one, his dreadlocks pulled back off his handsome face, which was screwed up with tension.

"Just trying to get this right," he said as Kate kissed his cheek.

"Great, aren't they?" said Nola.

Kate took in the work—large paintings, eight to ten feet wide, leaning against the gallery walls, all in Willie's signature style, his particular hybrid of painting and sculpture. She focused on a piece with beat-up, graffiti-covered metal trash-can lids nailed to the surface, surrounded by even more graffiti gouged into the heavily encrusted paint, the whole thing like some inner-city archaeological dig; then shifted to another, this one combining pieces of glass and mirror embedded into the paint, so that the viewer became part of the work, one's own face reflected in disorienting fragments.

Kate moved back and forth, from one painting to another. "They're amazing."

"You're not just saying that?"

"Of course not," said Kate, thinking that no matter how successful most artists became, they were always plagued by insecurity. She thought of Mark Rothko, who had ultimately slit his wrists, and his black paintings in the Rothko Chapel, all the mystery and uncertainty in them. "You've really pushed them," she said, trying to stay focused on Willie's work. "I love what you're doing with so many disparate elements at once, everything suspended, hovering in the rectangles of paint, unexpected, yet totally inevitable."

"They don't feel like a dumping ground, do they? You know, like just a mess of . . . of stuff."

Kate raised her hand as though hailing a cab. "Dr. Freud. Someone here needs you."

"Yeah, yeah." Willie laughed. "Preshow jitters, I guess."

"Relax." Kate touched his shoulder. "They're brilliant."

"You're really not just saying that?"

"Honestly, Willie, if you know me at all, you know I don't lie about art."

"Yeah, but I also know you'd never tell me if you hated them."

"I could never hate them because you are incapable of doing hateful work."

"I've already told him how good they are about a dozen times," said Nola.

"Who ever said a dozen times was enough?" Willie smiled. "But I love you both."

Kate looked past Willie, caught fragments of her own face shimmering in the painting with mirrors. It seemed a pretty good approximation of how she'd been feeling since she'd walked down that dark alleyway—in pieces.

"Love you too," she said. "Hey, what about switching those two paintings? I think the viewer should come upon the mirror piece unexpectedly, not when they first walk in."

"Good idea," said Willie.

"Forgive me," said Nola, rubbing her belly. "I've got to pee."

The installers were switching the paintings as Vincent Petrycoff strode into the room, dark suit fitting his frame as though it had been sewed on him, and very possibly it had. "So what do you think of our boy genius?" He air-kissed Kate's cheeks.

"I think he's great. And so are the paintings. Powerful. Rich. Smart."

"Sounds like you're describing *me*." Petrycoff ran a hand through his silver ponytail and snorted a laugh.

"If I had been, I'd have left off the last word," said Kate, and approximated the gallerist's snort-laugh, though she elbowed him good-naturedly. No way she wanted to piss off Willie's dealer just before a show.

Petrycoff laughed again, but sobered quickly. "I wonder if you wouldn't think about writing something about the work?"

Impossible, thought Kate. Everyone in the art world knew Willie was practically her adopted son, and she had already plugged the exhibition on her TV show—that was enough nepotism. She smiled noncommittally at Petrycoff and watched the assistants as they moved the mirror-and-glass painting into its new place, light bouncing off the reflective surfaces like stained glass in the middle of deep dark blue-black paint, which only now Kate realized contained shadowy faces and figures. "I'm intrigued by that painting," she said. "Is it available?"

"Oh . . . maybe. I mean, everybody's lining up for the work. I've got a huge waiting list," said Petrycoff. "The curator from Madrid's Reina Sophia was quite interested in that piece as well."

"Really?" said Willie. It was obviously news to him.

"Yes. He was in just yesterday, when we first unwrapped the piece." Petrycoff eyed Kate sideways. "He put a hold on it, but I told him if there was any serious interest I would have to sell it."

"Oh, I couldn't possibly take a sale away from a museum," said Kate. "That's too important to Willie's career."

"Right, of course not." Petrycoff seemed a bit flummoxed. "But I could call him. He expressed interest in several other pieces as well. I'm sure we can work something out."

Kate did not want to spoil a good sale for Willie—if it was true. But she was no rube. She knew when she was being manipulated by an art dealer. "Tell you what. I'll call Carlos. I know him quite well. Where's he staying in the city?"

"Oh—" Petrycoff was working his ponytail so hard, Kate was afraid he'd pull it off. "I'm afraid he's already left."

"Fine. I'll call him in Madrid."

"Yes, uh, right. Do that." Petrycoff's jaw muscles were twitching. He glanced across at the assistants moving Willie's painting and his face contorted. "Where the fuck are your white gloves!?"

The gloveless kid who was holding one side of Willie's painting six inches off the floor instantly let go, and it hit with a thud.

Petrycoff screamed. Willie gasped.

"You idiot!" Petrycoff marched toward the kid. "Out! Now! You're fired. Don't set foot in this gallery ever again! You hear me? Your last check is in the mail!"

The other assistants were quiet, scraping and painting those walls with a renewed intensity.

Willie checked out the painting. "It's fine."

"What a moron," Petrycoff was still grumbling as he examined Willie's painting.

"They're fairly indestructible," said Willie. "They're on wood, and the surfaces are so worked and heavy you'd need a hatchet to do any real damage. No need to fire the guy."

"Are you telling me how to run my gallery?" Petrycoff's face turned the color of beets.

"No. Just telling you something about my paintings."

Kate considered intervening. It was one thing for the art dealer to abuse his staff—Petrycoff was famous for his rages—but Willie was entirely another matter. But as she looked from Willie, who was maintaining a cool smile, to Petrycoff, whose features appeared to be smoothing out, she realized that Willie could handle the man all by himself. Maybe the art dealer was more shaken by the murder of his most successful artist than he'd appeared to be at the memorial service. Kate would cut him some slack.

She took another slow stroll around the perimeter of the gallery, noting things in Willie's paintings she hadn't seen at first glance. But thoughts of constructing a show for the psychopath at the Gallery of

Outsider Art began to infect her unconscious like a computer virus, scrambling her brain. *Good idea? Bad? Would he appear? Stay away?*

Kate forced herself to come back to the moment, to Willie's paintings. "Willie. They're great. Absolutely great. I'll see you at the opening. And remember, the day after, you, me, and Nola are having dinner. Just the three of us. Don't forget."

"I'll be there."

Nola padded back into the room, and Willie gave her an awkward hug, trying, and failing, to get his arms around her.

"Vincent." Kate signaled the art dealer over as soon as Willie was out of earshot, busy instructing one of the installers. "Why don't *you* call Carlos."

Petrycoff smiled. "Good idea. More professional that way."

"Yes. Of course," said Kate. "If he's interested in another painting, I'll take the glass and mirrors."

The art dealer beamed. "I'll get back to you. Let's keep our fingers crossed that Carlos will settle for another piece."

"Yes. Let's." Kate shook the dealer's hand. She'd had enough. She took one more look at the painting she had no doubt would be hers. It was indeed a mesmerizing piece, not only a metaphor for her recent, fragmented life, but for the world as well, all smoke and mirrors.

Outside, the clouds were threatening rain and a chill was coming off the nearby Hudson.

"God, it's almost like winter," said Nola.

"Yes," said Kate, putting her arm over the girl's shoulder. She was thinking that winter had set in two weeks earlier, but it had nothing to do with the weather.

Willie burst out of the Petrycoff Gallery and jogged the few feet to catch up with them. "Just wanted to say thanks again. I mean, for the encouragement. And I think I'm going to need it—with Petrycoff."

"You can handle him," said Kate. "The show is going to be a great success. Trust me. You have nothing to worry about." She was just giving him a good-bye kiss when her cell phone rang.

Brown, calling about the proposed exhibition.

Tapell had given the go-ahead.

Across the street, hovering beside a steel lamppost, sunglasses in place, trying hard to remain half hidden and appear nonchalant, he watches and tries to figure out the scenario.

A family? Her children? They never said she had any children. And they don't look like her, their faces dark, hers white. He scrambles through the TV Rolodex in his mind: *The Cosby Show, The Partridge Family, The Brady Bunch, Happy Days.* None of them quite right, though each of the theme songs has started playing in his head, all at once.

Clearly, she likes them, perhaps even loves them, though he is not sure what that emotion would require. He dares to slip out into the open for a better look at them. He can see they are far too engrossed in their love fest to notice him.

He feels a sudden flash of heat, a surge of jealousy so intense, Kate's hair, a minute ago all copper and chestnut, fades, and the redbrick buildings go muddy, his world, once again, smudged and colorless.

It's them. Their fault. They are ruining it. Destroying what the art *her-story-n* had given him.

He sags against the street lamp as the trio disappears down the gray street, and thinks that they will have to pay for their crime.

THIRTY-ONE

PBS had been airing the promo for the show on an hourly rotation. Herbert Bloom was making room in his gallery. Brown had gathered the troops.

"Remember," said Brown, scanning the crowd in the briefing room. "If he is the escaped patient from Pilgrim State, we're looking for a white male, early- to mid-twenties, may be wearing sunglasses; and if he's not, wearing sunglasses, that is, he'll be blinking and squinting. Oh, and he'll have a nasty scar on his wrist."

"And what if it's not that guy?" asked a young detective in the first row.

"Either way we're dealing with a psychopath," said Brown. "And he might be out of control at this point."

"That mean he's gonna come in shooting?" asked another cop.

"Doubtful. The shrinks think he's going to want a good look at his artwork before he pulls anything. But all of you are still wearing Kevlar." Brown tugged at his earlobe. "There will be at least twenty or so civilians in the gallery with you—art lovers and collectors that the dealer invited so the situation looks and feels kosher—so caution and judgment are the words of the day, people. The civies' names will be at the door. Of course anyone suspicious *will* be let in. That's the whole point."

Brown glanced over at Agents Sobieski and Marcusa taking notes for Grange, who was busy prepping a few new recruits for the operation.

"The Bureau's also going to have agents inside, wired, in contact with a van around the corner. There will also be an agent across the street at all times, and we'll have two men in a car as well. Oh, last thing. You gotta look the part." Brown nodded at Kate.

"The operative word," said Kate, taking a place beside Brown, "is black." She glanced over all the uniforms and detectives who would be playing art lovers at the Gallery of Outsider Art, a fairly equal mix of men and women. "Black is the unofficial art world costume. Anyone who shows up in floral prints or stripes is in *big* trouble. This opening has to look like the real thing because we have no idea if our unsub has ever been to an actual art opening. But on the chance that he has, all of you have to look authentic." Kate scanned the men. "Guys, it's perfectly okay to wear black jeans, just couple it with a decent black shirt or tee, or a plain white shirt is okay too. But absolutely no button-down collars."

"Jean jackets okay?" asked Brown. "They've got to hide their guns somewhere."

"Fine," said Kate. "But don't all of you show up in jean jackets. Some of you get your black sport jackets out of mothballs. And ladies, black too. Black jeans, pants, black tops; white's okay too, if it's a plain blouse. But keep it simple. Nothing too fancy, and absolutely nothing frilly."

A detective in the front row self-consciously patted down the ruffles at the cuffs of her pink blouse.

"And no comfy cop shoes or sneaks, girls." Kate took in the women cops, the uniforms and detectives, remembered what it had been like when she was in Astoria, and wanted to do something for them. "Listen, if you haven't got any, go out and buy yourselves a pair of really expensive black shoes. Go over to Jeffrey. It's just a few blocks south on Fourteenth Street in the old meatpacking district. It's known for its shoes, and it's where the art world girls who can afford to, go. And don't faint when you see the price tags."

A hand flew up. Second row. Youngish woman. Dyed blond hair.

"You'll be reimbursed," said Kate, anticipating the blonde's question. Kate nodded at Floyd Brown, just so he'd know she intended to pick up the tab for a dozen pairs of designer shoes. What the hell, she thought, regarding all the smiling women. She thought back to her cop days, shopping at JC Penney and discount stores. Why shouldn't these women own a pair of fancy-ass shoes? "Choose something you really like," she added. "'Cause you get to keep them. Just make sure they're black."

"Hey—" Burly detective, second row. "What about me? I could use me a pair of them Yves Saint Laurence shoes."

Everyone laughed. Kate too.

"Sorry," said Kate. "Black sneaks or oxfords will have to do. Let's face it, who gives a shit what you guys put on your feet?"

More laughs. First time the cops who weren't part of the "murder squad" were not giving her the cold shoulder.

Nicky Perlmutter threw her a wink.

"Okay," said Kate, trying to get their attention again. "A few rules about art opening behavior. One, it's okay to look at the artwork, but don't act like you're terribly interested. It's all about attitude." Kate glanced over at a corkboard wall covered with gruesome crime scene photos, lifted a brow, pursed her lips, crossed her arms over her chest, affected a look of total ennui. "See what I mean?"

"Like you just smelled a fart?" said the same burly detective, obviously the class clown in junior high and still playing the role.

"Not quite. But something like that." Kate didn't bother to smile this time. "And chat with your partner, say things like, *interesting,* or *fascinating,* but never—ever—say the artwork is pretty. That's a no-no."

Class Clown said, "Aw gee, can't I say you're awful purdy."

Brown locked the man in his gaze. "This is a killer, McGrath. A cunning psychopath, young and strong. Get it?"

The bulky McGrath seemed to shrink a bit.

"Weapons concealed, but easy to get at," Brown continued. "And do not overreact. We don't want to scare him off. We'd like this joker alive."

"Why's that?" asked a very young guy in uniform leaning against the wall.

"Because that way," said Brown, "he gets to answer all of our questions."

Hey, wait up." Kate called out to Nicky Perlmutter, who was heading down the precinct hall at his normal loping stride.

He turned, offered up one of his Huck Finn smiles, but it faded fast when he spotted Class Clown and his partner lumbering toward them, both in serious need of a gym membership. Class Clown whacked Perlmutter on the back. "Hey, Nicky-boy, you gonna go over to that Jeffrey place, get yourself a pair of shoes?" He elbowed his overweight partner, the pair of them giggling like ten-year-olds as they turned the corner.

"Dumb and Dumber," said Kate.

"You got that right," said Perlmutter, but he wasn't smiling. He fixed her with his twin blues, hesitated a moment. "I don't imagine you know what it's like to be a gay cop."

"No, but I know what it's like to be a woman cop, in Queens, no less, and what it's like to be a woman in general." She straightened and affected a radio announcer's voice: "All second-class citizens please raise their hands." And she did.

"Well, gay men are more like third-class, and gay cops—who knows?" He shrugged his broad shoulders.

His admission hadn't come as much of a shock to Kate.

"You know the old joke: What do you call an African American with a degree from Harvard?" Perlmutter waited a beat. "Nigger." He dragged a hand across his mouth as if wiping away the word. "Me, I'm usually about halfway out of the room when I hear 'Faggot' muttered under one of those assholes' breath. You heard what good ol' boy Agent Sobieski said, didn't you? 'One less faggot.' That was his assessment of the murder of that poor kid."

"Sobieski is a jerk," said Kate.

"Half the people in this country think guys like me are going straight to hell."

"Maybe, but the Supreme Court has condoned same-sex marriage and killed the sodomy laws."

"Yeah. And Pat Robertson is praying that the judges responsible for that vote die. Now there's a lesson for the kids. 'Hey, kids, if someone disagrees with your point of view, just ask God to kill them.' " Perlmutter sighed. "When I was ten, I was sitting in church with my mom, who remained devout even though she'd married a Jew. Go figure." He shrugged. "Anyway, I'm sitting there and the priest is up in front preaching about how homosexuals are going to hell. Never forgot it."

"Okay, I got one for you," said Kate. "There's a social worker, a lawyer, and a priest on the *Titanic,* and it's going down, fast. Social worker says, 'Save the children!' Lawyer says, 'Fuck the children!' Priest says, 'Do you think we have time?' "

Perlmutter sputtered a laugh.

"I'll bet hell's a lot more fun anyway." Kate looked into Perlmutter's open face, and got serious. "So how come you never said anything to me about being gay?"

"How come you never said anything about being straight?"

"Touché."

"Seriously?" He sighed. "Took me half my life to like myself, to accept who I am. And I do. But I don't feel like making announcements or being a poster boy. They wanted me to head up Hate Crimes, and I thought about it, but I didn't want to be known as the gay cop, which that would have ensured, though with all due modesty I am the best damn gay cop you, or anyone else, has ever seen."

"Never doubted it for a minute."

"You know, maybe McGrath is right. About Jeffrey, I mean. I could use a new pair of size thirteens."

Kate made a show of reaching for her shoe. "What the hell, I'll lend you mine."

A*m I dreaming?*
    He reaches out and touches the TV set to make sure it is actually there, that he is not hallucinating, feels the crackling static on his fingertips. He stares, transfixed, at one of his very own street scenes, while the art *her-story-n* says something about a gallery, but he is so bewitched by the image of his painting on the screen that he can just barely hear her. He blinks and squints, realizes he has been holding his breath and gasps. His ears pop and he hears her clearly now, quickly writes in his sketchpad in his childlike scrawl, and afterward, when she is gone from the set, he reads and rereads the fragments of her statement that he has scrawled in the sketchpad, and tries to believe it is real.

A promising new comer. A tail-ented painter. Her-bert Blume Gallery. In Chel-see.

He stares a full minute at his notes, at these things the art *her-story-n* has said, then calls out, "Donna! Tony! Dylan! Brenda! Everyone! Listen to this!" And he tells them in detail over and over about his painting on TV and how they will all be going to his exhibition. "She's seen them. My paintings. And she likes them!"

A feeling, like the embrace of a soft blanket, comes over him, but it doesn't last long.

How will he do this, see the show? After all, he can't just walk into the gallery and say those are *my* paintings. Do they think he is stupid? Would she try to trick him? He doesn't think so, but it's possible. People are always tricking him.

"What do you think, Donna?"

"I think you can do anything," says his Donna-voice.

"Sure, sure," says his Dylan-voice. "You can figure it out. You've done lots of stuff, and you always get away with it."

He thinks about that, a montage of images playing in his brain along with the static and jingles and radio-speak, and agrees that it is true. He *can* do anything.

He glances back at the TV, at a woman with mahogany hair and a wild-strawberry blouse drinking a Coke and walking across an emerald lawn, and falls back against the couch thinking about his exhibition, and he is so utterly and deliriously happy the tears in his eyes have blurred all the TV colors into a gorgeous streaky rainbow. It is truly a miracle— the exhibition *and* being cured. All of it.

His own show.

Celebrate the moments of your life.

Indeed.

He has to make a plan.

THIRTY-TWO

KILLER OF A SHOW

Just when you think you've heard it all, here is another one straight from the I-can't-believe-it file. Apparently, the NYPD is now in the art biz. The serial killer who leaves paintings at his crime scenes, you know the one, formerly of the Bronx and more recently of Manhattan with the slaying of artist Boyd Werther, is having his first one-man exhibition. That's right. A solo show of the killer's work will be opening at Manhattan's Gallery of Outsider Art.

We all know that economic times are tough and the NYPD is hurting for funds, but has it actually come to this?

Herbert Bloom, director of the gallery, offered this definition of outsider art:

"Outsider art is art made by the unschooled, untrained, and often the mentally ill." Sounds about right, particularly that last part.

Clare Tapell crumbled the *Post* into her fist and slammed it onto the conference table.

"The damn press gets stuff before *we* even know it." Brown shook his head.

"This might attract a crowd." Tapell exhaled a loud breath.

"We have a guest list," said Kate. "No one else gets in—except for suspicious-looking young men."

"Which could be a lot more than we expected," said Tapell.

"I don't think anyone in the art world will care about this." Kate tapped the paper. "You may get a few thrill seekers who want to gape at the killer's paintings, but basically New Yorkers are so blasé they won't bother. Besides, the killer's paintings have already been reproduced in the papers. It's not a big thing."

FBI Agent Grange marched into the room, the *Post* open in front of his face "You see this?"

"Just been through it," said Tapell.

"This reporter—" He regarded the byline. "He's toast. Over. Finito."

"Let's deal with the opening tonight and I'll help you ruin that reporter's life tomorrow, okay?" Clare Tapell sounded weary.

"I've got six agents for inside the gallery." Grange glanced at Kate. "And don't worry, they're all wearing black. Six men, two women. All wired. Wristbands. Very discreet. The van around the corner will be receiving. From five to seven I've got two agents dressed as tourists—New York map, the whole nine yards—across the street, in case he shows early. After that, one dressed as a homeless man will spend the night."

"I have a couple of detectives already at the gallery who will be there all day." Brown glanced at his watch. "At the opening, from six to eight, there'll be a total of twenty-six cops playing art collectors and critics, one more playing a waiter, another tending bar, both of whom will be staying the night. Two detectives in a car across the street as well."

"Everyone recognizes cops on a stakeout," said Kate.

"Unmarked car. Best I can do," said Brown. "The car stays all night. If he wants to look at his paintings after hours, he's gonna *have* to break in."

"I'll be there from six to eight," said Kate. "But I could hang around."

"No point in that," said Brown. "We just need you for the charade."

Charade. The word vibrated in Kate's mind. Richard's life? Her life? Was all of it a charade?

"Make sure you have your gun," said Brown.

"Of course," said Kate. "Though do you really think he'd try anything in a crowd?"

"You never know," said Brown. "I'll be nearby. Any vibe, you signal me or one of the other cops."

"I'll be nearby too," said Freeman.

"FBI shrinks now pack a weapon?" asked Brown.

"'Fraid not." Freeman looked a little sheepish. "You think I need one?"

"I'll protect you," said Kate, painting on a grin, though her palms were sweating.

"Floyd, you'd better install a few more plainclothes for outside the gallery," said Tapell. "You don't know who this newspaper item may bring out." She turned to Freeman. "Do you think this article will flip him out?"

"Could be," said Freeman. "But psychopaths can rationalize anything. They rationalize murder, remember? I don't think it will keep him away, if that's what's worrying you. I think he's going to try and take a look, soak up the adulation. My guess? This is one scene our boy has *got* to see."

He stomps across his darkened room, waving the newspaper. "Tony, Donna, did you see *this*?"

"It's grrrrrrrrrreat!"

"No, it's *not*, Tony! They think I'm mentally ill! Fuck! Fuck! Fuck!"

"It's okay," Donna-voice says. "You're smart. You'll figure it out."

"Sure," says Brenda-voice. "It's still your show. Your paintings. Lots of times they think great artists are crazy."

"That's true," he whispers, the idea taking root, soothing him. They thought all the great ones were crazy. He drags one of his Jasper Johns books over, flips pages with paintings of numbers and targets and cast body parts. He holds up a page, squints at the image—half a chair and a plaster cast of a human leg attached upside down to the top of a painting. "They *must* have called Jasper Johns crazy, right?"

"Right," says Donna.

"And he's famous now," says Donna.

"And he's afflicted, like you," says Brenda.

"That's true," he says.

"Yeah," says Dylan, deep-voiced. "Don't let it bother you, dude."

Good friends, he thinks, as he switches on the TV. That lady judge who is always yelling at people. No good. He switches the channel to find something calming, cartoons, watches a minute until he realizes that everything is dull gray, that the miracle has been lost—and it's all because of this, he thinks. He kicks at the newspaper and shouts and screams so loud that his friends run from the room.

Outsider? Mentally ill?

Did she do this, the art *her-story-n*?

Why would they say that about him? He thought she was different, but maybe she is just like the others. He thinks again of those two young people, the artist at the Petrycoff Gallery who kissed Kate, and the girl, the pregnant girl. If the art *her-story-n* is trying to trick him, he will pay her back, maybe take one of them away from her. He imagines opening up the girl's pregnant belly. Now that would be something. He touches himself and shudders.

Dylan slinks back into room. "They're just fucking with you, dude. Jealous, that's all."

"You think so?"

"Sure. You're smart, not crazy."

Images flood his mind like muddy brown water, a small room, all those doctors, the taste of rubber, and the pain.

But Dylan is right. He is smarter than they are. Surely smarter than some newspaper writer who is probably making it all up to hurt him. He kicks the balled-up paper again, stares at the tube, and tries to concentrate. He must figure this out. An exhibition of his paintings—no question he has to see it.

He tugs the revolver out of the cereal box where it has been stored for years, fingers wrapping around the barrel and the cylindrical silencer, which he is certain will come in handy. Sometimes things really do work out. He had taken the gun off the man, after the accident, and tucked it away. Never used it. Didn't think it would work the way he needed for learning more about his art. But this is different. Simply a way to get the job done. The good part, the pleasure, will come later. He likes the feel of it in his hands, the weight, and the cool smell of the metal. He runs his tongue along the barrel, believes he can taste a hint of turquoise mixed in with sparkling silver.

Oh, he will show them how clever he is, how talented, and while he's at it, since they already think so, just how fucking *mentally ill*.

THIRTY-THREE

Kate slipped a thin black cashmere sweater over her head, and the bedroom went dark, and with it an image took shape—Rothko's black paintings and then Boyd Werther's studio and all those slashed paintings, words in blood; and then another image, indistinct—a faceless young man, a killer, color blind. Kate thought about her announcements promoting his show and wondered if he had seen them—and then the newspaper article, and worried.

"Are you listening to me?" Nola's pretty face came into focus.

"Yes, of course."

"I didn't know you even liked outsider art."

Kate had not told Nola the truth about what was going down at the Gallery of Outsider Art, and wouldn't have bothered to mention it if Nola hadn't caught one of the PBS spots. "I'm helping Herbert Bloom. That's all."

"Since when do you do promos for commercial galleries? I mean, isn't that a conflict of interest?"

"Listen, my dear, it is merely a favor, I'm not getting a kickback on sales." Kate sat beside Nola on the bed while she slipped on a pair of black flats, tried to hide the fact that her hands were shaking. "I'll be home before you know it."

A small crowd had gathered on the sidewalk in front of the Gallery of Outsider Art.

That damn article, thought Kate.

One of the cops, appropriately dressed in black jeans and jacket, was checking names against a list.

"Private party, my ass," said a tattooed woman whom he had turned away. "You're letting all the guys in—what the fuck is that about?" She gave him the finger, muttered, "Queer," and swaggered down the street.

Inside, the gallery was warm. Kate would have removed her jacket if her gun were not strapped under it.

Brown squeezed past a couple who were studying the psycho's paintings, displaying that blasé expression Kate had demonstrated for the cops, many of whom were trying it too, though even in their artful black clothes they appeared somewhat out of place, wary cop eyes giving them away as they scanned the room.

Kate took in the chief of Homicide—white shirt, black sports jacket. "You clean up nice."

"I'm roasting," said Brown.

"Good to know. I thought it was my nerves—or hormones." Kate looked past him and checked out the room. "Anyone suspicious?"

Brown angled his chin slightly to the left. "Over there. Near the back."

"Guy in the shades. Gotcha. He looks a little old for the part," she said, eyeing the guy, whom she pegged at close to thirty. She could see a couple of the cops were watching him too.

A middle-aged man beside Kate, one of the invited art collectors, was taking in a Bronx street scene. "A true outsider in every way," he said. "Clumsy drawing, weird color." He cast a jaded eye at the paintings. "But totally fascinating."

"Love the obsessive doodling along the edges," said the much younger woman on his arm.

Herbert Bloom, Sir Elton glasses halfway down his nose, made his way over to Kate and Brown. "I had no idea there would be so much interest. I'm taking names."

"Names?" asked Kate.

"I've started a waiting list. I've already got two or three people for every painting."

Brown looked from Bloom to Kate, mild disgust tugging at his lips. "These paintings are evidence, Mr. Bloom. They are not for sale."

"Well, maybe not tonight, but . . . never?" The art dealer looked genuinely distressed.

A distinguished-looking woman indicated one of the psycho's still-life paintings. "I'll take the one on the end, Herb. It will look fabulous with my tramp art."

Bloom gave Kate a see-what-I-mean look. "I'll put you on the waiting list." He turned and whispered to Brown. "I can sell them discreetly. No one has to know. The NYPD, your favorite charity, whatever you like, can get a percentage. Talk to your superiors. Someone. Anyone."

"No," said Kate and Brown in unison.

An anorexic-looking woman in skintight leather pants looped a spindly arm over Bloom's shoulder. "These are *killer*," she said, and laughed. "True memento mori. But I don't think the color is going to work with my Native American paintings, you know, the ones you sold me last year, or my newest pieces with the tiny skeletons pressed into copper."

"I don't recall selling you any copper pieces," said Bloom.

"I got them on my trip through the rain forest. I can't remember the name of the tribe. But they're *fabulous*. The skeletons are human. *Babies*. Just weeks old. They press the bones into soft copper. I don't how they do it, but they're gorgeous. Of course they're illegal, but, really, I mean it's not like they kill them. They just die. Might as well make use of them, no?" Her dark lifeless eyes slid over the psycho's paintings. "Is it possible, Herb—I mean, doesn't he make any darker-colored pictures?"

Kate leaned in. "I just thought you should know I've written down every word you said and I'm reporting you to U.S. Customs and Import and Export, and—" Kate hadn't finished inventing her list when the woman bolted, Herbert Bloom trailing after her.

Nicky Perlmutter, sporting a black muscle-T and perfectly pressed black jeans, said, "Import and Export?"

"All I could think of," said Kate.

"How about Freaks Anonymous?"

"How about the League of Human Decency?"

"Fucking necrophiliacs. They actually want to buy the sicko's paintings. JFK's golf clubs and Marilyn's wedding band I can see, but—" Perlmutter spied a man leaning in close to one of the paintings, noted that several of the other cops were keeping an eye on him too. "You know, the Smithsonian supposedly owns Dillinger's *member*. Now there's a conversation piece I wouldn't mind having in my living room."

"Already bought it," said Kate, and would have laughed, but felt a chill as a young man came into the gallery and the cop at the door signaled. The guy moved just behind her, silver-mirrored shades reflecting part of a painting and Kate's own face right back at her. She slid her hand under her black blazer, fingertips flirting with her .45. Sunglasses guy was so close she could smell his cologne or whatever it was he used to spike his hair.

Perlmutter shimmied a bit closer, and so did Grange, the two men positioning themselves so that the guy was trapped between them.

"Hey, man," said Spiked Hair to Grange. "You mind?"

Kate moved in, Brown just beside her.

He was about the right age, tall and thin, good-looking.

"Isn't it difficult to see the paintings like that?" Kate asked, adding a smile to mask her anxiety.

"Like what?" He tossed his head a bit, and Kate's reflected face jitterbugged in his mirrored shades.

"With the glasses." Kate's adrenaline was kicking in, heart rate pumping up a few notches. "Thought you might want to see all the *color* these have to offer."

Perlmutter kept his eyes locked on the guy and another two cops caught wind of the scene and edged closer.

Spiked Hair whipped off his shades. "Don't know why I'd want to see this stuff any better."

"You don't like them?" she asked.

"No. I think they're awful."

Would the psycho say that about his own paintings? Kate didn't think so—unless he was a damn good actor. But she pressed. "What about the color?"

"It stinks." He made a face. "I just came here to check out a real live psycho's paintings, but truthfully, they give me the creeps." He turned and his eyes met Perlmutter's for a moment, then he flipped his shades back into place.

"Not our guy," Kate whispered to Grange and Perlmutter. "He's not interested in the paintings."

"Could be an act," said Grange.

"Not a blink or squint when he took off the shades," said Kate. "And check out his wrists. I didn't see any scars."

"I agree with Kate," said Perlmutter, eyes trailing after the guy.

Static emanated from Grange's palm and he put it to his ear, none too subtly, and took off.

"Smooth," said Perlmutter, staring after Grange.

"That's Grange."

"Cute, though."

"*Grange?*"

"No. The guy with the hair."

"Well, then, why don't you keep an eye on him for another minute."

"Fine," said Perlmutter.

Kate moved into the center of the room, pivoted slowly, tried to assess everyone as best she could. The guy in the corner, the only other man wearing shades, was now chatting with a young woman, obviously putting the moves on her, no interest in the paintings. Everyone else was engaged in conversation. Many were simply too old, she decided; others were obvious couples. And most of them had been on Bloom's guest list. Still, Kate could not relax, and that weird buzzing sensation had started and she wasn't sure if it was her natural cop instinct on alert, or if there was something she was missing. She focused on one person after another until the crowd began to blur and the room went still and all the voices commingled into a locustlike buzz. A hand on her back and Kate spun around fast, hand going for her Glock. "Jesus, Mitch. Don't ever do that."

"Sorry."

"It's okay. I'm just a bit on edge."

"Aren't we all." Freeman looked over the room, then glanced toward the entrance. "I hope they're keeping a watch outside. He could be enjoying this from afar."

"Don't you think he'd want to experience it up close and personal—his first and *last* exhibition?" Kate spotted another young man slip in through the front door, alone, baseball cap low on his forehead, face in shadow. She nudged Bloom. "He on your list?"

The art dealer shook his head no.

The young man slowly made his way into the room, awkward, arms hugging his sides, practically glued to the room's perimeter, carefully taking in each painting.

Kate and Freeman watched him, and they weren't the only ones. Brown had caught him too, and he'd registered on several of the cops' radar, their eyes trained on him as he inched his way around the gallery. Grange was closing in too.

He fit the description: early twenties, light hair falling into blinking eyes.

Blinking!

Kate cut across the room, fast.

Two cops, Class Clown and Dyed Blonde, moved in too, surrounding the kid, not making a move yet, though Kate saw Dyed Blonde's hand twitch toward the weapon in her handbag.

Easy now. Kate took another step, Perlmutter just beside her, Brown coming from the opposite direction, and almost at once there were six, maybe seven pairs of arms grabbing the kid, his blinking eyes opening wide.

The rest of the crowd quieted, everyone turning to see what was going on.

"Outside," Brown hissed. "Take him outside."

The air had cooled a bit, but there was heat coming off the cops.

"I didn't do anything." The kid's voice was soft and high, touched by the South. "I wasn't going to steal anything, I swear." His eyes were blinking and twitching.

Guns were out now, handcuffs too.

Class Clown slammed the kid up against the brick wall. A couple of the art patrons peeked out the door, but they got bored and turned back in. The two cops on surveillance had bolted out of their car and were tearing across the street, weapons drawn. The agent impersonating a homeless man was up too. Within seconds, every agent from inside the gallery had joined them on the street.

Grange was nearly shouting into his wrist and then the van was screeching around the corner and more agents joined the scene

Class Clown had the kid's arms stretched behind his back, pushing his face into the wall while Dyed Blonde slapped on the cuffs.

The kid strained to look over his shoulder, and there were tears gathering in his twitchy eyes.

"I didn't do anything."

"Let him talk," said Kate.

"Name," said Brown.

"Bobby-Joe Scott."

Kate could smell the fear coming off him.

"Why are you here, Bobby?" she asked.

"B-bobby-Joe."

"Bobby-Joe." She rested her hand on his arm, turned to Class Clown, who still had the kid's neck in his hand like a vice. "Ease up."

"Talk to me," said Brown.

"What, w-what about, sir?"

"You. All about you."

"I, I don't know what to say. I'm an artist, is all. I, I make things, you know. Outta wood." Tears were now streaming down Bobby-Joe's young face, along with a thin ribbon of snot from his nose.

"What are you talking about?" asked Grange.

"I w-whittle, sir. You know, with w-wood, and a knife."

"You got a fuckin' knife on you?" Class Clown grabbed him again.

"Easy, Detective," said Brown, then asked the kid, "Where you from?"

"Alabama."

"You got some ID?"

"Y-yessir." He swallowed hard. "My, my pocket. Back p-pocket."

Perlmutter fished a worn brown wallet out of the kid's jeans. Class

Clown eyed the maneuver like he was about to make a crack. Kate noticed, vowed if he did, to personally break his jaw.

"This, this is, m-my, my first trip here, to N-new York, and, and . . ."

"Relax," said Brown, tugging a driver's license from the wallet. "Looks like this is indeed Bobby-Joe Scott, from Tuscaloosa, Alabama."

Kate reached for Bobby-Joe's arm, and the kid flinched. "Just want to see something," she said, pushing up the sleeves of his jacket. "No scars," she said, and looked into his face. He was a goofy-looking kid, gawky.

"How old are you?" she asked.

Brown answered reading off the license. "Nineteen."

"I, I got my b-bus ticket in there too, sir. I just, just got here, yesterday."

Brown slipped the ticket out from between a few bills, and a couple of traveler's checks. "I think we owe you an apology," he said.

Perlmutter plucked the key out of Dyed Blonde's hand, undid the cuffs.

The kid rubbed his wrists.

Grange marshaled his agents, started sending them back to their posts.

Brown patted Bobby-Joe on the arm. "We're looking for a very bad man, son. And we made a mistake. I'm sorry."

"That fuckin' eye twitch could get you in some deep doodoo," said Class Clown.

"A tic is what my mama calls it," said Bobby-Joe, smiling a bit now, as each cop took a turn patting him on the back, mumbling "Sorry," cuffing him on the chin as if he were their kid brother.

"Call a car," Brown said to Class Clown. "Take Bobby-Joe wherever he'd like. You can tell your pals back home that you took a ride with the NYPD. Bet they'll be jealous of that."

"Yes, sir," said Bobby-Joe and shook Brown's hand.

Brown turned to Kate and Perlmutter and shook his head. "Waste of time," he said.

The gallery lights had blinked a half hour earlier and the place was empty now of art lovers dying to buy a piece of the death-related art. Grange was still huddled with a couple of his agents, but most of the cops had already left, the women exchanging their new black heels for running shoes before heading to the subways that would deliver most of them to the outer boroughs, to husbands and kids who had eaten take-out from Boston Market or Domino's Pizza. A bunch of the younger guys were taking their tired bodies but still active libidos to a singles bar to see if they might get lucky. Only the waiter cop and the bartender cop remained, and a couple of gallery assistants who were cleaning up. Herbert Bloom was making notes at his desk—probably figuring out how to sell the paintings without anyone knowing, thought Kate, gazing across the room, feeling disappointed, adrenaline oozing out of her as if she were donating blood. She stared at the psycho's paintings, the ones with her name encoded into the borders.

"The paintings will stay up for the next couple of days and there'll be cops here with them. There's still a good chance he's gonna show up," said Brown, though his heart wasn't in it. "Hey, Bloom," he called out to the art dealer, "you gotta get going." Then he turned his attention to the bartender and waiter cops, noted how young they were, two rookies who'd been assigned to him from General, felt like telling them what sort of life was in store for them, but didn't bother, they'd see for them-selves in a couple of years. "Replacements will be here at seven A.M. Have a good night, boys."

"I already picked out my chair," said bartender cop, angling his square jaw at an overstuffed leather number beside Bloom's desk.

"What's that leave me?" said waiter cop.

"Comfy-looking metal folding chair over there," said the bartender cop, and laughed.

"Don't forget. You've got Brennan and Carvalier in the car across the street. And Agent Homeless too," said Brown. "Call in if anyone even *sniffs* around the gallery—you got that?"

"Got it," said waiter cop. Bartender cop was already arranging him-self in the leather chair, sipping black coffee from a Styrofoam cup and trying not to yawn.

It is one-fifteen in the morning. No people on the street other than the homeless man who he knows is a cop and the car just across the street from the gallery with two guys in it, one with his face buried in a newspaper, the other one with his head against the backrest, maybe sleeping, also cops, no question. He'd watched them before, when all that commotion with the kid was going down.

This is the perfect moment, with the garbage truck halfway down the street, making a racket.

"I'll be back for you in a minute." It is almost black in the alleyway, but he can see perfectly. "Wait for me."

"Then what?"

"Do just like I said. Don't worry." He swings his arm into the night air. "You'll be grrrrrrrrrrrreat!"

THIRTY-FOUR

Nola was asleep in the chair, an old James Bond movie playing on the TV screen, Pussy Galore pulling a karate-type flip on a startled Sean Connery.

She woke up when Kate turned off the set. "How was the opening?" She yawned, stretched out her arms.

"Believe me, you didn't miss anything." *Had they missed something?* Kate wondered. Tonight, in the gallery, two or three times she'd had the feeling that something had happened but they just didn't know it. She'd been so sure that he wouldn't be able to resist, that he wouldn't be able to stay away.

"I'm starved," said Nola.

"Let's see what's hiding in the fridge." Kate laid her arm gently over Nola's shoulder as they headed down the hallway toward the kitchen. She wondered if Richard was home yet and was about to ask Nola if he'd called when she remembered.

Agent Marty Grange stared at the TV, some dumb cop show, a repeat, no less. He took a sip of his Budweiser and glanced at the file he had accumulated on McKinnon: her Astoria record, a couple of cases she'd botched, but plenty of commendations, which far outnumbered the fuckups. That, plus copies of her marriage certificate, phone records,

and bank statements with numbers he never even imagined possible—
none of it amounting to much. He wasn't entirely sure why he had bothered, just that the woman had gotten under his skin.

He finished the Bud, pulled himself up and went for another. Today
was his birthday. Fifty-seven years old. No family. No hobbies. No one
to celebrate with. A life devoted to the Bureau—and for what?

He needed this operation to go well. He needed to be the one to catch
this guy, this psycho. He had to show the Bureau—and his new superior—
that he still had what it takes.

Grange took another slug of Bud, then he shoved the papers back
into the file, closed his eyes and pictured McKinnon—green eyes, shiny
hair, the way she held herself, poised, regal, the kind of woman who
wouldn't give a guy like him a second glance.

Vonette Brown was curled up in a corner of the couch in the living
room of the Park Slope apartment that she and her husband had
lived in long before the area had become chic.

Floyd kissed her cheek lightly and her eyes fluttered open.

"What time is it?"

"Time for me to retire," said Floyd.

Vonette Brown rolled her eyes. "I've heard that before." She patted
her husband's cheek. "You eat anything?"

"Not hungry," he said, thinking about Bobby-Joe Scott and what a
welcome to the big city they'd given that poor kid. At least no one had
shot him. But the thought brought him little solace. They had three
more days to wait around and see if the psycho would come see his
paintings. Floyd was surprised he hadn't shown tonight. In the past,
when McKinnon had a hunch, particularly when it came to artists—sane
or insane—she'd been right.

Vonette gripped Floyd's hand, and pulled herself off the couch. "I've
got some meatloaf I can microwave."

Brown followed his wife into the kitchen, sat heavily into a chair, and
leaned his elbows onto the table.

"Everything okay?" Vonette asked, setting the timer on the microwave.

"Just tired." He was thinking that in a few minutes he would call those rookies inside the gallery, and see how they were doing. "Maybe a little hungry too." He managed a smile for his wife.

He watches a moment, then sprints down the street. The homeless agent, who is practically asleep, blinks awake and sees him coming. The agent is just going for his gun when he gets a bullet between the eyes. The silenced gun makes a small popping noise lost in the din of a New York City night—that garbage truck churning away, distant sirens, the underground rattle of a subway. It is only a few yards to the car and though the cop who has been reading the newspaper has sensed him coming, it is too late. Through the open car window he fires off several shots.

The beeper went off and Nicky Perlmutter reached for his pants crumpled on the floor beside the bed in a heap. He tugged the pager out of a pocket. Brown's telephone number glowed iridescent in the dark room.

"Gotta go," he whispered.

"So soon?"

"Work calls."

Spiked Hair gazed up at him, reached out and ran his hand over Nicky's muscled chest. "Glad I went to that opening tonight."

Perlmutter pictured the psycho's paintings on the gallery walls, the disappointment they'd all felt just a few hours ago when the guy hadn't showed up. But there was still time. He just hoped to God that they wouldn't lose anyone else before they finally caught the creep.

"You okay? You looked far away for a minute there."

"The job. You know."

"Not me. Never actually had a real job. Just a poor starving artist, is all."

"Lucky you," said Perlmutter, ruffling the guy's spiky hair. "I'd like to see your art sometime."

"That mean you want to see me again too?"

"Yeah." Permutter pulled his black tee over his head, down over his chest, regarded Brown's number glowing on his beeper again. "I gotta get moving," he said. "But I'll call you."

The bartender cop is on the floor, gasping for breath, eyes wide open, glazed, staring at the blood pouring out of his gut, his life along with it. The waiter cop is nearby, shot through the heart, already dead. Any minute the bartender cop will be dead too, just like the homeless cop and the two in the car, shot right through the open car window, pop, pop.

He gazes at the bodies on the floor, all the blood, magenta with a hint of razzle dazzle rose. *Beautiful.*

But nothing compares to his paintings on the wall.

No need to turn on a light. For him, it is better this way, just the soft illumination from the street lamps. How elegant they look, shimmering with color, perfect.

The only thing missing is the art *her-story-n* to talk to him about them.

He goes from painting to painting, the colors blurring a bit from the tears in his eyes. He is content, happy—believes those are the emotions he is feeling—and something else, sadness, loss. But he can cope with them; has his whole life.

He knows what he must do and has the strength to do it. He uncaps the tin, the smell in his nostrils a bit sickening, sprinkles some onto the floor, splashes more onto nearby walls, leans over a dead body, shakes the liquid onto the face and hands, draws his leg back and delivers a swift mean kick directly into the lifeless mouth, teeth shattering and splintering, then remembers something important and takes a moment to do it before splashing a bit more gasoline onto the body, for good measure.

One last look at his paintings. The colors are fading—or is it just the tears in his eyes washing the color away? Doesn't matter. Not any longer.

It's a sacrifice. Necessary.

This part of his life is complete, finished.

He's had a triumph tonight. Outsider, indeed.

His mind is clear. No ads or jingles or noise to distract him. Everything makes sense now, has had a purpose.

He sees her perfectly, the one who hurt him, starved him and sold him. *Sara Jane.* Fifteen years old when he was born. Of course he did not know her then, or know that he was born addicted to heroin, or that he had gone through withdrawal, DTs, just days after entering the world. Nor has he any way of knowing that the reason he so often feels as though he is suffocating is because, as a baby, his mouth was taped shut to stifle his cries. But soon enough he knew her, this girl, his mother, a runaway. *My daddy used to fuck me, you know, and Mom, where was Mom? In hell, I hope.* How many times had he heard that?

He remembers the man whom she brought home that night, who destroyed his artwork and stomped on his crayons and chalks, and Sara Jane did nothing.

He touches the crescent-shaped scar hidden beneath his light brown hair. He remembers the struggle to save his drawings, the man's heavy black boot connecting with his head and everything going black.

Was it hours, minutes, he'd been unconscious? He'd never been sure.

When he awoke, Boy George was crooning, "Do You Really Want to Hurt Me?" and there were two figures on a bed, blurry, but clear enough, Sara Jane and the man. Disgusting. Not that seeing her, his mother, fucking a stranger shocked him. He'd seen it before. What shocked him was that their flesh had gone gray, two cadavers, grunting and groaning.

For just a moment the Francis Bacon painting *Two Figures* glows in his mind, and then he is back in that room, watching his mother fucking that man, everything gray.

How could it be?

Sara Jane's colored bulbs still burned, but the light they cast was no longer blue or red or green. He raised his hand; it had also turned gray, and touched his aching temple and when his fingers came away sticky and stained black, he knew it was his eyes and not the bulbs that had failed, and nausea rose in his gut and his head throbbed, the floor tilting, room spinning.

That was when the man noticed he was awake, and pushing Sara Jane aside, lumbered over, naked and leering, and called back to Sara Jane, "He's prettier than you—I'd rather fuck him," and she shrugged, and said, "Suit yourself," and started rolling a joint. And then this man, this monster, grabbed him by the shoulders and hoisted him up and shoved his half-erect cock into his bleeding mouth, and though he had been forced to do this so many times as a child, and lately had been doing it for money, he could not detach, was absolutely incapable of imagining a garden or rainbow—not now, when the real world had gone gray. He smelled her on the man's cock and thought he'd be sick.

The penknife burned in his pocket. He wanted to slice the man's cock off, pictured him darting around the room bleeding and squawking, a wild, headless chicken, but he was not sure the small knife was up to the task and could not risk failure, and so he continued the chore, scrutinizing the man's face, and when his eyes closed and he knew he was close, he drew the knife and inflicted the blows, three quick jabs, stomach, lung, heart—*thwack thwack thwack*—and blood poured from the man's wounds and streaked down his belly and coated his cock and then splattered onto *his* face and into *his* eyes, and for a brief moment he wondered if that was why everything had suddenly turned red.

The man was making wild, pathetic efforts to stanch the blood loss, hands pressed into gashes, eyes wild, deep crimson stripes against pale apricot flesh. Everywhere he looked—floor, ceiling, walls—was now radiant with Sara Jane's colored lights—periwinkle, shamrock, and royal purple—which, if he had been able to think clearly about it, was impossible—there were no purple bulbs. But then the colored lights began to fade and the man's flesh went white and the blood deepened to black, and the man keeled over and hit the floor, the whole time Sara Jane screaming, until he turned the knife on her.

Afterward, when they were both quiet, he smoothed the hair off Sara Jane's face and noticed all of the razzmatazz blood had turned ebony, her goldenrod hair ash, the walls, everything, a wan gray, and he barely remembered that, minutes ago, when he killed them, the room had been dazzling.

The radio was humming in the background—*This is Casey Kasem with the top . . ."*—as he placed Sara Jane on the floor and dragged the man's body beside her and put the knife in his hand, and imagined what Jessica from *Murder She Wrote* would say: "A fight between a prostitute and her customer; they must have killed each other, right, Sheriff?"

When he was going through the man's clothes, looking for money, he'd found the gun, wasn't sure what he would do with it, but thought it might come in handy one day and decided to keep it.

Then he cleaned up and changed his clothes so that people would not stare at him in the street, gathered his money, and made his way to Port Authority, where he stashed the cash and the gun in a locker, the whole time staggered by a world gone gray, the pain in his head growing worse, legs weak. When he awakened in the white room he thought he was dead—and was glad.

But he wasn't dead. And the colorless world remained.

The doctors stitched his head and bandaged his wounds and told him what they thought had happened—*some sort of brain damage*. But he wouldn't tell them anything. Ignored the plates of gray sludge that was supposed to be food and stared out the window at a dull pewter sky, and tried to pretend that one day he would see color again, but somewhere inside he knew that he would not—and that his dream of becoming an artist was over.

He returns to the moment, staring at his brightly colored paintings, and smiles. He has proved them wrong. He is cured.

He moves from one painting to another, so close, nose practically grazing paint and canvas, inhaling the sweet scent of oil, once or twice drags his tongue across an area of thick impasto paint—a long wet kiss good-bye.

Tears are streaming down his cheeks now, everything in front of him streaking like visions through a rainy windshield, but the images in his mind have started to play again, that awful woman and man, and now music chimes in along with the jingles and ads and radio-speak—a jumble of white noise. That's it. Enough.

Strikes a match.

A sound like wind through a hollow heart.

Flames dance. Heat.

He gazes straight ahead, almost hypnotized, as the flames lick his paintings and the canvases begin to blacken and curl, reaches out for a farewell touch, fingertips singed. The fire twirls around his shoes, bottoms of his pants begin to smoke and burn.

THIRTY-FIVE

S irens cut through the night and arcs of police beacons swept the street, intensifying the scarlet of the dying fire as Kate gazed across at the Gallery of Outsider Art, water pouring over blackened brick, half the facade gone, dark gray smoke and mist belching out of the ruins.

One of the Crime Scene crew handed Floyd Brown a Baggie with a heavy chain coiled inside. "Necklace we took off the body. You wanted to see it, Chief?"

Brown nodded at Kate. "Wanted *her* to see it."

Kate gripped the bag, held it up toward a street lamp, stared through the plastic.

"Kid was wearing it," said Brown. "Think it fits the description of the chain missing from Boyd Werther's neck?"

Kate pictured the artist in his studio, running his paint-stained fingers under the chain, displaying it for her, the individual links like crosses. She slid the chain back and forth inside the bag, felt as though she were trying to channel the dead artist, and it made her want to cry. "Yes, I'm pretty sure it's the one. But you should contact Werther's first wife for an absolute ID." Kate reached for the chain around her own neck and grasped Richard's wedding ring in her fingers.

"Not all that much left of the body," said Brown. "Face is a mess, sunglasses melted right into flesh. Weapon in his hand ended up in better condition than the rest of him. At least someone got off a solid punch or kick—knocked half the kid's teeth out." Brown sighed. "It's not gonna be an easy ID." He stroked his forehead, thought about the two young rookies dead, Brennan and Carvalier, also dead, and the agent. "Fucking mess." The last of the fire was reflected in his dark eyes, but it didn't mask the pain. "Did he come in shooting? Catch them off guard? I'm trying to see it," he said. "He comes down the street, shoots Agent Homeless, then shoots the two in the car, then what? Walks across the street to the gallery, knocks on the gate, and they just open up?" He dragged a hand over his head. "It doesn't make sense."

"Wouldn't the cops inside have heard the shots and come running out of the gallery?" asked Perlmutter.

"Gun had a silencer," said Brown. "Crime Scene says the gate was halfway up, so they must have let him in. Either they didn't know who he was, or they thought they could handle it. Obviously they didn't know Brennan and Carvalier were dead."

"Did either of them call in?" asked Kate.

"At midnight. To say everything was quiet."

Tapell headed toward them, backlit by the glow of the dying fire. "Press conference in the morning, Floyd."

Brown nodded.

"Sorry about the men." She started away, then turned back. "You going to call the families, or—"

"Already did," said Brown. "Couldn't take the chance of them seeing it on the news." He motioned toward two camera crews filming the fire, newscasters standing in front of the gallery broadcasting, appropriate frowns in place along with every hair.

"Right." She turned away, dodged a couple of reporters.

"Too bad we didn't have the chance to interrogate him," said Kate as they headed toward Perlmutter's car. She was feeling incomplete and anxious and sad all at once.

"Guess it will remain a mystery," said Perlmutter.

There wasn't much reason for Kate to come into the precinct in the morning, but when the daylight cut in through her bedroom windows after three hours of non-sleep, the last thing she wanted to do was hang around her apartment and think about what she was going to do with the rest of her life.

Clean out her locker? A lame excuse. But she used it.

At the station, she and Perlmutter watched the press conference on a TV in the briefing room; Tapell presenting the good news—that the serial killer was dead, Brown left with the not so good news of lost lives, "heroes"; then the two of them fielding questions, trying to put the thing to rest. The press had obviously gotten some information because they kept referring to the kid as the *color-blind killer*.

"Do we know who he was yet?" Kate asked, as Perlmutter shut off the television.

"Prelims show the kid was a user, heroin. But they haven't been able to ID him. I can't imagine anyone coming forward to claim the body. Would you, if he was your kid?"

"Good point," said Kate, though she thought she would.

"The Bad Seed," said Perlmutter. "A fifties howler about an evil little girl. You ever see it?"

"No. Think I'll pass too."

"Tired?" asked Perlmutter.

"Aren't you?"

"Dead Man Walking," he said. "Now there's a movie that proves two things. One, that a good-looking actress is assured an Oscar if she plays a part without makeup, and two, it makes me happy that our psycho is dead."

"What do you mean?"

"No trial. No bleeding hearts to say he shouldn't be put to death."

"You're in favor of the death penalty?"

"Suppose we'd brought him in alive. No question he cops an insanity plea. They subpoena the therapist from Pilgrim State. The lawyer brings the jury to tears over the way the poor kid was just a victim himself, right? He spends maybe a dozen years in a *facility* zonked out on Thorazine. Gets out, stops taking his meds, kills again."

"You're oversimplifying," said Kate. "No way they'd have ever let him walk the streets again."

"Maybe not."

"And you know what—and don't call me a bleeding heart—but he probably *was* a victim. Sure, he's a monster, but it takes a lot of work to create a monster like that."

"Lots of people overcome really bad shit," said Perlmutter.

"No question," said Kate, thinking of most of the kids who had managed under incredible hardship to get through Let There Be a Future and create amazing lives for themselves. "I'm just saying that you never know. Plus there's always the chance that you might execute the wrong man."

"Another great flick, Hitchcock's *The Wrong Man*."

"Very smooth. The way you changed the subject."

"Me?" Perlmutter's blue eyes widened with innocence. "No. Just like to think of life as fiction. It's easier that way."

Life as fiction. Kate wondered if that phrase might define her life?

"You with me?"

"Yes. Sorry. I think I'll clean out my stuff—for the second time. Then head home." Though she wasn't quite ready to go home or give up her NYPD status, not with so many questions about Richard's death unanswered.

Perlmutter walked her toward the women's locker room. Halfway there they met up with Marty Grange and they all played an unintentional game—dodging to the right, then left, one blocking the other. "I'll stand still," Kate said to Grange. "Then you go, okay? On the count of three."

Grange almost smiled.

"Back to the Bureau?" asked Kate.

"Guess so," said Grange, who looked into her eyes for about a second, then immediately away.

Kate nodded. Grange nodded.

Perlmutter looked from Kate to Grange.

"Well then," said Kate, and took a step.

"Hey, I—" Grange stretched out his hand. "No hard feelings, huh?"

Kate figured her face was registering some small amount of shock, but she took his hand. It was warm and moist. "Sure. Who needs hard feelings?" Kate slid her hand out. "Good-bye."

Grange didn't say anything, just nodded, this time closer to a bow, then quickly straightened up, awkward, tapping his pockets. "Keys," he said. "Just looking for my keys. Ah, here they are." He produced a heavy metal ring laden with keys.

"You a warden in your spare time?"

"No. I, uh, have a place here, in New York, and then the place in D.C., so I have a lot of uh . . . keys."

"I was kidding," said Kate.

"Oh. Sure. I knew that." Grange set his features into a sober mask, then took off down the hall.

"Whoa," said Perlmutter, once Grange had disappeared around the corner. "Agent Grange has got a thing for you."

"Oh, sure."

"Hey, when a man goes all bumbling and goofy around a woman—"

"Nicky," said Kate, with what she hoped was a good-natured smile. "Shut up."

The San Remo apartment seemed bigger and emptier than ever, like a tomb, or a museum with art and objects that Kate and Richard had collected that she couldn't bear to look at, every one of them setting off another memory.

Kate wandered from the den to the living room, into the library, perused a few art books, considered the idea of writing a new book, which at the moment seemed totally impossible, then finally stumbled into her bedroom, a sideways glance at Richard's laughing photo beside the money clip on her dresser, a constant reminder of her failure to get answers—and maybe his failure too. But would she ever know for sure?

The money clip felt cold in her hand, just a piece of metal, not much of a talisman, neither conjuring the man nor his spirit. Kate laid it back onto the dresser, wandered down the hallway into the den, folded herself into a soft leather chair, caught up on calls. First, Richard's mother, who continued to insist that she come to Florida for a visit, which Kate said she would after Nola delivered, maybe all three of them. A quick call to Blair, who wanted to plan a lunch, all the girls, at one of their uptown haunts, but Kate begged off. "Next week," she said, though Blair complained it was always *next week*.

Kate stared at the bookshelves filled with the novels Richard liked to read, thrillers of any kind, mysteries, whodunits, the irony not lost on her. But she couldn't sit still. Down the hall again, into her office, where she sat and gazed at a blank yellow pad, finally picked up a pencil and started free-associating, compiling a list of what she knew, or thought she knew, about Richard's death.

Painting found beside Richard's body painted by Leonardo Martini.

Martini worked for Angelo Baldoni.

Baldoni commissioned painting from Martini.

Lab confirms hair on Martini's shirt belonged to Baldoni—likely Baldoni killed Martini.

Kate stopped a moment, pencil poised in midair, then started again, allowing the thoughts to dictate themselves.

According to Grange, FBI has a file on Baldoni—history as freelance hit man.

Baldoni number 1 suspect in killing Richard.

The words throbbed on the page.

Kate wasn't sorry she'd shot and killed him. She took a breath, then wrote:

Baldoni—Giulio Lombardi's nephew.

Lombardi—well-known crime boss.

But Lombardi had disappeared without a trace. Neither the NYPD nor the Bureau could find him.

So what else? Kate glanced out the window, down at the treetops of

Central Park, a blur of fall color beginning—greens going brown and orange. It brought the Bronx psycho's paintings to mind, and the arrangement in Boyd Werther's studio, and the idea of the exhibition, which she had thought made sense, but now nothing made sense. The color-blind killer. Another mystery. Over. But not solved. Kate tapped the pen lightly against her chin and started writing again.

Andrew Stokes—defended Lombardi, continued to see him posttrial.

Lombardi—Baldoni's uncle.

Kate wondered: Did Stokes know Baldoni?

Stokes—Baldoni?

Stokes killed in Lamar Black's apartment.

Rosita Martinez identified Stokes as Suzie White's regular.

Suzie White killed by Color-blind Killer.

Andy Stokes—Lamar Black—Suzie White—Angelo Baldoni. What's the connection?

Kate thought about talking to Noreen Stokes again, pictured the woman in her hospital bed—and how she had screamed at her—and knew it was impossible.

Kate scanned the notes she had written. So many of the players were dead.

So who was alive who might give her something she didn't already know? If not Noreen Stokes, who?

Kate stared at the wall a moment, then checked her watch.

Her *watch*. Baume et Mercier. Baume, the private detective. Of course.

Baume Investigations was in one of those tall, nondescript Midtown Manhattan buildings, the eighth-floor hallway long and harshly lit, doors every few feet, gray walls that may once have been white, worn brownish carpet that suggested it had started life as a color.

"Appointment?" asked the receptionist, middle-aged, hair the color of ripe Florida oranges.

"Sorry," said Kate. "But if Mr. Baume can give me a minute . . ."

The secretary whipped a paper off her desk. "You'll have to fill this out."

One page. NAME. ADDRESS. PHONE. DATE. PURPOSE OF VISIT. METHOD OF PAYMENT.

"I only need to talk."

"Mr. Baume, my husband"—she smiled, but it was slightly sour—"works by the hour. A hundred and twenty-five. Plus expenses. First consultation is free. Eugene, that is Mr. Baume, won't charge you if he doesn't take the case."

"Have you worked with your husband long?" Kate asked, taking a moment to smile up at the woman while she filled in the form.

"Forever." The woman waved a hand through the air. "But from what I've seen in this line of work, it pays to be around. You know what I mean, hon?" She laid a finger across her lips. "Oh, sorry. You're not here about your husband, I hope."

"Excuse me?"

"Husbands. Wives. Eugene's specialty. Keeping an eye on them."

Kate tried not to think about the word *husband*. "Oh, no. That's not my problem. I was referred by . . . Mrs. Stokes. Noreen Stokes."

"Sounds familiar. But I'd have to check the files."

Kate was about to ask if she would when the office door swung open.

Eugene Baume was a small bald man with a jutting jaw and hooded eyes that made him look like a turtle.

"Used to work for one of those big investigation firms, lots of partners and associates," said Baume as Kate arranged herself in a chair opposite his desk. "But I prefer working alone."

"How long have you been off the force?"

Baume almost smiled. "It shows?"

"Just a little. I used to work Astoria. Missing Persons. Homicide. Retired now ten years." Kate smiled too. "Something about you just said *cop*."

"Eighteen years, I guess. Needed a change of pace." He gave her the once-over. "Looks like you did okay."

"Well enough," said Kate.

"So you're a friend of Mrs. Stokes?"

"Do you remember her?"

"I remember all of my clients."

"Well, it's her husband I'd like to ask you about."

Baume sat up straight, his jutting jaw pronounced. "I never discuss a case."

"Of course, and I respect that." Kate slid her temporary police ID onto his desk.

"Thought you were retired," said Baume.

"So did I," said Kate. "It's a long story."

"Confidentiality's the name of the game, you know that—unless you've got a warrant."

"To be honest, Mr. Baume, this is really more personal than official." Kate tried on a smile. "Just a few questions. Between you and me."

"What is this?" Baume's hooded eyes narrowed. "Some sort of NYPD sting?"

"Oh, no, not at all. Like I said, it's personal."

"Sorry. No warrant, no talk."

Baume held the door open for her. "Franny," he said. "No charge."

*D*amn. She hadn't handled that very smoothly. But she was impatient, sick of not getting answers. Kate glanced up and down busy Broadway as though the solution were out there, hiding in the traffic. No way she could get a warrant. She was no longer part of the team, not even temporary. And Brown and Tapell both considered Richard's murder closed. In a few weeks it would be just another *cold case*.

She flipped open her cell phone.

"Sounds like you're in the middle of traffic," said Liz.

"Times Square, to be exact."

"Slumming?"

"Don't even go there. Listen, I need a favor." Kate explained, hoped her friend could make a few calls to Quantico that would open doors without a warrant.

"Sorry, no can do. Not unless I was on the case. Otherwise there's going to be a whole lot of questions that are going to get me into a whole lot of trouble, and I'm certain you don't want to do that."

"Don't be so sure."

"Listen, honey, I'd love to help, but . . . the case is over, isn't it?"

"This is about the other case, Richard's case."

"Oh." A moment of silence. "Well, you need someone who is involved."

"Like who?"

"How about Marty Grange? The way the Bronx psycho case ended wasn't so good for him. Rumor has it they'd like to retire him."

"Grange wouldn't give me the time of day."

"Don't be so sure. He's an odd one, but deep down he has a sense of what's right and what's wrong."

Kate shut her cellular and stared at the traffic. *Marty Grange?*

Liz must be out of her mind.

THIRTY-SIX

FBI Manhattan. Streamlined. Quiet. No smell of bad coffee. No peeling paint. No perps screaming about their rights.

Kate headed down the corridor until she found the door, slightly ajar, with his name on it, peeked in and saw him bent over, inserting a file into a low drawer, another one between his teeth.

Agent Marty Grange looked up, did a double take, and the file dropped out of his mouth. He quickly straightened up, smoothing neatly pressed pants.

Kate took a quick breath, thought she must be out of her mind to be here. "I need a favor."

"A favor?"

"Yes."

"Well?" Their eyes met and Grange quickly glanced to the side.

"I'd like to see the FBI file on Angelo Baldoni. You mentioned that the Bureau had been compiling one for years."

"And you want *me* to get it?"

"Yes."

"And I should do this because . . ." Grange stared at the file that had fallen to the floor, then went to retrieve it just as Kate did, the two of them bent over, almost eye-to-eye for an awkward moment.

"Timing"—Kate straightened, file in hand—"is everything." She smiled.

Grange took the file, but didn't seem to know what to do with it.

"I'm asking for your help. I'm not satisfied with how my husband's case ended."

"And you want to open it up?"

"No, I want to close it. But I'd like to know what really happened. Wouldn't you? Wouldn't the Bureau?"

Grange seemed to be considering that. "And you think Baldoni's file might help?"

"Maybe." Kate took a step closer and Grange caught a whiff of her perfume, felt his muscles twitch.

"Okay."

"Okay?"

"Okay I'll get you the file."

"Really?" She was genuinely shocked.

"It's not such a big deal." Which was true—especially if they were re-tiring him, which was what he sensed was just around the bend. *Fuck them, after all these years.*

Kate continued to stand there, just a few feet from him, and Grange thought if she didn't move soon he would have to run down the hall to the men's room and splash cold water onto his face, maybe his entire body. He could feel the sweat beading up on his brow.

"That it?" he said, drawing the back of his hand across his forehead.

"Well, actually, no. I was wondering, I mean, while you're at it, how about Uncle Giulio Lombardi's file too?"

"Jesus, McKinnon. What do want? Full access to the Bureau's files?"

"That would be nice." Kate laughed, pushed her hair behind her ears, and Grange heard himself say, "Okay," and the next thing he knew she'd grabbed his hand and was shaking it and he knew that at that moment, if Kate McKinnon had asked him to walk into the White House and shoot the goddamn president's dog, he'd say okay again.

"You're a doll," said Kate. Words she never imagined saying to Marty Grange.

A smile twitched at the corners of his lips.

"I'll get the files to your home. Address?"

"One Forty-five Central Park West. But I can come get them. I don't want to put you to any trouble. When will you have them?"

Grange checked his watch. "Couple of hours." He thought about another lonely night in his one-room Midtown efficiency, drinking warm beer. He took a breath and tried to sound nonchalant. "I have to be up there, on the West Side, so I could bring them by."

"You don't have to do that, I can easily—"

"I *said* I'd drop them off. Like I was saying, I, uh, have to be on the Upper West Side anyway." A lie. He did not have to be anywhere.

"Okay. Thanks." Kate smiled and she meant it. "I was wondering . . ."

"What now? Another file?"

"No."

"Good."

"But . . ." She shook her head. "Never mind."

"What?" Grange had the awful feeling that McKinnon was about to tell him not to come and now that he'd said it there was nothing in the world he wanted to do more than simply sit across from the woman in her apartment. "I said I'd bring the files."

"No, that's not it. I, uh, well, there's something else, but . . . I've already asked too much."

"I said what, didn't I?"

"There's this private investigator, the one who trailed Andrew Stokes—remember, his former employer mentioned it? I think he might be helpful, but I can't get him to open up without a warrant."

"So you've already talked to him?"

"Afraid I have. I know what you're thinking, that I—"

"How do you know what I'm thinking?" He wiped his damp palms along the sides of his pants. "Where's this PI work out of?"

"Midtown. Forty-sixth and Sixth."

A block from the efficiency hotel that Grange had no desire to return to any earlier than he had to. "Give me a half hour to get on the phone so those files will be ready by the time we get back."

N ot much of an office," Grange said loud enough for Baume's receptionist-wife to hear.

She pursed her lips. "Eugene is busy at the moment."

Kate tried a smile, leaned over the woman's desk. "Look, it's kind of important, and—"

Grange didn't bother to wait. He stepped past her and pushed open the door to Baume's office.

The PI glanced up, and saw Kate. "You got the warrant?"

"Well, no, but—"

"I told you," said Baume, "I can't say anything without it. That's personal and private information and protected under article H of—"

Grange planted his hands onto Baume's desk. "Forget article H, or Q, or P, or F—as in fuck all of the articles."

"And who are you?" Baume looked into the dark marble eyes Kate had so often had trained on her, though now she was beginning to see it was an act Grange had perfected, his own form of protection. "I already told your friend—I need a warrant."

Grange relished the phrase, *your friend,* then slapped his ID onto Baume's desk. "You know, lately, the FBI has been working pretty closely with the IRS. Checking on small businesses, PIs specifically. You'd be surprised how many they had to close down."

Baume sighed. "What was the file again?"

"Stokes," said Kate. "Andrew Stokes."

Baume rolled back in his chair, wheels squeaking, pulled open the lower drawer of an old metal file cabinet, came up with a dog-eared folder, and plopped it onto his desk.

Kate flipped it open and started shuffling through a stack of black-and-white photos.

"Speak," said Grange.

"About?"

"The story on Stokes. I hate to read. And don't leave anything out."

Baume sighed again. "I followed Stokes for about a month. Real low life, though he had a fancy address and a fancy job. He was into hookers, gambling, drugs. Regular party boy. Occasionally scored his drugs on the street. I've got a picture of that in there somewhere," he said. "His wife didn't care about any of that. Just the girls, the hookers, you know."

Kate perused the photos, all a bit grainy, obviously taken with a tele-photo lens and from some distance, but still she recognized Suzie White.

"His main squeeze," said Baume tapping the picture of White. "Stokes was very hot for that little number. Would pick her up in Midtown and take her to a hotel couple of times a week."

"Midtown?" Kate asked, thinking that Suzie worked out of the Bronx.

"Yeah. Worked the tunnel crowd, corner of Tenth Avenue and Thirty-ninth. I remember because I used to take time out to get myself a cup-cake—you know, there's that famous place on that corner, the Cupcake Café. I nicknamed the hooker Cupcake because of it. Good thing that case only lasted a month or I'd have gained twenty pounds." Baume laughed, but no one laughed with him. "Other days Cupcake would meet Stokes on a corner near his fancy law office. Name's in there some-where."

Kate managed to say it. "Rothstein and Associates?"

"Yeah. That was it. Cupcake, the hooker, worked for that guy there." Baume tapped another photo.

"Angelo Baldoni," said Kate, staring at the photo. She turned to Grange. "So Baldoni was Suzie White's Midtown pimp, the wise guy Lamar Black mentioned, the one she was hiding from up in the Bronx."

"That guy, Baldoni, was running a small stable of girls, very young ones," said Baume. "I used to see him collecting money from them. He'd rough them up too. A real pig, that guy. I didn't know who he was right away. But when I found out, hell, I didn't want anything more to do with the case." Baume eyeballed Grange. "You know about Baldoni?"

"Yeah. I know."

"Read that he died," said Baume. "Good riddance to bad rubbish, huh?" He took the remaining photos from Kate, sorted through them and selected one. "How about this guy? You recognize him?" He pointed at a blurry picture of two men coming out of a bar, one of them Stokes.

"Guilio Lombardi," said Grange.

"Bingo. Stokes was hanging with mobsters! Jesus H. Christ. Once I realized that, I quit. I wasn't going to fuck with the likes of Giulio Lombardi."

"Smart move." Grange took the photos. "You have any of Lombardi and Baldoni together?"

Baume shook his head. "Just Stokes with each of them. Baldoni was the one who supplied Stokes with drugs, both curbside and home delivery. Saw Baldoni going up to Rothstein and Associates with a brown bag a couple of times."

"What about the partner, the boss, Richard Rothstein?" asked Kate, taking a deep breath.

"Never met the guy. Saw him go in and out of his building, but I wasn't being paid to watch him."

Grange had to ask: "You ever see Rothstein with Lombardi or Baldoni?"

"No. Never."

Kate let out her breath.

Grange fingered the edge of another photo. "Where'd you take this?"

Baume thought a moment. "It was the last on a roll. I remember because I was pissed that I'd run out of film. I'd been trailing Stokes, who had just met with Baldoni, and then that guy showed up, and either Stokes met with him or Baldoni did. Can't really remember. Like I said, I ran out of film. And that was like the last day because I didn't want to work a case that had anything to do with the mob, and so I took the money and ran."

"You mind if I keep this?" asked Grange, already sliding the photo into his jacket pocket.

"Doesn't much matter what I mind, does it?" said Baume.

"Not really." Grange leaned toward Kate. "Maybe you'd better take the whole file. I don't think Mr. Baume has any use for it."

That was great," said Kate when they were outside. She squeezed Grange's arm, and he let out a tiny gasp, which was lost under the noise of the traffic. "So who is that in the photo?"

"This," said Grange, recovering and removing the photograph from his pocket, "is none other than Charlie D'Amato, aka Charlie D. Well-known crime-world underboss, a *capo bastone*."

Kate stared at the photo of a man who looked to be in his late sixties, white-haired, kindly, like someone's grandfather. "What's that, like a godfather?

"More like a vice president. But still very powerful. And still very dangerous—even though he's doing life in Sing Sing."

THIRTY-SEVEN

"McKinnon, you are one surprising woman," said Perlmutter, steering Kate's Mercedes onto the New York Thruway. Kate was too anxious to drive, and Perlmutter was more than happy to exchange his NYPD Crown Victoria for Kate's upscale auto.

"I try."

"What'd you do to Grange?"

"Sorry, my lips are sealed."

"Bet they weren't."

"Don't be crude. Agent Grange and I have a new understanding, that's all."

"Uh-huh." Perlmutter took his eyes off the road to shoot her a fishy look. "Well, your new beau sent me in his place, and I'm happy to take the ride. So whatever it is you're doing, keep doing it."

Kate peered through the windshield at cars and road signs and wondered what it was she had done to convert Agent Grange.

"The Taconic is a nice route," said Perlmutter. "And I'm going to drive real slow. Might as well use up as much of the day as possible." He laid his arm onto the edge of his open window.

Small patches of blue sky were playing peekaboo with gray clouds.

"Brown condoning this little excursion?" Kate asked.

"Absolutely. It was Brown who made the phone call to the warden after he had a chat with your new best friend, Agent Grange. If anything pans out, both he and Grange come out looking good. If not, well, nothing lost, nothing gained."

Kate had no idea what she might gain or lose, but she needed to know, whatever it was—good news or bad—to get on with her life, if that was possible. She recalled Grange's instructions about the forthcoming interview: what he was interested in knowing, and what she could trade for it. She'd listened attentively and memorized it all. Now she stared out her side window, trees sliding by, slabs of green as if someone were dragging a squeegee over them.

"Just think of me as your driver." Perlmutter shot her a smile. "This is a CL 500 Coupe, right?"

"It's just a car," said Kate.

"Twenty-four-valve engine. Three hundred and two horsepower at fifty-six hundred rpms." Perlmutter laid his foot on the accelerator. "A lot more than just a car."

"How on earth do you know all that?"

"Boy stuff," said Perlmutter. "By the way, Brown didn't have to ask me twice. I've got a thing for prisons—and I don't mean a sexual thing, so don't even go there. I'm into their history."

"You mean there's something you know other than movies?"

"Hey, you can't beat a good prison movie. *The Defiant Ones*—Tony Curtis chained to Sidney Poitier, very interesting possibilities there—*Bird Man of Alcatraz, The Shawshank Redemption*." Perlmutter tapped the steering wheel. "Okay, here's one for you, and it's not a movie. Who were the most famous people executed at Sing Sing?"

"Haven't a clue."

"Come on. Give it a shot."

Kate rolled her eyes. "Al Capone?"

"*Al Capone?* No way. Try Julius and Ethel."

"The Rosenbergs?"

"Fried to a crisp. Here's another—one of my all-time favorite fun couples, Martha Beck and Raymond Fernandez."

"Oh, yes. The Lonely Hearts Killers. Made into a B movie, remember?"

"Remember? I own it. Tony LoBianco, Shirley Stoller."

"Nicky, a mind is terrible thing to waste. On garbage."

"Garbage?" He exaggerated a sigh. "Sacrilege."

They drove a while not speaking, then Nicky switched on the radio. It played over the static of police codes, and Perlmutter had no trouble keeping up with Jay Z, rapping along perfectly.

"What are you, like seventeen?"

"I wish," said Perlmutter.

"Can't you find something just a bit more . . . mellow?"

Perlmutter played with the dial, tuned into the middle of an old Dylan song, "Simple Twist of Fate." "Dylan okay?"

The song reminded her of Richard, and she wasn't sure she wanted to hear it, but Perlmutter was already singing along and so she said, "Dylan's fine."

Dylan. The photo enlargements of the borders in the killer's paintings played in her mind, and the names: Dylan, Tony, and Brenda. Who are they, she wondered?

Kate pinched a piece of Nicorette out of the packet and popped it into her mouth.

Soon after the bridge, they cut off the Thruway and headed into the town of Ossining, down Main Street with so many of its historic buildings still intact, a few turns, then headed up a hill and the Sing Sing tower came into view.

"You ever wonder where the name Sing Sing came from?"

Kate nodded, only half listening. Now that she was here she wasn't sure she wanted to go through with it.

"It's from the Indian, *sin sinck,* which means *stone-upon-stone.* The whole southern part of Ossining, which, by the way was called Sing Sing until the residents wanted to distance themselves from the prison, has these extensive limestone beds."

"You're just a font of information, aren't you?"

"That's me. What else you want to know? How many people they've electrocuted, types of torture they used before prison reform . . ."

The prison was presenting itself before them, and Perlmutter stopped at the locked gate and showed the guard his ID. For once Kate was glad he was quiet.

Inside, Kate and Perlmutter were brought into a small square room by a guard who looked Kate over as if she were a piece of lemon meringue pie.

Once he'd left them alone, Perlmutter said, "This is your gig. I'm just here to keep it official."

Kate nodded, took in the room. Ten by ten, no window, just a small pane of glass in the door, overhead fluorescent flickering, two metal chairs, a NO SMOKING sign, which made her exchange her old Nicorette for a new one.

"Quite a habit you got there."

"Tell me about it. It's more expensive than cigarettes."

A moment later the guard brought him in, the old man in Baume's photograph, wrists and ankles cuffed. "Sit," he said, then cuffed the man's feet to the bottom of one of the metal chairs, the one bolted into the cement floor. "I'll be right outside," the guard said, throwing Kate a wink.

In person, Charlie D'Amato was smaller than Kate had expected, looked older too, the white hair not so thick, face sagging like a basset hound's, liver spots dotting his manacled hands, which were gnarled with arthritis.

He glanced at Perlmutter, who was leaning against the wall, staring at his shoes.

"And you are?"

"Detective Perlmutter." He pulled the *Daily News* from his back pocket, unfolded it, and started to read. "Just pretend I'm not here."

D'Amato raised his eyebrows, shrugged, then looked Kate over. "Not sure what you think I can tell you about your husband's murder."

Kate tried to keep the shock from registering on her face. "So you know why I'm here."

"Word gets around." A brittle, sardonic smile cut across his face, and Kate imagined he brought it out when he wanted to make someone feel small. "Let's just say me and the warden . . . we understand each other."

"Good," said Kate. "That saves me some time."

"I like that in a woman. No crap." He bobbed his head toward ciga-rettes in his breast pocket. "Can you get those for me, sweetheart? I'm a bit tied up at the moment." He hacked a laugh.

Kate tugged the pack out, placed a Winston between his lips and lit it for him.

D'Amato had some trouble getting the cigarette to and from his mouth, the weight of the irons made every hand movement an effort. He eyed her through the smoke. "You're about my daughter's age, Teresa's her name, lives out in New Brunswick. Jersey, you know? Got a real nice house, couple of kids, one of them almost a teenager, the boy, Charlie. Named after his grandpop. Haven't seen him in a while." He smiled a slightly less toxic version of the one before. "You got any kids?"

Kate figured he knew the answer to that too, which was probably why he asked. "Mr. D'Amato. I've got limited time here, and—"

"Me?" D'Amato exhaled a plume of smoke. "I got plenty of time."

"Not the way I hear it," said Kate. According to Grange, the man was sick. Terminal. But she hadn't meant her comment to sound so brutal. "Look, if you know why I'm here, then you also know that I must have a few bargaining chits. Why don't you just tell me what you want?"

"Who says I want anything?"

Kate offered the man her own version of a knowing smile. "We all want something, Mr. D'Amato." She dragged the free metal chair over, sat across from the old man.

"Call me Charlie," he said, donning his grandfatherly persona.

"Let's not play games, okay, Charlie? You tell me something. And I'll tell you something. You know how it works. You start."

D'Amato puffed on his cigarette a moment, blew a couple of lopsided smoke rings into the already stale air. His eyes flitted over toward Perlmutter before he spoke. "Angelo Baldoni killed your husband," he said. "How's that for a start?"

It felt like a slap, even though she'd expected it.

Perlmutter eyed Kate, saw that she could handle it. She sounded cool when she asked, "Why?"

"I think it's my turn, sweetheart." He leaned forward in the chair and his leg irons clanked. "They won't let my grandkids see me."

"I think a visit can be arranged," she said, recalling that Grange had told her visitation rights were a bargaining tool to use at her discretion.

"In a room, with a guard, not through the glass. I don't want them to see their old grandpop like that."

"Okay. I can arrange that. My turn." She took a deep breath. "Why did Baldoni kill Richard?"

The old man shrugged, bored, or acting it. "He got in the way."

"In the way of *what*?"

"You should see the cell they've got me in, sweetheart. So dark. I get maybe a half hour outside, to see the sun, breathe the air, that's it, once a day. Unless I go to the doctor, which is no fun, I never get to see anything. I hear they got some cells over on the north side that got windows."

"And you'd like one of those."

"Let's say the idea of it makes me talkative."

"Maybe I can do that." The fact was that Grange had already arranged for something better if the man cooperated, but Kate wouldn't tell D'Amato that, not yet.

"I hate that word *maybe*."

"I hate games."

"You're the one who set the rules, not me." That brittle, sarcastic smile was back on his thin lips.

"Mr. D'Amato—"

He shook a gnarled finger at her, not easy with the cuffs. "Charlie."

"Charlie."

"I'd really like a room with a view. I'm an old man. A dying man. Is that so much to ask?"

He didn't need the act, which Kate wasn't buying anyway, but she'd let him play it. "Yes. I believe I can get that for you."

He smiled, and it appeared genuine. "Your husband was making trouble."

"What sort of trouble? For who?"

"It makes that much difference to you?"

Kate looked into his rheumy eyes. "Yes."

"Okay. But only because you remind me of my daughter." He glanced over at Perlmutter. "Maybe you can wait outside, give me and the young lady some privacy? You can watch through the glass in the door. Just like the guard is doing."

Perlmutter's eyes met Kate's, and she nodded.

D'Amato smiled his saccharine, grandfatherly smile. "That's better, isn't it?" he said, after the door had closed behind Perlmutter.

"Go on," said Kate. "You were telling me what happened—to my husband."

D'Amato sighed. "That creep, Stokes, he's your villain, not Angelo Baldoni. Angelo?" He blew air out of the corner of his mouth. "A nothing. A pip-squeak. A *sgarrista,* a common foot soldier, what your television shows call a *made man.* But he was just a stupid kid. He may have pulled the trigger, but it was Stokes who ordered the hit." D'Amato dropped his cigarette to the floor, tried to step on it but couldn't lift his cuffed foot to do so. "I'm not saying Angelo was a saint. But it was just a job to him. He didn't have nothing against your husband."

Kate's heart was constricting in her chest. Just a job. To kill her husband. *Just a job.*

"A hit's a hit," said D'Amato, as if he were talking about the weather. "Baldoni's uncle, Lombardi, he okayed it because of the favor. He wanted to clean the slate with Stokes, was getting sick of the guy, always giving him money, and the guy snorting up his nose and spending it on hookers. He wanted to finish up the favor. Finito. Ciao. You know? So when Stokes called in the big favor—kill Rothstein—Lombardi figures okay, this will do it, this is it, the last favor. He tells Angelo to do it. Angelo gets creative, hires the schmuck who works for him to do a painting, make it look like your husband was killed by that psycho."

"And then Baldoni killed him, the artist, Martini, right?"

D'Amato nodded. "Apparently Martini got greedy. Money makes people crazy, you know." He shrugged. "Stokes was cooking the books at the law firm, getting a lot more than his salary. Your husband, apparently he got wise, and was not only going to fire Stokes, but worse, turn him in to the *authorities*. Stokes went whining to Lombardi, told Lombardi that Rothstein was going to give up some names too, that Rothstein knew who Stokes had been playing with. Got Lombardi all fired up. Wanted to make sure they wanted Rothstein dead too. You know how it is."

Wanted to make sure they wanted Rothstein dead too. You know how it is. The words were burning in her ears. But she needed to hear it all, and now that D'Amato had started, he appeared to like talking. Kate nodded for him to continue.

"They deserved each other, Baldoni and Stokes. Angelo says, yeah, he'll take care of Rothstein, but he wants fifty grand for the job, and Stokes has the balls to say, fine, and skims a little more off the law office books. Ironic, you might say, that it was your husband's own money that paid for his hit, huh?"

Kate was feeling sick. Andy had ordered Richard's death, and paid for it with money from Richard's firm. "How do you know all this?"

"Sweetheart, there's very little I don't know." He smiled his malevolent grandfather smile at her. "Lombardi reports to *me*. You see, later, it was me that ordered the hit on Stokes."

My God. She was sitting across from the kingpin, the man who pulled all the strings. The man who could have said no, don't kill that man—her husband.

"You shouldn't be telling me that."

"Why? You gonna put me away for life? You gonna kill me?" He snorted a laugh, then sighed. Kate smelled the tobacco on his breath along with something sour. "I hear the Bureau is looking for Lombardi. I'll let you in on a secret, sweetheart. They ain't gonna find him." Another knowing smile.

Kate didn't have to ask the obvious—Lombardi was dead.

"You can tell them—from me—to stop wasting their time," said D'Amato. "As for Stokes, he was bad news, a loose cannon. He wasn't going to stop getting into trouble, and he had a big mouth. And all the favors were paid back, right? And me, I never owed the schmuck anything, did I? So, fuck him." He punctuated the word with a stab of his arthritic finger.

"You ordered it from here?"

"Why, you think I can't?"

"I imagine you can do plenty, Mr. D'Amato."

"That's right. And let me tell you something, sweetheart. You almost got yourself killed, being in the way like that."

"Does that upset you? That I killed Baldoni?"

"Everyone's expendable." D'Amato shrugged. "But I was talking about you— you being killed."

Kate's words came out without thinking. "That would have been okay with me."

"Easy to say. You're sitting here with me. Alive. Next time you might not be so lucky."

Kate thought about that. Was she glad she had lived? It felt like everything in her life was behind her. She looked into D'Amato's eyes. "I learned to take care of myself from a very early age." She thought about her mother dying and then her father, and then Richard. Richard, who was innocent.

Innocent.

Kate took that in for the first time, and when she did, realized that she was happy she had not died.

"About the new cell?"

"You'll get the reassignment," said Kate. "And you want to hear something funny?"

"Sure, sweetheart. Entertain me."

"I had the authorization all along to move you to another, lower-security prison. Room with a view too. All you had to do was give something up. Lucky for you that you did."

"Sweetheart." D'Amato flashed her his shrewd, malevolent smile. "You think I would have said one single word to you if I didn't already know that?"

Outside, Perlmutter and Kate walked to the car, neither one of them speaking. He'd seen and heard it all, knew Kate would appreciate the quiet.

Kate was trying to process the good news and the bad. Richard killed

as a favor to Andy Stokes. A worthless, senseless death. And Richard
had been guilty of nothing more than poor judgment—not going to the
police before he confronted Andy Stokes.

She had done it, gotten the answers, the ones she wanted, hoped for—
that her husband was innocent—and that she had killed his murderer.
So why didn't she feel better?

Kate glanced up at the sky, more blue than gray now, her eyes filling
with tears. It was going to take some time to start healing. The truth
might have lifted the veil of suspicion from Richard, but it also made his
loss that much greater, her pain more acute. She had been right. But
what did that change? An innocent Richard would still not be coming
back. She watched the wind tear a cloud apart like cotton candy.
Perhaps tonight, she thought, she might sleep.

THIRTY-EIGHT

H ad they made the aisles in D'Agostino's narrower, or did it just feel that way to Nola? She felt as though her girth was about to knock the packages of Oreos and Pecan Sandies and a whole rack of Pepperidge Farm cookies right off the shelves and onto the floor. She tossed a couple of boxes of Mallomars into her wagon. *What the hell?* It wasn't like another dozen cookies were going to make a difference, not at this point.

"Those are my favorites too."

Just what she needed, some creep to annoy her. But when she turned around, Nola decided that maybe she didn't mind being annoyed, because the creep was, in fact, a very cute guy.

"You like them too, Mallomars?"

"Nothing better, except maybe Oreos. Sometimes. Depends, of course." He smiled.

Nice mouth. "Tough contest," said Nola. "By the way, I'm pregnant, not fat."

The guy laughed. "I sorta figured that."

"Oh. Good." She shifted her impressive weight from one foot to the other, and smiled.

The guy smiled too, then said, "See ya," and continued down the aisle.

I'm pregnant, not fat. What a jerk. Like any fool could not see that. Well, forget it. She was dreaming anyway, that any halfway decent guy would even look at her. Nola sighed, watching the handsome young man pluck a box of pretzels off the shelf. For a moment she considered going over to him, offering him a cup of coffee and some Mallomars, but she didn't, and then he was gone. Too late. And in a few weeks, really too late. A baby. *A baby.* She must have been out of her mind.

At the checkout she realized she had bought too much, milk and juice, two heavy bags, but it was too late and it wasn't like she was infirm or anything, she could handle it. Not worth a delivery guy. It was only a few blocks.

"Hey."

"Hey."

The cute guy, one aisle over, collecting his one bag. "You gonna carry those bags all by yourself?"

"Thought I would."

He scooped one out of her hand, then the other. "You shouldn't be carrying heavy bags. Not in your condition. You've gotta think about your baby, you know. Babies need taking care of."

"I guess I'm about to find that out."

"Where are you headed?"

"Central Park West. It's just four blocks over."

"Yeah. I know. Come on. I'll walk you."

After a block, Nola's lower back was aching and she was glad someone else was carrying the bags, particularly this cute guy, even though she had sworn off men, especially white men, after Matt Brownstein.

"You live there, on Central Park West?"

"Temporarily."

"The park is nice."

"That's an understatement."

"Is it?"

"Sure is. I'm staying with a friend. Until I have the baby, then I'll see. I have some things to figure out."

"Uh-huh."

Nola could just about hear his thoughts: *Knocked up. No husband.*

Living with a friend. Pathetic. "I'm at Barnard," she added, as they crossed over Amsterdam Avenue.

"What's that?"

"Barnard, the school. You know, the women's part of Columbia, or was. It's just its own thing now."

"Oh, right. Cool."

He seemed a bit embarrassed about not knowing Barnard, though not everyone did. So he was uninformed, maybe even a little goofy, but sweet too, and his looks made up for a lot.

"Well, I *was* at Barnard, I mean. I'm taking a leave." She patted her belly.

Just at the corner, a half block from the twin entrances to the San Remo towers, he stopped. "I should get going. I, uh, live in the other direction." He handed the packages back to her.

"By the way, I'm Nola. And you are—"

"What?"

"Your name?"

"Oh. Right. Dylan."

"Nice name."

"Thanks. So, uh, what are you doing later?"

"Later? Well, I'm going to this opening tonight, an art opening, in Chelsea, a sort of big deal, a friend of mine—"

"Art opening?"

"Yes, you know, a show, an exhibition. My friend is a painter. It's at the Petrycoff Gallery, on Twenty-fifth Street."

"WLK Hand?"

"You know Willie?"

"Willie? Is that his name?"

"Yeah. WLK Hand was his *handle,* you know, his graffiti name, when he was back being a wild child in the projects." Nola laughed. "He kept the handle, but believe me, he's come a long way from there. So you know his work?"

"I saw it. On TV."

"Oh. Of course. On Kate's show?"

"That's right."

"You should come tonight."

"Yeah. I might."

"I'll tell Kate I met a fan. Isn't Kate wonderful?"

"Yeah." He lifted his wraparound sunglasses for a second, blinked, smiled, than set them back in place. "She's grrrrrrrrrrrrrreat."

I met the sweetest guy," said Nola, hoisting her shopping bags onto the kitchen island.

"Why are you dragging heavy bags around?" Kate gave the girl a stern maternal look.

"To annoy you?" Nola grinned.

"You can have them delivered, you know."

"I didn't carry them. That's where the guy comes in."

Kate started unloading the bags, orange juice and milk into the fridge, cookies onto the counter.

"We started chatting in the cookie aisle, about Mallomars. Then at the cash register we bumped into each other again and he offered to carry my bags home." She patted her belly. "Guess he took pity on me."

"And?"

"And nothing. But he was cute. Very." Nola went for the Mallomars. "How any cute guy could look at me—"

"You look beautiful."

"For a baby orca." She took a bite of the cookie. "I should stop eating these. What am I going to wear tonight? I'm so sick of being fat."

"You're not fat, you're pregnant."

"That's what I told the guy."

"We'll wrap one of my pashmina shawls around you. You'll look gorgeous."

"You better start sewing two of them together."

Kate laughed, but wasn't particularly cheery, her emotions in a state of chaos, one minute euphoric over Richard's innocence, the next despondent over his death. That, plus a mix of excitement and anxiety about Willie's opening, all the people she would have to see, when all she wanted was to be alone, to try and sort out some of these feelings.

Nola dusted cookie crumbs off her chest. "I think I'll lie down for a few minutes so I can stand up at the opening. Wake me in a half hour if I'm not up, okay?"

Kate took her time dressing. She wanted to look good for Willie's show—and for Richard, too. It was the first time since he had died that she cared about her appearance.

Nineteen days. Less than three weeks. A lifetime.

"What do you think, honey?" she asked Richard aloud as she perused her closet, pushing aside dresses until she found the answer.

She slid the charcoal-gray top off a hanger, a simple Armani number that Richard had bought her for absolutely no reason other than he'd been passing the elegant Madison Avenue shop, had seen it in the window, and imagined her in it.

It fit perfectly, the scoop collar showing off her long neck and sculpted collarbones, the smoothness of her skin against which the chain and ring rested.

Pencil-thin black pants and charcoal heels to complete the outfit.

Kate brushed out her hair and let it rest gently on her shoulders, simply, the way Richard liked it. Some blush on her high cheekbones. Gloss on her lips. A soft smoky shadow on her lids and mascara on her lashes.

She grasped Richard's ring as she regarded herself in the mirror, noting how Richard had always known just what she liked and what she looked good in.

She pictured him smiling his approval.

There." Kate finished arranging the steel-gray shawl around Nola's shoulders.

"You're sure all this gray doesn't make me look like the Goodyear blimp?"

Kate stood back, closed one eye, peered at her through the other. "No. The blimp's definitely smaller."

"I hate you."

"You look great. What's the big deal anyway? You know how people are at art openings. They only care about how *they* look."

"Yeah, but . . ." Nola played with the shawl, tying it loosely, then un-
tying it. "I sort of invited Dylan, and he said he might come."

"Dylan?"

"From D'Agostino's."

Did his name have to be one that reminded her of the psycho?

"What?" asked Nola, catching Kate's faraway look.

"Nothing. Forget it."

The shower is just what he needs. He wants to look good, to feel and
smell good—for her, the art *her-story-n*.

He's tired of waiting. It's time.

He pictures the pregnant girl, Nola, and what it will be like to open
up her belly. He could see she liked him, that she will go anywhere
with him.

He thinks about where he should take her, and decides that he will let
her take *him*. What a good idea.

It's grrrrrrrreat!

"Thanks, Tony."

The WLK Hand exhibition. The Petrycoff Gallery. It all makes perfect sense.

He towel-dries his hair and stares at his reflection in the mirror. His
flesh is still slightly gray, but his hair has a brownish cast with just the
slightest hint of sunglow. He is almost cured. And after he sees her, talks
to her, Kate, the art *her-story-n,* the cure will be complete. He is certain
of it.

The Vincent Petrycoff Gallery was humming, wall-to-wall artists
and dealers and collectors and hangers-on, a sea of black and
gray, scattershot bits of Willie's paintings playing peekaboo in between them.

Kate tried to see around a couple blocking her view.

"I'm telling you it's the muscle that lifts the testicles," said the man.

"Are you sure? I thought Cremaster referred to the testicles themselves," said the woman.

"No. I looked it up after I saw the film. It's the *lifting* muscle."

"So the film is about lifting balls?"

"Not that I could see. But Ursula Andress was in it. Remember her, *Dr. No*?"

"No."

"James Bond? The girl on the beach, in the bikini?"

"Whatever." The woman shrugged. "I remember the artist's first video, the one where he climbed the gallery walls, which I think were covered with Vaseline, in his jockstrap."

"Hmmm . . . sort of like being inside the womb."

"Could be that the jockstrap connects to the Cremaster idea, the idea of lifting the testicles?"

"That's brilliant. I hadn't thought of that."

"Excuse me," said Kate, trying to get past them, wishing she could think of something witty to say, but she was preoccupied, definitely on edge. She looked around the room. Everything seemed in order, and yet that odd buzzing sensation had started—*why?*

Petrycoff came through the crowd to greet her, face glowing with artificial bronzer, silver hair slicked against his skull, ponytail gelled into a spear. "It's yours," he proclaimed. *"Harm's Way."*

"Harm's Way?"

The art dealer pointed toward the mirror-and-glass painting mostly hidden by a mass of bodies.

"Oh, I didn't know the title." Kate wasn't sure she liked it either. There had been a bit too much harm coming her way recently, though she wasn't sorry to own the painting. She got a peek of it through the crowd, dozens of fragmented faces and bodies reflected in the bits of mirror, and felt another chill. *What is it?*

"All sold. Every one," said Petrycoff.

"What?"

"I said the paintings are all sold. The Reina Sophia will just have to wait until our boy genius does a few new pieces."

Kate wasn't sure she believed him, but she hoped that at least half of the hyperbole was true, for Willie's sake.

Petrycoff excused himself, and Kate watched him slither into the crowd like an eel.

"Kate, darling." A hand on the small of her back. "I knew I'd find you here."

Kate turned and kissed Blair's cheeks, which she could not help notice were smoother and glossier than ever. She scrutinized her friend's face. "Okay, what's the deal? You look fifteen, and you haven't had time for another face-lift—and I don't see any bruises or new scars."

"The magic of Botox. I just hope it doesn't give out in the middle of some important event." Blair laughed, mouth opening slightly, nothing else on her face moving. "You should try it, darling. Your forehead's becoming a map."

"I had it chiseled into my skin so I wouldn't forget my way home."

"Is that supposed to be funny?" Blair frowned; maybe. "Old age is no joke. You'll see."

Kate thought sixty-year-olds masquerading as sixteen-year-olds wasn't a joke either, but maybe she was wrong. Who knows what she'd think in a couple of years, when her skin really started to sag, in this culture where youth and beauty were worshipped above anything else—except perhaps money.

Willie leaned between Kate and Blair and accepted kisses and compliments, and Kate felt proud and happy and sad all at once, wished that Richard were here to see Willie's success; Richard, who had been the first to step up to the plate and buy one of Willie's paintings.

"Divine," said Blair. "But I don't have the walls for them. They're all so huge. Can't you make smaller ones?"

"You could get bigger walls." Willie flashed a grin. "But check out the drawings in the back. They're small."

"Very classy." Kate smiled, and in her mind said to Richard, *He's something, our Willie, isn't he?* She patted Willie's cheek, and as she did felt another chill. Was it thinking of Richard? Or . . . she wasn't sure. Kate attempted to scan the crowd, but it wasn't possible. The place was jammed. And what was she looking for? She had no idea. She spotted Nola, the back of her head, anyway, talking to someone whom she could not see, and that buzz seemed to intensify, though it didn't make any sense. Maybe it was just the excitement in the room and the thrill of the evening, but it was definitely there, that odd sensation she always got when she was on to something. Perhaps it was just the horror of the past weeks getting to her, and her emotions playing with her psyche. She smiled again at Willie, but a museum director was talking at him a mile a minute, and Kate knew business when she saw it, and eased away. She tried to get Nola's attention, but Nola didn't see her waving, still rapt, talking to some guy, his back to Kate; Nola smiling, maybe flirting. Could be Mr. D'Agostino, thought Kate. Better to leave the girl alone. She wished that feeling would leave her alone too, but it had intensified, along with a chill that felt as if someone were running ice cubes along her spine. She needed a good night's sleep, that was all, maybe even that trip to Florida, sit on her mother-in-law's porch for a full week and stare at flamingos.

Then, one after another, there were artists and curators, art critics and associates, even a few real friends, many she hadn't seen in a while, and they talked of museum shows and movies and this artist and that film-maker and a poet she knew who was collaborating with a painter, and before long Kate forgot about that buzzing sensation, distracted by this theatrical production known as the art world, in which she was happy to play a supporting role.

"Hey, you."

"Well, well, well." Kate shook her head. "Just goes to prove that any-one can crash an art opening."

Nicky Perlmutter laughed, his bright open face somewhat out of place in a room full of people who had elevated ennui to a high art. "Daniel thought a little culture would be good for me." He threw his arm over a slender young man with spiked hair whom Kate recognized from the de-bacle of the other night.

"Really cool work," said Daniel.

"You should tell the artist," said Kate.

"You know him?"

"Right over there. Go introduce yourself. Tell him you like the work. You'll make a friend for life."

"Cool," he said and bopped off in Willie's direction.

"Daniel's a painter," said Perlmutter, his eyes trailing after the young man.

"Finger painting? At preschool?"

"Ha. Ha."

"Sorry." Kate took his arm. "Couldn't help myself."

"Let's say he's old beyond his years," said Perlmutter. "And a serious painter."

"You ever read *Death in Venice*?"

"No. But I saw the movie—old man stalks young boy through plague-ridden Venice. Very nice analogy. Thanks. I'll get you back one day."

"I'm not going to show up with a teenager."

"Hey, you never know—Mrs. Robinson." Perlmutter smiled, then looked at her more closely. "You okay?"

Kate forced a smile. "I'm fine."

Perlmutter patted her arm and then went off to reclaim his boy toy.

Kate was tired. She cut through the crowd, found Willie, watched him juggle a dozen people all talking to him at once, finally cut in, gave him a hug and quick kiss. "I'm taking off."

"You're not staying for the party at Bottino?"

"Forgive me, honey. I'm exhausted. Nola can be your date."

"Don't think so. She took off with her new friend, Dylan."

That name again. *Couldn't he have been a David or a Doug?* "I wonder how many kids have been named after ol' Bobby Zimmerman?" she said, thinking aloud.

"That's Bob Dylan's real name, right?" asked a pretty young blonde beside Willie.

"Right," said Kate. "I think Bob named himself after the poet Dylan Thomas."

"Oh, really?" said the blonde. "Anytime *I* hear the name Dylan I think of *Beverly Hills 90210*. You know, Dylan, the bad boy? Brandon, the good boy, Brandon's sister, Brenda, and—"

"Donna," said Kate, on automatic.

"That's right. Donna. God, how I loved that show. I was like, totally addicted. Truth?" The twenty-something giggled. "I still watch the reruns."

Those black-and-white photographic details, all those names—*Brenda, Brandon, Donna, and Dylan*—scribbled to create the borders in the psycho's paintings, were vibrating in Kate's mind, and that icy hand was playing a tune on her vertebrae.

But it was absurd. It was just a name. Why was she letting it get to her?

"Where did they go?" she asked, trying to maintain her cool—and why shouldn't she? After all, the psycho was dead.

"Don't know," said Willie, who was pulled back into the throng by one of his many admirers. He threw her a kiss.

I'm overreacting, thought Kate, as she weaved her way through the crowd, suddenly anxious to be out of there.

THIRTY-NINE

Nola?" Kate called out and shut the door behind her.

Damn. She had hoped Nola would be home.

The hallway was dark, but Kate didn't bother with the lights. The click-clack of her heels against the hardwood floor seemed louder than usual. She made her way past the den, also dark, no sign of Nola, no glow from the TV set, her heart beating fast. *Stop it.* She was working herself up over nothing, a name, for Christ's sake. *Dylan.* It was ridiculous. She really did need that vacation.

What was that? A voice? Or just the old San Remo creaking? "Nola? You home, honey?"

Kate peeked into the girl's room, also dark, empty.

She's fine. Gone off for coffee with Mr. D'Agostino, that's all. She'll be home any minute.

So why couldn't she shake the feeling that something was wrong? Kate didn't want to act like a worried mother, but she was being one and so might as well give in to it. She opted for the cell phone in her bag, hit the auto-dial for Nola's cell, and when she heard the phone ringing somewhere in the apartment, she felt relieved. *Probably in the kitchen, gorging on milk and cookies.* "Nola?" Kate called out again.

The living room was dark. Kate went for the light switch, but when she tapped it nothing happened.

Was that breathing, or the sound of her own blood rushing in her ears?
"Nola?"

Kate hit the dimmer again. Nothing. She knew her paintings, an-
tiques, and furniture hovered in the shadows, waiting to be illuminated,
but she felt blind. She pictured the room: twin sofas straight ahead,
square low table in front of them, other tables with lamps on either side.
But where exactly? And what was wrong with the lights? Not another
blackout. She should call the doorman—see if something was wrong
with the building's power—it wouldn't be the first time the old landmark building had blown a main fuse. Kate squinted toward the windows and realized the shades were almost completely drawn, just thin
rectangles of ambient city light at the bottoms of each. Had Lucille
pulled them closed? Kate almost always kept them open.

She caught a whiff of Nola's musky perfume, and became conscious
of the fact that the darkness had sharpened her senses. Had the girl been
home and left? Without her cell?

Kate took a few steps, bumped her knee against one of the side tables,
reached out for the lamp she knew was on it, and as she did something
crunched beneath her heel that sounded like peanut shells or dried
leaves. The lamp was dead.

Kate dragged her fingers along the floor to see what she had stepped
on. She felt a jab, then pain.

Glass. Broken glass.

"Damn."

Kate sucked on her finger; the blood tasted strong and sweet. She
stood perfectly still, allowed her other senses to do the work.

That's when she heard it, the slightest intake of breath, a sigh, and yes,
smelled Nola's perfume, too strong to be just a trace. And then the darkness opened up and the room began to reveal itself—twin couches, deco
lamps, an African mask, its shell-teeth glinting.

Kate's eyes came to rest on the oak counter that separated the living
room from the dining area, a normally flat slab, eight feet long, but the
silhouette had changed, morphed into an irregular mass, and from it
came that sound she had been trying to locate: *whimpering.*

Kate took another step into the living room, and the mass was unmistakable: Nola stretched out on the counter, hands and feet bound with tape, more across her mouth, the silhouette of a man behind her, one of Kate's carving knives in his hand.

Oh, God.

"Sorry about the lights. But it's easier for me this way. They'll be okay, the lights, I mean. You can get new bulbs." For a moment, colored lights swirled in front of his eyes, artificial blues and greens, Sara Jane's bulbs. But he blinked them away.

Kate took another step. More glass crunched under her heels. She knew the .45 was in her bag, just hanging on her shoulder. She had to distract him.

"I needed to talk to you," he said.

"Yes. Okay." Kate was holding her breath. "But I can't see you."

"I can see you."

"Don't you want me to see you?"

"This is better. Let's talk."

"Okay."

"Were you trying to trick me?"

"Trick you? No. No. Of course not. I would never." *Think. Think.* "Why would you think I'd try and trick you?"

"All those police, waiting for me."

"That wasn't up to me. I couldn't stop them. But it was my idea to give you the show. I thought you would like it. I hope you did."

"Yes, it—it was beautiful." His voice cracked. "But it's over now. They're gone."

"The paintings?"

"Yes."

"But I saw them, and so did a lot of other people."

"Did they laugh?"

"Oh, no. No. They wanted to buy them."

"Why would they do that?"

Because they're a bunch of sick fucks. "Because they liked them so much. But I wouldn't let them because I didn't think it was right. I wanted you to have them back. And I would have, but—"

"Donna said it was for the best."

"Your friend?"

"Yeah."

"A good friend, I'll bet."

"The best." He swung the knife over Nola's belly and Kate gasped. "Please. Don't."

"I won't hurt her if you'll talk to me. Sometimes people won't talk to me unless I force them."

"Of course I'll talk to you. As long as you'd like." She had to get her gun, but couldn't chance it. Not yet. Even if she got a shot off, he would need only seconds to use the knife on Nola. She could just make out the girl's face, and the terror on it. *Flatter him.* "I really liked your paintings."

"Did you?"

"Very much."

"I'm a good painter, right? A pepper—a painter—a pepper—a painter!"

"Yes, yes, you are." Kate shivered.

"I did the last ones for you. I'm glad you liked—" *Have you driven a . . . Betcha can't eat . . . Coke is it!* He pressed a hand to the side of his head. "Stop!"

"What?"

"Your name."

"Yes, in the borders, I saw it. Thank you. I was very flattered. But may I ask you, why? I mean, why did you paint them for me?"

"Because you cured me."

"How did I do that?" Kate's hand was sweating on the cell phone. *The cell phone. Was it still on? Did I turn it off after calling Nola? No, it's still on.* Her fingers played over the raised circles. Could she figure out the numbers without looking? *Brown is on auto-dial, but what number?*

Celebrate the moments of your— "Stop it! Please."

"Stop what?"

"Kodak moments. Not you." He squinted, blinked. "That painting over there, it's a beautiful blue, isn't it?"

"Which painting is that? It's a little dark for me to see it, but I'm certain you're right."

"You wouldn't kid me?"

"Never."

"I didn't think you would." A flash. *Her* face. Laughter. And music. "Every breath you take," he sang.

"I like that song."

"Do you?"

"Yes, don't you?"

"No. She liked it."

"Who was that?"

"*She.* The one. And the others, like her."

"What others?"

"The others. You know. The ones who helped me to see. I had to do that to them, to her. To see."

His victims, the eviscerated bodies. He thinks he had to do it.

Dr. Schiller's statement flickered in her mind: *He thought that killing enabled him to see color.*

"But why Boyd Werther? Why hurt him?"

"I didn't mean to. Not at first. I just wanted him to help me, but he wouldn't." He sang again: "Every breath you take."

"I thought you didn't like that song."

"No, but Brenda does. And she's a good friend."

"Is she here? Now?"

"Of course."

"You're lucky to have such good friends . . ." The slightest hesitation then she added, "Tony."

"Why are you talking to him?"

"I thought, maybe, that Tony was *your* name."

His laughter sliced through the dark room. "That's funny, isn't it, Tony?"

Kate joined him in the laugh. She was still thinking of Dr. Schiller, and her patient, Tony the Tiger, a name he said he had borrowed from a friend. "Hi, Tony?" she said. "I didn't realize you were here too. I think you are grrrrrrrreat."

"See that, Tony. What did I tell you? I knew she'd understand."

"Yes, I do." *Keep him talking, distract him, then go for the gun.*

"I've wanted to talk to you for so long, and—*here's the story, of a lovely lady, who was—*"

"I know that show. *The Brady Bunch,* right?"

"Show?"

Oh, he thinks it's real. "Tell me your name, okay?"

"I don't have a name."

"Everyone has a name."

"She called me Jasper."

"Shall I call you Jasper, would you like that?"

He considered that a moment. "You can call me Jasper, because . . . it's like the artist, Jasper Johns."

"You like him, Jasper Johns?"

"He's one of my gods. Same name, and . . . he's afflicted, you know. Like me."

"Is he?"

"Oh, yes. But I'm better now and I'm going to help him get better, and maybe you can help him too."

"Yes, of course." Kate glanced at Nola, could almost make out the panic in the girl's eyes. She inched her hand toward her bag. "I was worried we'd never get this chance to talk. I thought you were dead."

"Oh, that wasn't me." A short laugh. "It was a trick."

"And smart. The way you fooled the cops. How did you do that?"

"Easy. I paid him, you know, the kid, a street punk. After I killed the cops outside, I sent him in just ahead of me, into the gallery. Made him wear the sunglasses and all, go right up to the door. They were so excited. They thought they'd caught him. Me. Then it was easy, you know, to go in while they were all so distracted, not expecting me to show up a minute later, and then, *bang bang,* you're dead; not you, them, and the others, the ones in the car, they were already dead, kaput, goners, *pop pop.* I liked the sound the gun made with the silencer on it, *pop pop.*" He aimed the knife like a gun, and Kate debated a quick run, tackling him, but the knife was still only inches from Nola. "They never saw it, me, coming. *Pop, pop. Plop, plop, fizz, fizz*—Sometimes I can be invisible."

"Really?"

"Yes. But not now." He seemed to shudder, and the knife quivered in his hand, and Kate had to hold back from leaping across the room. "Made me sad. I mean, like Prince says—when doves cry—but then I got to look for a while and it was so good, I mean it felt really . . . fine, my paintings, on the gallery walls, where they belonged, and—" His voice cracked again. "Sometimes you have to sacrifice, right?"

"Yes." Another inch toward her bag.

"It's all about the work. I mean, I kind of knew it was *counterproductive,* but I had to, I mean, I just had to. And it was good—*Hurts so good!*—and the right thing to do, right, right, right?" He licked the tips of his burned fingers, still throbbing, thick scabs on several of them.

"Right. You were very brave."

"I am brave. Tough as nails. Hard as steel. Able to leap tall buildings!"

"Superman?"

"Superman. Right. And you're Lois Lane."

"Am I?"

"No." He laughed. "I know who you are. Don't confuse me."

"I wouldn't do that."

"People are always trying to confuse me. Hurt me."

"I'm sorry about that."

"Are you?"

"Yes."

"You cured me."

"So you said. How did I do that?"

"You made me see. It was a miracle."

"Show me."

"What do you mean?"

"Show me how you can see."

"I don't know."

"I really want to see how well you can do. I'm so happy for you, that you can see, and proud of you, really proud of you. But I could be even prouder."

"How?"

"You can show me what you've learned. How I've helped you, cured you." Another step closer, broken light bulbs crunching.

"Please stay away. I don't want to hurt you, don't want you to hurt me—*come on, baby, make it hurt so good*—"

"I won't hurt you."

"Everybody hurts. Do you know what they did to me?"

"Who?"

"In that place. The doctors. My head and—" A series of sensations: cold steel on his back, needle in the arm, rubber in his mouth. "My head."

Kate knew what he was referring to—the electroshock therapy Dr. Schiller had spoken of. But she did not picture *him* in that place, on a gurney, *his* body receiving enough electricity to trigger a grand-mal seizure; rather it was her mother she saw, who could not hold on to words or thoughts after only a few treatments, her mother, whom the treatments had failed, who committed suicide in the very hospital that was supposed to have saved her.

Kate looked at him and saw his pain and sadness. But then he swung the knife, and Nola squirmed and moaned.

"Don't. Please."

"You should know me. I thought you would from the things I put in the paintings."

"What things?"

"The faces I drew—with the tape."

"Yes, I saw them, but . . ." The image shimmered in Kate's brain, but it made no sense.

"I thought that would help you know. Help you remember."

"I'd like to. But . . . Why don't you tell me?"

He didn't answer, just swung the knife like a pendulum above Nola, playing with it, a toy.

"Please. Don't you want to show me how you can see?"

"I do, but . . ."

"There are other lights behind you, in the dining room. The switch is just on the wall, to your left. It won't be much light. Just enough. See those shell-like forms, that's all, there are small lights inside them, but it will be enough to see."

"I can see."

"But I can't. How will I know if what you say is right?" Kate was putting it together. The words. The colors. The paintings. Everything a test for him. A challenge to see the colors. She'd play the game.

"Okay. For a minute. Just to show you."

"Grrrrrrrrreat," said Kate.

"Don't make fun of Tony."

"I wasn't. I thought Tony would like that."

"You never know with Tony."

The switch was six feet from where he stood. Maybe enough time when he went for it, for Kate to make her move, get the gun.

He jagged to the side, hit the lights, and leaped back fast, knife stopping only inches from Nola, who tried to pull back, strangled noises emanating from her throat. Not nearly enough time.

Arcs of soft light fanned out of the crescent-shaped sconces, washing the walls and the room in a diffused glow, blurring edges, paintings merging with furniture, shadows holding on to their secrets, but Kate could see him clearly now, handsome, baby-faced, shaggy brownish-blond hair falling into large sad eyes. A boy, she thought. Just a boy. How is it possible that this person, this young man, this smooth-cheeked boy was responsible for so much pain, capable of such horror?

"You'll show me now—how I cured you. It can be a game."

"I'm tired of games." His boyish face seemed to grow older for a minute. *Old men and their games. Pants down. Face in a pillow. Atta boy. Feels good, doesn't it. Pain.* "Help me. Somebody. Please. Help!"

"I'll help you," said Kate. "Please. Let me."

His eyelids fluttered, more blinking. "You did already. You rescued me. *Do you really want to hurt—Grrrrrrrrrreat—Double your pleasure— It's Casey Kasem with the American Top Forty— Wolfman Jack here—*" His mind, splintering. "No! Shut up! Shut up! Shut up!" The knife was swinging, nipping at Nola's blouse.

Oh, God. "Listen to me. Listen." Kate was trying to make contact, took a step closer. She could take him now. Maybe. But if he panicked, Nola was a goner. "Talk to me. Tell me how I saved you."

He closed his eyes a moment, and Kate made a move to her bag, fingers inching in.

"What are you doing?"

"Nothing." She showed him her empty hand. "Nothing." *Damn. Have to keep him talking.*

"Look at me," he said.

"I am."

"It was *me*. Don't you remember? *Look.*"

"No, I— What do you want me to see?"

"I want you to see *me*. Then. That time." His eyes, a moment ago twitching, lost in some mental chaos, were now so sad.

"I see you, but . . ." Kate tried to imagine what it was he wanted from her.

"You *saved* me. Why can't you remember?" He sounded close to tears.

"I'm trying to remember, but . . ."

"Think!"

Kate's mind was scrambling, but she had no idea what it was he wanted from her, what he wanted her to remember. Was he simply rambling? "Yes, I'm thinking. But help me out. I need help too."

"Why do you need help?"

Kate thought a moment. "Because, like you, I'm sad. Very, very sad. My husband is dead. They killed him. Hurt him. Hurt *me*. And all I want to do is cry. All the time."

"I'm sorry you're sad."

"Me too. Now tell me what it is you want me to remember. *Please.*"

"That man. He's the one. One of many. Snake. Drake. Fake. Bake. Stake. Lake. *Snake.*" His eyes blinked violently, then stopped, and he seemed to become perfectly lucid. "The man, remember? The one she sold me to. He had us tied up. And he took pictures, and he touched me—me and that other boy."

Oh my God. What he'd been trying to let her know, those faces drawn in the borders of his last painting, with tape across their mouths. *Of course.* She had seen it but not understood. But now she did. Long Island City. She and Liz on the stakeout for that child pornographer, Malcolm Gormely. She could taste the sugary Dunkin' Donuts on her tongue, feel the sweat on her palms as they waited, and remembered

what she had thought when they found those poor kids, Denny
Klingman and the other boy, bound and gagged, naked and shivering,
that she would kill the guy, if she could, and almost did, the beating
she'd given Gormely after Liz had taken the kids to the station.

"When I saw you and remembered, I knew you would save me all
over again. And you did. I'm cured now." His whole body trembled a
moment. "But how could you let her take me again? Sara Jane, you
know. My . . . m-mo-mother— motherfucker, cocksucker! She took me
to Snake. But I took care of her—and the ones like her."

The whore, just a kid herself. His mother, whom he had murdered.
And the other victims, the hookers, like her.

Kate tried to reconstruct the young woman's image, his mother, but
could not. "It was a mistake," she said. "That she took you. I didn't want
it to be, and I would never have allowed it, but—it happened. I'm
sorry."

"Sorry?"

"Yes."

"Everybody's always sorry. *Who's sorry now—sorry, wrong number.*
Sorry! Sorry! Sorry!" His face was contorting, hand wavering, butcher
knife shaking above Nola's pregnant belly, the tip tearing her blouse.

The girl emitted a strangled moan, and Kate made eye contact with
her, tried to telegraph that it would be okay—though she didn't know if
it would be. She had to get to her gun.

"She sold me. Sold me. More than once. To Snake. To others. Give it
to me, that's right, so big, so strong, shut up shut up. *Today's weather
will be partly cloudy with . . . where's the beef?* Shut up shut up shut
up . . ."

He seemed to be falling apart in front of her eyes, his brain splitting
into fragments. But he would stab Nola if she blew it. Kate's eyes fell on
the vial of Ambien beside the counter where she'd left it the other night.
But how could she possibly get him to take it?

"It was horrible, I know. You were just a child." Kate pictured him
perfectly. The pretty little boy with the pouty lips who did not cry when
they rescued him. How many more like him were out there? "Please. Let
me help you."

"Help you, help me. Help me. Help me. Help me."

Kate went for the gun. She had to try.

But he instantly came back to the moment. "Stop! What are you doing? You want to hurt me!"

"No, I—I—" Kate let her hand drop from the bag. "You said I saved you, remember? I took you away from that man. You know that. And you said I saved you again. How did I do that?"

"The miracle. Miracle Whip. *I can't believe it's not butter!* Butter shutter whatter mutter. Mutter. Mother. Motherfucker! Baby sucker! Baby fucker!" His blinking eyes were rolling up, the whites gleaming, and his hands were quavering on the knife as if he might drop it.

The gun. Could she get it now or would he snap back into reality? She didn't know what to do, the knife looked ready to take a plunge. "Jasper. Jasper." Kate said his name softly and it seemed to pull him back, and he focused on her. "Listen to me. We have to figure this out. You and me. Together. Okay? Are you listening?"

"I'm listening." His face muscles convulsed along with his eye tics. Was she losing him again?

"Tell me about the miracle."

"It's all fine now. Everything is . . . restored." He smiled and the spasms abated and even his eyes stopped blinking and for a moment his face was like the face of the little boy in that Long Island City house of horrors. "I knew if I saw you, talked to you, it would be okay, that it would stay forever, the miracle. And it has. I can see everything. Perfectly."

"That's wonderful. I'm so pleased. You see there's no need for this. You don't have to hurt anyone to see anymore."

"Maybe . . ." He glanced over the room, eyes blinking again. "All the paintings, the rug. So beautiful. All the color. I'll show you." He used the butcher knife as a pointer. "There. In that painting. The top is all green, pine green. Right?"

Dead wrong. It was a deep blue. But did he want her to lie, or tell the truth? Kate had no idea.

"And there . . ." He aimed the knife at the rug. "Lots of colors, magenta and fuchsia and, oh yeah, a whole lot of laser lemon."

The rug was a mix of tan and gray.

"And your eyes." He smiled at her. "Your beautiful blue eyes. They are blue, right?"

Kate didn't know what she should say, opted for a noncommittal, "Uh-huh."

"You're not lying to me, are you? Please, don't lie. Not you." He steadied the knife directly over Nola's heart.

Kate swallowed a gasp. "No. I won't lie to you. Ever. You don't have to do that. Please."

"That's good." He smiled at her across Nola's swollen belly, and waited.

"I'll only tell you the truth, Jasper." Kate took a breath. "My eyes are green."

"They're blue."

"I'm sorry. But they're green."

"That can't be." The veins in his temples were bulging.

Oh, God. Had she miscalculated? But what choice did she have?

"They *have* to be blue. Don't you understand? Can't you see that? They *have* to be!" His eyes were twitching and blinking furiously. "Blue blue sniffing glue. Touch me there, no, there, here, there, everywhere!" The knife was only an inch from Nola's heart, hovering, ready to dive.

"No, Jasper, *listen* to me." She had to keep him with her. "I can help you to see that my eyes are green, that the painting is blue, that the rug is tan and gray."

"Nooooooo!" He raised the knife above Nola's belly. "You're wrong. I'll prove it to you!"

"Stop!" Kate's heart was racing, and she felt sickness rising in her throat. "Wait. Don't do that. Look at me. Look at me. I can help you. Listen to me. I saved you once, didn't I? Let me save you again." She sought out his twitching eyes. "Let me save you. *Please.*"

"Please squeeze tease. Tease me. Please me. Touch me. Suck me. Fuck me."

"Jasper." Kate spoke with quiet authority. "You *must* listen to me. Stop it at once."

He glanced up at her, mouth slightly open, eyes blinking, but her tone had worked, had brought him back to reality, at least for the moment. "But I have to do this. Don't you understand? It's the only way I can see the colors." He gripped his other hand around the knife, poised, ready. "It's the only way."

"No, it isn't. I know another way."

"You do?" He was squinting now, skeptical, but Kate knew he wanted to believe her.

"Yes. There, right beside you. Those pills. Do you see them?"

He shifted his blinking glance and saw the vial of Ambien.

"I take them. To see. They help me to see the colors. And I know a lot about color, don't I?"

He glanced from the pills to Kate. "They tried to give me pills in that place. But I fooled them."

"Yes, you did. And you were right. But these pills are different. These are special pills." Kate thought about Mitch Freeman's description of the drug—a hypnotic—and his words: *You have to believe in it.* "These pills will make you see. I promise." Kate could see him weighing it, wanting to believe her.

"You take one." He took one hand off the knife and tossed her the vial.

Could she fight off the effect? She knew a pill would slow her reflexes, maybe even make her hallucinate. But it would do the same for him. At the very least calm him. She pried off the lid. There were four pills left. She had hoped for more, and that she could convince him to take enough to knock him out. Kate placed a pill on her tongue.

"Don't hide it," he said. "I did that. I fooled them. *Just for the fun of it!* I need to see you swallow it."

Kate's throat was dry and the pill stuck a moment, but she managed it. She tossed the vial back to him, and it landed on the counter just beside Nola.

"Oh, wow," she said. "The colors are so . . . amazing."

"It works so fast?"

"Sometimes. Yes. The more pills you take, the faster it works."

"You wouldn't lie to me?"

"I have never lied to you—and never will."

"Promise?"

"I promise."

"And you won't hurt me?" Kicks, slaps, hunger, pain, a montage of images playing in his brain.

"No. I will not hurt you."

"Do you swear?"

He seemed to regress, looked so much like that helpless little boy she had once rescued.

"Yes. They work. You will see color. *Believe* me."

He pried the top off with one hand just as Kate had done, shook all the pills into his mouth, and swallowed.

Silence. The knife still above Nola's pregnant belly. Hand gripping it. Knuckles going white.

"Sometimes it takes a few minutes. Trust me." Kate was holding her breath.

Jasper was still blinking and squinting, muttering bits of jingles and ads and songs.

"Patience," said Kate.

Minutes like hours. But time for Kate to think, to remember that Brown was number five on her auto-dial—she had programmed him in by the number of letters in his name. Right. Her fingertips moved over the tiny embossed circles, counting them, and she pressed what she hoped was five.

Jasper was still blinking, but in slow motion now. She could see the pills were having an effect. He licked his lips. His head swayed a bit. His muttering had stopped. Shoulders eased. "I see them," he said. "The colors. The true colors."

"I knew you would. Look at me. My eyes are green, aren't they?"

He blinked slowly in her direction. Kate could see he was having some trouble staying awake. "Yes."

She had no idea what he was seeing, if he was making it up, or if the drug had him hallucinating. Kate was feeling it too, a slight dizziness, her eyes begging to shut.

"They're the most beautiful . . . sea green," he said, his words coming slowly.

"Yes. Go back to that painting on the wall, there. I want you to see the blue. It's a dark blue. Do you see it?"

He stared at the paintings, his lids only slightly twitching, going heavy. "Yes. It's . . . midnight blue."

"That's it, midnight blue. Perfect." *Was he really seeing it?* Kate had no idea. "Keep looking at it. Now just below the blue is a beautiful orange." She slipped her hand into her bag. "Do you see it?"

"Orange . . . Yes."

He was still holding the knife, but he was distracted, his slightly twitching lids half closed. Kate's fingers touched the edge of her gun just as the soft crackling of a voice, like a radio, filtered into the room. She froze.

"What was that?" His eyes blinked open.

"I don't hear it," said Kate. A voice on her cell phone. "I don't hear anything."

"It's . . . noise," he said. "Noise. Like she always had going—"

"It's okay." Kate spoke clearly, careful to enunciate every word. "You're safe here, with me, in my apartment on Central Park West. You don't have to hurt anyone anymore. Put the knife down. Don't talk anymore," she said, but not to him, to that voice on the other end of the phone. "Understand? *Do not speak.*"

Jasper cocked his head to the side, listening, but the voices, all the noise in his head had stopped. "I'm so . . . tired."

Kate hoped Brown had heard her. "It's time to rest," she said. "You've seen enough colors. You know now that you are cured."

"But . . ." He squinted at her. "I think they're . . . fading."

"That's because you're tired." Kate's hand was on her pistol again, a solid grip. She could shoot him now. It would not be difficult. He was going under. She hooked her finger into the trigger. *Do it.* But when she looked into his face and saw the sad little boy from Long Island City, she hesitated. She had made a promise not to hurt him. And seeing him now, mouth slightly open, lids closing, she knew she wouldn't have to.

"The knife, Jasper. Put it down. Carefully."

He regarded the knife in his hand as if surprised to see it and lowered it slowly toward the counter. Kate watched Nola's belly rise and fall with her breath. "That's it." *Needs support and love.* "You're a good boy. A wonderful boy. A smart and talented boy."

He let go of the knife, and stared at it, his face gone slack, then glanced up, and his half-closed eyes were filled with tears.

"Leave the knife there and come to me. Let me take care of you."

Kate still had her hand on the gun, but he didn't seem to notice. The drugs had subdued him. She let go of the cell phone and offered him her hand.

He stared at it a moment, eyes blinking slowly, then took it, and Kate slid her arm around his slender waist, and he rested his body against hers, any strength he had left, gone. Kate plucked the knife off the counter and cut the tape from Nola's wrists and ankles and carefully tugged the piece off the girl's mouth and very quietly said, "Go." She watched Nola run from the room, hugging her belly, terrified, but fine.

The warmth of his body burned against her side, and Kate thought of all he had done, this sad, ruined man-child, but she was not afraid. She could see something had broken in him as she led him to the couch, where he curled up and began to ramble again, but in a soft whisper, "Do you . . . really . . . want to hurt me—sometimes you . . . feel like a . . . nut—double . . . your . . . pleasure . . . double . . . ."

Kate still had the .45 gripped tightly in one hand, but she put her other arm around him, and still mumbling bits of familiar jingles and songs, he laid his head on her shoulder and she could smell a soapy detergent coming off his hair. His reddened eyes opened and twitched. "Tell me . . . about them. Make me . . . see them again. The colors."

Kate pressed her fingers lightly to his lids. "Close your eyes," she whispered. And he did. "Now picture a flower."

"What kind . . . of flower? I don't know any flowers." His eyes flicked open and there was an edge of panic in his drugged voice.

"Shhh. Close your eyes. I'll choose one for you, okay?"

"Yes." His breath tickled her neck, warm, as he curled against her again.

"This is a favorite of mine," said Kate. "It's a small flower, about the size of a silver dollar. Can you picture that?"

"Yes."

"It's called a pansy. They grow in groups, close to the ground, clustered together like a group of friends."

"Friends," he said.

"That's right. And each flower is made up of just a few petals, but the most beautiful colors, rich and varied, indigos and blue-violets, and magentas. Can you see them?"

"Yes. Magenta and . . . blue-violet. I *can* see them."

"Pansies are almost like faces, big bright faces, made entirely of color, carnation pinks and purples and—"

He lifted his head off her shoulder with some effort. "And . . . razzmatazz?"

"Yes, razzmatazz too."

He let his head drop back to her shoulder, eyes shutting by themselves. His words came slowly, oozing out of him as he drifted toward sleep. "I can . . . see them. I . . . can. And . . . they're . . . so . . . beautiful." He put his thumb in his mouth.

Kate saw his eyes twitch beneath the closed lids, and then go still.

She was feeling the effects of the pill herself and trying hard not to forget that the sad young man lying in her arms was also a monster. "That's good," she said. "Very good."

I know what you think." Kate and Nicky Perlmutter watched Jasper being led out of her apartment handcuffed, dragging his feet, a rag doll, two uniforms on either side of him, each with an arm around him, holding him up, trying to balance their weapons, though they hardly needed them; Floyd Brown and a medic beside them. "I know you think I should have killed him when I had the chance." Kate was straining to keep her eyes open.

"Why didn't you?"

"For one thing, I didn't need to, the drug had kicked in. He was going under. And I think he wanted an excuse to stop, to rest." Kate stifled a yawn. "I gambled that I could handle him."

"Dangerous gamble."

"I had my gun."

The medic, who had been talking to Brown, called over to her. "What's he on?"

"Sleeping pills," Kate said. "Thirty milligrams of Ambien."

Perlmutter took him in again. "He doesn't look like much, does he?"

"No," said Kate. "Not much at all."

Another medic strode into the living room from the hallway. "She's fine, but her water's broken."

"What? Oh, Jesus." Kate was fully awake as Nola waddled into the room.

"I think it's time," said Nola.

FORTY

T he sun, a bright canary yellow, dapples through verdant trees, over the grass, and scatters diamonds onto the picnic blanket. Richard uncorks the champagne, light glittering off the bottle into Kate's eyes, and for a moment the world goes white, then slowly, patches of green grass and blue sky begin to fill in like a paint-by-number oil, and Richard is smiling again, and Kate knows what he is about to say.

"Marry me."

"Why not?" she says.

They both laugh and the picnic scene dissolves, replaced by a room crowded with people, walls covered with the psycho's bright, garishly colored paintings. Kate accepts a cigarette from the man beside her, Charlie D'Amato, then stares at the paintings and the borders until her scribbled name tears free and floats into the room like a charmed snake bringing with it the small pencil-drawn faces with taped mouths, and she can't remember what it is she is supposed to know about them and feels panic surge through her body.

Richard cuts through the crowd, and Kate notices that he is oddly transparent. "I wish you wouldn't smoke," he says.

"I quit," she says.

D'Amato grins, offers her a light, and his handcuffs glisten as a flame shoots out of his lighter and swells into a blaze. The room goes orange, then fades, and Kate believes she is awake, and it is a normal morning like any other, with Richard beside her in bed, and she feels relieved.

Richard smiles at her and says, "It's okay, you know."

"Is it?"

He touches her face and his fingertips are warm. "I love you."

"Do you?"

"Very much. But I have to go."

"Please. Stay with me."

Richard smiles and it is the most beautiful smile Kate has ever seen, his face radiant. "No, I can't. But I'm always here when you need me."

"Okay," she says. "I understand."

She can still feel his fingers on her face, but they've grown cold. "Thanks," he says.

"For what?" she says, and looks toward the window. The shade rolls up to display an indigo sky with stars winking like Christmas lights.

"For caring so much."

"It wasn't so much."

The stars gather into a nebula and swirl into the room.

And when Kate looked across her pillow there was no Richard and bright sunlight was streaming in through her bedroom windows for the first time in weeks, and she did not feel like she needed to stay in her dream but could get out of bed and face her life.

She showered and washed her hair and dressed. A quick spray of Bal à Versailles, rather than Richard's aftershave.

The burned-out votive candles were still on the dresser beside the photo of Richard. Kate gathered them up and took them into the kitchen, tossed the candles into the trash, and when she found the empty vial of Ambien on the floor beside the dining room counter she reflected for a minute about the young man she had held in her arms, and she was glad she had not killed him. There had been way too much killing, far too much death. Maybe Nicky Perlmutter was right, that someone like Jasper should not be allowed to live, but had the boy ever really lived? Kate thought about that night, so many years ago, in the Long Island

City apartment, and wondered if Denny Klingman had survived. He had a family, a real family, and that, Kate knew, counted for something. At least he had a chance.

Sunlight was streaking in through the living room windows, a beautiful dawn filled with promise. Kate was anxious to see Nola and the baby, but it was far too early to go to the hospital, and she was due at the station to fill out reports and hand in her badge, which she was happy to do, but even that was hours away. She put up some coffee, gathered the *Times* from outside her apartment door, and when she saw the story on the first page of the Metro section—"Serial Killer Captured"—she wondered how they always got the news so fast, and decided not to read the story, and skipped to the Arts section, where a small piece recounted the fact that Herbert Bloom was renting a newer, bigger gallery, with the slightest hint that he still had a few of the psycho's paintings, which Kate figured he was either painting himself, or farming out to one or more of his outsider artists to make for him.

Willie's show had not only been reviewed the day after the opening— a coup—but had snared the picture—another coup—at the top of the first Arts page. The caption read: "*Harm's Way,* WLK Hand, at Vincent Petrycoff," and the review, two columns, was glowing.

Kate went for the phone, anxious to congratulate him, then stopped. It was unlikely he would appreciate a call at 6:30 A.M.

She read the review for a second time, this time for Richard, then sat a moment, memories of their life together coming faster than a Hollywood chase scene, and she worried because some of the memories were already blurring at the edges.

In the den she found a CD Richard had bought just before he died, and never played, *Jools Holland & His Rhythm & Blues Orchestra,* slipped it into the player, hoping the music might clarify his image, but it wasn't until the CD was half over and the Stereophonics haunting version of "First Time Ever I Saw Your Face" started playing, that she saw Richard's face, and remembered the first time she saw him, in a courtroom, the young lawyer in his suit and tie, tall and handsome and commanding, and how he had looked at her and the way he had smiled, and she knew then she would never forget.

Kate finished typing up the report, felt that there was a lot more to say, but the NYPD wasn't interested in her feelings, though she figured she might get a chance to state them—at the trial, which would undoubtedly be a media circus that she did not look forward to.

Mitch Freeman leaned into the cubicle. "Didn't think I'd find you here."

"Didn't think I'd see you here either."

Freeman smiled, pushed his sandy gray-streaked hair off his forehead. "Just finished a few reports. I'm heading back over to the Bureau in a few minutes." He glanced at his watch. "You have a minute to grab a coffee?"

"As long as it's not here."

They settled into a Starbucks on Eighth Avenue, Kate sipping a latte, Freeman devouring a crumbly scone. "I haven't had breakfast," he said.

"No excuses necessary."

"By the way, Agent Grange said to send you his best. He's back in D.C. And very happy about it too. Your getting that info out of Charlie D'Amato didn't hurt."

"He wasn't so bad."

"D'Amato?"

"No, Grange." Kate thought a moment about how the agent had helped her, though she still wasn't sure why. Maybe Nicky Perlmutter had been right, that Grange did carry a bit of a torch for her. Whatever. She was glad it had worked, and glad it had helped Grange too.

"And you? Feeling somewhat better than when we last talked, I hope."

"Is that a question, Dr. Freeman?"

"Sorry, I didn't mean it to sound like therapy. I was asking as a friend."

Kate thought back to their previous conversation about whether or not she wanted to go on living. She set her latte aside, thought a moment. "Nola's had her baby. And there are the kids for next season's Let There Be a Future. I'll be busy."

"That's good."

"You don't like my answer, I can tell."

"It's a fine answer. I was just wondering about *you,* that's all, and you told me about other people."

"And you said this *wasn't* a therapy session."

"It isn't." Freeman smiled. "I'm just worried about you."

"But those things *are* me—Nola's baby, the foundation." Kate glanced into Freeman's gray eyes, then out the window at the passersby and the traffic. "Well, they're something to wake up for, to care about, right?"

"Absolutely."

"I know I've still got a lot to sort out." Kate looked back at the FBI shrink. "It's sweet of you to worry about me, but I can take care of myself."

"I'm sure you can. But, listen, if you ever need anyone to talk to—"

"As a patient?" Kate picked a bit of scone off his plate and popped it into her mouth.

"No, as a friend." He reached over and dusted a crumb off the corner of her lips.

Kate looked into his eyes, noticed they were actually more blue than gray. "Uh-oh. Was I drooling?"

"Hardly." He touched her hand briefly, almost as though it were an accident, then picked up his napkin. "I was thinking we could have dinner sometime. Just to talk, but nothing professional, I promise." He crossed his heart.

"Damn. And here I was hoping for some more free therapy."

Freeman smiled, and for a moment neither one of them spoke. "Hey, I hear you were quite heroic," he finally said.

"Depends on who you talk to. I think some people would have preferred I just shot him."

"Well, he's safely locked up in Bellevue, then he'll be shipped off to some maximum-security facility for the criminally insane, get some treatment, if possible. But he'll be studied, for sure."

The image of Jasper in her arms came into Kate's mind, and she hoped that maybe his tortured life would come to mean something after all.

Daylight cut through the blinds, painting broad stripes across the hospital bed.

"Have you seen him?" Nola asked.

"He's beautiful," said Kate.

"And long, did you notice? I think he's going to be tall."

"There are worse things."

Nola smiled, though she looked worn out. Was it simply the ordeal of birth, or the trauma that had preceded it? "Are you okay?" Kate asked.

"I guess. For a while there I wasn't sure I was going to make it, you know?"

Kate nodded, laid her hand over Nola's, had a flash of the knife swinging above Nola's belly and knew for certain that she would have killed the boy if she'd had to.

"I was thinking that maybe, when my life gets back to normal—whenever that will be—that I might switch my area of concentration from something other than surrealism. I mean, what happened was surreal enough to last me a lifetime."

Kate was about to agree when the door opened and the nurse carried the newborn into the room. She placed him into Nola's arms. "The jaundice is just about gone. You can take him home tomorrow." She adjusted his head at Nola's breast.

"I don't know if I'm doing this right," Nola said to Kate.

Kate watched the baby fasten his lips onto Nola's nipple and begin nursing. "Looks like you're doing just fine."

"Feels a little weird."

"You'll get used to it," said the nurse. "Buzz me if you have a problem."

Nola petted her son's dark chestnut curls. "He's got a lot of hair, don't you think?"

"He's gorgeous," said Kate. "So, have you settled on a name?"

"Oh. Hadn't I told you?"

"No."

"Richard."

"Richard," said Kate, laying her hand onto the baby's back as tears cut smooth paths down her cheeks. "Good name."

"It's okay? I mean, you don't mind, do you?"

"Mind? No, of course not." Kate dabbed at her tears. "I think Richard would have been thrilled."

Nola glanced down at her nursing baby and frowned.

"What's the matter?"

"Nothing. I'm just a bit terrified. I mean, I want to go back to school, and I still have that semester abroad to deal with, and how am I going to do it? How am I ever going to do *anything*? Oh, God, you must think I'm awful."

"Not at all."

"It's just that I don't know how I'm going to handle it all."

"You don't have to do everything at once, sweetie." Kate caressed the back of the baby's head. "And I'm here. You can go to school, and I'll watch the baby."

"You're busy too."

"Not that busy." Kate pictured the baby in the room she had just redecorated, the painted clouds on the ceiling, the new crib. "You do what you have to do, Nola. I can handle this little fella."

Nola smiled, and yawned.

A few minutes passed and the baby's lips fell from Nola's breast and first the baby's eyes closed, and then Nola's. Kate gazed at the two of them until the baby started to fuss, then she lifted him off Nola's chest and wrapped him in her arms.

ACKNOWLEDGMENTS

Thanking people who have helped me along the way is always a pleasure. Thanks to my amazing agent, Suzanne Gluck, who always comes through. Trish Grader, a compassionate editor who makes rewriting (almost) a pleasure. To the many people at William Morrow/Harper Collins: Jane Friedman, Michael Morrison, and Cathy Hemming for taking me into the fold; George Bick, Brian McSharry, Mike Spradlin, Brian Grogan, and the rest of the hardworking sales force; Juliette Shapland for having gotten my first novel into many languages I can't read; Lisa Gallagher, who was a supporter from the very first meeting; the incredible Debbie Stier and the wonderful PR staff, including Heather Gould and Suzanne Balaban, among others; Erin Richnow, Libby Jordan, Betty Lew, Tom Egner, Richard Aquan; Dan Conaway for coming in at the eleventh hour; and everyone else at Morrow/Harper who works behind the scenes and deserves praise.

Many thanks to those friends who threw spectacular parties and dinners for my first novel—Jack and Jane Rivkin, Sydie and Gerrit Lansing, Bruce and Micheline Etkin, Kevin and Elaina Richardson, Jill Snyder, Allison Webb, Nana Lampton, Helen and Ed Nichol.

More thanks to . . . Marcelle Clements, Janet Froelich, Nancy Dallett and Richard Toon, Marcia Tucker, Adriana Mnuchin, Shay Youngblood, for their help with the first novel and more; S. J. Rozan, for her generous guidance through the mystery world; Judd Tully, who always lends a hand and is there to have a drink; Glenn Brill for his expertise and help with Crayola facts and more.

Special thanks to my friend Janice Deaner for her generosity and help with this book.

Once again, thanks to the Corporation of Yaddo, which has provided me with the most gracious and inspiring home away from home for many years, and the entire Yaddo staff, among them Candace Wait, who understands what a whiny guy from New York needs to be comfortable, Peter Gould and all of the Yaddo "suits" who give so much and so generously, Lynn Farenell and the office staff, and Elaina Richardson for her dedication to Yaddo, her friendship, enthusiasm, humor, and editing suggestions.

A big kiss to my brilliant and beautiful daughter, Doria, who helped me plot this book (any complaints, please call her).

And finally, to my wife, Joy, for her reading, editing, commentary, support, intelligence, and love.